It has only been a few months since Nathen and Authia won their battle and became the new Lord and Mistress of the Jelani Tribe. With Tammy and Hansen at their side, they have made Africa their new home. However, their life of peace and tranquility is about to be threatened. Greed, hatred, and revenge are at their doorstep, and Nathen will have to call upon an unlikely ally if he is to have any chance of winning this battle.

Discovery of the Lion People
Copyright © 2018 Christine Frances
ISBN: 978-1-4874-2272-1
Cover art by Angela Waters

Published by eXtasy Books Inc or
Devine Destinies, an imprint of eXtasy Books Inc

Look for us online at:
www.eXtasybooks.com or www.devinedestinies.com

Discovery of the Lion People
Lord of His People Book 3

By

Christine Frances

DEDICATION

My books will always be dedicated first and foremost to the teacher who saw in me a raw talent for writing. She cultivated my talent and made me who I am today. Though she is no longer with us, Sister Lambert will always be my mentor, my guiding light. I also dedicate my book to my Granddaughter Paige who came up with the name Discovery of the Lion People. My sister Pat continues to play an integral part in the writing of my books. Her unwavering support and encouragement are appreciated more than she will ever know.

I want to also thank Jay, EIC of Devine Destinies, and especially my editor, Laura McNellis. Your support, your patience, all the knowledge that you have shared with me is appreciated far more than mere words can express.

CHAPTER ONE

Congo Region, Africa 1992

Zane's breathing was rapid. Fear enveloped him as he pressed his back tight against the slimy wall of the narrow walkway hidden behind the waterfall. His clothing hung on him, drenched from the spray of the falls. The roar of the falling water reverberated inside his head. His eardrums felt as though they were going to explode. However, he would much rather suffer the deafening sound of the falls than to step one foot inside the Valley of the Lion People. Sensay, one of the elders of his village, had sent him with a message for the Lord of the Lion People—a message that was to be delivered in person. Zane knew the importance of delivering the message, but he also knew he was unfamiliar to the Lion People. And the Lion People didn't like strangers. If only Sam or Tomas were available to deliver the message. The Lion People knew them and considered them friends. But unfortunately, they had been given a mission of their own. They were miles away from the village and couldn't be of any help to Zane.

Zane knew that Sensay would be very angry with him if he didn't deliver her message. So he took a deep breath and nervously entered the valley. Once inside, Zane was overwhelmed by the beauty that lay before him. The jungle floor beneath his feet was lush and green. The plant life and the trees grew taller and were richer in color than the ones in his valley. He was lost in the beauty of his surroundings until he heard a noise—the sound of a bow being pulled back. Slowly he turned until he was face to face with four Lion People. Three bows were aimed at his chest. These men all

1

stood at least six feet tall. They had shocking red hair that fell in waves to their shoulders. Their faces were slightly elongated and covered with a fine layer of red hair. Their cheekbones were quite high, the bridge of their noses was unusually wide, and there was a slight cleft in their upper lip. The hands that held the bows had long fingernails, curved and pointed. Zane recognized these features, for he had seen them once before in his village.

Tuval, the leader of the group, approached the man who dared to enter into their territory. He held his bow downward, at his side. But still, it was pulled back, ready to fire. He looked at the man who stood before him, drenched in his own clothing. He was short, standing a good six inches shorter than himself. His hair was quite dark and disheveled. He wore jeans cut off at the knee and a buttoned shirt with the sleeves cut off. He appeared to be from the village on the other side of the falls. Tuval stood in front of the man, towering over him. "Who are you?"

He bit at his lower lip. "I'm Zane. I come from the village that protects you. I have a message for your Lord."

Tuval was amused that Zane thought that his little village could protect the Valley of the Lion People. "And tell me Zane . . . how do you protect us?"

"We guard the entrance to your valley. We make sure it remains hidden."

"That's very noble of you. Providing that you're being truthful."

"I am!"

"What's the message?"

"Sensay tells me that I must deliver the message in person."

Tuval could tell that Zane was frightened. Beads of sweat

ran down his face, and his entire body was trembling in fear.

"Well . . . Zane . . . you don't appear to be a threat. I'll take you to our village. You'll speak with my Mistress. She'll decide if you are truthful or not. But be forewarned. The punishment for entering our valley without permission is death."

Zane looked as though he was going to faint. He had no way of knowing that since the rule of the new Lord, the punishment of death had been abolished. It was only an empty threat.

Tuval turned to his men. "Stay here. Watch the entrance in case anyone else decides to pay us a visit." His men disappeared into the jungle, while Tuval escorted Zane to his village.

Nathen, the new Lord of the Jelani Tribe, was standing in the entrance to the gathering hut as he surveyed his village. The gathering hut was the largest of all the huts in the village. There were over thirty circular huts, all of varying sizes, and all made of sapling trees and palm leaves. Hardened dirt served as the floor to the huts. A flap made of palm leaves covered each entrance. The huts encircled a large open area, and in the middle of that open area was a communal fire pit, which was considerably larger than any other fire pit in the entire village. The tribe would cook their meals there, but most importantly, the priestesses of the village would perform special ceremonies around the fire pit, especially those that were meant to vanquish evil spirits.

Nathen hadn't come by his title as Lord of the Lion People with ease. He wasn't born to the tribe, even though he was similar in appearance. As Nathen observed the men of the village, he compared himself to them. He stood well over six feet tall. His broad shoulders, muscular arms and legs, curved fingernails and emerald eyes mirrored the appearance of the men of the tribe. The only difference separating Nathen from the rest of the tribe was that his hair was a golden red and not the fiery red of the rest of the tribe.

Nathen had spent the first twenty-nine years of his life living in a sanctuary hidden in the northern regions of the Rocky Mountains in British Columbia, a sanctuary christened Burwood. He lived his early years in turmoil, hiding from the outside world while wondering who and what he was. It wasn't until his twenty-ninth year that Nathen discovered the truth behind his birth. A powerful priestess from the Jelani Tribe had cursed Nathen and his father back to the seventeen hundreds. For two centuries Nathen lived at the mercy of a cruel and vindictive priestess named Serena, a priestess who lived in the spirit world controlling the spirits to do her bidding. Then, one day, a woman possessing gifts somewhat like that of Serena's came into Nathen's life. She was what the Jelani Tribe considered an outsider, for she didn't resemble them in appearance. She was a beautiful brunet with rich brown eyes and a loving smile, and her name was Authia.

Nathen and Authia shared a common gift. They could meld their minds and speak to each other from great distances. Nathen's gift also allowed him to sense auras and emotions. However, Authia's talents were much more developed. By just a simple touch, Authia could see into the very soul of the person she touched. She could see their past, present, and future. Through these gifts, Nathen and Authia fell in love, and together they battled Serena. After several months and suffering great sacrifice, they were victorious. Nathen, free of the curse, lived his life as he saw fit. He and Authia were married, and two months later, Authia gave birth to their son.

Through an age-old parchment, Nathen became aware of the possible existence of a village of people not unlike himself.

It was written that they lived in a hidden valley in the Congo region of Africa. With their son Joshawa, Nathen and Authia made the trek to Africa in search of Nathen's origins. Once again, they faced a priestess who ruled the Jelani Tribe with anger and hatred. The people of the tribe lived in fear while waiting for the return of their rightful Lord—waiting for the return of Nathen. Authia played an integral part in defeating the High Priestess Casandra. Once her rule was vanquished, Nathen became Lord of His People. Unfortunately, it came at a great cost, with the death of a trusted friend and loyal supporter.

As their new Lord, Nathen ruled the Jelani Tribe with honesty, respect, and strength. For the second time in the history of the Jelani Tribe, the Lord didn't take a priestess as his mate. Instead, Nathen appointed a High Priestess to rule with him as an advisor to the spirit world. And not just any High Priestess. He chose Tamara, daughter of Casandra, and the priestess who played an integral part in defeating her mother. Tamara was one of the strongest priestesses of her time, though her strength was not reflected in her appearance. At five feet eight inches, she was considerably shorter than the other women of the tribe. She was twenty-two but still maintained a youthful, almost innocent look about her.

Even though Authia was an outsider, the tribe accepted and honored her as Nathen's chosen mate. When their son Joshawa turned thirty, there would be an elaborate ceremony where he would be ushered into manhood. At that time, he would become the new Lord of the tribe and choose a mate of his own.

Nathen's rule had been relatively uneventful. The tribe was at peace and lived in harmony with the three outsiders who had chosen to live in the Valley of the Lion People.

Arman, leader of the warriors, joined Nathen, and the two

men entered the hut. They wanted to discuss the practicality of keeping men at the entrance to their valley. The village on the other side of the falls was not a threat. And with the removal of Casandra as leader of the tribe, there was no threat within their village. Before they could come to a final decision, Tuval entered the hut.

Nathen looked at him curiously. "I wasn't expecting you back so early, Tuval."

Tuval bowed before him, then stood to face him. "A man, a stranger, from the village on the other side of the falls, entered our valley. He has a message for you, my Lord. One that apparently only he can deliver."

"Where is he now?"

"I left him with three guards just on the border of our village."

"If he is from the other village, then he means us no harm. Bring him to me, please."

"If I may speak, my Lord. I would be more comfortable if my Mistress could read him first, be sure that he is being honest."

Arman added his opinion. "I agree with Tuval. Outsiders are easily swayed. Trust needs to be earned, my Lord."

"Of course, you're both right. Arman, where is my wife?"

"She's at the pond. Cameron watches over her and your son. I'll send someone to get them."

"That won't be necessary." Nathen reached out to Authia, his mind joining with hers. *Can you hear me, my Love?*

Yes. I'm at the pond with Joshawa and Tammy.

I need to see you. I'm in the gathering hut.

Is everything okay?

Yes. I just need your special talents. Nathen smiled to himself. *The ones you can demonstrate in public.*

Authia laughed. *I'll be right there.*

Twenty minutes later, he watched as Authia approached

him. Even though she was an outsider, she had chosen to dress as the tribe did. She wore a skirt that covered her from her waist to her mid-thigh and a top that resembled a halter top. Both were made of animal skin and tanned a soft brown. Nathen, as well, had given up his favorite jeans and wore only a large loincloth that also covered him from his waist to mid-thigh.

Nathen drew Authia into his arms and tenderly kissed her.

Authia smiled up at him. "My Lord, should you be showing such affection in public?"

"I'm Lord of this tribe. I'll show affection where and when I please." Once again, he pulled Authia tight against his body and passionately kissed her. Seductively he allowed his tongue to playfully seek out hers.

Authia giggled as she pushed him away. "You always want to play. You needed me for something?"

"There's an outsider that I need you to read."

"What outsider?" Authia scanned the gathering hut, looking a little confused.

"He's at the border of our village. Come, I'll take you there." Nathen took Authia's hand in his and started to walk away when Tuval stepped into his path. "What are you doing?" Nathen asked.

"My apologies, my Lord. But I feel you should stay behind, protected. We don't know with any certainty that this outsider isn't a threat."

"I'm not putting Authia into a situation that I wouldn't enter myself."

"She'll be well protected. Your place is to remain here, my Lord."

Authia placed her hand on Nathen's chest and looked up into his eyes. "It's all right. I don't sense any trouble. I'll be fine." She turned to face Tuval. "Lead the way."

Nathen scowled at Tuval as he escorted Authia to the

outsider. He didn't like someone else doing his job of protecting Authia.

Zane stood with his three guards, patiently waiting for the Lord of the Lion People. He wondered why Sensay had sent him on such a perilous mission. He wasn't a brave man, a fact that didn't go unnoticed by his guards. They didn't seem overly impressed by his short stature, nor did they show any fear of him. Zane reasoned that it was probably a good thing. If he wasn't a threat to them, then the chances were good they would not feel the need to harm him. After quite some time had passed, he was greeted by the Lord's mate. He remembered her from the village. Respectfully he bowed to Authia. As he stood up, he became painfully aware that the Lord was not with her. "Where is your husband?"

Authia smiled at Zane. "He's in the village. I need a favor of you."

"I'll do anything for you." Once again, he bowed.

"Well, for starters, you don't need to bow to me."

"I must. It would be disrespectful if I didn't."

Authia was taken back several months to a time when she'd heard those words before. Sam, another man from Zane's village, had spoken those very words to her. "Well, bow if you must, but once is plenty. May I take your hands?"

"My hands?" Zane looked puzzled.

Authia held out her hands. "Please. I'll not harm you."

Zane wiped his hands on his pants, then presented them to Authia.

Tenderly she took his hands in hers, closed her eyes, and then gazed into his very soul. At first, the visions bombarded her as they chaotically danced within her mind. Then she focused on Zane, and the visions cleared. She saw what he saw. The message was cryptic, but that wasn't what caught her attention. She saw the lights like fireflies scattered all over the jungle floor. There was danger in the lights, and the scent of death permeated her mind.

CHAPTER TWO

Tammy and Hansen were still at the pond watching Joshawa. Tammy, an outsider, was a nurse who had accompanied Nathen and Authia to Africa. She had been there to help with the delivery of Joshawa and to watch over him while Nathen and Authia went on their journey to find Nathen's people. Tammy smiled as she gazed over at Hansen. She found him to be an incredibly good-looking man, with pitch-black hair, brown eyes, and a fit physique which he had earned from years of working on the freighter.

As Tammy let Joshawa play in the pond, she marveled at the beauty of her surroundings. Besides the waterfall that guarded the entrance to the valley, there was one other waterfall located north of the village. The tribe christened the waterfall Shasha, which Tammy was told meant precious water in the language of the Lion People. The falls stood hundreds of feet high. Majestically it rose high above the substantial canopy of the jungle. And at its base, a large pond formed. The tribe retrieved their drinking water from the crystal-clear waters. The pond, which was the size of a small lake, was where the tribe would bathe, swim and fish. Tammy learned shortly after she arrived in the Valley of the Lion People that the falls had a unique meaning to Nathen. It was at the falls where he was conceived, and under the trees that lined the pond was where he was cursed.

Hansen, also an outsider, had met the trio on the freighter to Africa. He was the Captain's first mate, and he fell in love with Tammy the minute he met her. She was the prettiest girl he had ever met. To Hansen, her honey-blonde hair, hazel eyes, tanned complexion, and petite frame made her the total package. She was everything he ever desired in a woman.

Hansen stood a good six inches taller than Tammy, which pleased him. It felt good to embrace Tammy, holding her head against his chest, and resting his chin on top of her head.

Hansen was sitting at the edge of the pond watching Tammy as she played with Joshawa in the water. Joshawa was only seven months old but had the development of a two-year-old. According to the Jelani Tribe, their children developed quite rapidly for the first two years. Then the development slowed to what would be considered normal in the outside world. Joshawa had his mother's dark hair and eyes, but the rest of him was all Nathen. Hansen smiled as he watched Tammy throw Joshawa in the air and then catch him just before he touched the water. Every time she caught Joshawa, he would squeal with laughter. Hansen sighed as he smiled to himself. He thanked the heavens every day for the courage that allowed him to tell Tammy he loved her. As he watched her play with Joshawa, he rehearsed the proposal he planned to make in the very near future.

Zane still held Authia's hands as she stared deep into his eyes. "What are the lights?"

Zane's eyes went wide with fear. "How do you know about the lights?"

"I saw what you saw. What are they?"

"Only Sensay knows. Can I see your husband now?"

Authia let go of his hands. "Sure. Follow me." She led Zane into the village and straight to the gathering hut.

Zane looked about the village in wonderment. There were so many Lion People, more than he'd ever imagined. They appeared to be startled by his presence, which made him very uncomfortable. Zane was led to the gathering hut where

11

Nathen was waiting. When he saw Nathen standing by the entrance to the hut, he immediately bowed. Slowly he looked back up as Nathen approached him.

Authia walked over to Nathen and stood by his side.

Without taking his focus off Zane, Nathen addressed Authia. "So, my Love, what did you see?"

"He's telling the truth, but, Nathen, there's something very evil going on."

Nathen looked over to Authia. "What are you talking about?"

"Zane, tell us about the lights."

"I know of the lights, but I know nothing of what they are. Sensay wants you, my Lord, to come see her. That's my message."

Nathen took a step closer to Zane. "That's all she told you?"

What little courage Zane had was spent, and all he wanted to do was turn and run. "That's all she told me. So, if you'll come with me, my Lord, she wants to see you now."

Nathen looked up at the evening sky, and Zane followed his lead as he too looked up. The sun was setting, and soon darkness would encase the village. "We'll leave in the morning."

Zane interrupted. "No, my Lord. We must leave now!"

Nathen shook his head. "We'll not travel in the dark. The jungle's too dangerous, and you haven't given me a good reason to risk my life and the lives of my protectors." Nathen turned to Tuval. "Find him a hut to spend the night and make sure he's fed. Authia and I are going to get Joshawa." The conversation was over as Nathen took Authia's hand in his and headed away.

Sensay sat cross-legged in front of the fire pit located in her hut. She knew she looked awful, as she was dressed in a long brown robe stained with age and sweat. Her gray hair that fell just past her shoulder blades was dull and badly knotted because she was more concerned about her people than about her own appearance. Her eyes felt weary from years of seeing too much as she stared deep into the fire contained in the fire pit. She had been an elder of her village for as long as she could remember. Ever since she was a child, she could see things and feel things that were beyond the sight of ordinary people. Her gift of sight was what kept her village safe. But unfortunately, it couldn't penetrate the depths of the valley where the Lion People lived. She closed her eyes as she listened to the popping and snapping sounds that came from the valley below. Though she couldn't see them from inside her hut, the lights still danced within her mind. She needed to show the Lord of the Lion People. She needed to warn him of the danger.

A very weak voice spoke to her. "Sensay . . . help me."

Sensay's head shot up. Sam was standing at the entrance of her hut. He took one step toward her, then crumpled to the ground.

Nathen laid Joshawa in his bed, then went to sit with Authia on their sleeping mat. Nathen had started a small fire in the fire pit and was heating a pot of coffee in the embers.

"You're not going to get any sleep if you drink that much coffee."

"I need to think."

"I know. It's been so peaceful for the past few months. I feel like I can breathe. But now . . .I don't know . . . Nathen, I think something's going on, and it isn't going to be good."

Nathen stared deep into the embers of the fire. "I'll go visit Sensay first thing tomorrow and see what she has to say." He looked over to Authia. "I want you to stay here with Joshawa."

"But what if you need me?"

Nathen smiled as he placed his fingers on Authia's chin. He leaned in and tenderly kissed her. "Is there something that you wanted to tell me?"

"How did you know? I wasn't even sure myself. I was blocking you. Do my blocks no longer work?"

"Your blocks work fine. Your body gave you away. I know every inch of your body, intimately. I can see, I can feel the changes."

"Casandra just confirmed it for me yesterday. We're having another baby. I'm about six weeks along."

Nathen wrapped Authia in his arms and whispered into her ear, "And that's why you are staying here."

"All right." Authia looked up into Nathen's eyes. "I'll stay, but I'm not happy with it." Her smile let Nathen know that she wasn't all that upset with his decision. "Now, skip the coffee and come to bed."

Nathen lay on their sleeping mat cradling Authia in his arms. He listened to the rhythmic sounds of her sleeping, sleep that evaded him. Once again, his stomach was in knots, as if warning him of the danger that was waiting on the other side of the falls.

As the sun poked its head above the horizon, Zane made his way to the gathering hut. There he patiently waited for the Lord to appear. It wasn't long before the courtyard came alive with the inhabitants of the village. Everyone went about their morning activities, totally ignoring Zane, for which he was eternally grateful. Arman and Tuval made their way over to the gathering hut. Arman gestured toward Zane. "Someone's in a hurry."

Zane looked at Arman, then turned to look behind him, not really sure who he was referring to.

Tuval just shook his head as he approached Zane. "You're up early."

"We must leave now. Sensay's waiting. She needs to speak to your Lord. It is very important."

Arman looked at Zane as if he were sizing him up. "And why is it so important that our Lord go see this woman you speak of?"

"Sensay doesn't tell you more than you need to know. We're already late. Where's Lord Nathen?"

No sooner had he spoken those words than Nathen and Authia came from around the corner of the gathering hut.

Zane, as well as Tuval and Arman, bowed to their Lord and Mistress. Nervously Zane stood up, not taking his focus off Nathen. He took a deep breath, then approached Nathen, stopping just a few feet away. "My Lord, I mean no disrespect, but we must leave."

"All right, Zane, but I warn you. The evil that my wife senses, it had better not involve you."

"It doesn't, my Lord. The evil has nothing to do with me or my village."

Authia stepped closer to Zane. "So, you do know that evil exists?"

"Yes. That's why Sensay needs to see Lord Nathen."

Nathen spoke to the entire group. "Arman, you'll stay here and keep my family safe. Tuval, you'll come with me. Bring four warriors with you. We leave in ten minutes."

"Ahh . . . my Lord . . . it's supposed to be just you. I'm not to bring anyone else back with me."

"Sorry Zane, but I'm not entering the outside world by myself. Sensay will have to understand. She has no choice. If she wants me, she'll get me and my protectors." Nathen turned, put his arm around Authia's shoulders, and headed away.

Zane stared after Lord Nathen. *Sensay won't be happy. She'll not like this show of force.* But there was nothing Zane could do, so he sat cross-legged on the ground, patiently waiting to return to his home — something he so desperately wanted to do. As he waited for Lord Nathen, he scrutinized his surroundings. The Lion People were primitive people. They had no modern conveniences, not that Zane knew of many himself. He watched as they cooked their meals on an open fire. The only weapons he saw were bows, spears, and machetes. However, the Lion People with no weapons were still very dangerous. True to his word, Nathen returned in ten minutes along with Tuval and four men. Everyone, with the exception of Nathen, carried a bow, spear, and machete.

Nathen took one last look at his village, then followed his warriors into the jungle. Zane was close behind while Tuval took up the rear, machete in hand, bow at the ready. Nathen knew Tuval didn't trust Zane, and he also knew that Tuval would be ever mindful of the dangers that lurked in the shadows of the jungle.

Once they reached the falls, the four warriors led by Zane went ahead, while Nathen and Tuval waited in the safety of their own valley. One of the warriors, Dameon, returned to announce that it was safe for them to cross.

As Nathen entered the outside world, his loincloth and hair drenched from the spray of the falls, he immediately noticed something different. The voice of the jungle had an almost mechanical tone to it. He strained to hear the strange noises, though the roar of the waterfall was doing its best to drown them out. He walked over to the edge of the pond, then stood perfectly still as he focused on the mechanical echoes that filtered their way through the jungle separating the falls from the village. However, the dense foliage of the jungle was muffling the sounds, and Nathen still couldn't distinguish what they were.

It wasn't until he entered the clearing surrounding the village that he could distinctly hear what was filtering up from the valley. He paused and focused on the popping and snapping that was resonating from the valley below. He knew what those sounds were. As if in a daze, he walked toward the very edge of the clearing and stared down hundreds of feet to the valley below them. He was concentrating so hard on pinpointing where the sounds were coming from that he didn't hear Sensay come up behind him.

"If you are trying to locate the sounds, you are wasting your time, Lord of the Lion People."

Nathen turned to face Sensay. She looked worried and fearful. It was as though she had aged years since he last saw her only months ago. "And why is it a waste of my time?"

"You know what those sounds are. To truly appreciate the danger, you must look upon the valley at night. Now come with me, my Lord, I need your help." Sensay turned and slowly made her way toward her hut. Nathen and his men followed, leaving Zane alone in the clearing.

Nathen couldn't help but notice that the village was empty. "Sensay, where is everyone?"

Sensay stopped and sadly turned to face Nathen. "My Lord, my people have found a new home."

"A new home? Why would your people need a new home? And why are you and Zane not with them?"

"You are full of questions, Lord of the Lion People. Help me first, then I'll answer your questions."

"Help you how?"

Sensay turned back toward her hut, shaking her head as she continued walking. "And yet another question." She entered her hut and gestured Nathen to follow, which he did.

Inside he found Sam, asleep on a mat, obviously injured, his shirt stained with blood. "What happened to him?"

"You tell me. I do not recognize his injuries."

Nathen went and knelt beside Sam. Carefully he opened Sam's shirt to find three round holes. Two were located in his chest and one in his shoulder. Nathen left the shirt opened and looked back as Sensay. "How long has he been here like this?"

"He returned at dusk last night."

"Tuval, bring me the medical satchel."

Tuval handed the satchel to Nathen. "I don't recognize those wounds. Do you, my Lord?"

"Unfortunately, yes. He's been shot. The sounds you hear are gunfire. And a lot of it."

Tuval looked as if he didn't understand. "What is gunfire, my Lord?"

"It's a weapon. Either a gun or a rifle. And by the sounds coming from the valley, I would say both are being used." Nathen looked up at Tuval's blank expression. "Tuval, a gun has a barrel." Nathen drew a gun in the dirt that made up the floor. "Put a projectile in it, and when you fire the gun, the projectile flies through this barrel and into whatever you are aiming at. And it does so at great speed." Gently Nathen lifted Sam to a sitting position, and as he did, he lifted his shirt to examine Sam's back. Sam moaned in pain as Nathen laid him back on the sleeping mat. "Sorry, Sam." Nathen directed his attention to Sensay. "I don't see any exit wounds, so I'm certain that the bullets fired at Sam are still in him. I just hope that none have done any permanent damage." Nathen opened the satchel and looked for something he could use to remove the bullets. There were two long, thin rods made of what looked like to be bamboo. They would have to do. Nathen carefully placed the rods into one of the holes made by the bullets. Sam was visibly in extreme pain. His back arched in agony as Nathen pushed the rods deeper into the hole. Nathen looked over to Sensay. "These bullets are deep, and they have to come out if he's going to have any chance of survival. Is there anything you can give him so he'll not feel the pain?"

"Yes. It will take a few minutes to prepare."

Ten minutes later, Sensay had made a broth with herbs and spices. She leaned closer to Sam as she raised his head with one hand and poured the foul-smelling broth into his mouth. Nathen held Sam's mouth open so he would swallow as much of the broth as possible. Before the bowl of broth was empty, Sam had passed out. Sensay sat back and looked lovingly at Sam. "He will be fine now. He will not feel any pain or have any memory of it."

Nathen worked diligently over the next couple of hours as he carefully removed all three bullets. After they had been extracted, he filled the holes with a mixture of herbs and tree sap. Sensay watched with great admiration on her face. "You have done well, Lord of the Lion People. Will he live?"

"I have no idea, Sensay. The bullets were deep. I've no way of knowing if they did any damage or, for that matter, how much blood he's lost. We'll just have to wait and see. Now, why did you summon me?"

"You have many questions, and they can all be answered tonight. When the village is blanketed in darkness, that is when you will get your answers. Please have your man tell Zane that he is no longer needed, he can join our people." Nathen watched as Sensay sat in front of her fire pit, crossed her legs in front of her, and rested her hands on her knees. She closed her eyes and started to chant softly. The conversation was over, and Nathen knew not to pursue it.

"Tuval."

"Yes, my Lord."

"Send one of your men back to the village. Tell Arman and

Authia that we'll not be returning until sometime tomorrow. And tell Zane that Sensay wants him to join the rest of his people."

Tuval bowed before him, then left to do his bidding.

A few minutes later, Tuval returned and took his place sitting on the ground next to Nathen. He looked over at Nathen, smiled, and shrugged his shoulders. "I guess we wait."

Nathen nodded in agreement as he casually gazed about the hut. The sounds of gunfire were echoing throughout the village. Three of his warriors remained standing outside the hut door, ready to protect him. However, Nathen knew there was no need — they weren't in any immediate danger. The fighting in the valley below them was miles away. But that didn't lessen the threat. His focus shifted to Sam, who lay quietly on his mat, his breathing shallow, his wounds swelling from the invasion of removing the bullets. Sam must have known of the danger, for he'd witnessed first-hand the travesty that consumed the valley below. Then Nathen's gaze fell on Sensay, who was still sitting cross-legged in front of the fire. Such a frail old woman . . . but yet a woman who had the strength to save her village and attempt to save the village of his people. "Sensay, how long has the fighting been going on?"

Sensay opened her eyes, her gaze etched in sadness as she looked upon Nathen. "There has always been fighting. For as long as man has walked this earth, there has been war. Up to now, our home and the home of your people have been safe from the cruelties of the outside world. But that is no longer to be. Each night that passes, the lights keep getting brighter, and as each new day dawns, the sounds get louder."

"So, you're saying that we don't have much time."

"Time is not our friend. Your strength will be tested, Lord

of the Lion People. For the question is not if the fighting will find your doorstep, but rather when."

Sensay's words repeated themselves within the confines of Nathen's mind. He had a very good idea of what was coming, and he knew there was no way he could defend his people against such weaponry. The group remained quiet, listening to the sounds of gunfire, waiting for darkness to envelop the village.

Just before sunset, Sam became feverish, his body drenched in sweat. Nathen wanted to believe it was part of the healing, but he knew it would depend on whether the fever broke or not. He had his guards retrieve a bucket of cool water from the pond. Tenderly he laid cool cloths on Sam's forehead. An hour later, Dameon entered the hut. He bowed to him. "Darkness is upon us. You might want to see this, my Lord."

Nathen stood to follow Dameon. He looked over his shoulder at Sensay. "Are you not coming?"

"I have seen the lights. Go. See them for yourself, then I will answer your questions." Sensay smiled at Nathen. "That is after you answer mine." Sensay closed her eyes, once again ending the conversation.

Nathen followed Dameon, and as he stood in front of the hut, he could see a glow rising from the valley floor. Nathen and Tuval approached the edge of the clearing. Cautiously they looked down. The valley floor was alive with lights. Some smaller... some larger. White and yellow lights, exploding in unison.

Nathen stood back from the edge of the clearing. He closed his eyes and sadly shook his head. He and Authia had just finished the second of two battles. They'd fought for peace. They'd fought for Nathen's freedom. For his right to live a normal life. And now his valley, his home, existed at the edge of a war. Not his war, an outsider's war. A war, according to

Sensay, that would end up on his doorstep. It was only a matter of time.

CHAPTER THREE

The sound of gunfire resonated throughout the jungle. Rick pinned his back tight against a giant Kapok tree. The sheer girth of the tree concealed him from the rebels who were firing at him and his men. The rebels had worked their way between Rick's platoon, effectively cutting their numbers in less than half. For the entire night, bullets peppered the area surrounding Rick. He dared not move. Even with his camouflage gear and blackened face, the rebels would still be able to find him.

Hours later, as the sun rose over the horizon, Rick still didn't feel safe. The area was still being targeted, though it didn't appear that the rebels were advancing toward them. Rick was Captain of his platoon and had earned the respect of his men not only because he was a fair and just leader, but also because he was intimidating. Rick hadn't planned on leading his own platoon in this insanity of human carnage, but that was the position he'd been given. He led a group of men he'd never met before, and he knew that being over six feet tall and weighing over two hundred pounds of pure muscle definitely worked to his advantage. Plus, his dark black hair and piercing eyes kept people from challenging him.

Rick and his men had been hired as peacekeepers for the resistance. They were fighting to help usher in a new government. When Rick joined, his definition of peacekeeping was quite different than that of the men who hired him. He and his platoon had been thrown into the jungle, armed to the teeth. They were battling not only rebels but also sweltering heat, insects as large as their hands, and the four-legged predators who patiently waited to strike at any given moment. Some of his men were used to the harsh conditions, but not Rick. He came from central Canada and had joined the cause because the price was right. As he pulled his gun from its holster and checked the clip, he was seriously questioning his decision to back the new government that meant nothing to him. The money was of no use to him if he died in the God-forsaken jungle.

Rick looked over to his right, and from his vantage point, he could see Adam, one of his Lieutenants. Adam had also taken cover behind a Kapok tree. He was shorter than Rick, standing just under six feet, and his physique was pure muscle. His tanned complexion complimented his brown hair and eyes. Rick was out of earshot of the rebels, so he took a chance and yelled over to Adam.

"Adam, are you okay?"

"Yes, sir. And you?"

"I'm fine. How many men do you have?"

"Five, sir."

"Any injured?"

"Not that I know of, sir."

"I want you to retreat. Head back to the bunker."

"What about you, sir?"

"I can see Travis. He's about a hundred yards from here. I'm going to get him. I'll meet you back at the bunker."

Adam nodded his head, then motioned to the five men surrounding him. Rick watched on as, in unison, they all dropped to their bellies and started crawling south, away from the fighting and toward their bunker. The gunfire continued to spray the area. Anything five feet or taller was in danger of being hit. Rick holstered his gun, dropped to his belly and started crawling toward Travis, his second in command. Rick kept Travis in view as he dragged his body over the jungle floor.

Travis was a little shorter than Rick with blond hair and

hazel eyes. He weighed almost the same as Rick, though he was much broader in the shoulders and leaner at the waist and hips. Rick had crawled about fifty yards when the rebels decided to pepper the area just above him. As the bullets flew over his body, Rick stopped and clasped his hands over the back of his neck. He'd hoped by doing so he would protect himself from any falling objects. He was just about to continue when something heavy hit him square in the middle of his back. Frightened, Rick rolled over onto his back and kicked at the object. He looked down at his feet to find a black and white colobus. It was a monkey, smaller, with his chest ripped open from the barrage of bullets. Rick closed his eyes, said a silent prayer, then continued crawling toward Travis. After what seemed to take forever, Rick reached his objective. Travis was sitting on the ground, his back firmly pressed against a Kapok tree. Even with his ample size, he was dwarfed by the two-hundred-year-old tree.

Rick sat next to Travis, just staring out into the jungle. "Where the hell did they come from? There weren't supposed to be rebels anywhere near this area."

"Obviously, somebody gave up our position."

"How many men do you have with you?"

"Seven, but a couple of them have been injured."

"Shit! That means that there are over forty of our men on the other side of the rebels."

"What are your orders, sir?"

"We need to regroup at the bunker."

Travis looked concerned at his Captain. "But what about the men trapped north of us?"

"There's nothing we can do for them right now. We need to regroup and plan a strategy to get the men back. Colin is with them. He'll get them to safety until we can reach them."

Travis stared deep into the jungle. As with Rick, the jungle was foreign to him. He'd grown up in Kansas, where the worst thing he had to deal with were the tornadoes. Travis knew the fury of a tornado, having experienced an F-four just one year earlier. However, with all the threats in the jungle, animal as well as man, he would gladly face an F-five tornado rather than the hell the jungle was dishing out to him. He felt fortunate that he'd been assigned to Rick's unit. They were very much alike in their thinking and their beliefs. The main belief was that they'd made a terrible mistake signing up to fight a war that wasn't theirs.

Rick scanned the area around him. Seven of his men were hidden on the jungle floor. Knowing that all eyes were on him, he raised his right hand in front of his body and used hand signals to tell his men what to do. The ferns before him started to rustle as his men crawled on their bellies heading south toward their bunker. The bunker that Rick was sending his men to was located an hour south from their present location. They had found it quite by chance over six months previous. It was a hut that appeared to have been used as a temple by the locals. However, after a thorough check of the area, Rick had determined that the hut was uninhabited. If there were any locals, they were long gone and had been for quite some time. Rick used the hut to store all their weapons, ammunition and explosives.

The group crawled until the gunfire was barely discernable. At that point, they felt safe to stand and double-time it to the bunker. When they arrived, the five men that Adam had brought were there waiting. Rick had his medic attend to the wounded. Then he, Travis, and Adam went inside the hut for privacy while they discussed their next move.

Nathen woke as the rays of the sun rose over the horizon and into the morning sky. He listened for the sounds of the jungle, but the only ones he could hear were those of gunfire. The wildlife of the jungle remained quiet, as though they knew not to make a sound. Everyone had spent the night in Sensay's hut. The guards took turns watching over him. Nathen glanced over at Sam and found Tuval tending to Sam's wounds.

"How is he, Tuval?"

"His fever broke in the night. I think he'll make it, my Lord."

Nathen sat up. "That's good to hear. Okay, we have to get back to our village. We'll take Sam with us." Nathen looked over to Sensay, who was awake and sitting by the fire she'd built earlier in the morning. "You too, Sensay. You're coming with us."

"Is that an order, my Lord?"

Nathen smiled at Sensay. "It's a strong request. No offense, but I highly doubt that you're in any condition to follow your people to your new home. And I can't, in good conscience, leave you here to be found by whoever comes out of that jungle. We could use your wisdom, Sensay."

"I am too old to be of any use to anyone. I am prepared to die, and I choose to die here."

Nathen stood towering over the frail woman. "Then let me put it this way. You're coming with us. Whether you walk, or we carry you, it's your choice."

Sensay stared deep into the embers of the fire. "I am not strong enough to cross into the falls." She looked up to Nathen. "My people lived here for the sole purpose of protecting the entrance to the Valley of the Lion People. I know that this village will be overtaken. I do not know when

27

or by whom, only that it will. Tell me, Lord of the Lion People, do you think an old woman such as myself will be of any use to you and your people?"

"I have no doubt that you'll play an integral part in our survival." Nathen turned to face his men. "Dameon, you'll carry Sensay to our village. Cameron, you and Zaire will stay in back of us and protect our group." Nathen was about to address Tuval, but he already had Sam cradled in his arms. "I think it would be best if I carried Sam and you lead our group back to our village."

"Of course, my Lord." Tuval handed Sam to Nathen, picked up his spear and bow and headed outside of the hut. Both Tuval and Nathen went to the edge of the clearing and looked down upon the valley below. "Do you think the fighting will stay in the outsider's valley?"

Nathen looked at Sam, who was fast asleep cradled in his arms. "I can only hope." Nathen looked back up at Tuval. "I fear for Tomas. He might still be out there. If he does make it back, I only hope he'll know to come to us." Nathen walked away from the clearing and into the jungle, hoping beyond hope that Sensay was wrong and the fighting would remain on the valley floor.

Authia woke to the sounds of her son gurgling in his bed. She reached over for Nathen, then remembered he was on the other side of the falls. She lay back on their sleeping mat, closed her eyes, and reached out to her husband. *Can you hear me, Nathen?*

Yes, my Love.

Where are you?

Heading back. We're just entering the falls. I have Sam with me, and he's been badly injured. Can you have Casandra meet us at the priestess' hut?

For sure. Is he going to be all right?

I believe so, but he has a lot of mending to do. We're entering the falls. I'll see you shortly."

Authia got up from her mat, dressed in her animal skins, and went over to Joshawa. He smiled up at her and raised his tiny arms for her to pick him up. After Authia changed Joshawa, placing a clean diaper made of animal skins on him, she happily obliged and lifted her little man into her arms. "Daddy will be home soon. How about we get you something to eat?" As she left her hut, she reached out to Casandra. *Casandra, are you awake?*

Yes, my Mistress. What can I do for you?

Do you remember the outsider Sam?

Yes. The little man from the other side of the falls.

That's right. Nathen is bringing him here, and he's been injured. Nathen wants you to meet him at the priestess' hut.

Of course, my Mistress. I'll be right there.

Authia ended the meld and went in search of Tammy and Hansen.

Casandra was at the birthing hut, a place of healing, but most importantly, a place to bring new life into the village. The birthing hut was located outside of the village where the occupants could heal in peace. Quickly, she gathered what she needed, then headed back to the village. Casandra had not always been so cooperative. She was the priestess who had once ruled the tribe under a veil of deception and threats. It was Authia who'd bested her, which allowed Nathen to become the rightful Lord of the Jelani Tribe. Casandra's punishment for the deception and cruel treatment of the tribe should have been death. But that was not Nathen's way, and he spared her life on the condition that she would become the tribe healer, that she would mend her evil ways and prove to him and the tribe that she was sincerely regretful for her past actions. Casandra was so taken aback by Nathen's generosity that she accepted him and Authia as her Lord and Mistress and lived her life proving her gratitude.

Authia found Tammy and Hansen sitting around the communal fire pit enjoying their breakfast. A large animal resembling a boar was cooking over the open fire in the pit. The animal would feed the tribe for their breakfast as well as lunch. Contained in bowls around the pit were freshly baked bread and fresh fruit. Authia sat cross-legged on the ground next to Tammy, placing Joshawa between them. He was strong enough to sit up on his own and also to walk away if Authia wasn't watching. She placed a bowl of bread and fruit in front of him, hoping to keep him occupied, even if it was for only a short time.

Hansen passed her a chunk of meat skewered on a stick. "Have you heard from Nathen?"

Authia took a bite of the meat. It was tender, almost melting in her mouth. "Yes. He's on his way back. He's bringing Sam with him. Apparently, Sam's been injured."

"Injured? How?"

"No idea. But Nathen has asked for Casandra."

"That doesn't sound good." Hansen stood up and brushed the dirt from his jeans. Then he leaned over and kissed Tammy on her forehead. "I'm going to the priestess' hut and wait for Nathen there."

Authia placed more fruit in Joshawa's bowl. "I'm going to stay here and finish feeding Joshawa. Please tell Nathen I'll catch up with him when he's finished with Casandra."

"Will do. How about you, Tammy, are you coming?"

"No, I'll stay here with Authia." Hansen nodded and headed over to the priestess' hut.

Hansen arrived at the hut just moments after Casandra. He watched as she knelt on the ground and carefully placed a sleeping mat in front of the cold fire pit. At five-feet eleven-inches, Casandra was of average height for the women of the tribe. Her blue eyes sparkled like sapphires, and she always wore her hair braided. When she stood back up, she looked over at Hansen. "Would you start a fire? I need to boil the broth I'm making for Sam."

Hansen didn't say a word. He left the hut to gather the firewood he would need. He didn't have to go far, for there was a generous stockpile of firewood right outside the priestess' hut. Hansen returned and started the small fire as instructed. When he was finished, he watched Casandra, who was at the back of the hut standing in front of a long table. Above that table were four shelves all lined with clay pots. Hansen had been told by the High Priestess Tamara that inside the clay pots were the herbs, oils, and powders that the priestesses needed for their spells, incantations and for the remedies used to heal the sick. Casandra took an empty clay pot and started filling it with herbs and oils. When it appeared that she was satisfied that she had the right dosage, she placed the clay pot over the fire Hansen had built. Hansen and Casandra sat in silence as they watched the liquid in the pot slowly come to a boil. Once it had boiled for a few minutes, Casandra removed the pot from over the fire and set it aside to allow it to cool. Minutes later Nathen entered the hut with Sam cradled in his arms. He walked over to the sleeping mat and gently laid Sam on it.

Hansen looked down at Sam. "What happened to him?"

"He's been shot."

"Shot! By who?"

"Fill you in later. Casandra, can you help him?"

Casandra knelt by Sam's side and opened his shirt, revealing the three bullet holes. With a narrow flat stick, she removed the herbs from one of the holes. Casandra looked up at Nathen obviously puzzled by what she saw. "What made these wounds?"

Nathen handed Casandra a leaf packet. Inside were three bullets, still covered in what appeared to be blood.

Casandra looked at them in wonderment. "How did these stones enter his body?"

"Long story. Can you help him?"

Casandra closed her eyes and moved her hands over Sam's chest. She started to sway back and forth, chanting in the language of the priestesses. Hansen's attention was focused entirely on Sam as his chest seemed to take on a glow, as if a light was emanating from within his body. A few minutes later, Casandra stopped her chanting and looked up at Nathen.

"Yes, I can help him. The healing spirits are confident that he will survive. Much thanks to you, my Lord. I'll clean out his wounds and place fresh herbs within them. However, the healing spirits cannot help his friend."

Nathen looked puzzled at Casandra. "What are you talking about?"

"The other small man that was with Sam. He's beyond our help."

Nathen knew she was referring to Tomas. "He's alive?"

"Barely, my Lord. I'm very sorry, but there's no help for him." Casandra turned from Nathan and started working on Sam. She gave him the cooled broth to help him sleep. Then she flushed his wounds and repacked them. "He will sleep until tomorrow. I'll stay and watch over him. There's nothing you can do here. Go to my Mistress . . . it's time to start planning the protection of our village."

Nathen looked at Casandra. "How do you know our

village needs protecting?"

"I know because Sam knows. He's afraid for our village. You, my Lord, must find a way to protect us."

How was Nathen going to protect his village against men with guns and rifles, and God only knew what else? Not to mention the sheer number of men that could be heading their way. Nathen turned to leave, Hansen at his side. He stopped and looked over his shoulder at Casandra. "Besides your daughter, you're one of the strongest priestesses in our village. I'm going to need you before this is over."

"And I'll need you. You and I both will have difficult decisions to make, ones that will forever affect our village, our home. We'll need each other. Now go, my Lord, there is much planning to do." Casandra turned her attention back to Sam as Nathen left the hut.

Nathen stood outside surveying his village. Hansen stood quietly at his side. What did Casandra mean by difficult decisions? She spoke of planning. How did you plan against an enemy that you knew nothing about? What Nathen did know was that if the war came into their valley, it would be a blood bath. And it wouldn't be in favor of the Lion People.

CHAPTER FOUR

R ick, Adam, and Travis left the hut to find the men gathered around a small fire they had started. Rick took a deep breath as he addressed his men with what he knew would be a difficult choice to make.

"Okay, we have a decision to make. We are fifteen men. Two of us are injured. There's an army of rebels separating us from the rest of our platoon." Rick scanned the group of men, desperate to find the right words to say. "Look at us. No one here is from Africa. No one here knows the jungle, knows the predators that stalk our every move. Don't get me wrong— we have two of the best trackers you could hope to find. But they're expertise is in the United States, not Africa. I don't know about you, but when I came here, I came to be a peacekeeper. I didn't sign up for this. I'm not a killer. I don't murder people because of what their beliefs are. No amount of money is worth this. How many men have we lost? And you know why we lost them? Because, like us, they were here to be peacemakers. They had no military experience. No experience with a gun. The men who are paying us lied to us. They wanted soldiers to fight their war for them. They threw us to the wolves knowing full well that we probably wouldn't make it out of this God-forsaken jungle to collect what's owed to us. Each of us has a decision we have to make. No one can make it for us. My decision is simple. I'm not going back to the fighting. I'm heading south, as far as I can go. When the rebels have moved further northeast, then I'm heading west to Cabinda. I'm jumping a freighter and taking my ass back to Canada."

The group of men was quiet. Then Taylor, one of the trackers, stood to face Rick. "And what about you, Adam,

Travis? Do you agree with our Captain?"

Travis nodded his head. "I'm with Rick on this. I don't want to die in this damn jungle."

Adam walked over to stand with Rick and Travis. "Colin is like a brother to me. I can't walk away from him. I have to try to find him. I'm probably signing my own death warrant, but I have to do this. That being said, I wouldn't blame any one of you if you want to follow Rick. As a matter of fact, I hope you do."

One of the injured men also stood. "So, you want us to run and hide like cowards?"

Rick shook his head. "No. Are we cowards if we choose not to be lambs heading for the slaughter? If we go back and fight, there's no way we're coming out of this jungle alive. Colin and the rest of the men . . . well, the majority of them . . . are soldiers. They made a choice to fight. We weren't given that option. There is no shame. No one will label you a coward if you follow me. If you want to join Adam and try to find Colin and continue the fight, then my prayers are with you. Okay, no more speeches. A show of hands. All those that want to continue the fight?" Rick scanned the group of men. Not one man put his hand up. "And those that want to follow me?"

Every man raised his hand. "All right . . . south it is."

Nathen called a meeting in the gathering hut. Only a selected few were invited. The High Priestess Tamara, Casandra, Tuval, Arman, Sensay, Tammy, Hansen and of course, Authia. Normally, the entire village would be present, and Nathen and Tamara would take their place on the raised platform at the back of the gathering hut, but not today. The village was unaware of the evil that waited for them outside of their valley. Nathen felt it best to keep them unaware until he had a plan. Nathen and Tamara didn't take their place on the platform, for today, everyone was on equal ground. Everyone had a say in this meeting. The group sat on the ground forming a circle.

Nathen started the meeting. "All right, we all know why we're here. According to Sensay, our valley is at risk of being attacked. There's a war going on in the valley below us, and it just might be heading our way. Sensay, tell us exactly what you saw."

"What I saw was a large group of men entering my village. I saw hatred, torture, and death." Sensay closed her eyes as she relived the vision. Tears started to run down her cheeks. "I saw my people betraying you." She looked up at Nathen. "They led the men right to the entrance of your valley. That is why I sent my people away. When the men come, there will be no one there for them to torture."

"Did you see them enter our valley?"

"No. My gift does not allow me to see past the waterfall."

"Do you know when they're coming?"

"Soon, my Lord, very soon."

Arman interjected. "Soon doesn't give us much. My Lord, I think we should plan as if they were on our doorstep."

Nathen nodded in agreement. "Problem is, how do we plan against the weaponry that they'll bring with them."

"What we need is an early warning system." Authia stood up and started to pace as she always did when she was deep in thought. "With the village empty, they might not even find us. But we can't take that chance. We need to know when they arrive, how many there are and what weapons they have."

Nathen smiled at Authia. "It sounds like you have a plan, my Love."

Authia grinned. "I do." She stopped her pacing and looked at the group. "Tamara, Casandra and I are the strongest melders in the village."

Nathen frowned at Authia. "I don't think that I'm going to

like where this is going."

"Hear me out, Nathen. Say that Cameron, Tamara, and Hansen hide in the trees just outside our valley. Tamara can meld with you and me and let us know when anyone enters the village and if so, how many. Hansen will be able to tell us what weapons they have. Cameron will be there for protection. We'll know if they come anywhere close to the entrance to our valley."

Tammy raised her hand. "Umm, not to be disrespectful, but we *are* talking about men, on edge, with guns. If they do enter our valley and get a glimpse of you, they may shoot first, ask questions later. Like, you guys are . . . intimidating . . . and some of you are downright scary."

Nathen laughed. "Not exactly the way I would have put it, but you do have a point. They could feel threatened if they see us."

The group was quiet until Authia spoke of something from the not so distant past. "Just a minute. Tamara, what did you say to Nathen when he asked you why he couldn't just come into the village and confront Casandra?"

Tamara shrugged her shoulders. "I do not remember."

"Well, I do. You said he couldn't do that because your mother could easily cast a spell that would have your people see Nathen as she wishes them to see him. Isn't that right?"

Casandra answered. "Yes, I could. What does that have to do with anything?"

"Don't you see? You can cast a spell so that if the men enter our valley, they'll see the Jelani Tribe as they see me."

All eyes were on Casandra. She looked at everyone in disbelief. "No, that's not how it works. I can cast a spell on one person, not on the entire tribe. I'm not strong enough for such a complex spell."

Tamara thought for a moment. "Maybe not you alone, mother. But what if all the priestesses and our Mistress and

Sensay cast the spell together? Would we not be strong enough if we were to be as one?"

Again, all eyes were on Casandra. "Yes, that could work. However, there are always great risks with performing such intricate spells."

Authia walked over to Casandra and knelt by her side. "What kind of risks?"

"The kind that you can't take back. For myself and Sensay, at our age, it could weaken us, weaken our gift or take it away altogether. For that matter, a spell as intense as this one could very well take its toll on all of us."

"If it means our survival, I'm willing to risk it." Authia looked over to Tamara. "What about you? Are you willing to risk your gift?"

"Yes, of course."

Authia turned to Sensay. "And you?"

"I am old. If what little I have to offer can save the Lion People, then I will gladly sacrifice it all."

Nathan looked at his wife with such pride as Authia stood up and looked around at everyone. "Great. Then we have a plan. Casandra, how much time do you need to prepare?"

"A few hours. The ceremony itself is quite involved."

Authia looked over to Sensay. "How much time do you think we have, Sensay?"

Sensay frowned as she slowly shook her head. "The evil is close. I can feel it. I can smell it. It creeps upon us like an animal stocking its prey." Sensay looked up at Authia. "The Lion People are in great danger. They have no time."

"Well then, we'll need to perform the spell sooner than later. Casandra, talk to the other priestesses. If it's okay with them, then we'll perform the spell tonight."

Casandra stood to leave, then reconsidered and turned to face Authia. "For this spell to work, neither of them can be present." Casandra pointed to Hansen and Tammy.

Hansen looked dumbfounded at Casandra. "Why? We're not your enemy."

"Mabey not. But you are still outsiders. And as an outsider, you can't attend."

Authia spoke up. "I'm an outsider, and so is Sensay. If we can attend, why can't they?"

"My Mistress. You are no longer an outsider. You're one of us, chosen by our Lord to be his mate. And as far as Sensay goes, she's gifted, so the Gods will look kindly on her."

Hansen stood up and offered Tammy his hand, then gently pulled her to her feet. "No worries. We'll stay in our hut. Come get us when it's all over."

Casandra watched the two of them leave, then turned to face Authia. "One other thing I should mention, my Mistress. When performing a spell such as this one, all those involved are entwined with that spell. The death of just one will dissolve the spell."

"Well, then we'll just have to make sure that none of us dies."

Rick's men all stood, waiting for orders. He didn't know what he was doing. Basically, he was flying by the seat of his pants. Head south. *What an ingenious plan.* He stared off to the north, where he could hear the gunfire. He could hear the screams of men dying in battle. Taylor came over to him and stood by his side. "You look deep in thought."

"Can you hear it?"

"The gunfire? Yeah, I can hear it."

"No, I can hear the sounds of men dying." He turned to look at Taylor. "I can't get their voices out of my head. I need to get out of this damn jungle. Get Greg and head south. See what's ahead of us. We'll pack up here and catch up with you."

"You got it." Taylor and Greg grabbed their gear and headed out.

Rick turned to face his men. "Okay, I want to take as many of the firearms, ammunition, and explosives as we can. What we can't carry on our backs, we'll carry on litters. I want to be out of here in twenty." Rick watched as his men scrambled to get everything packed.

Twenty minutes later, they were on the move. It took four litters and twelve backpacks, but they managed to clean out the bunker. They headed south through the worst jungle that they had ever seen. It was closing in all around them. Their machetes barely cut through the dense vegetation. The high humidity caused the camouflage gear they were wearing to cling to their bodies. The stench of body odor and fear hung like a heavy veil, surrounding them, choking them.

Two hours later, they met up with Taylor and Greg. Rick gave the order to break. The men carefully lowered the litters, trying not to jostle the explosives they were carrying.

Rick slipped his backpack off and then went over to Taylor and Greg. "What did you find?"

Taylor handed Rick a canteen of water. "There's a trail about twenty minutes from here. Looks like a migrating trail, though it hasn't been used in quite some time. At least not by animals."

"What do you mean?"

"There are signs of a truck, same truck, coming down that road at least three times. There're also signs of a campsite. I'd say five maybe six people."

"How far ahead of us are they?"

"Signs are old. Whoever camped there is no longer in the area. I say we head for the trail, camp there the night."

"You want to camp out in the open?"

"Right now, our enemy is the four-legged variety. I would rather be in the open, so I can see my enemy coming."

"You're right. I'll give the men another ten. Then we'll head for the trail. Tomorrow morning, I want both of you to continue heading south. See what's waiting for us."

Both Taylor and Greg nodded in agreement, then went to join the rest of the men. Rick stared out into the jungle. He was taking a considerable risk, not only with his life, but with the life of every man that followed him. He knew who led the rebels, and he knew the carnage, the mutilation, the man left in his wake.

CHAPTER FIVE

Darkness fell on the Jelani Tribe. Torches lit up the area that surrounded the communal fire pit. The village was quiet—there wasn't a soul in sight. Everyone was in their huts, waiting, preparing themselves for the ceremony that was to be held later that evening. Hansen was starting a fire in his hut while Tammy sat on their sleeping mat watching him. He looked up and smiled at her. "You're staring at me."

She looked down at the ground, then back up at Hansen. "Sorry, didn't mean to."

Hansen walked over to Tammy, sat down beside her, and put his arm around her shoulders. "Okay sweetheart. What's bothering you? I know that look."

Tammy looked over at Hansen, tears forming in her eyes. "I'm scared. I don't want to lose you. Can't someone else go climb trees and be a lookout?"

"Tammy, besides Nathen, I am the only one here that knows anything about guns and whatever other weaponry these men might be bringing. I probably know more than Nathen. I have to go."

"Well, I don't like it. I love you so much."

Hansen moved in front of Tammy so that he would be facing her. Tenderly he held her hands in his. "Do you love me enough to be my wife?"

Tammy's eyes went wide with her mouth gaped open. "Oh my God!" She threw her arms around Hansen. "Yes, yes, I'll be your wife."

Hansen gently pulled her away. "This isn't exactly how I was planning to propose to you. I don't even have a ring."

"I don't need a ring."

"Let me finish. And yes, you do need a ring. How about,

42

after all this is over, you and I head into Cabinda, buy you a ring, find a justice of the peace and get married?"

"That sounds amazing. But that doesn't change the fact that I'm still very afraid for you."

"There's nothing to be afraid of. Cameron will be there to protect me. Really, sweetheart, I'll be fine." Hansen drew Tammy into his arms, and as he hugged her, he looked past the village, past the waterfall to the trees that grew like skyscrapers into the sky, and the same fear that held such a tight grip on Tammy resonated deep within Hansen.

Inside Nathen and Authia's hut, Nathen watched as Authia played with Joshawa. She was lying on her back, legs up in the air and she was balancing Joshawa by placing her feet flat against his stomach and chest. She was holding on to his tiny hands as she glided her legs back and forth as if he were a plane in the air. Then she would separate her feet, catching Joshawa as he fell toward her. Joshawa would squeal *again*, and Authia gladly gave him another *airplane ride*.

Nathen walked over and picked up Joshawa, who was sitting on his mother's belly saying *again, again*. "All right little man. Daddy has to speak to Mommy." He placed Joshawa down among his toys, then went to sit next to Authia. "I need to speak to you about tonight."

"Okay?"

Nathen drew a deep breath and slowly let it out. "If this spell works then, for the first time in my life, I'll appear normal."

"Okay, I'm going to stop you right there. I know where you're going with this. Nathen, you're already normal. All this spell is going to do is make you look different. Nothing else is going to change."

"But what if you like what you see? I wouldn't blame you

43

if you would prefer not to have to look at this" — Nathen circled his hand over his face — "every day of your life."

"Nathen, I didn't fall in love with your face or any other part of your body, as magnificent as it may be. I fell in love with you. Or have you forgotten that I was head over heels in love with you before I even saw your face? And when you finally did reveal yourself to me, I didn't turn away from you . . . I embraced you. Nathen, when all this is over, I want you back, as you are now." Authia reached up and gently caressed the side of Nathen's face. "This is the face that I want to look at for the rest of my life. Nothing's going to change that."

Tears welled up in Nathen's eyes. "What did I ever do to deserve such an amazing wife?"

"You just got lucky." Authia leaned closer to Nathen and placed her arms around his neck. "We both got lucky." She brought him closer to her and gently kissed him.

Nathen, overwhelmed by emotion, pulled her tight against him as he gently laid her down on the sleeping mat. Their kiss deepened as Nathen went to undo the straps that held Authia's top in place.

Authia's hand covered his as she pulled away from the embrace. Playfully she smiled at him. "Joshawa is still awake."

Nathen sat up and looked at his wife. Her animal skin halter top and skirt were seductively hiding what he so desperately wanted to explore. He smiled at Authia. "Maybe Tammy and Hansen will watch him."

Before Authia could answer, Tamara's voice could be heard from outside of their hut. "My Lord, may I enter?"

Authia quickly sat up as she answered Tamara. "Of course. Come in."

Tamara entered caring a robe and mask. She was dressed in her ceremonial robe complete with a mask that covered the upper half of her face. "I brought this for you to wear, my Mistress. My mother tells me that she and the other priestesses are ready."

Authia stood up and took the gown and mask. "I'll be right there." Tamara bowed to him, and her Mistress then left the hut. Authia turned to Nathen. "I guess this is it." Authia pulled the gown over her head, then positioned the mask over the top half of her face.

Nathen picked up Joshawa and took Authia's hand in his. He met her gaze, knowing full well that he couldn't hide his fear from her.

Authia looked up at him. "You have nothing to fear. At least not from me. Don't worry about us. Worry about what's out there. What's heading our way." She leaned up and kissed Nathen on his cheek. "Now let's go and get this over with."

The sun was just beginning its descent in the western sky when Rick and his men broke out of the jungle and onto the trail that Taylor and Greg had found earlier. It was badly rutted, and there were obvious signs that someone had camped there before. Rick took off his backpack and walked over to where the previous campfire had been. He looked over to Travis. "What do you think? Do we risk a fire?"

"I think we should. At least a small one. We're far enough south. I don't think a fire will be visible to any rebels. And besides, it may keep the animals at bay."

"I agree. Get the men settled. I want at least five men on guard at all times."

"You got it." Travis went to carry out his orders while Rick scrutinized his surroundings. The sun was quickly disappearing, cloaking the area into darkness. The sounds of the jungle seem to intensify as the moon shone above their heads. Rick closed his eyes and concentrated on the various animals and birds conversing with each other. It was as if the jungle was alive. As if it had a mind of its own. And it was laughing at them—mocking them. He walked over to the edge of the trail and stared into the depths of the jungle. "You're not going to win. I'm not going to die here." The campfire lit up behind him, and the jungle grew quiet.

A two-hour walk north of the abandoned bunker was where the rebels could be found. Their numbers were growing with every village they raided. Innocent young men and boys were forced to take up arms. The majority of the rebels were from Africa, fighting because they believed they were defending their home, when in reality they were fighting for a government they knew nothing about. One such rebel was Obasi. He was only twenty and had been fighting for his survival since he was ten. He had been fighting for the rebels for over a year. Obasi had proven himself to be ruthless, cunning, and very knowledgeable of the Congo. He only took prisoners who could provide a tactical advantage to him. Anyone else, he killed. The prisoners that he did capture were beaten upon until they had no willpower left, no strength to fight back. They were beaten until they gave him what he wanted. Obasi was a loner with only one true friend. He commanded over forty men but didn't associate with any of them. He liked keeping his distance. If there were no attachments, then there was no reason to mourn when you lost a man in battle.

Obasi cared little for his appearance. He felt he was average looking for the men of his village. As he sat on the ground among the ferns, waiting for his meal, he took mental stock of his attributes. He knew he wasn't a very big man, being of medium height and build. On the ground next to him was a dinner plate that was made of metal. He held it up and gazed at his reflection on the shiny surface. His skin tone was very dark, his nostrils flared and his hair, cut short, was thick and curly almost to the point of being matted. He was missing two of his front teeth. To him, none of that was intimidating. He had to find his own way to control his men, and he did that by being ruthless, cruel, and unforgiving. Obasi would not waste time on his personal hygiene, nor would he weigh himself down with unnecessary clothing. He looked down at his camouflage pants, stained with blood and dirt. Not his blood, but the blood of those he'd tortured. His chest was bare and scarred from the many altercations he had with the enemy.

The day was settling into the evening as the last rays of sunlight vanished behind the horizon. Obasi sat on a ridge that overlooked his men. Several fires had been started, and he could smell the scent of cooked meat wafting in the air. His second in command, Saburo, walked over and sat next to him. He handed Obasi a large palm leaf that was wrapped around a chunk of meat. Obasi turned to face Saburo. He found Saburo to be what he referred to as a pretty boy. Saburo was lighter in complexion, mostly due to the fact that his mother was white, something Obasi didn't approve of. Saburo was slightly taller and stockier than Obasi, but every pound was pure muscle. His black hair was shoulder length and wavy. He was also dressed in camouflage pants and always wore the same dark green t-shirt. Obasi accepted the meal, then returned his gaze out to where his men were camped. Saburo also looked out over their camp as he addressed Obasi. "I think we have all we're going to get out of our prisoner."

Obasi continued to stare out into the night. "Do you believe him?"

"Yes, I do. After the beating he took, he's not likely to lie to us. He watched all his men die. He knows that no one's looking for him."

"Except for maybe the men that ran to the south. So, do you think we should abandon the fight to the northeast and follow the men that escaped to the south?"

Saburo looked over to Obasi. "You normally don't allow men to escape. I think we should follow them and kill them before they can reach reinforcements."

"I agree. We'll head out at first light. Let the prisoner lead the way. But keep him on a short leash."

Saburo stood up. "I'll let everyone know." He left Obasi to be alone with his thoughts.

And his thoughts were running wild. Heading south took him away from the fighting. But it could possibly lead him to a discovery that would bring him more wealth than he could ever imagine.

CHAPTER SIX

Nathen stood just outside of his hut and watched as his people started to gather around the communal fire pit. Tammy and Hansen remained secluded in their hut. The ceremony was not for them. The villagers left a ten-foot-wide open area around the pit for the priestesses. Already standing at the pit was Sensay. When everyone was in attendance, the priestesses left their huts and walked single file toward the fire pit. They stopped for only a second when they reached Nathen and Authia's hut, just long enough for Authia to file in behind Tamara and for Nathen to take the lead. Each priestess, dressed in her ceremonial gown complete with mask, carried a clay pot, which Nathen knew would contain the leaf covered packets of each priestess. These packets were what the priestesses used to conjure and cast spells. When they reached the fire pit, they formed a circle around it, each priestess standing an arm's length from the next. Nathen, holding Joshawa, took his place standing a few feet behind Authia. As everyone watched, the priestesses started placing the green leaf packets inside the fire pit. They were careful as they laid each packet right beside the next without overlapping. When they were finished, and the fire pit was filled with packets, they laid the clay pots in front of them.

Nathen looked on, his mind running wild, his thoughts taunting him. He was scared. He knew what they were doing was best for the tribe. And he knew that Authia loved him for who and what he was. But he just couldn't stop the fear that coursed through his body. What if Authia did change her mind? What if she decided that she preferred the new Nathen? He looked around at the people, his people. They were oblivious to the real reason for this ceremony. As far as they were concerned, the priestesses were cleansing the village, nothing more.

Authia had her back to Nathen, but she could feel him, feel his uncertainty, his fear. She wanted to hold him, to reassure him that everything was going to be all right. Instead, she melded with him. *Nathen, my dear, sweet Nathen. You must be strong. Strong for your people, for your son and for yourself. Trust in me, and most importantly, trust in us.*

Authia watched as Tamara motioned toward Nathen, who indicated he understood and walked over to her. Tamara then lifted her hands to silence the crowd. Nathen looked at his people, then at Authia, who smiled at him, hoping to give him the courage he needed to address his people.

"We are here tonight for one purpose, and that purpose is to protect our home and our way of life. There have been rumblings of an evil existing outside of our valley. Those rumblings are true. Outside our valley, there's a war being waged. And this war just might be heading our way." There were audible gasps in the crowd as fear swept over them. "There is nothing to be concerned about, at least not at this moment. The village on the other side of the falls has been emptied. We are going to place our people in the trees that separate the village from the falls. We're going to watch the village, and if outsiders do show up, we'll know they're there, and we'll be ready. If by some miracle they find their way into our valley, the ceremony we're performing tonight just might help us. Tonight, the priestesses will cast a spell so that when the outsiders look upon us, they'll see us as if we were one of them. Hopefully, by doing this, we'll not appear as a threat to them. Over the centuries, there have only been two incursions into our valley. The chances that whoever is coming will find the entrance are very low. However, it will not hurt for us to prepare, to be ready."

There was stunned silence among the crowd as they listened to their Lord.

"Trust me. Trust that I'll do everything in my power to keep you safe . . . to keep our valley safe." Nathen looked over to Tamara. "High Priestess Tamara, if you would start the ceremony." Nathen went back to his spot located behind Authia.

Authia looked over her shoulder and smiled at him. "You did good." She winked at him. "Now it's my turn." Authia turned to face the other priestesses.

Tamara addressed her people. "As High Priestess, I formally request that my mother, Priestess Casandra, lead this ceremony. Bow if you accept this request or stand and be heard."

Each priestess, including Authia and Sensay, as well as the entire tribe, bowed to their High Priestess. Casandra, her arms outstretched before her, looked up at the sky. "Hear me, spirits of loved ones long since gone. Help us reach out to the spirits of deception. Help them to hear our pleas. Become one with us as we become one with you." Casandra lowered her hands and looked upon the other priestesses. "Sit with me, my sisters. Join hands so that we may conjure as one." All the priestesses, including Authia and Sensay, sat cross-legged on the ground and joined hands. "Now close your eyes and empty your minds. Allow only my words, my thoughts to occupy your mind. Hear me, listen to me. Seek out what is hidden from us."

The priestesses closed their eyes and bowed their heads. Casandra started speaking in the language of the priestesses. Authia listened to the words, though they meant nothing to her. She cleared her mind, focusing solely on Casandra. The priestesses started to sway back and forth, and as they did, Authia could feel an energy flow through her body, an energy that connected her to all the other priestesses. Then, as she listened, she could understand what Casandra was saying. The words became clear.

"Oh, spirits of deception, hear our cries. See our torment. See the enemy that is at our door. We ask that you protect us. Conceal us with your trickery. Have our enemy see us as they would see themselves. Spirits of deception, hear our pleas. We beg of you to protect us, to conceal us. Reach out to the Jelani Tribe. To the children of this valley." The priestesses, including Authia and Sensay, started swaying faster and faster, side to side, then suddenly stopped and in unison reached forward until their foreheads almost touched the ground. They were bowing to the spirits they sought out showing their respect. "Spirits of deception, protect us, conceal us . . . protect us, conceal us . . . protect us, conceal us . . ."

Nathen watched on as the priestesses swayed faster, back and forth. Their chanting grew louder, their voices blending together. But still, Nathen could make out Authia's voice. She was speaking in the language of the priestesses. *How did she know to do that?* The ground started to swirl around the priestesses. Nathen took a step forward, only to be held back by Arman, who slowly shook his head side to side. Nathen stepped back in place. Nathen tightened his grip on Joshawa as he watched the dirt that they walked on come alive and dance around the priestesses. The dirt formed an impregnable barrier, separating the priestesses from the villagers. Through the dirt and small stones that swirled around them, Nathen could see the packets that lay in the fire pit. They started to glow, but not with fire. An intense light was building up inside the packets—a white light growing so bright that Nathen could no longer look upon it. The chanting stopped, and as Nathen looked back, he saw that all the priestesses were looking upwards toward the sky. Then the packets exploded, sending the light high into the clouds and turning night into day. The pure force of the explosion sent the dirt and stone flying into the villagers, knocking most of them off their feet. Within seconds, the light was gone, and darkness enveloped the village.

Rick and his men started a small fire on which to cook their supper and hopefully to ward off any animals that might be a threat to them. As Rick gazed deep into the red-hot embers of the fire, his mind registered every noise that surrounded his small group. The jungle was anxious. Its natural inhabitants were wary of what was transpiring around them. Rick looked up at the evening sky. He was just about to turn and address Travis when the southern sky lit up as if it were the day.

Then as soon as it was there, it was gone. Rick sprang to his feet. "Did you see that?"

Every man stood and stared off to the darkened skies. Travis stood next to Rick. "How could you miss it? What the hell was that? What kind of weapon could have caused that?"

Rick shook his head. "None that I'm aware of. Whatever it was, it's gone now." Rick turned to his men. "Okay, show's over. Get some sleep. We've a long day tomorrow." Rick turned his attention to Travis. "Maybe south isn't such a good idea."

"There's no fighting to the south. It's still our best bet."

Rick stood by and watched as Travis climbed into his sleeping bag. All Rick wanted to do was go home, leave this God-forsaken jungle behind him. He returned his gaze to the southern skies. *What was that light?* It was as if it were a beacon revealing to him his destination. As if some greater force was controlling his destiny. Rick slowly shook his head. It was a light . . . that was all it was. And even though something deep inside of Rick was telling him there was much more to that light, Rick climbed into his sleeping bag, dismissing the light altogether.

Obasi laid on the ground cushioned by the ferns and moss that grew there. He stretched his massive arms in front of him, then laced his fingers together and placed them behind his head. He stared up at the stars that shone brightly in the sky. He thought of the hut that his prisoner had told him about. The prisoner tried to pretend that he was unaware of what was contained in the hut, but Obasi knew. He was confident that it was filled with guns and ammunition, just there for his taking. His prisoner had also pleaded with him that the men that headed south were no threat. *Does he take me for such a fool?* Obasi had implied that there were no survivors, that the men who had headed south had all been killed. And then there were the moments when the prisoner was delirious, rambling on about a valley protected by the Gods. A valley where no man dared set foot. *Until now.* Obasi smiled to himself as visions of untold wealth danced in his mind. And that was when he saw it. A great light was shining in the southern skies. Quickly he sat up, only to see the light disappear as suddenly as it came.

Saburo came running up to Obasi. "Did you see the light? The entire southern sky lit up."

Obasi answered, not taking his eyes off the night sky. "Yes, I saw it. It was a beacon from the Gods showing us the way."

"The way to what?"

Obasi turned to face Saburo. "Only the Gods know that answer. We leave at first light. Saburo, I want the men that headed south. I want them dead."

CHAPTER SEVEN

Nathen turned his back to the flying dirt and pebbles, tucking Joshawa closer to his body, shielding him from any injury. He glanced over his shoulder at the brilliant light that shone high above the fire pit and deep into the evening sky. In the time it took Nathen to blink, the light was gone, blanketing the village into darkness. As the dust settled, Nathen could see his people slowly getting up from the ground, looking at each other, wondering if the spell had worked. Arman was immediately at his side.

"Are you all right, my Lord?"

"Yes. Light up the torches." Nathen turned his attention to the fire pit. "Authia? Where are you?"

He could feel her hand on his shoulder. Slowly he closed his eyes as he turned to face Authia.

"I'm right here." She placed her hand on the side of his face. "Open your eyes, my Love. The spell didn't work. You appear to me exactly as you did before."

Nathen opened his eyes and scanned the crowd. Everyone was exactly as they were before the spell. Arman relit the torches bringing to light the sad realization that their pleas to the spirits had gone unanswered. Their attempt to hide within themselves had failed.

Nathen sought out Casandra. "Why didn't the spell work?"

Casandra smiled, giving Nathen the impression that she knew something he didn't. "And who said it didn't work?"

"Look around you, Casandra. Nothing has changed."

"Are you sure about that, my Lord? I think it's time for Hansen and Tammy to rejoin us."

Nathen wasn't too sure what Casandra was getting at but

decided to play along. He sent Tuval to retrieve Hansen and Tammy. As he watched them approach, he couldn't help but notice the stunned look on both their faces.

Hansen looked around at the faces he once knew. They were dressed the same, they had the same physical build, even their eye color remained the same, but everything else had changed. Their shocking red hair was dark brown. Their faces appeared no different than anyone else from the outside world. Their long fingernails were short and rounded. Hansen walked over to Nathen. He knew it was Nathen, for the man who stood before him resembled Nathen, just an outsider version of him. "The spell worked. Wow! You, everyone here, looks as though you came from the outside world."

Nathen appeared confused by Hansen's comment. "What are you talking about? We all look the same as we did before the spell."

"Well, I don't know what you are looking at, but believe me, you look no different than me."

Nathen turned to Casandra. "What's going on? Why does Hansen see what I'm not?"

"My Lord. We asked the spirits of deception to hide us from our enemy. However, the spirits don't know who our enemy is because we don't know who our enemy is. They can only assume that the people participating in the ceremony are our friends. Anyone outside this circle is considered the enemy and will see us as they see themselves. That's why I requested that Hansen and Tammy remain in their hut. How else would we know if the spell worked?"

Nathen smiled as he shook his head. "Smart. So, we'll see each other as we are, but anyone else will see what they want to see?"

"Yes, my Lord."

"Will the spell work outside of the valley?"

"No, my Lord. The magic is confined to our valley. That is true of any spell."

Authia reached over and took Joshawa from Nathen, kissing Joshawa gently on his forehead as she wrapped her arms around him. "My handsome little man." She looked up to Nathen. "So, when do you want to start monitoring the village?"

Tamara removed her mask as she approached her Lord. "We should leave for the falls first thing in the morning." Tamara turned her attention to Hansen. "Will you still accompany us?"

"Sure. Just give me a time and a place, and I'll be there."

Authia shifted Joshawa's weight to her left side. "Well, that sounds good to me. I think we should all call it a night. The next few days are going to be very stressful."

Hansen lay on his sleeping mat, staring at the roof of the hut. He looked down at Tammy, who was wrapped protectively in his arms. Tenderly he kissed the top of her head, then continued to stare at the roof. From what Nathen described, Hansen knew what was coming—firepower beyond anything that the tribe had ever seen. *How are we going to fight?* Bows, arrows, and spears against guns, rifles, and God knew what else. The tribe had performed a ceremony to the spirits of deception. Maybe they should have been praying to the spirits of protection. God only knew they were going to need it. Hansen closed his eyes and dreamt of a battle overrun with blood and death.

The sun was just beginning to poke its head above the horizon, basking the village in the light of a new day. Joshawa woke up and rolled off the pillows that made up his bed. Nathen, awake but still lying on his mat, watched Joshawa as he sat up and looked around the hut until his gaze fell upon him. He giggled with delight as he stood and waddled toward his mother. With a pudgy hand, he poked awkwardly at her head. "Plane ride . . . plane ride."

Authia rolled over to face Nathen. "Your son wants an airplane ride."

"I thought he was your son?"

"Not at this time in the morning."

Nathen leaned over and kissed Authia. "Sleep, my Love. I'll take Joshawa and get him some breakfast."

"Perfect." Authia curled up into a ball and fell back to sleep.

"All right little man. Let's get you something to eat."

Nathen put on his loincloth, put a fresh diaper on Joshawa, then picked him up and headed toward the communal fire pit. There was already a bush pig roasting over the open fire. The aroma of ham laced with herbs wafted throughout the village. Large bowls of fruit and bread were situated around the fire pit. His people were sitting around the fire, talking about the evil that lurked just outside their valley. Nathen could sense the uneasiness and fear that consumed the tribe's every thought. He scanned the area for Tamara until he found her walking in the direction of the priestess' hut. She was dressed in her ceremonial gown without the mask. He caught up with her and joined her as she entered the hut. Casandra, dressed in her animal skin, was sitting next to Sam as she spoon-fed him some broth. Sam was propped up against several pillows. His right arm was in a sling, immobilizing the shoulder that had been wounded. He still appeared very pale and looked as though he had little to no energy.

Nathen put Joshawa down and walked over to Sam. "How are you?"

Sam lowered his head in a weak attempt to bow before Nathen. As he looked up and met Nathen's gaze, he smiled. "I'm doing well, thanks to you, my Lord."

"Good to hear. Do you know where Tomas is?"

"I saw him running, and then there was a loud noise, and he fell to the ground. I couldn't get to him." Tears started to well up in Sam's eyes. "I just left him. And I ran, and I ran until I could no longer run. I was hurt. All I could think of was getting home." Tears were streaming down his cheeks. "I don't deserve to live. Tomas was my friend, and I just left him to die."

Nathen knelt next to Sam. "There was nothing you could do. But you can help me now."

"How?"

"What did you see when you were in the valley?"

Nathen watched Sam stare past him to a place that was obviously uncomfortable for him. Then Sam closed his eyes, the tears continuing to stain his cheeks.

"If it's too painful, we can speak later."

Sam gently nodded his head, and Nathen respected his wishes. He stood up and walked over to Joshawa, picked him up, and held him securely in his left arm. He looked over at Sam. "That's fine, Sam. You need time to come to terms with what you experienced. I'll come back later." Nathen then turned his attention to Tamara. "Can you find Hansen, Tammy, and Sensay and meet me at the gathering hut? I'm going to see if Authia's awake yet. I want to hold a meeting before you head out."

Tamara bowed to him. "Yes, of course, my Lord."

Nathen turned to face Casandra. "I'd like you there as well."

"Yes, my Lord. I'll finish tending to Sam and then join you there."

"Thank you." Both Tamara and Casandra bowed to

Nathen as he left the hut.

Nathen headed to his own hut to find Authia awake and dressed.

She reached over and took Joshawa. "Did your father feed you?" Joshawa smiled at his mother, leaned closer to her, and ran his hands through her hair.

"No, I haven't. We can grab something on our way to the gathering hut."

"We're going to the gathering hut?"

"I thought we'd start planning our protection of the village before we start sending anyone to the other side."

"Sounds good. I'll get something for Joshawa and meet you there." Authia leaned up and kissed Nathen, then headed for the communal fire pit, where he watched as she picked up some fruit, meat, and bread for Joshawa.

The atmosphere in the gathering hut was solemn. *How do you prepare for a fight when you don't know who your enemy is? When you know the odds are nowhere near in your favor?* Masking their appearance would only buy them time . . . maybe. There was no guarantee. Nathen looked around at the group that sat on the floor of the hut alongside him. He was their leader, their Lord. It was his job to protect his people, but Nathen knew, deep down, that he was out of his league. He was not a warrior as his father was. Nathen drew a deep breath. "So, what do we know?"

Hansen spoke first. "It's what we don't know that's the problem. We don't know who's coming, when they're coming, or for that matter, even if they are coming."

Sensay shook her head. "You have no faith in my gift of sight?"

"Sensay, I meant no disrespect. Okay, let's all agree that someone is coming."

"Not just someone. It will be a large group of men . . . only men. They seek what is not theirs to have. They are guided by hate and death." Sensay closed her eyes and took a deep breath. When she reopened her eyes, she stared directly at Nathen. "Lord of the Lion People, I have done everything in my power to protect your people. It is now on you. You must be strong, and you must be prepared to fight for your people."

Nathen's mind tried to digest all he knew about the coming events. If only his father were there to guide him. He would know exactly what to do. Then from deep within himself, a voice came to him. A voice he knew only too well.

Well, Nathen, I see that you have succeeded in taking your place as Lord of our People.

Serena, what are you doing here?

Apparently atoning for my . . . shall we say, indiscretions.

Well, you can atone for your indiscretions somewhere else. Get out of my head!

Sorry. Neither you or myself have any say in this matter. You see, neither your father, and especially not your mother, have the skills required to help you in your time of need. I, however, do. And if I want to join my ancestors, I must perform a deed of honor, protecting those that I have hurt in the past. You see, my Ancestors are none too pleased with me. Apparently, everything I did to secure the rule of my family was looked upon with great disdain. Now, they are sending me back to the spirit world so that I may help you protect our people. So that maybe I can earn their forgiveness and become one with the great spirits of my past.

Nathen looked over to Authia, but she showed no signs that she could hear Serena. *Can Authia hear you?*

Right, Authia. No, she cannot. And she will not until you and I come to an agreement.

What kind of agreement?

You have to agree to play nice. My only purpose in being here is to help you. I cannot accomplish that if you fight me.

Serena, you are not to be trusted. What proof can you offer me that you are being truthful?

I told them that you would be difficult. You always were. You want proof. Close your eyes Nathen. Empty your mind. See what I have to show you.

Casandra entered the hut and observed that everyone in the group was staring at Nathen. He appeared as though he was in a trance. Authia was about to gently shake him when Casandra realized that Nathen was in something deeper than just a trance. "No! You mustn't disturb him." Casandra walked over and sat between Nathen and Authia. "I'll watch over him."

"What's going on, Casandra?"

Casandra didn't take her eyes off Nathen. "My Mistress, he's in communication with a spirit. I can feel the spirit's presence." Casandra turned to face her daughter. "And you, my daughter, what aura do you sense?"

Tamara concentrated on Nathen as she crooked her head to one side. "I sense a very strong aura. One that I have sensed before." Tamara's eyes went wide as she looked over at her mother. "It is Serena. She is with him."

"What!" Authia tried to get to Nathen, but Casandra stopped her using all her weight to pin her to the ground. "Let me go. She'll hurt him."

"No, my Mistress." Tamara's voice was soft and soothing. "I do not sense evil. Serena's aura is weak. She is there to speak with our Lord, not harm him."

Authia quit struggling. "Let me up." Casandra moved aside, and Authia sat up. "Are you sure, Tamara?"

Tamara smiled at her Mistress. "Yes, very sure."

Nathen emptied his mind. He allowed Serena in, and she filled his mind with the jungle he knew from past melds. In the middle of the jungle was a fire pit filled with leaf covered packets. Serena came into view dressed in her ceremonial gown.

What are you showing me, Serena?

Humm . . . it is not so much as what I am showing you . . . but rather who I am showing you. Serena stood aside, and from the furthest recesses of Nathen's mind, a figure approached. Nathen looked on in disbelief as his father walked into the jungle.

Father, what are you doing here? I thought that I would never see you again.

As a past Lord of the Jelani Tribe, I have some influence with the High Priestesses of our past. I have sought them out to demand that they help you in your time of need. They have insisted that Serena be the vessel that they use to offer you this help.

Of all the Priestesses and Lords that they have to choose from, they choose her?

Yes, my son. They know of your past history. It is a test, not only for you but also for Serena. If she wishes to join us, she will have to behave. She will have to prove herself.

And I'm to be the guinea pig?

Believe me, my son. The Priestesses and Lords that are our Ancestors do not look lightly upon your situation. There is wisdom in their choice of Serena. She was one of the strongest priestesses of her time. She will be a strong ally.

I guess we just have to learn to trust her.

As you learned to trust Casandra. I have a gift for you. Or rather, your Ancestors have a gift for you. Joshawa, Nathen's father, extended his hand toward the shadows. A woman appeared to stand next to Joshawa. Nathen gaped at this woman, who was an outsider. She was stunning with long, honey-blonde hair that cascaded in gentle waves to her waist. Her eyes were a dazzling blue, and she had the most beautiful smile.

Hello, my son. It's so good to look upon your face.

Mother? Father, is that really my mother?

Yes, my son. I thought it was time that you met her.

Julia took a step forward. *We haven't much time. I just wanted you to know that I have loved you since I first held you in my arms on the day you were born. I have watched you grow into a man so many times, and each and every time, I was so proud of you. I am proud of you now.*

Tears ran freely down Nathen's cheeks. All his life, he wanted to know who his mother was. And now she stood before him. *I can't believe that I am finally meeting you. I only wish that I could hold you. That you could meet my family.*

Joshawa smiled at Nathen. *Trust me, son, we have met your family, for we watch over you all the time. We must go. Trust Serena.* Nathen's parents faded into the jungle. Then once again, Nathen's mind became blank.

Are you still here, Serena?

Yes. Of course, I am. Are you going to trust me now?

Trust is earned. I will try, but know this . . . it won't be easy . . .

Good. Tell everyone in this hut of my existence. Though I sense they already know. In order for me to help you, I must co-exist with a living soul. Preferably someone who is gifted. Find that person, then find me.

Serena was gone, and as Nathen opened his eyes, he saw that everyone was staring at him. They appeared concerned. Maybe Serena was right, and they did know of her existence.

Authia moved over and sat in front of Nathen. "What happened? You were in a trance. Tamara thinks that Serena was with you."

"And Tamara would be right."

"What? How's that possible?"

"My Ancestors are not pleased with Serena and those that followed her. They have punished them and are not allowing them to join wherever it is that they go to after death until they atone for their behavior."

Casandra's face went pale. "Does that include me as well?"

Nathen shook his head. "You weren't mentioned. It's possible that your new approach to life is giving credence to your wish to better yourself. That being said, our Ancestors want to help us. And they choose to offer that help through Serena. We are to trust her, to trust that she will use her gifts for the betterment of the entire tribe. I, for one, will have difficulty believing that she has changed. Our past history doesn't allow much room for trust."

Casandra thought for a second. "Serena is dead. A true spirit. In her present state, she has no powers."

"True. She told me that she needs to co-exist with a living soul. Preferably someone who's gifted. That means that one of the priestesses has to volunteer. Authia's out of the question. So is Sensay."

"Are you kidding me?" Authia poked her finger at Nathen's chest. "How many times do I have to tell you that you can't control me. It's not up to you to decide what I do."

"You're pregnant. I can't allow you to risk yourself as well as our child."

Tammy blurted out, "You're prego? Awesome! Congrats!"

Hansen put his arm around Tammy. "I don't think now is the time for congratulations."

"Right." Tammy frowned. "Sorry."

"No need to apologize, Tammy. Nathen, we agreed that we would make all decisions together."

Nathen sighed. "You're right. What do you want to do?"

"That's better. However, I do agree with you. I've already gone through one pregnancy with Serena rattling around in my brain. I don't need to do it a second time. Sorry, but I can't participate."

Casandra reached over and took Authia's hands in hers. "There's no need to apologize. You are our Mistress, the mate to our Lord. We would never expect you to put yourself in such danger. I know Serena. I think it's best that she joins with me."

"But, mother — she could kill you."

"Oh, Tamara, she'll not kill me. She and I are of kindred

spirits. She was the strongest priestess of her time. Besides you, I'm the strongest priestess of our time. Combined, our powers could be what keeps our village safe. Besides, we both have much to make up for. This could be a way for me to make amends." Casandra turned to face Nathen. "Tell Serena she has a willing host."

They might not have man-made weapons such as the army that threatened their doorstep. But they did have sorcery on their side. Nathen wasn't entirely convinced that he would have control over the sorcery. He needed to trust in Serena as well as Casandra if he was going to wield such a weapon. He knew he couldn't falter — he couldn't doubt. Only then would he be strong enough to control a force that was greater than what any man could produce.

CHAPTER EIGHT

The morning sun rose above the horizon, finding Rick already awake and sitting cross-legged in front of the fire pit. He stared into the embers still warm from the previous night's fire. Heading south was the most sensible move to make. The fighting was heading northeast, far from the direction he and his men were headed. But if that was the case, then what the hell was that light? Was someone testing weapons in the area? But what kind of weapon made no sound? He was so engrossed in his thoughts that he didn't hear Travis walk up behind him.

"Planning on making coffee on those embers?"

Rick looked up at Travis, shook his head, and smiled. "Lost in my own thoughts."

Travis placed some kindling in the fire pit, knelt and started softly blowing on the embers that lay underneath the kindling. It didn't take long before the embers came alive and the kindling caught fire. Travis placed a couple of larger logs on the fire, then hung the coffee pot from the makeshift pole that was secured two feet above the pit. He sat next to Rick as he stared at the flames that licked the bottom of the coffee pot. "So, what do you make of that light we saw last night?"

"I have no idea. Possibly a weapon?"

"I don't think it was a weapon. At least not one that I've ever heard of. A flash of light, no sound, no aftermath. Just there one second, gone the next." Travis looked over at Rick. "Maybe it was aliens." Both men laughed. "But seriously Rick, we're still heading south, right?"

"Greg and Taylor returned late last night. They found a trail, overgrown. It hasn't been used for quite some time. So, unless you have a better idea . . . then yes, we're still heading south."

"Good. I'll get Taylor and Greg to continue scouting ahead."

"Don't bother. I've already sent them. They left a couple of hours ago."

"Okay. When do you want to head out?"

Rick stood up and wiped the dirt from his pants. "Give Greg and Taylor another half-hour." Rick didn't wait for a response, he just turned and walked toward the edge of the jungle. There he stood and stared at the wall of foliage that was his barrier between him and whatever was waiting for them to the south.

Nathen and Authia walked hand in hand toward the falls that separated them from the outside world. They were joined by Tammy, Hanson, Tamara, and Cameron. Joshawa remained behind under Casandra's watchful eye. Tamara and Cameron were dressed in their animal skins, while Hansen wore his jeans and a dark t-shirt. Their exposed skin had been completely covered with soil which had been tinted a dark green color. The camouflage would allow them to blend into the foliage of the trees in which they would be hiding. Cameron carried a bow, spear, and machete. Tamara carried only a bow. Hansen, unfamiliar with either a bow or spear, carried two machetes. Nathen knew that after years of working on a freighter, Hansen knew how to handle a knife. The question was, could he use one to take another's life?

When they reached the narrow opening that led to the falls, Nathen stopped to address the small group. "Okay, you know what you have to do. Stay hidden. If anyone enters the village, under no circumstances are you to confront them. You are to only watch them. Keep in constant contact with Authia and Casandra. When we better understand their intentions, then, and only then will we decide a course of action. You will return to our village before nightfall."

Hansen had a look of puzzlement on his face. "But Nathen, what if they come at night? Shouldn't we be watching the village twenty-four seven?"

"I doubt that anyone would travel at night. Especially in uncharted areas. Sensay's visions have always been clear. What she saw, she saw in the daylight. There's no way she could be so descriptive if she were looking upon these men at night. Trust me, these men are coming, and when they do, it'll be in the light of day."

"Okay. Second question. Shouldn't we have put this muck on after we went through the falls?"

Tamara smiled at Hansen. "The *muck* needs time to totally dry in order for it to remain on our skin and not rub off on the trees. Follow me. I will clear a path that will keep us dry." Tamara removed a leaf covered packet from her waistband then glanced over her shoulder at her comrades. "Coming?"

Hansen cupped Tammy's chin leaned in and kissed her. "Wait up for me. You can help me take this muck off when I get back."

"You better come back."

Hansen smiled at Tammy, then joined Tamara and Cameron at the opening to the falls. Tamara held the packet in the palm of her right hand as she raised it to face the opening in the rock. She closed her eyes and started chanting in the language of the priestesses. The packet began to vibrate in her hand as it split open and encased the three in a soft, yellow glow.

Nathen and Authia looked on in utter disbelief. They've seen that glow before. It had protected them more than once. They watched as the group entered the falls and continued to watch them until the yellow glow disappeared.

Tammy pointed toward the falls. "What the hell was that?"

Authia turned to leave. "Not sure. But I can almost guarantee you that they stayed dry. Now let's head back." Authia turned her attention to Nathen. "Maybe Sam is well enough to tell us what he saw."

Obasi and his forty men headed south. It wasn't long before they came across the area where they had encountered the resistance, effectively splitting the platoon up. They had forced part of the platoon north, coming at them from all sides. They left none alive with the exception of their prisoner. Obasi sneered as he gazed upon the bodies that littered the ground. Saburo approached him but remained quiet until Obasi acknowledged his presence. "What have you found?"

"You might what to come see this." Saburo led Obasi a few hundred yards south. He stopped and pointed to the ground. A colobus monkey was lying dead on the ground. Obasi moved it onto it's back with his foot. He smiled at the sight of the monkey's chest ripped wide open. Saburo continued. "There was a man here. He crawled from that direction." Saburo pointed to his left. "There were about half a dozen men hiding there. They crawled off to the south. The man that crawled here continued about a hundred yards in that direction." Saburo pointed to his right. "There were about seven to ten men hiding there. It appears that one or more of them were injured. They also crawled off to the south. I've sent a couple of men to follow the tracks, see where they lead. These are most likely the men that the prisoner spoke of."

Obasi stared off into the jungle. "I thought that there might be more."

"Not that we can tell, Obasi. I think that this is all that is left of their platoon."

"Good. We'll follow them. When we come upon them, I want all but one killed." Obasi went to turn away but stopped and looked back at Saburo. "No one is to tell the prisoner there are survivors. Hope can be very dangerous. I would prefer if he had none."

Nathen and Authia headed back to the priestess' hut. When they arrived, they found Joshawa sitting in Sam's lap staring at him wide-eyed as Sam told him a story of his village. Sam's arm was still in a sling but, other than that, there was color in his face, and he was able to sit up without the aid of pillows to support him. Sam looked up at Nathen and Authia, then bowed his head. As he looked back up, he nodded in Nathen and Authia's direction. "Look, Joshawa, your mother and father are here."

Joshawa turned around and raised his arms toward his parents. "Mama"

"Hey, little man." Authia bent over and picked Joshawa up. "I'm going to head out to the pond and bathe Joshawa. You stay and talk with Sam." Authia reached up and kissed Nathen on his cheek. Quietly she whispered into his ear, "I'll listen in." She smiled at him, then left the hut.

Nathen turned his attention to Sam. "You look better. Where's Casandra?"

"She left for the birthing hut. Someone needed her attention. She left Joshawa with me. I hope you are not displeased, my Lord?"

Nathen went and sat down next to Sam. "No, not at all. We need to talk. What happened out there? What happened to Tomas?"

Sam's face went pale. He lowered his eyes and slowly shook his head. "Sensay sent Tomas and me to find out where the lights were coming from. To find out what they were. The further north we traveled, the louder the noise. We found a hut filled with boxes and strange weapons. We followed the

71

noise and then somehow it was all around us. Men screaming, the ground blowing up in front of us. We climbed a tree . . . as far up as we could go. We could see men fighting, dying all around us. Then Tomas got scared. He jumped out of the tree and ran. Something hit him, and he fell to the ground. He didn't get up." Sam started sobbing. "I started to climb out of the tree when something hit me. It burned my shoulder. I fell to the ground. I got up, and two more times I was hit, but I kept running. I left Tomas to die alone." Sam hung his head, sobbing uncontrollably.

Nathen placed his hand on Sam's uninjured shoulder. "There was nothing you could do for Tomas. If you had stayed with him, you would have been killed as well."

Sam looked up at Nathen. "My Lord, you don't understand."

"What don't I understand?"

"I saw Tomas fall. He didn't move. But I didn't check to see if he was still alive. I just ran. There were so many men. I was so scared. He was my friend, and I left him alone with those men."

"Are you saying that Tomas could still be alive?"

Sam shrugged his shoulders. He looked up at Nathen, his eyes filled with tears, his voice barely audible through the sobs. "I don't know."

Saburo followed Obasi as he and his men continued south following the tracks the men they pursued had left. A half-hour later the men that Saburo had sent ahead returned. They immediately approached Saburo, avoiding Obasi all together. Not one of Obasi's men would address him directly.No one had the courage to. They spoke to Saburo, then went to the front of the group to lead the men. Saburo caught up with Obasi and walked alongside him. He did not look at Obasi—

he kept his focus straight ahead.

"The men came across a hut about half an hour from here. It appears that the men we are following stayed there."

"How long ago?"

"The fire is cold. They've been gone for some time."

Obasi's mind was unsettled. Usually, he would be quite excited about hunting his prey. The thought of capturing, torturing, and killing his enemy aroused him. He lived for the climax of watching his enemy take its last breath. Beast or man, it didn't matter. His desire to maim and kill overrode all other thought. With the exception of one thing, Obasi was a deeply religious and superstitious man. He believed he was killing for the Gods, and the Gods guided his hand, his every move. So when he heard about a valley protected by the Gods, he knew that was where he had to be. The light he saw was the Gods showing him the way. He didn't share his thoughts or desires with anyone, not even Saburo. A valley protected by the Gods had to contain great wealth, and the valley, the wealth, would be his and his alone.

Obasi and Saburo continued to walk side by side, not speaking one word to each other. A half-hour later, they entered the clearing that their scouts had discovered earlier. There was a circular hut approximately ten feet in diameter situated at the back of the clearing. In the middle of the clearing was a small fire pit. The embers contained in the pit were cold and lifeless. Obasi headed straight for the hut. Once inside, he scrutinized his surroundings. There were obvious signs that crates had been stacked on the ground. He could see the imprints made from the butt of several rifles that had been propped up against the circular wall. Obasi called out to Saburo, who he knew would be standing just on the other side of the entrance.

"Bring me the prisoner." Less than a minute later, Saburo entered the hut, his right hand firmly grasping the prisoner's left arm. The prisoner's head was down, his shoulders slumped. His clothes were ratted and torn, and dried blood caked his face and clothing. His feet were bare and covered in cuts and bruises. Saburo unceremoniously threw him to the ground at Obasi's feet. The prisoner drew his knees to his chest, wrapped his arms around his knees and lay there, not making a sound.

Obasi, hands resting on his hips, towered over his prisoner. He spoke to Saburo, not taking his attention off the small man who lay at his feet. "Leave us."

Saburo nodded his head and left the hut.

Obasi walked around the prisoner deciding on how he was going to extract the information he so desperately wanted. After several minutes, he knelt on his haunches facing the prisoner. "Look at me."

The prisoner didn't move.

Obasi balled up his fist and punched the prisoner as hard as he could on the side of his face.

The prisoner moaned in pain as he spat out the blood that was pooling in his mouth. He lifted his head ever so slightly and looked at Obasi through eyes that were black and blue and nearly swollen shut from the repeated beatings. His face was covered in bruises, his nose, jaw and right hand were broken. He could barely breathe and spoke with great difficulty.

Obasi smiled down at his prisoner. It pleased him to see his handiwork so vibrantly displayed on the poor man's body. Obasi sat on the ground and placed his hands on his lap. He wanted his prisoner to see his hands, to know how close they were, to know how close they were to hurting him. "As you can see, we found the hut you spoke of. However, it's empty. Tell me again, what did the men hide in here?"

The prisoner tried to speak, but with his broken jaw, it was extremely difficult. "Boxes. I saw metal sticks. I know not what they are."

"Liar!" Obasi punched the man in his arm, causing him to recoil in pain. He stared at the man who lay before him, and then what the man said finally made sense to him. *Metal sticks, who calls rifles metal sticks?* "You are not dressed like the rest of your men. But they weren't your men, were they?" Obasi did not wait for an answer. "You are not dressed as they are, and you don't speak as they do. What were you doing in the jungle?"

"Watching."

"Watching who?"

"Everyone"

"You're not from around here. Where do you come from? Where is the valley you spoke of?" Obasi leaned in closer and whispered into the man's ear. "Tell me what I want to know, or I'll hurt you until you beg me to kill you. And then I'll hurt you some more."

The man lay still, not wanting to utter a sound. He had been beaten every day for as many days as he had been with these men. How many days that was, he didn't know. He had lost all track of time. The man who beat him wanted to know about a valley. *What valley? Where am I?* His head pounded. It felt as though it was going to explode. He could hear his captor talking to him. He wanted to know his name. *My name?* He searched his mind for something familiar, something he could hold on to. He remembered the tree, it was tall, and he was sitting in it. No . . . he was hiding in it. He fell. The tree was speaking to him. The man concentrated on the memory. Tried to hear what the tree was saying to him. One word came to him. He was not sure what the word meant, but he would tell his captor, and maybe it would keep him from being beaten. Painfully he looked up at Obasi and said one word . . . *Tomas.*

CHAPTER NINE

Nathen stared at Sam in shock—Tomas could be alive, a fact which changed everything. "Sam, you rest." Nathen gently helped Sam lie back on his sleeping mat, then placed a couple of pillows underneath his head. "If Tomas is out there, I promise I'll do everything I can to find him."

As Nathen was about to leave, Casandra returned from the birthing hut. "Casandra, I need to speak with you."

Casandra bowed to him, then placed the clay pot she was carrying by the fire pit. "Of course, my Lord." She stood facing him, folding her hands in front of her. "What did you want to know, my Lord?"

"Have you heard from Tamara."

"Yes, she says that the village is quiet."

"Good. Casandra, when you were tending to Sam, you said that the other small man with Sam was beyond our help. What did you mean by that?"

"Simply that he was hurt beyond my capabilities to heal."

"So, he could still be alive?"

"Yes, his heart still beats, but his mind and body are sick. The healing spirits say that he has gone to a place far in the recesses of his mind. A place that I can't enter."

"What are you telling me? Is he in any condition to betray us?"

"My Lord. I can't answer you. However, Serena may be able to venture where I can't. Not to tell you your business, but I think we should perform the ritual that will join Serena's presence with mine as soon as possible. Tonight, perhaps, when the others return."

If the truth was known, Nathen didn't want to join forces with Serena. In his mind, she couldn't be trusted. However, combining her strengths with Casandra's could create a priestess with abilities far greater than anything the tribe had ever seen. "I won't lie to you. You and Serena together . . . is not a union I would choose. How do I know that you'll remain faithful to me, and to the people of this tribe?"

"Well, my Lord, you are just going to have to trust me, and Serena. I know that'll be a difficult task, but it's one that you have to undertake. For the good of the tribe."

Nathen thought for a moment. Trust was earned, and even though Casandra had done everything in her power to prove her loyalty, the question was, would she be swayed by Serena when they were joined? A lot was at stake, and Nathen knew he didn't have much choice. "When the others return, we'll meet in the gathering hut. We'll perform this ritual, but I warn you, Casandra." Nathen took a step closer to Casandra. "If you and Serena betray my trust . . . I just might bring back the death penalty."

"I promise you, my Lord. I'm here to serve you, and I will control Serena." Casandra smiled at Nathen. "Serena has much to learn if she thinks she can control me."

Authia and Tammy sat on the lush blanket of vegetation which covered the ground around the pond. They watched as Joshawa chased a butterfly in among some ferns. Authia had heard the conversation between Nathen and Sam. If Tomas was alive and tortured, as Sensay said these men would do, he could lead them straight to the entrance to the valley. Authia turned to discuss the new information with Tammy. However, one look at Tammy's face, and she could tell Tammy's mind was focused somewhere else.

"Tammy? Are you all right?"

Tammy turned and looked blankly at Authia. "Huh? Oh sorry. What were you saying?"

"Okay, what's going on? You've been distracted the entire morning."

Tammy turned and stared out at the pond. A group of children were playing in the water. Further along the banks of the pond, a few men of the tribe were catching fish for the evening meal. A half dozen women from the tribe were either swimming with the children or were laying on the ground, enjoying the warmth of the sun as it peeked through the canopies of the large trees that surrounded them. Tammy turned back to face Authia. She sighed, her eyes sad, her usual canter gone. "I'm so scared, Authia. Scared for Hansen. Scared that we might die."

Authia placed her hand on Tammy's forearm. "Nobody . . ." Authia stopped short as a vision bombarded her. "Oh my God, Tammy. You're pregnant!"

"What! No, I'm not. How do you know?"

"I can see your baby. She's beautiful. A beautiful, healthy baby girl."

Tammy looked stunned. "How could I've not have known?"

"You're early in the pregnancy. Six weeks, maybe. This is a good thing, isn't it?"

Tammy smiled as she placed her hands on her belly. "Yes, it's amazing. Did I tell you? Hansen has asked me to marry him."

Authia wrapped her arms around Tammy. A hug Tammy eagerly returned. "I'm so happy for you. We're going to have our babies together. How wonderful is that? I can't wait to tell Nathen."

"I've got to tell Hansen first."

"Of course. Let's head back. Nathen received some disturbing news. I'm sure he's going to want to talk about it."

Tammy stood to leave as Authia called Joshawa over. "News? What news?"

"Apparently, Tomas might still be alive." Authia bent down to pick up Joshawa. "And he might be with the men that Sensay saw."

"Well, Tomas wouldn't give us up . . . would he?"

"Not willingly. However, Sensay also mentioned that the men were torturing her people to tell them what they wanted to hear."

"Oh, that's not good." The girls walked back to the village in silence, their happiness overshadowed by the thought that the men in Sensay's vision could have a key to their village.

Rick and his men packed up and headed back into the sweltering jungle. As they traveled deeper, Rick's fears played on him, causing him to feel as if the jungle were closing in all around them, as though the jungle had a mind of its own. The vegetation grew thicker with every step they took, and the heat and humidity clung to them like a blanket wrapped too tightly. Sweat dripped from their foreheads, stinging their eyes and blurring their vision. Rick watched the men who were carrying the litters and could see they were experiencing difficulty maintaining their grasp as the sweat built up in the palms of their hands. One of the litters was weighed down with a large crate containing dynamite, highly unstable when damp and jostled about. Rick and his men desperately tried to ignore the horde of insects buzzing around their heads, biting at any exposed skin they could find. They were extremely careful as they walked the jungle floor that was littered with roots, vines, and vegetation. The group had been walking a couple of hours when the man at the back of the litter laden with dynamite tripped over an exposed root and fell onto one knee. Miraculously, he kept the litter level, even though each and every man held their breath, expecting the blast from the explosion that would take their lives. The man that had fallen looked up to Rick, fear etched deeply across his face.

Rick took a quick look at his men. They were tired and scared. "Okay. Let's take a break before someone blows up. We'll wait here until Greg and Taylor return." Rick felt uneasy. They had no clear line of vision. There could be all kinds of predators waiting just a few feet away from them, and they wouldn't know it. He needed to find a safe haven until the fighting was far beyond their reach. Rick and his men sat quietly, listening to the sounds reverberating throughout the jungle — sounds of animals, sounds of distant gunfire, sounds of death.

Obasi left the hut, his right hand swollen and raw from the beating he had just given Tomas. There was nothing more he could get from his prisoner. Tomas had fainted, giving him a reprieve from the beating. Obasi walked up to Saburo. "What do you know?"

"I know that there are about twelve, maybe fourteen men heading south. They are weighed down with the supplies they took from the hut. I'd say three maybe four litters. It's going to slow them down, and with the amount of supplies they took, they'll be easy to follow. Should we head out?"

Obasi looked back at the hut. He needed more information from the prisoner. He would give him a couple of hours, then revive him, find out what else the prisoner could tell him. "No. We will leave at first light."

"Tomorrow?"

"You said yourself, they are slow and easily tracked. We will keep our distance. Make them feel at ease. Then, when they least expect it, we'll attack." Obasi ended the conversation and returned to the hut.

Nathen sat alone in the gathering hut. He didn't sit on the raised platform located at the back of the hut but instead sat cross-legged on the ground in the middle of the hut. From where he sat, he could see his people walking about the village through the entrance to the hut. But none of that registered. He was oblivious to all that was going on around him, his mind focused on one thought. *How am I going to save my people? Serena said the Gods wanted to help me. If that's the case, then help me. Speak to me directly. Tell me what's needed in order to protect my tribe.*

You seem troubled, Lord of our People.

Nathen closed his eyes and sighed. *What do you want, Serena?*

I told you. I am here to help you.

Well, that's yet to be seen. Casandra has agreed to be your host. We are performing the ritual tonight.

Casandra? I would have preferred Tamara. But then I guess I do not have a choice in the matter.

No, you don't.

Fine. I will see you tonight. Oh, by the way, your mate is on her way.

Serena's tone didn't go unnoticed by Nathen. She had to behave herself, but she was still bitter, angry over something that had happened centuries ago. Angry because Nathen had outsmarted her. Trusting her wasn't going to be easy. He opened his eyes to find Authia standing at the entrance of the hut. He watched as she passed Joshawa to Tammy. who then turned and headed in the direction of the communal fire pit.

Authia came to sit in front of him, tenderly placing her hands on each side of his face. "You looked so troubled. What's bothering you, sweetheart?"

Nathen's hands covered hers. He brought her fingers to his lips and gently kissed them. He held them there for just a second, then lowered them to her lap. He continued to hold her hands as he looked deep into her eyes. "Tomas may still be alive."

"Yes, I heard. Do you think he'll betray us?"

"Not willingly. Casandra tells me that his body and mind are broken. I promised Sam that I would do everything I could to find him. Such an empty promise. Authia, I feel lost. What am I doing here? I'm not a Lord or a warrior. I have no right to lead these people. I have no idea how to protect them. To defend them. What was I thinking? I came all the way to Africa, dragging you along with me, to do what?"

"You have every right to be here. Your people love you. You have brought peace and contentment to this village, something that has been lacking for a very long time. No, you're not a warrior. But do you think that your Ancestors would be able to handle this situation any better than you? There have only been two incursions in all the centuries that this tribe has existed. And neither of those two incursions were a threat. You're facing a group of men, not one or two. And they are going to be armed to the teeth with weapons that this tribe has never seen. Did you ever think that maybe you were meant to be here? How do you think the tribe would be dealing with these men if you weren't here?" Authia didn't wait for a response. "I'll tell you how. They would have had no warning. It's because of you that Sensay knew how to reach us and warn us. Whoever's coming would be walking straight into this valley, and it would be a bloodbath. Your people have no chance without you. You know that. Instead of brooding about what might have been or should have been, become the Nathen I know. Protect your people as if you were protecting Burwood."

"You're right, as usual. But I can't do it alone."

"You're not alone." Authia smiled at Nathen. "You have an arsenal at your disposal. You just have to learn how to use it."

"You're speaking of Serena and Casandra, aren't you?"

"Yes. Two of the most powerful priestesses combined as one. Think about it. How better to keep your promise? With their gift of sight, they just might be able to find Tomas."

"You're right. Their gift of sight could give us the upper hand. Especially if Serena can see beyond this valley."

"Well, she could before. I don't see any reason why she couldn't now."

"We're going to join them tonight when Hansen and the others return. What I have to do is direct Serena's anger away from me and toward the men that are coming here."

"Now you're talking. If you can do that, those men won't know what hit them."

Nathen smiled at Authia. "You're the most amazing wife. I love you so much."

Authia leaned closer to Nathen and affectionately kissed him. "And I love you. We have a while to wait before the others are back. Tammy has Joshawa." Authia smiled seductively at Nathen. "How about we go back to our hut, and I'll relieve some of that pent-up tension?"

Nathen didn't have to be asked twice. He stood up, pulled Authia to her feet, and the two headed for their hut.

Rick and his men spent what felt like hours waiting for Taylor and Greg to return. They sat quiet, rifles resting across their laps, ready to use at a moment's notice. Rick could easily see the tension etched across each one of his men's faces. He could actually feel it, like an aura dancing around his men and taunting them to shoot at anything that moved. A half-hour later there was movement just in front of them. Immediately twelve rifles were raised and aimed. Rick scanned the area. "Who's there? We can hear you, and we're armed."

Rick could hear Taylor's voice. "Whoa. It's just us."

Rick turned to face his men. "Put those away." He looked

back to see Taylor and Greg emerge from the jungle.

Taylor turned to Rick, looking shocked. "What the hell! You could have killed us."

"Sorry. The men are a little tense."

"No shit! Look, we found a place we can hold up. There's a large cleared area and a freshwater pond. Looks like somebody stayed there, but not recently."

"Good. Can we make it before nightfall?"

"If we leave now, it'll be dusk when we get there."

"Okay. Taylor, you lead the way. Greg, I want you to backtrack and make sure we're not being followed."

Greg shrugged his shoulders. "Sure, but who would be following us?"

"I don't know, but I'm not taking any chances."

Greg picked up the backpack that he'd placed on the ground. "See you in a couple of days." Greg disappeared into the jungle.

Rick addressed Taylor. "Do you need to rest, or can we head out right now?"

"Right now, is fine with me."

Rick watched as his men strapped on their backpacks, slung their rifles onto their backs and picked up the litters. They were tired, and when people were tired, they made mistakes. Taylor led, while Rick took up the rear. He looked over his shoulder at the obvious trail they were leaving in their wake. And as Rick faced forward, he had a gut feeling that the fighting was not over. At least not for them.

CHAPTER TEN

Nathen lay naked on his sleeping mat. He placed his hands behind his head as he watched Authia get dressed. The last few hours had been spent in sweet rapture. Authia had such a hold on him, her very touch could excite him. Just watching her dress caused his manhood to throb with desire. Authia walked over to him as she tied her halter style top at the back of her neck. She smiled at him, shaking her head. "Really? You still want more?"

Nathen sat up and gently pulled Authia onto his lap. He wrapped his massive arms around her as he gazed into her eyes. "I could never get enough of you."

Authia leaned in and kissed Nathen ever so softly. "So, how's the pent-up tension?"

"What tension?"

"Good. Now get dressed, and we'll go find Joshawa." Authia stood up and went to pick up Nathen's loincloth which had somehow ended up by the entrance to the hut. "Good thing the flap to the entrance was closed." She picked it up and threw it in Nathen's direction. "By the way, are you going to *abstain* from this pregnancy as you did with the first one?"

"Absolutely. When you are into your fourth month, then I will no longer make love to you. I don't want to hurt you or the baby."

"You do realize that you can't hurt the baby or me just by making love to me."

"Sorry." Nathen wrapped his loincloth around his waist then walked over to Authia, drawing her tenderly into his arms. "I couldn't live with myself if I in some way, injured you or our baby because I couldn't control my own strength.

You know what happens when I lose control."

"You've never lost control with me. And you can't keep beating yourself up for something that happened so long ago. You know it was self-defense."

"Self-defense or not, I would rather play it safe. Let's go find Joshawa."

Nathen and Authia left the hut hand in hand and went in search of Joshawa. They didn't have to go far.

Joshawa and Tammy were sitting on the ground in front of Tammy and Hansen's hut. Tammy was patiently trying to teach Joshawa to play pat-a-cake.

Authia giggled. "Having fun?"

Tammy looked up, her eyes bright and her demeanor carefree. "He's catching on." Tammy returned her attention to Joshawa, who still had the palms of his tiny hands facing outward, trying desperately to connect with Tammy's hands. "A little FYI. The walls of these huts are not exactly soundproof."

Authia appeared horrified. "Are you saying you could hear us?"

"The entire valley could hear you."

Nathen's eyes went wide, and he could feel his face turn red as Tammy laughed at him. "Don't worry, everyone ignored you. I know its mid-afternoon, but Joshawa and I haven't had lunch yet. Care to join us?" Tammy stood and reached over to close the flap to her hut.

Nathen bent down and picked up Joshawa. "We'd love to."

"When do you expect Hansen back?"

"Not till nightfall."

"Really?" Tammy's look of disappointment did not go unnoticed.

With Joshawa sitting securely on Nathen's left arm, he placed his free arm around Tammy's shoulders. "There's nothing to worry about. According to Tamara, the village is quiet. Now let's get something to eat." The four headed toward the communal fire pit in silence. Nathen had a new attitude toward their possible confrontation. Authia was right, he had to harness the power that Serena and Casandra would possess once they were combined. Maybe, just maybe, sorcery would be the answer to keeping the valley safe.

Obasi sat on the ground of the hut staring at the little man that lay unconscious before him. He had much to learn from his prisoner, but he was afraid that he might have pushed him too far. It had happened before, men that had become idiots, lost in a world of their own after days of being beaten almost to death. If he was going to learn about the valley protected by the Gods, then he might have to change his tactics. Obasi called out to Saburo, but it proved unnecessary, since he was already entering the hut. Saburo stood by the entrance, hands behind his back, waiting for his orders. Without taking his focus off the little man, Obasi spoke to Saburo. "Bring me water. And bring me our medic."

"Our medic?"

Obasi looked up at Saburo. "You have a problem with that?"

"Are you injured?"

Obasi looked back at the little man. "Medic!"

Saburo left, returning within minutes accompanied by the medic. He placed the canteen of water he'd brought next to Obasi. "Is there anything else you need?"

"No. Leave. I'll call you when I need you." Obasi knew that Saburo wouldn't question him — he wouldn't dare.

Saburo left the hut, leaving a very nervous medic standing by himself. The medic's name was Daktari, which, in his language, simply meant healer. The men in the group called him Dak. He stood a few inches shorter than Obasi and was slight in build. Obasi stood, took a couple of steps back from his prisoner, then focused his attention on Dak. Beads of sweat were running down Dak's forehead. He was fidgeting and shifting his backpack from one arm to the other. The backpack was large, being two feet wide and three feet high, and there was a large red cross on the front of the pack. Obasi smiled at his medic. It gave him pleasure knowing that his men feared him, for fear made them easier to control. "Revive him."

Dak nodded his head then went to kneel by the prisoner. He reached into his bag and brought out a small container. From inside he withdrew a vial of smelling salts. He snapped the vial and then waved it under the prisoner's nose. It took a few seconds, but Tomas finally came to.

Tomas' mind was clouded in a fog. He tried to open his eyes, but they were almost swollen shut from the last beating. He could just make out that there was a man next to him. Tomas tried to look at the man, but what he could see was blurred. He could hear voices, though they sounded as if they were miles away. Tomas tried to focus on the voices. *What were they saying?* One voice, in particular, was familiar to him. His heart started racing as he recognized the harsh, demanding tone of the voice. Tomas closed his eyes and focused more intensely on that one voice. He was asking the other man a question. They were talking about him. Tomas knew what was coming, so he instinctively slowed his breathing and went to a place far in the recesses of his mind.

"Can you mend him?"

Dak looked questioningly at Obasi. "Mend him how?"

"So he can heal. I need him awake, and his mind focused.

Can you do that?"

"I can try to set his hand and nose, though they've been broken for several days now. There is nothing I can do for his jaw, at least not with the tools I have. I can clean his wounds, give him painkillers to ease his suffering. As far as his mind being focused, that's out of my hands. The mind is a tricky thing. When a person is being attacked, and there is no end in sight, then the mind takes over. It protects by shutting down. As long as he believes he's in danger, I don't think you'll get him to focus on anything."

Obasi listened to what he was being told. He had to make this little man feel safe. That was not something Obasi knew how to do. He was at his best when people feared him. He needed someone who the little man would feel safe with. Obasi thought of Saburo; however, that would mean he would have to tell him about the valley. "Do everything you can to heal him and make him comfortable."

Dak's expression went from fear to shock.

Obasi shot him a warning glance, which was all he needed to do.

Dak immediately went to work on Tomas. And as Obasi watched, he came to the realization that the only way he was going to make this man talk was to let Saburo in on his little secret.

Rick's men trudged through the merciless jungle. As the day progressed, the heat sored, and the insects attacked with a vengeance. Tsetse flies flew about their heads, taking what felt like large chunks of flesh every time they bit. Welts formed on the men's exposed skin. Then finally, as dusk was approaching, they arrived at their destination. The men gladly put their litters down, stretching out their hands that were cramped from tightly holding on to the litters for so long.

Their *safe haven* had apparently been used as a campsite before. But by who and how long ago, no one knew for sure. Rick surveyed their new home. It was remote, keeping them far from the fighting. It was large enough to accommodate all his men, and there was a freshwater pond, so they had plenty of drinking water. A small smile graced Rick's lips as he slowly nodded his head. *Finally, something in our favor.* "All right, everyone, set up camp. Get those litters as far from the campfire as possible. Once we're set up, you can go to the pond in groups of five." Rick turned his attention to Taylor. "Any chance of rustling something up for dinner?"

"Consider it done." Taylor retreated into the jungle, emerging half an hour later with four small animals, skinned and ready to cook.

By the time the sun disappeared behind the horizon and the moon shone brightly in the evening sky, the atmosphere in the camp had gone from fearful and exhausted to carefree and relaxed. Maybe even a little too relaxed. As the majority of his men curled up in their sleeping bags, Rick paid attention to the five that were guarding their campsite. They were sitting around the fire, rifles laying on the ground, their backs facing the jungle. They were softly talking and laughing among themselves. Rick walked up to them, and as they looked up, they could tell that something wasn't right.

"Not that I would begrudge you a little peace of mind. But you still need to be on guard. Walk the perimeter and have two men check the pond at regular intervals. I doubt there's anyone this far south. That being said, this was someone's campsite — they may want it back. And don't forget our four-legged friends. The fire should keep them at bay. However, I don't want to take any chances. The odor from our supper may entice them." Rick looked at the carcasses left over from their dinner. "Get rid of those." Rick watched as the five men dutifully followed his orders. He walked over to his sleeping bag, crawled in, then lay on his back gazing at the stars that filled the night sky. It was so peaceful. The sounds of the jungle were not so chaotic. As Rick rolled over onto his side, he acknowledged the gut feeling that this was just the calm before the storm.

As night approached, Tammy became overly anxious. She nervously paced at the edge of the village waiting for some sign that Hansen was coming back. Since the village was surrounded by jungle, it was very difficult to see beyond the ferns, vines, and trees. A half-hour later, Authia joined Tammy.

"Relax. They're on their way back."

"Thank God. Are they okay?"

"They're fine. The village was quiet. Nothing happened."

"That's a relief." Tammy and Authia stood in silence as they waited for Hansen, Tamara, and Cameron to return. Ten minutes later, they could hear the three of them approaching. As soon as Hansen was clear of the jungle, Tammy ran up to him, throwing herself into his arms.

"I'm so glad you're back. I was so scared for you." Tammy had wrapped her arms around Hansen's neck and was hugging him so hard that he had to pull her arms away.

Hansen chuckled as he placed her arms around his waist. "Trying to kill me?"

"I'm just so happy to see you." Tammy put her arms back around Hansen's neck, only this time she drew him closer to her and passionately kissed him—a kiss he eagerly returned.

Authia smiled as she addressed Tamara. "Walk with me." Tamara joined Authia as they headed back to the gathering hut, the rest of the group following close behind. "You saw no movement at all, Tamara?"

"No, my Mistress. The village was unoccupied, but the aura surrounding the village is not as it should be."

Authia stopped and looked directly at Tamara. "What do you mean?"

"My Mistress, there is an evil residing in the village. But it is not whole. It waits for someone, a special someone, that it can control. On its own, it is trapped inside its own aura. While it is trapped, it has no power. When it becomes one with a living soul, then it will be very dangerous."

Tammy raised her hand as if requesting permission to speak. "I don't get it. Isn't that what we're doing with Serena and Casandra? Joining them to become one. Are they going to become dangerous?"

"No. My mother is a strong priestess that can control Serena, and Serena is being monitored by our Ancestors. The aura that I sense at the village is on its own. There is no greater power watching over this aura. That is what makes it dangerous. It answers to no one."

Authia thought back to when Serena was controlling her and Nathen's lives. "Can you tell who this aura is? Could it be Serena?"

"It is not the Priestess Serena. It is a strong aura, and it is very old. I could try to connect with this aura, if that is what you wish."

"How dangerous would it be?"

"Not dangerous at all. The aura is weak and, as I have said, powerless in its current form."

"Can you connect from here, or do you have to be in the village?"

"I will not know until I try. When do you want me to approach this aura?"

"We'll try tomorrow. Tonight, we're performing a ritual to

combine Serena and Casandra." They continued walking over to the gathering hut, where Nathen was waiting. Tamara and Cameron bowed to their Lord.

Tamara stepped forward. "If it pleases my Lord, we would like to go to the pond and clean up before the ritual."

"Of course. Casandra says the ritual is best performed at night, when the village is in darkness. We'll meet back in three hours."

The moon shone brightly in the night sky. It looked down upon the sleeping village basking the huts in a pale-yellow hue. Nathen stood at the entrance of the gathering hut, his arms folded across his chest, waiting for Casandra. Tamara, Hansen, Tammy, and Authia were already in the hut. Joshawa was being watched by one of the priestesses in Nathen's and Authia's hut.

A few minutes later, Casandra approached, dressed in her ceremonial gown. She bowed to Nathen. "Good evening, my Lord."

"Good evening Casandra. Are you ready?"

"Oh, I think the question is, are you?" Casandra entered the hut, leaving Nathen to ponder her question.

Was he ready . . . he didn't believe so.

Nathen entered the hut to find everyone sitting in a circle with Casandra kneeling in the middle. Tamara, dressed in her ceremonial gown as well, stood between Authia and Tammy. She motioned Nathen to stand next to her. When he took his place, Tamara passed him a clay pot she'd been holding. Nathen looked inside to find several green leaf packets. He looked back at Tamara, waiting for an explanation, but none was given.

Tamara merely stared straight ahead as she began the ritual. "Inside this pot are the packets that have been combined with the essence from Casandra, healer of this village, and myself, High Priestess of this village. With these packets, we will create a pathway for our sister Serena to follow. It is the desire of our Ancestors that Serena helps us in our time of need. We will combine her spirit with the living soul of my mother, Casandra. It is time to show Serena the way." Tamara reached into the pot, touched one of the packets, then withdrew her hand. She looked over at Nathen. "My Lord, will you take these packets and lay them before Casandra."

Nathen reached into the pot and took hold of one of the packets, but before he could remove it Tamara placed her hand over his and shook her head. Nathen let go of the packet and removed his hand.

Tamara looked over to Authia. "My Mistress, will you take these packets and lay them before Casandra." Authia stood, took the clay pot from Nathen, then reached in to retrieve a packet. Quickly she withdrew her hand and turned to face Tamara. Before Nathen could react, Tamara placed her hand on his forearm, assuring him all was well. "My Mistress, you were given a vision?"

"Yes, but I don't know what it was."

"Serena has chosen you to be the one to guide her."

"What! Me?"

"For each packet you touch, a vision will be granted to you. Each vision is a steppingstone for Serena to find her way to my mother. Take a packet, empty your mind, fill it only with the vision that is granted you. Live in that vision."

As Authia went to step inside the circle, Nathen held her back. He glared at Tamara. "This isn't some trick to enable Serena to harm Authia, is it?"

"Why no, my Lord. Serena cannot harm my Mistress. If she but tries, our Ancestors will punish her. She will remain a lost spirit for all eternity."

"I'm not convinced."

"My Lord, I have done nothing but protect my Mistress since I first met her. I promise you, no harm will come to her, or your child."

Authia reached over and placed her hand on his forearm. She smiled up at him. "I'm not afraid. It'll be all right, Nathen." She turned and went to kneel next to Casandra. She placed the clay pot on the ground and looked up at Tamara. "Should I start now?"

Tamara did not respond. Instead, she looked up toward the roof of the hut as she raised her arms high above her head. "Ancestors from long ago times, hear my plea. Open the gateway so that my sister Serena can find her way home. Use my Mistress as the vessel and show her the path that must be traveled. Ancestors from long ago, hear my plea." Tamara started to swirl her arms in a circle, and as she did, a thick fog began to come out of the ground. It completely encircled Casandra and Authia as it whipped faster and faster around them, growing until it reached the roof of the hut.

The fog became so thick that Nathen could no longer see through it. The sound it made as it formed a funnel was deafening. Everyone stood, then stepped back, shielding their faces with their arms from the dirt and debris that was being thrown about the hut. That was, everyone but Nathen. He tried to get closer to the fog that was acting much like a tornado, but the sheer force of the wind kept pushing him back.

Tamara grabbed his arm and turned him to face her. As loud as she could, she yelled at Nathen. "My Lord. My Mistress is fine. They are in the calm of the storm. Step back. Protect yourself." Tamara let go of Nathen's arm and raised the hood to her gown, shielding her face from the ferocity of the wind.

Authia glanced all around her. The fog grew so thick that she could no longer see Nathen. She gingerly raised her hand and touched the fog with her fingers. The result was a slight shock. She immediately withdrew her fingers and looked over to Casandra. Casandra was still kneeling—however, her shoulders were slumped over and her head hung down with her chin, almost resting on her chest. She appeared to be completely oblivious to her surroundings. Authia took a deep breath, reached into the clay pot, and withdrew a packet. The vision danced in her head. It was of Serena, and she was in a very dark place. Authia could feel her fear. She placed the packet on the ground, and as she did, it lit up and became a brilliant blue. Authia reached into the clay pot and withdrew another packet. This time the vision was of Nathen, Serena, and Joshawa, Nathen's father. It was when Joshawa and Nathen killed Serena. Her screams echoed inside of Authia's head. She placed that packet down, and again it became a brilliant blue. The next packet she withdrew came with a vision of when Nathen was born and Serena had captured his parent's souls. Authia finally realized what was happening. She was reliving Serena's life, only in reverse. As she laid each packet down, she was given another glimpse into Serena's life. With the last packet, she saw Serena sitting at Joshawa's side on the platform in the gathering hut. And for the first time, Serena was actually happy. Authia looked into her empty clay pot and then glanced over at all the packets laid out before her, glowing a brilliant blue. *Now What?*

Authia's question was answered as an apparition appeared hovering just above Casandra. A voice that Authia didn't recognize echoed within the confines of the fog. "Serena, you must walk the path of your life. You must feel the pain you caused to so many others. Only then will you be allowed to join with Casandra and redeem yourself."

The voice was gone. Authia looked up at the apparition as it started to take on a female shape. Though its features were indiscernible, Authia knew it was Serena. The apparition lowered itself onto the first packet, and as it stepped from one packet to another, she could see its body contorting in pain. When it finally stood on the last packet, it turned to face Authia. Authia could have sworn that it smiled at her.

Then the apparition turned into nothing more than a mere wisp. It circled Casandra's head until Casandra lifted her head and slightly parted her lips. The wisp wasted no time and flew into her mouth. Casandra's head shot straight up, her back rigid. A second later, Casandra heaved a heavy sigh, turned to face Authia, then smiled. A voice Authia knew only too well spoke to her. "Hello, Mistress of the Lion People. It is good to see you . . . alive. So, tell me, Mistress of the Lion People, are you afraid? For, if you are not, you should be."

CHAPTER ELEVEN

Obasi had left Dak to attend to his prisoner. He needed to speak with Saburo. As he left the hut, the first thing he noticed was that the sun was already beginning its descent into the western sky. He had been with the prisoner longer than he realized. Besides the existing fire pit, two other fires had been started with pigs roasting over all three. Obasi ignored the hunger pangs brought on by the sweet smell of the succulent pigs. He ignored the fact that the men sitting around the campfires had grown quiet as he approached. He didn't care, because his only focus was on Saburo. Obasi found him sitting at one of the fires. He made eye contact, then turned his back to his men and walked into the jungle. Saburo immediately joined Obasi, and the two men walked in silence for over five minutes before Obasi stopped and faced Saburo. "I need to speak with you about the prisoner."

"Is it time? You want me to dispose of him?"

"No. We have a lot to learn from him still."

"He's a babbling idiot. What do you think you'll learn from him?"

Obasi was quiet. He still wasn't ready to share in the wealth that he was confident was waiting for him in the valley the prisoner spoke of. However, he also knew that the prisoner wasn't about to confide in him. "He mentioned a place. A place that I want to find."

"What place?"

"It is a special valley. One that is protected by the Gods."

"Where's this valley?"

"That's what I need you to find out."

"Me? How am I supposed to do that?"

"Make friends with our prisoner. Put him at ease." Obasi

took a step closer to Saburo. "Find out what he knows . . . your life depends on it." Obasi started to walk away only to stop. Without turning around, he imparted one last warning. "Tell no one of what we have discussed. The punishment will be severe if you do."

Saburo watched as Obasi returned to the campsite. He didn't believe in the Gods as deeply as Obasi, but he didn't want to incur Obasi's wrath, so he would humor him. He knew Obasi was crazy, but Obasi had never threatened him before. *Where is this valley he spoke of? Could it be the prisoner's home?* If it was, then the Gods weren't doing a very good job of protecting him. Saburo went back to the campsite to finish his dinner. When he was done, he wrapped a large piece of meat in a palm leaf, then went to the hut to check on the prisoner. Dak was just finishing up. The prisoner was awake, but not very lucid, and Obasi was nowhere to be seen.

"How is he, Dak?"

"I'm surprised he's still alive." Dak walked over to Saburo and noticed the piece of meat wrapped in the palm leaf. "If that's for him . . . you'd better chew it for him before you give it to him."

"He can't chew for himself?"

"He has a broken jaw. I can't even get his mouth open wide enough to see if there is any damage to his teeth. So, no, he can't chew for himself."

"What do you suggest we feed him?"

Dak looked questioningly at Saburo. "Obasi wants to feed him?"

"Yeah. He wants me to take care of him."

Dak snorted. "Are you kidding me? Why?"

"It's not my place to ask."

"If Obasi wants him fed, then I can make something for

him. But you'll have to spoon feed him. His one hand is broken, and the other is swollen so bad that I don't think he can use it." Dak looked back over at the prisoner. "I can't believe that Obasi is actually going to show him kindness." With that comment, he left the hut.

Tomas lay quietly on the ground. The heavy shroud of pain was lifting, his body was relaxing, and he could breathe normally. Tomas listened to the two men talking. They wanted to take care of him. *What did the one man say? Show me kindness?* Something in the back of Tomas' mind told him not to trust the men. No one had shown him kindness since he was taken captive, so why should they now? The voice inside his mind beckoned him to retreat to a safe place, to lose himself in the comforting seclusion of his mind. Tomas listened to the voice and went to a place in his mind where he felt no pain. A place far beyond anyone's reach.

The wall of fog that separated Authia from Nathen slowly dissipated. As soon as it was clear, Nathen rushed to Authia's side. He wrapped his arms around her and drew her close to him. "Are you all right?" Gently he pulled her away, examining her body for any injuries. "Are you hurt?"

"Nathen, I'm fine. It worked. Serena and Casandra are together."

Nathen gently let go of Authia and looked over to Casandra.

Cassandra simply stood in place, a smirk of satisfaction on her face. "Well, hello Nathen. Or should I say *Lord of our People?* Where are my manners?" Serena bowed, then glanced back up at Nathen. "I never thought that I would be bowing to you."

"I assume I'm addressing Serena."

"Yes, you are."

"Where's Casandra?"

"She's here."

"And who controls her body and mind?"

"Well . . . unfortunately . . . that would be her. She's just allowing me some *quality* time with you and your girlfriend . . . I mean with my Lord and Mistress."

"That would be my wife."

"Wife? A lot has happened since you killed me. I'm assuming congratulations are in order. You are a father now, right?"

"Yes. I'd like to speak to Casandra now."

"But we are having so much fun."

"Now, Serena."

"Oh, all right. Not that I have much choice in the matter." Authia stepped forward. "Wait!"

Nathen looked over to Authia.

"I have a question for Serena." Authia went and stood next to Nathen. "You said that I should be afraid. What am I supposed to be afraid of?"

Serena smirked at Authia. "Now that would be telling." Serena went quiet for a moment, then slowly shook her head as she rolled her eyes. "All right, Casandra." She looked back at Authia and Nathen. "Apparently, I'm not playing nice. This is going to be such a bore."

Nathen took a step closer to Serena. "Authia asked you a question."

"Yes, she did. While I was still a lost spirit and waiting for you to finish laying out the packets, I took a little peek outside of our valley. There is much death and greed in the valley just outside of ours. And it is heading our way. However, in among all the anger and hatred, I sensed an ally."

"What do you mean *an ally*?"

"Somebody that could possibly help us. There is fear surrounding this person, but also good and compassion. We need to find him."

Nathen spoke up. "And how do you suppose we should do that?"

Serena closed her eyes for just a minute, and when she opened them, it was Casandra that stood before Nathen and Authia. "Serena's resting. I promise you, my Lord, she will behave. However, her attitude . . . well she is Serena, and she does have a wicked tongue."

Nathen thought back to his previous encounters with Serena. "Yes, she does. Are you going to be able to control her?"

"You have nothing to fear, my Lord. Part of her agreement with our Ancestors is that I control this body. She's a visitor, nothing more. Now, if it pleases my Lord, I would like to retire for the night."

"Of course. But I want to see you first thing in the morning. I'll meet you in the priestess' hut."

Casandra bowed to Nathen. "Yes, my Lord." Casandra left the hut under Nathen's watchful eye.

Hansen approached Nathen. "So, do you think you can trust this Serena person?"

"I don't know. It's hard to trust someone that used to rule her life with hatred and anger, mostly directed toward my father and me. And then there's Casandra. She has done everything in her power to make atonement for her past. But with Serena taking residence in her mind . . . I guess we're just going to have to wait and see."

"Well, if you need anything, just let me know. Tammy and I are going to head back to our hut. See you in the morning."

Nathen watched as Tammy and Hansen walked hand in hand toward their hut. Authia came to stand next to him, wrapping her arms around his bicep. "He's asked her to marry him."

Nathen looked over to Authia. "Really? That's great news."

"Yes, but I know something even better." Authia grinned at Nathen.

Nathen smiled at Authia. "What are you not telling me?"

"I guess it's okay to tell you now. I'm sure Tammy's going to tell Hansen the minute they get to their hut."

"Tell him what?"

"That she's pregnant."

Saburo sat cross-legged in front of the prisoner. He was supposed to make friends with him. But why would the prisoner trust Saburo? Saburo might not have beaten him, but he was present at most of the beatings. "Are you awake? Can you understand me?"

The little man didn't respond. He simply lay still, quiet, his chest barely moving as he breathed.

Saburo sighed as he stared at the prisoner. *How am I going to make this man talk?* His life depended on him being able to do just that. Obasi didn't make idle threats . . . he would kill Saburo if he didn't get what he wanted.

Tomas was awake, but he was hiding. His mind registered that someone was speaking to him, but from within the confines of his hiding place, he could not interpret what was being said to him. Maybe he should listen, just for a moment, hear what's being said. He recognized the voice, though he didn't fear it. Tomas crept a little closer to where he was most vulnerable.

The man continued to question him. "Are you in pain? Do you need something for the pain?"

Tomas knew what pain was. He tried to remember when

there was no pain. He tried to remember where he was, who he was. He searched his mind, but all he could find was darkness. He retreated to his safe place, and from there, he could no longer hear the voice. He looked around, and in the darkness, he could see a sliver of light, and in that light stood a tree, tall and strong. The tree called out to him, its branches reaching out to him. He tried to go to the tree, but he couldn't move, and then the darkness overtook him, leaving him once again lost in his hiding place.

Saburo could hear him faintly mumbling something. His jaw could not open very wide, so it was difficult to understand what he was saying. Saburo leaned closer until his ear was just above the prisoner's mouth. He was saying one word over and over. Saburo was desperately trying to make it out. Tons . . . no . . . not Tons . . . Toms. Saburo strained to hear the word then it became abundantly clear. "Tomas! Is that your name? Is your name Tomas?" The little man's head slumped closer to his chest. "Okay. I'm going to call you Tomas. Don't worry, Tomas. I'm going to take care of you. I won't let anything bad happen to you. At least not anymore." Saburo stretched out on the dirt floor. He would spend the night with Tomas. He wanted to make sure he didn't miss anything this little man had to say.

Tammy watched as Hansen started a small fire in the fire pit that was located in the center of their hut. It was just large enough to light up the hut, but not so large as to give off any heat. Tammy was sitting on their sleeping mat, staring at Hansen. He meant everything to her, and she hated that he was putting himself in danger, even if it was for the sake of the village.

Hansen looked up at her as he stood away from the fire. "You're staring at me . . . again."

"Can I help it if you're so damn good-looking?"

Hansen smiled at her as he shook his head. "You're crazy." He sat down next to her, placed his arms around her waist, and lifted her onto his lap. She giggled as she put her arms around his neck, leaned in and seductively kissed him. As she did, she could feel his arousal harden underneath her. Tammy turned to face Hansen, straddling her knees on either side of him. Her loincloth skirt rode high above her thighs. Tenderly she placed her hands on the back of his head, bringing him closer to her body. Hansen hungrily kissed her neck, her shoulders. He couldn't seem to get enough of her as he slowly made his way down to her breasts. At the same time, his hands explored her thighs, lifting her skirt to her waist, revealing the fact that underneath her skirt, she was naked.

Tammy didn't want to hold back any longer. She undid Hansen's jeans, exposing his engorged manhood. Hansen held onto Tammy's hips as he lifted her off his lap and then slowly brought her down on top of him while his mouth and tongue tantalized her nipples. Tammy arched her back in erotic passion as his ample manhood filled her. Hansen lay down on the sleeping mat, keeping Tammy sitting on top of him. He held his hands on her hips as they slammed against each other, harder and faster with each thrust. Then, finally, the sweet release, sending both over the edge as Tammy crumpled into Hansen's waiting arms.

Tammy rolled over onto her side, snuggling close to Hansen. "You're amazing!"

He softly kissed the top of her head. "You weren't so bad yourself."

Tammy chuckled. "I seem to remember telling Authia and Nathen that these walls aren't soundproof. I guess they'll know what I mean now."

"It's late. The whole village is probably asleep. I doubt anyone heard us. Not that I care."

Tammy's mind was running over different scenarios for how to tell Hansen she was pregnant. For her, the direct approach always worked best, but blurting out that she was pregnant didn't sit well with her. Tammy looked up to face Hansen. "You know, I really enjoy playing with Joshawa."

Hansen gave Tammy a look as if to say *where did that come from.* "Yeah, he's a cute kid. It's amazing how fast he's developing."

"Apparently, that's normal for the tribe." There was a moment of awkward silence while Tammy was thinking of what to say next.

Hansen beat her to it. "Would you ever want children?"

"Would you?"

"Sure. A combination of you and me would be great."

Tammy leaned up, resting on her forearm as she gazed down at Hansen. "That's good to hear, because, according to Authia, I'm pregnant." Tammy held her breath as she waited for his reaction. Hansen's eyes went wide as he jolted up. Tammy sat up next to him. "Are you happy?"

"Happy!" Hansen threw his arms around Tammy and hugged her tightly. "I'm ecstatic!" Gently he pulled her away. "How far along are you?"

"Not long. Just a few weeks. Did you want to know the sex?"

"You know?"

Tammy smiled. "Yes, I do."

Hansen thought for a second. "Sure, what are we having?"

"A girl. A beautiful baby girl."

CHAPTER TWELVE

Sam slowly opened his eyes and looked around at his new home. He saw the morning sun streaming in from the entrance to the hut. He could see Casandra over by the table at the back of the hut. She was preparing something in a large clay bowl as she softly chanted. He groaned as he awkwardly sat up, which caught Casandra's attention.

She looked over her shoulder at Sam. "How are you today?"

"Shoulder is still sore, but I feel better." Sam was shirtless, exposing the three bandages that covered his injuries.

"That's good to hear. Our Lord will be pleased." Casandra put the clay bowl aside and walked over to Sam. She knelt next to him, then carefully removed the bandages, checking the injuries as she did. "These are healing nicely. I think we'll leave the bandages off, let the wounds have time to dry." Casandra suddenly became quiet, staring right through Sam. A minute later she smiled, but not as Casandra would.

Sam looked at her suspiciously. "Casandra?"

"Actually, Serena. So, your friend is causing quite a stir."

"My friend? You know of Tomas?"

"You are an outsider, just like the other two. I never thought I would witness the day that outsiders would be allowed to live among us. Normally we would just kill you. Rid our valley of your filth." Serena paused for a second. "But that was another time, and as I am repeatedly reminded, I must embrace the new Lord and his rules. To answer you, yes, I know of Tomas. But only what you know. I can see into your mind." Serena leaned closer to Sam. "You deserted your friend. Left him for dead. I wonder how forgiving he will be?"

"That's enough Serena." Nathen's voice bellowed

throughout the hut. "Behave yourself, or I will send you back where you came from." Nathen stood not two feet from Serena, glaring at her as he towered over her. "Consider this your one and only warning."

Serena stood and bowed to Nathen. "Message received and understood. You wanted to see me this morning?"

"Actually, I came to see Casandra. But since you're here, can you travel outside of our valley as you did before?"

"Yes. Where would you have me travel to?"

"I need you to find Tomas. We need to bring him home."

"You believe he is still alive?"

"Casandra believes so, and that's good enough for me."

"Well, since I have been stripped of my powers, and I am no longer a *true spirit,* I can no longer venture to the outer realms of the outsider's world."

"You just told me you could."

"Ugh . . . you were never one for patience. As I was about to say . . . in my present state as a wisp, I can venture into the outsider's valley that is to the north of us. But no further. And I can only remain outside of my host for a couple of hours. Any longer and I will be lost to the wind."

"Only a couple of hours?"

"As a wisp, I can travel a great distance in a short time. I know where to start looking. This little man here has shown me where he deserted his friend."

"Serena!"

Serena rolled her eyes and sighed. "Well, that is what he did. However, if that offends you . . . I will just say the last place he saw him."

"That's better. I want to speak to Casandra now before you leave."

Casandra bowed to Nathen. "Good morning, my Lord. What is your bidding?"

"Where you privy to the exchange between Serena and

myself?"

"Yes, my Lord."

"Can we control her while she is outside of your body?"

"No. But that being said, she can't remain outside of my body for long. She needs a host to survive, a host that she is linked to, which means only me. And believe me, our Ancestors are watching her. One step out of line, and she will be a lost spirit for eternity. And that is not something you would want to endure."

"Okay, release her, and then find me the minute she returns."

"Yes, my Lord."

Nathen started to leave, then changed his mind. "Casandra, have Serena also check how close anyone is to us. And how many."

"Of course."

Sam and Nathen watched as Casandra closed her eyes, then looked up at the roof of the hut. She parted her lips ever so slightly, and as she did, a brilliant blue wisp flew out into the open. It darted around the hut, then flew past Nathen.

If Sam didn't know better, he could have sworn he heard it giggling as it flew by.

Serena felt as free as the wind as she sored through the valley, past the falls and into the valley of the outsiders. It didn't take long for her to find the tree Sam had been hiding in. The memory was vividly implanted in his mind and therefore vividly implanted in hers. Serena circled the tree, then rested on one of the lower branches. There were rotting corpses littered all over the ground. However, that didn't bother Serena. They were outsiders, so their death, to her, was meaningless. She scanned the area looking for the place that the man, Tomas, had fallen. She darted to the ground, then did something no one expected. She took on a physical form. It was the form of herself from centuries before. She wore a gown unlike anything that the Jelani Tribe had ever seen. It was light blue and almost sheer. It clung seductively to her breasts, then fell in layers to just past her knees. The jungle breezes playfully swirled around the skirt, causing the layers to flutter around Serena. She held her hands in front of her and slowly turned them about so that she could examine them. She took a couple of steps, feeling the lush jungle ground beneath her feet. Her sorcery knew no bounds. It took most of her energy to take on a physical form, but it was worth it. At least now she knew what she was capable of doing, which would serve her well ... when the time was right. Serena turned back into a wisp and hovered over an area on the ground where the ferns had been flattened, and blood had been spilled. *This is where Tomas fell.* She flew closer to the blood, grazing it as she went by. Tomas' memories bombarded her, causing her to dart among the trees wildly. She saw what he saw, and she felt what he felt. She knew of the brutality of the men that had him. She knew the direction he went, but her time was spent. She had to return.

Tomas slowly began to wake up. He wasn't in his hiding place, but instead, he was just waiting on the brink of reality, close enough to see who was with him, but far enough in that he could retreat at a moment's notice. He was lying on his side, curled into a fetal position. He tried to open his eyes, but they still would not cooperate. They were mere slits, allowing him only a glimpse of the world that surrounded him. He could see a man sleeping on the ground just a couple of feet from him. Other than that, the hut appeared to be empty. The pain that had been so mercifully taken away was now, once again, enveloping his body. He tried to lie on his back, but the pain was too great. He loudly moaned which woke up the man who laid so close to him. Tomas could see the man leaning over him, but something was different. The man didn't appear angry, and his hands weren't balled up into fists. He was speaking to him, softly, as if he was concerned. A voice deep within his mind told him to be leery. Told him not to trust the man hovering above him. But Tomas was curious—he wanted to know who he was and what he was doing here. He wanted to know why he was being hurt. Tomas left the safety of his hiding place and listened to what the man had to say.

"Tomas? Are you all right? Do you need pain medication?"

"Who is Tomas?"

Saburo looked at the little man in bewilderment. "You said your name is Tomas."

"I do not know Tomas. Why am I here? Where is here?"

"You have no idea how you got here? Or what's been going on for the past few days?"

"I remember a tree. I remember a strange voice followed by pain. But that is all."

Saburo figured that this complete loss of memory could work in his favor. He could tell Tomas anything he wanted to, and Tomas would believe him. But first he had to take care of Tomas' pain. "Look, you just lie here. I'm going to get you something for the pain and something for you to eat and drink."

Tomas didn't answer. He just curled back into a fetal position, crying out in agony as he did.

Saburo left the hut in search of Dak. He found him by one of the fire pits drinking his morning coffee. "Dak, I need you."

"What do you want?"

"Meds for Tomas. He's awake and in a lot of pain."

"All right. I'll just finish my coffee . . ."

"No. You'll do it now." Saburo turned and went in search of Obasi. He found him at the edge of the clearing, on his own, just sitting on the ground while he watched his men. Saburo walked over to him, sat next to him, but kept his focus straight ahead. "Obasi, I think I have a way to get through to Tomas . . . I mean the prisoner."

Obasi was silent, as he kept his focus on his men. He waited a couple of minutes then addressed Saburo. "Who is Tomas?"

"That is the name the prisoner gave me. Though he doesn't recognize it as his own."

"And how do you plan to gain his trust?"

"He has huge gaps in his memory. He doesn't know who he is or where he is, only that he has been hurt. I plan to ease his pain and feed him. Hopefully, by doing this, he will look upon me as a friend, someone he can trust. Then just maybe he'll crawl out of that dark hole he's living in and start remembering what you want to know."

"How long will it take?"

Saburo turned to face Obasi. "I have no way of knowing. His mind is sick. Dak says that there's no guarantee that this will even work."

Obasi stood and glanced down at Saburo. "We will remain here one more day. You have till then."

Saburo closed his eyes and sighed as Obasi walked off. It was already late morning. He had twenty-four hours to perform a miracle, one day to make Tomas remember. If he failed, he knew that Obasi would kill him.

Serena raced through the valley of the outsiders, making her way back to her host. She flew over an old migrating trail and right into a clearing filled with outsiders. Serena quickly hid in among the trees, hoping that the men did not get a glimpse of her. As she rested on a branch of a large Kapok tree, she scrutinized the men that sat on the ground below her. Fourteen men all dressed alike. She sensed their fear and frustration, and she knew these were not the men that had taken Tomas. Then she saw *him* walking into the clearing — it was the man she had sensed before. She watched him as he walked over to the fire pit and sat with the rest of his companions. *He is the one!* The one that would save her village — her home. She was getting weaker, and in her weakened condition, she could not easily read him. There was only one way to ensure that she was right and he was the protector.

Serena left the safety of the branch and flew down toward the men. She fluttered around them, giggling as she did. The men all stood up watching her as she flew about them. Some of the men ducked as she swooped down among them, some tried to catch her, but she was too fast. Serena then zoned in on her target. She buzzed around his head, keeping out of his reach as he tried to swat at her with his hands. Just as he was about to speak, Serena took the advantage and flew inside of him through his slightly parted lips. She possessed him, taking control of his body and mind. She felt his body as it collapsed to the ground, and she was very much aware of the men that ran to his side.

Serena was giddy. It had been a long time since she had controlled an outsider's mind and body. It felt so good — it was a vision of things yet to come. She entered his subconscious, soaking in all his memories, learning who he was. She smiled, for she knew she had found the right outsider.

So, you are Travis.

Though Travis lay still on the ground, his eyes closed, his breathing shallow, Serena knew he would be very aware of what was transpiring inside of his own mind. *Who or what are you?*

I am Ser . . .

Serena stopped short. Oh, she had to be careful. One wrong move, one wrong word could end everything she was planning. *I am your spirit guide.*

Spirit guide? Guide to what?

Your destiny.

And what is my destiny?

To protect a village of . . . people . . . that are unable to protect themselves. There is a great evil in this valley, and it is coming this way. You know of the evil I speak of.

You are talking about the rebels, the ones led by Obasi.

Yes. They are following you. You must head South, then climb to the top of the mountain that stands before you. At the top, you will find a deserted village. Wait there for me. I will find you there.

We are just a small group of men. How are we going to fight Obasi?

There is a strength at the top of the mountain. Go there now. Protect the people that cannot protect themselves.

Travis repeated what he heard. *Protect the people.*

Protect the people that cannot protect themselves. I will find you on top of the mountain.

Protect the people.

Serena smiled. *Yes . . . protect the people.* Her work was done. She left his body and continued on her way home to her host.

Rick knelt at Travis' side. He was repeating something. *Protect the people.* He said it over and over again. Rick watched as the blue wisp left Travis' body. Gently he shook Travis' shoulders. "Travis. Can you hear me? Travis."

Travis slowly shook his head as he took a deep breath and then released it. "What the hell happened?"

"Whatever that blue thing was, it flew inside of you. Are you okay?"

Travis sat up and stared off in the direction of the mountain that towered before them. "I think we need to head further south."

"What are you talking about? We're staying here. It's a perfect place."

Travis turned to face Rick. "No. We need to head south. There are people there that need our help."

"What the hell are you talking about?"

"I just know that there are people that need our help. They're on top of that mountain." Travis pointed in the direction of the mountain. "We need to go there. Obasi is following us. These people will not have a chance if we don't help them."

"What people? How do you know that there are people up there?"

"That wisp spoke to me. She told me that her people needed our help. Rick, we were hired as peacemakers. But most importantly, to protect a village of people that are unable to protect themselves. We are being given the opportunity to do just that. I can't explain it. I just know that these people are in desperate need of our help. Look, I don't expect you to believe me, or to follow me for that matter. But I'm going to that village. I have to."

Rick stood up and looked down at Travis. "If that wisp needs our help, why didn't she speak to all of us?"

"Who knows." Travis stood next to Rick. "I'm heading out. This is something I have to do."

"Just wait a minute." Rick turned to face his men. "I haven't a hot clue as to what just happened here. But you all saw it, you all heard it. I don't believe in ghosts or fairies or wisps that fly around our heads. But there was something here, and it made a big impression on Travis." Rick was quiet for a minute. He ran his right hand down his face, cupping his chin for just a second. Then he placed his hands on his hips. "Okay. Speaking for myself, I can't ignore what Travis was told to do. What if there are people that are in need of our protection? What if Obasi is on his way? What if we do nothing, and an entire village is destroyed because of our inaction? I know, a lot of *what ifs*. But if I do nothing, all I am going to think about for the rest of my life is *what if*. And God help me if I hear of a village that was destroyed at the hands of the rebels. I'm going with Travis. You men can do whatever you feel is right. I will not judge anyone of you if you decide to stay here."

Taylor spoke up. "Well, you guys won't get a hundred yards without getting lost if I don't go with you. I know Greg will feel the same way. I'm in."

"All right. Show of hands. All those that want to remain here?" Not one man raised his hand. "And those that want to follow Travis?" Every man raised his hand. Rick looked over to Travis. "So, where are we going?"

Travis nodded in the direction of the mountain. "We have to climb that mountain to the very top. There's a deserted village there. I'm to wait for her at that village."

Rick looked up at the mountain, and from his vantage point, he could only see the top portion of it. "Okay, we should head out. We have a long hike ahead of us. Kill the fire, fill up everything you can with water. We head out in twenty."

Rick watched his men as they double-timed it packing up. He'd been hoping to be finished with the fighting. But apparently not. And according to Travis' wisp, he was going up against Obasi. God help them all.

Serena made her way back to the Jelani Tribe. She entered the priestess' hut, where she found Casandra, dressed in her animal skins, placing ingredients into a clay pot. Serena buzzed around Casandra's head.

Casandra stopped what she was doing. With her hands still holding onto the bowl and pestle, she closed her eyes and slightly parted her lips.

Serena flew past Casandra's lips and into her body, causing Casandra's entire body to shudder as she accepted Serena's entity. Casandra gave her head a shake then spoke with Serena. "You're back early."

"I did not want to risk taking too long. Besides, it was draining being in the outside world."

"You do seem to be very weak. Did something happen?"

"Yes. I found someone to help us. We should go see Nathen . . . sorry, I mean our Lord. I have much to tell him."

Casandra placed the pestle down on the table and turned to leave the hut. Something was nagging at her. Serena wasn't being totally honest—Casandra was sure of it. But how could Serena be deceitful? The Ancestors were watching her. She wouldn't be permitted to do anything to hurt the village or their Lord and Mistress. As Casandra left to find Nathen, a disturbing thought entered her mind. One that went unnoticed by Serena. One that involved treachery at its highest level.

CHAPTER THIRTEEN

Saburo entered the hut, where he found Dak administrating morphine into a vein in Tomas' left arm. He withdrew the needle, placed the syringe back into his brown leather kit, then acknowledged Saburo as he zipped the kit closed. "He should be feeling the effects within minutes."

"How often can we give him the morphine? I'd like to keep him out of pain, but I don't need his mind any more clouded than it already is."

Dak stood and faced Saburo. "You can't have it both ways. If you want him pain-free, then I have to inject him before the previous injection leaves his system. If I do that, then the morphine will affect his mind. If you want him lucid, then there will be pain."

Saburo went to sit next to Tomas. "Bring me whatever it is he can eat. And some water." Dak left the hut, leaving Saburo alone with Tomas. Saburo sat cross-legged on the ground and scrutinized Tomas' body. Tomas was shirtless and wore jeans that were cut off at his knees. He was also barefoot. His body was tattooed with bruises that were so purple they were almost black, and there were signs of old bruises layered underneath the new bruises. Saburo couldn't tell if Tomas's eyes were open or closed, his nose was broken, and his jaw sat at an odd angle. *How does anyone survive this?* Saburo sat quietly, waiting for the morphine to kick in. Dak returned with a bowl of what appeared to be mush and a canteen of water.

"I ground some anti-inflammatories and mild painkillers into the food. It should help prolong his comfort." Dak placed the bowl of food and canteen next to Saburo then left.

Saburo remained at Tomas' side, just staring at him,

waiting for some sign that the morphine was doing its job. Finally, after several minutes, Tomas began to wake up. Saburo gently laid his hand on Tomas' forehead. "Can you hear me? Are you okay? I have some food and water for you. Would you like some?"

He could feel the pain lifting from his body, and his head was starting to clear. He looked around to see where he was, but there was only darkness. He could just make out a voice, though it seemed to be so far away. Was it speaking to him? He couldn't tell. As he glanced around in the darkness, a faint sliver of light started to appear off in the distance. It was beckoning him to come closer. It was as if a curtain had been parted, allowing the light into the darkness. Slowly, within the confines of his mind, he approached the light. Inside the light was a large tree. It was calling to him, its branches reaching out to him. As he got closer, the voice that lived inside the darkness spoke to him—warning him of what was waiting for him inside the light. He was confused. He wanted so much to know who he was, where he came from. He was sure that the answers were inside the light. Maybe, if he just stood on the edge, kept his feet firmly planted, it would be safe. The voice told him no, it was not safe. It warned him to stay in the darkness. But he ignored the voice and stood at the edge of the darkness as he gazed into the light. Waiting for him, inside the light, was a tall, muscular man with golden-red hair that flowed to his shoulders. Though he couldn't see his face, he knew the man was smiling at him. Then he spoke to him. "Come with me, Tomas. I will take you home. Home to my valley. The valley that is protected by the Gods."

Saburo gently lifted Tomas into his arms, cradling him mostly in his left arm. With his right hand, he reached for the canteen of water. "Tomas, if you can hear me, I'm going to give you some water. Try to swallow it." Carefully he poured the water between Tomas' lips that were parted ever so slightly. The water ran down Tomas' chin and onto his chest. Saburo eased up on the water so that more of the water would stay in Tomas' mouth. It took a few minutes, but Saburo finally could see Tomas' throat in motion as he swallowed the water. "Good, Tomas. Take a little more." He fed Tomas the water until Tomas could no longer swallow. Saburo placed the canteen back on the ground and continued to cradle Tomas. "Don't suppose you want to talk?"

Tomas' voice was hoarse, barely discernable. "Have you come to save me?"

Saburo looked down at Tomas in disbelief. "Yes, I'm here to save you."

Tomas looked at the man. "Please, take me to the valley that is protected by the Gods."

Saburo couldn't believe what he was hearing. *Oh my God . . . there is a valley. Obasi was right.* "Yes, Tomas, I will take you to the valley protected by the Gods. But I have forgotten the way. Can you help me?"

"Yes, my Lord. It is my duty." Tomas' voice grew faint, and his body became limp in Saburo's arms as he drifted off to sleep.

Casandra went in search of Nathen and Authia. She found them in the gathering hut with Tammy and Hansen. She heard them celebrating the news of the pregnancy and the upcoming marriage. Casandra remained standing at the entrance of the hut. "Excuse me, my Lord." She bowed as Nathen and Authia acknowledged her presence. "Serena has returned. She wishes to speak with you."

Nathen approached Casandra. "I thought she would be gone longer."

"Apparently, she was trying to be cautious." Casandra went quiet as she stared straight through Nathen.

She gave her head a little shake, then smiled smugly at Nathen. "I was testing the waters, so to speak. I do not want to push my luck."

"And what did you discover?"

"I found where Sam and Tomas parted. I know the direction that those awful men took him."

"Did you find him?"

"No. I was not risking staying outside of my host any longer than I had to."

"You mean Casandra. Your host has a name."

Serena rolled her eyes. "You and your father, so stubborn when it comes to names. I will look for the little man . . . Tomas . . . tomorrow."

"Why not later today? It's not even noon yet. Every hour he is with those men, he becomes further out of our reach."

"There is nothing they can do to him that they have not already done. I need time to regain my strength. And before you ask, leaving at night is totally out of the question."

"And why is that?"

"A bright blue light flittering around the darkness of night. How am I to conceal myself?"

Nathen pondered the ramification of Serena traveling at night. Somehow, he didn't believe it was as great a challenge as she made out. "Fine. You'll leave at first light." Nathen went to rejoin the others when Serena interrupted him.

"Are we finished? I guess you are not interested in the group of men I found."

Nathen whirled around in anger.

Authia was immediately at his side. She took a step closer to Serena. "Quit playing games. What men are you talking about?"

"I am not playing games. It was Nathen, I mean my Lord, who turned his back on me."

Nathen held back and allowed Authia to take the lead. "Enough, Serena. Tell us about the men."

"Yes, my Mistress." Serena's tone dripped with sarcasm. "There is a clearing at the base of the mountain, close to a pond."

Authia nodded her head in recognition. "Yes, we stayed at that place."

"There are fourteen men there. They are warriors, though I sensed that the fighting displeased them. I managed to convince one of them to help us."

"One of them? And how did you convince this one man?"

Serena giggled. "I rattled around in his brain. You remember what that is like, do you not?"

Authia glared at Serena. "Unfortunately, yes I do. I thought you weren't allowed to do that."

"I am not allowed to enter your mind, or his." Serena motioned toward Nathen. "Or anyone else in the tribe." Serena took a step closer to Authia. They now stood only a couple of feet apart. "However, if I am to help the cause, then I must be able to enter the mind of whomever I feel is necessary outside of the tribe."

It was obvious that Authia was reaching her boiling point, something Nathen noticed that Serena was taking deep pleasure in. Nathen stepped forward, took Authia's hand, and gently pulled her back so he could step in front of her and face Serena. "You've made your point. Now, what about these men?"

"I have convinced the one called Travis to help us. He is to meet me at the village on the other side of the falls. How many men he convinces to follow him is beyond my realm of sorcery."

"Then your sorcery is very much diminished. When are you to meet him?"

"When he arrives." Serena closed her eyes.

Nathen looked at her questioningly. "Casandra?"

"Yes, my Lord. Serena has left. If it pleases my Lord, I must rest." Casandra stepped forward, placing her hand on Nathen's forearm. "Perhaps a visit to my daughter is in order." Nathen could see the uneasiness in Casandra's eyes.

"Yes, a visit to the High Priestess is long overdue. Go rest. We'll speak later."

Nathen watched as Casandra made her way to the family priestess' hut. There was a warning in her eyes. Maybe she didn't have as much control over Serena as she believed she would. Nathen took a deep breath and slowly let it out. Serena, left unchecked, would be a greater enemy than any force from the outside world.

Rick and his men headed south. Travis led the way, following a path that was ingrained in his mind. The jungle didn't disappoint and was as unyielding as ever. The heat and humidity clung to them like a heavy cloak. The insects were continually swarming around their heads. The men carrying the litters dared not swat at them, for their cargo was far too unstable to try to carry with just one hand. As they climbed higher, the air became thinner, causing the men to suffer headaches and shortness of breath. After several breaks and hours of hiking, they reached their destination. Travis looked about in disbelief. Everything was exactly as the wisp had shown him. The deserted village, the view to the north where he could see the canopy of the jungle spread out for miles. The litters were gently placed on the ground, and the men, exhausted and overheated, set down their backpacks, then used them as pillows as they too lay on the ground.

Rick approached Travis, who was standing at the edge of the clearing looking out to the valley below. "Now what?"

Travis looked over at Rick. "We wait. Someone will come to get us, take us where we need to go."

"And where do we need to go?"

Travis shook his head. "I don't know. Somewhere close." He looked past Rick to the jungle that separated the village from the falls. "There's freshwater just over there."

Rick looked behind him. "More jungle."

"You can see the water from the edge of the jungle. It's not far." Travis started walking in the direction he knew only too well. It was as if he had been there before. He knew what to expect, he knew there would be a waterfall and a pond. When he reached the pond, he looked at the waterfall with suspicion. There was something about that waterfall, a secret, disguised, hiding what was in plain sight. The arrival of the other men brought Travis back to reality as they stripped naked and ran whooping and hollering into the cool, clear waters of the pond.

Saburo had laid Tomas back on the ground and allowed him to sleep for an hour. Then he gently poured some water on his face to revive him. He watched, not saying a word, as Tomas slowly came to.

Tomas opened his eyes slightly and smiled as much as his jaw would allow him. "What is your bidding, my Lord?"

Saburo had to play his cards right. Tomas was obviously mistaking him for someone else, someone he felt safe with. "You promised to show me the way to the valley protected by the Gods."

Tomas closed his eyes as he lay still on the ground. "Yes, I did, my Lord. When would you like to leave?"

"As soon as possible."

With his eyes barely open, Tomas gently moved his head as if he were looking for something in the hut. "I do not know where I am, my Lord. There is so much darkness. I must find the tree. Please, help me find the tree."

Saburo had no idea what he was talking about. *What tree? Does the tree mark where the valley is?* "Tell me what tree you are looking for, and I will help you find it."

Tomas opened his eyes wider than Saburo even believed he could. "The tree where it all began."

Chapter Fourteen

It was noon, and the smell of roasting meat filled the village of the Jelani Tribe. Nathen and Authia left Joshawa with Tammy and Hansen, then made their way to the priestess' family hut in the hope of finding the High Priestess Tamara. They didn't have to go far, for Tamara was looking for them as well.

Tamara, dressed in her animal skins, bowed to him and his wife. "I was looking for you. I sense that my mother is conflicted. She is worried, and I believe she wants me to help you discover what troubles her."

Authia smiled at Tamara. "You are truly gifted. Walk with us." The three walked in silence as they headed toward the outskirts of the village. They only stopped once they were sure that they were alone and no one would overhear their conversation.

Nathen turned to Tamara. "Are you certain that Serena is secure within your mother?"

"Yes, my Lord. She cannot leave her host without permission. Right now, my mother sleeps. And while she sleeps, so does Serena."

"Your mother made it quite clear that something's not right. And I'm certain it involves Serena."

"I do sense that my mother is troubled, but I cannot see into her mind. I cannot hear her thoughts as I once did. I believe that Serena is blocking me from seeing what there is to see."

Nathen frowned, for he knew Serena only too well. "If Serena is blocking you, then there has to be something going on. She's planning something. Is there any way that she can exist outside of your mother?"

"Only by the grace of our Ancestors would she be allowed

to take human form outside of my mother's body. And our Ancestors are adamant that she must help in saving our village or suffer by their hand. I cannot believe they would allow her such freedom. However, even if she were allowed outside of my mother's body, she will always be attached to my mother."

Nathen was quiet, listening to everything that was being said. "What do you mean by attached?"

"She lives through my mother. She and my mother are joined by my mother's life force. Nothing can change that. Not even our Ancestors."

Nathen's mind was full of questions. But one question stood out from all the others. "These Ancestors that you speak of . . . are they all the ancestors of the Jelani Tribe, or just a selected few?"

"The Ancestors that watch over us and decide the path that we are to follow once we die are only a selected few. They are chosen from all the Lords and High Priestesses that have ruled us over the centuries. Every hundred years, new Ancestors are chosen."

"Who chooses these Ancestors?"

Tamara looked puzzled as she looked at Nathen and Authia. "I do not know. I have never given it much thought."

Authia must have caught on to where Nathen was going with this. "How do we find out who the ruling Ancestors are right now?"

"I do not know. The rule of the Ancestors has never been brought into question."

Authia took a step closer to Tamara. "There must be a way to find out. We need to know who these Ancestors are, and we need to do this without Serena discovering what we are up to."

"There may be one way. In times of need, the priestesses can meld, join as one, and communicate with the Ancestors.

At that time, they are visible, and you can see who they are."

Authia looked over to Nathen. "If that's true, then we'll know if these Ancestors think as your father did or as Serena does."

"Seeing our Ancestors will not tell you what their beliefs are. As I said, the Ancestors that rule over us now are at least a hundred years old. Neither my mother or I would know who they are. However, if that is what you seek, then it might be possible to see into their minds during the meld."

Authia looked at Tamara in disbelief. "How can we see into their minds? Why would they allow that? And how would we accomplish this without Serena finding out?"

Tamara smiled at her Mistress. "You are always so full of questions. To begin, when we meld with our Ancestors, we become one with them. That is the only way we can communicate with them. If your reason for communicating with them is sound, then there would be no reason for Serena to doubt our motives."

Authia thought for a moment, mulling over the many reasons she could use as an excuse to meld with the Jelani Ancestors. "Why not play on their vanity."

"Vanity? What is vanity?"

"Simple. We thank them for the gift of Serena but insist that we need a more powerful form of sorcery to defeat our foes. A sorcery so powerful that only they could provide it."

Nathen looked at Authia then back to Tamara. "Would they use their sorcery to help us?"

"No, my Lord. If they have not already offered, then they never will. Serena is all we get. But making this request would give us the opportunity to see into their minds and keep Serena in the dark."

Authia smiled. "Perfect! How about we arrange it for the

next time Serena leaves our valley."

"Yes, my Mistress, that could work. We should not mention our intentions until after Serena has left. Then we will summon the priestesses along with Sensay, yourself and my mother." Tamara looked over her shoulder in the direction of the village. "My mother wakes." She looked back to Authia and Nathen. "We should return before Serena becomes suspicious." She did not wait for an answer, but instead turned and headed back into the village.

Authia almost stopped her but thought better of it. She wanted to learn more about the aura that resided in the other village, but possibly that was also something to be mentioned after Serena had left the valley.

Serena rested within the confines of Casandra's mind, regaining her strength. She lay in a state of perpetual bliss. She felt confident in her plan to once again walk the lush green carpet that served as the floor to her valley—so confident that she was unaware of the nagging doubt that skirted the edges of Casandra's mind. A voice no louder than a faint whisper echoed within Serena.

I see into your thoughts. I feel your desires. Do not forget that I control you. Do not attempt to alter your destiny. Your existence is allowed as long as you do my bidding. Your ability to take human form is only because I choose to allow it.

The voice left shivers down her spine. Serena, a priestess who once controlled everything and everyone around her, was, in the mind of the voice, nothing more than a mere puppet. A puppet with a mind of her own. To Serena, the puppeteer was a fool to think that anyone or anything could control her.

Travis sat cross-legged on the outcrop of rocks that edged the pond. He stared at the waterfall knowing that it was important but not knowing why. Something about it was just not sitting right with him. There appeared to be a glimmer in the darkness of the rock that formed the back wall of the waterfall. He was so focused on his own thoughts that he didn't hear Rick approach him.

"You look intense." Rick sat on the rocks next to Travis.

Travis continued to stare forward. "I don't know or understand what that wisp did to me, but what I do know, without a doubt, is that there is a village of people who need our protection."

"Protection from Obasi?"

Travis shifted his gaze toward Rick. "Yes. Who else could it be?"

"He's the most likely candidate. You know, the people of this village aren't the only ones who will need protection if Obasi is following us. Do you know where the village is or how many people we're supposed to be protecting?"

Travis stared back at the waterfall. "Like I said, someone is coming to show us the way. And no, I don't know how many people there are. I have a deep-seated feeling that these people are defenseless against the firepower that Obasi is bringing." Travis turned back to Rick. "They need us to even the odds."

Rick glanced over in the direction of the men that were dressing after their plunge into the pond. When he returned his attention to Travis, a look of concern clearly evident on his face. "We were running from the fighting. Now, with Obasi hot on our heels, we'll not only have to fight, but we'll also have to be prepared to kill. That's the only way to win over Obasi. Are you good with that?"

Travis stood and nodded his head. "I came here to protect the innocent. To protect those that could not protect themselves. I knew when I signed the contract that the protection could, and would most likely, involve killing. Rick, killing a man to protect a child or woman that is in danger is something I can live with. Killing out in the jungle just because the person is not on our *team* is ... well, it's something I can't live with. But now we are going to be given the opportunity to do what we came here to do. So yes, I'm good with that."

"All right, but don't forget, it's not just your life on the line. We'll check this village out, but I'm not going to risk the lives of every man here to protect something or someone that is impossible to protect. We're not going on a suicide mission. Do you agree?"

"No one is impossible to protect. It's our duty to help this village. Can you walk away and leave this village to Obasi?" Travis didn't wait for an answer. He just turned away and walked back to the deserted village. He couldn't explain it, but he knew that these people he was asked to protect were not entirely defenseless.

Saburo sat on the ground staring at Tomas. He was supposed to take him to the place where it all began. *Where what began?* And what tree was he talking about? This was not going to be easy, and with the threat of death hanging over his head, Saburo was motivated. There had to be something he could do to get the information he so desperately needed. As he focused on Tomas, Dak entered the hut.

"How is he?"

"Better. A little more lucid. Are you here to give him another shot?"

"Yes." Dak knelt by Tomas, opened his kit and started to tie a rubber band around Tomas' bicep. Tomas opened his eyes as much as the swelling looked like it would allow.

"Are you here to help me take my Lord to the tree? To the

place where it all began?"

Dak looked up to Saburo, confusion written on his face. "What the hell is he talking about?"

"I have no idea. I have to find this place where it all began. Do you have any idea what he's talking about?"

Dak retrieved the syringe from his kit and inserted it into the vial of morphine. Slowly he drew the plunger back as he filled the syringe. "If you want to figure out what he's saying you got to think like him." Dak gently slapped the inside of Tomas' elbow and then inserted the syringe into the bulging vein.

"What do you mean, *think like him*? How am I supposed to know how he thinks?"

Dak returned the syringe to its resting place in the kit, zipped it up and then looked up at Saburo. "Put yourself in his shoes. What if you were being beaten merciless for days on end? What if you escaped to a place in your mind where you could hide from the pain and abuse? What would you know when you came out of that place?"

"I don't know. You're the doctor."

"Medic." Dak stood and looked at Saburo with a smirk on his face. "He has hidden in his mind from everything that has happened to him for the past few days. He has no idea where he is. Right?"

"Right."

"If I had to bet money on it, I would have to say the place where it all began is the place that you captured him. The last place he has a conscious memory of." Dak reached over and patted Saburo's shoulder. "My Lord." Dak laughed as he left the hut.

CHAPTER FIFTEEN

Serena could feel Casandra's energy coursing throughout her own being. Casandra was waking, and all Serena wanted to do was to leave Casandra's body, to be free and to live her life as something more than just a wisp, an apparition of what she used to be. But she had to be patient—she had to wait for the right time. There was a plan set in motion, a plan that would correct what she felt was a great injustice dealt to her. Casandra had dressed and was leaving the family priestess' hut, and even though Serena couldn't see, she could sense her surroundings. Casandra headed for the gathering hut, and in the hut, Serena could sense Nathen. He wanted to speak with her. She felt Casandra opening the barrier that kept her locked inside her host. Serena took over Casandra's body, and with Casandra monitoring the conversation, Serena addressed Nathen.

"You were looking for me? Oh, where are my manners." Serena bowed to Nathen. "My Lord, I do not see Authia. Did she loosen that leash she has around your neck?"

"You'll address her as your Mistress. And if you disrespect her again, I'll send you back where you came from."

Serena snorted at Nathen. "You cannot. You need me to fight this battle."

"Actually, we need the men that you're bringing here. Not you. Unless, of course, you're capable of much more than you're telling me."

Serena shrugged her shoulders. "I am what I am. Nothing more . . . nothing less. However, you still need me to find Tomas. Or have you given up on him?"

"No, I haven't. And that's why I sent for you. I want you to leave now. You have at least four hours before night falls.

Find Tomas, and then, on your way back, I want you to see if the man you call Travis has reached the village yet."

"I thought that I was going to be allowed to rest until the new day dawns?"

"You've rested enough. Leave. Now!"

Serena scowled at Nathen. "Very well." Casandra's eyes closed, and she parted her lips slightly. Serena flew out of Casandra and raced around the confines of the hut.

Serena could see the disapproval etched across Nathen's face. "Conserve your energy, Serena. Leave. Find Tomas."

Serena flew out of the hut and headed in the direction of the falls.

Cassandra turned to see Nathen looking at her and smiled at him.

"Casandra, are you with me?"

"Yes, I'm with you, my Lord."

"Just you, or is Serena privy to what transpires between us?"

"No, my Lord. As soon as she leaves my body, she's only aware of her surroundings, nothing more."

"Casandra, I sensed that you are troubled by something. Tamara feels the same. Serena is blocking her from seeing your thoughts or sensing your feelings."

Casandra was shocked. "How's that possible? She has no powers. At least she's not supposed to."

"Well, Tamara can't connect with you, and she assumes it's Serena that's blocking her."

Casandra melded with her daughter. *Tamara, can you hear me?*

Yes, Mother. What can I do for you?

I'm at the gathering hut. Come to me, and bring our Mistress.

Yes, Mother.

Casandra looked up at Nathen. "This shouldn't be

happening. I'm going to get to the bottom of this. You're right, my Lord, I am troubled. Something isn't right. There's a strange aura that surrounds Serena. Sometimes it's very strong, and other times it's faint, as if it's just resting on the edge of my consciousness."

"Can you find out who this aura belongs to?"

Tamara answered Nathen as she walked into the hut. "Yes, my Lord." Both Cassandra and Nathen turned to face her. Standing there was Tamara dressed in her ceremonial gown. Authia was at her side dressed in her animal skins, with Joshawa resting on her right hip. Tamara approached them with a look of trepidation on her face. "I can reach out to this aura, try and see what it hides from us. But if I do this, then the aura will be aware that we know of its existence."

Authia placed Joshawa on the ground, then turned to face Tamara. "Is that a bad thing or a good thing?"

"It is neither. The aura is too weak to do any serious harm. It must first take over a host. One that I am sure it has already picked out."

Nathen was trying to weigh out in his mind which of the many dangers he should deal with first. "Tamara, do you believe that the aura at the village is the same aura that Cassandra senses surrounding Serena?"

"I am sorry, my Lord, I cannot tell. I must meld with both auras to see if they are the same or not."

"And how do you meld with both auras?"

"I will first focus on the aura that lives in the village. Then, when Serena returns, Mother will tell me when she can sense the aura that surrounds Serena. I will meld with that aura, and I will know if it is the same aura as the village or not."

Nathen's attention was averted to Joshawa, who was struggling to stand. He didn't take his focus off Joshawa as he addressed Tamara. "Then I need you to meld with the aura at the village as soon as possible." Joshawa gained his footing, then he half wobbled, half ran to his father, who scooped him up into his arms. Joshawa sat securely on Nathen's forearm, then wrapped his arms around Nathen's neck and rested his head on Nathen's shoulder. Nathen smiled as he looked over at his son who was trying to snuggle just a little bit closer. Then, when he appeared to be content, he closed his eyes and fell asleep.

"My Lord, I can do as you wish at this very moment, but I will need Sensay and my Mistress to strengthen my vision."

Authia spoke, "What about Casandra? Won't you need her too?"

"No. I do not want to chance that the aura my mother senses is lurking anywhere within her. If it is, then I may confuse the two." Tamara faced Casandra. "I am sorry, mother, but you should not be present when I reach out to the aura at the village."

Casandra smiled at Tamara. "I understand. I'll wait for you in the priestess' hut." She looked up at Nathen. "If it pleases my Lord, come see me when you have your answers." Casandra didn't wait for a reply. Instead, she left the hut, apparently heading for the priestess' hut.

Authia spoke, "Where's Sensay? I haven't seen her all day."

Tamara replied, "She secludes herself inside her hut. She prefers to spend her time in meditation."

Authia shrugged her shoulders. "Well then, we'll go to her."

Tamara bowed to Nathen and Authia. "As you wish." She left the gathering hut and headed for Sensay's hut, followed closely by Nathen and Authia.

Saburo left the hut in search of Obasi. He found him in his usual place, sitting on the ground at the edge of the camp watching over his men. Saburo sat next to him as he kept his focus straight ahead. "I think I've found a way to get Tomas to lead me to this valley you want so bad."

Saburo was uncomfortable, for Obasi wouldn't acknowledge him. Usually what Obasi did or didn't do meant nothing to Saburo, but as the threat of death loomed over his head, every action or inaction that Obasi took played on Saburo's fears. He held his breath as he waited for Obasi to speak.

"You mean the prisoner." It was a statement, not a question.

"Ah, yes, the prisoner."

"Do not name the prisoner. Do not get close to the prisoner." Obasi turned to face Saburo. "Otherwise it may prove difficult for you to kill him when he's no longer of any use."

"You want me to kill him?"

Obasi turned back to face his men. "Yes. When it is time. Now, how are you going to get him to cooperate?"

Saburo's mind was reeling. How could he do as Obasi commanded and not get close to Tomas? He took a deep breath—he would figure it out when he needed to. Right now, all that was important was appeasing Obasi. "He keeps asking to go back to where it all began. From there, he can show me the way to the valley. According to Dak, he's probably asking to go back to where he was captured."

"And what good can come from taking him back to where we slaughtered his people?"

"Dak thinks that Tom... the prisoner's mind is not allowing him to remember anything since the time he was captured. Apparently, it's the mind's way of dealing with the torture. If I take him back to that area, hopefully, he'll remember how he got there."

"Hopefully?"

"Obasi, there are no guarantees here. He's damaged. He's not in control of his own mind. This is our best shot."

Obasi remained quiet for several minutes . . . minutes that dragged forever for Saburo. "Take him, and we'll follow you."

"How close do you plan to follow?"

Obasi once again turned to face Saburo. "Very."

"Not a good idea, Obasi. If the prisoner sees you, or any of our other men for that matter, he may shut down, and we'll never find this valley. Give us a day's head start. Keep us a day ahead of you. That's the only way this is going to work."

Obasi returned his gaze toward his men. Saburo could tell Obasi was mulling over his options. He knew that Obasi didn't want him to find the valley first. "Leave now. I'll give you your day. Do not enter the valley until I'm with you. Your punishment will be severe if you betray me."

Sensay sat cross-legged on the ground in front of the small fire pit that was in the center of her hut. The hut that was assigned to her was small, with no openings other than the one that served as her entrance. She felt comfortable in her little hut for it reminded her of the hut that was her home in her village. Her eyes were closed, and her hands rested in her lap. She allowed the aura of the hut to surround her, become one with her. The aura was a mixture of sadness, fear, and strength. The signature was undeniable — it belonged to Authia. Authia had once called this place home, though Sensay could sense it wasn't a pleasant time. She was so engrossed in the feelings of the aura that she didn't hear when Authia called out her name. It wasn't until Authia entered the hut that the aura dissipated and Sensay opened her eyes.

"Welcome, Mistress of the Lion People."

Authia looked around the hut. "You know, Sensay, we could find a larger hut for you."

Sensay smiled at Authia. "No, that is not necessary. What brings the Mistress of the Lion People to my hut?"

"May Tamara and Nathen enter?"

"Of course."

Sensay looked on with avid curiosity as Tamara, dressed in her ceremonial gown, and Nathen entered her hut. Cradled in Nathen's arms was his son, who appeared to be fast asleep. Tamara sat on the ground at the edge of the fire pit, directly across from Sensay. "It is an honor to have the High Priestess of the Lion People in my home."

"Sensay, I need your help."

"And what can this old lady do for you?"

"You have sensed the aura that hides in your village. Is that not true?"

"You know it to be true."

"I need your help to meld with the aura. To discover who or what it is, and hopefully, what it wants."

Sensay stared wide-eyed at Tamara. The aura frightened her—she didn't want any part of it. "The aura that you speak of covers my village in a shroud of darkness. It is evil. No good can come from it."

Authia sat on the ground and gently placed her hand on Sensay's knee. "That's why you emptied your village. You knew about the aura. You didn't want any harm to come to your people."

"Yes. But also, I sensed the men that were coming. I saw what they were capable of doing. The aura waits for them. When my people left, it did not follow them. It waits for someone else."

Smiling at Sensay, Tamara moved over to sit closer to her, then reached over and took Sensay's left hand in hers. She covered Sensay's hand with her right hand and closed her eyes. Tamara could sense the turmoil and fear that was part of Sensay. Fear of the aura, fear of what could happen to the people that she had protected for so many years. Tamara opened her eyes but continued to hold Sensay's hand.

"We need your help. Through you and my Mistress, I will hopefully be strong enough to be able to see who or what this aura is and what it wants. With this knowledge, we will know how to fight it."

"You are a powerful priestess. I am but an old lady. I have not the strength or the courage to approach an aura as dark as the one that lives in my village."

Tamara gently squeezed Sensay's hand. "You are stronger and braver than you let on. Was it not you who warned my Lord of the impending invasion? Was it not you who sent your people to safety only to remain behind to face what comes out of the jungle all alone? I know your heart. You want to help us . . . to save us. Meld with me and my Mistress. Help us protect our home as you have done for so many years."

Sensay remained quiet as she gazed upon Tamara. Patiently Tamara waited for Sensay to realize what she already knew. "You have much faith in me, High Priestess of the Lion People. I cannot say how much help I will be to you. But if you request it of me, even though it frightens me, I will help you in your search."

"Thank you, Sensay. I know this is difficult for you." Tamara looked over at her Mistress. "Please join us. Take our hands in yours." Tamara removed her left hand from Sensay's and reached over to hold Authia's hand. Authia, in turn, reached with her free hand and gently took hold of Sensay's right hand. Nathen remained quiet as he stood behind Authia. Tamara took a deep breath and slowly let it out. She wasn't certain what they were going to find. The aura was weak, but without knowing its true strength, there was no way to gauge its weakness. Even in a weakened state, the aura could prove to be a threat—a fact Tamara was not willing to share.

"Close your eyes. Join your mind with mine. See my thoughts . . . feel my thoughts. We will approach the aura as one. See the aura through my eyes and my eyes only. Do not falter, do not allow the aura to build on your fears." Tamara could sense the presence of Authia and Sensay. They became one with her mind, and together they traveled outside of their valley to the village that was home to the aura. Tamara slightly tilted her head to one side as she focused on the village.

The aura was there, but she couldn't meld with it. She concentrated harder, opening herself to allow the aura to reach out to her. It happened with no warning. The aura collided with Tamara, swirling around her as if the aura was the storm and Tamara was in the eye of it. Tamara gasped as the aura penetrated her mind. Tamara was right, the aura did have strength. Not enough to break the bond that she shared with Authia and Sensay, but enough to allow it to communicate with her.

You are a fool if you think you can destroy me! I have lived a lifetime waiting to be whole once more. Waiting to regain my place. Be warned! The Destroyer *is coming, and he will show no mercy.*

CHAPTER SIXTEEN

Saburo packed his backpack with provisions and what pain medication Dak could spare. He swung the pack over his right shoulder and went to collect Tomas. As he entered the hut, he watched as Tomas struggled to sit up. "Are we leaving, my Lord?"

"Yes, Tomas. I'm taking you to the place where it all began. Then I'll need you to take me home."

Tomas managed a slight bow. "As you wish, my Lord."

Saburo went over to Tomas and helped him to his feet. "Are you going to be able to walk?"

Tomas steadied himself and stared deep into Saburo's eyes. Saburo tried to figure out the expression on Tomas' face. He appeared almost relieved. It was as if Tomas felt safe in his presence. Obviously, Tomas' mind was imagining that Saburo was someone else, someone he trusted. He referred to Saburo as *Lord*. Maybe Tomas thought that he was the Lord of the valley Obasi was looking for. *Whatever.* "So, are you able to walk?"

"Your presence gives me strength. However, I will need your help, my Lord."

Saburo placed his arm around Tomas' shoulders. "Lean on me. I'll help support you until you are strong enough to walk on your own."

"Thank you, my Lord."

"You don't have to always call me *Lord*."

Tomas looked up to Saburo. "But I must. It would be disrespectful if I did not."

Saburo shook his head as he helped Tomas leave the hut. To Saburo's amazement, the camp was empty. Obasi and his men were gone. *Obasi's not taking any chances. He's going to stay out of Tomas' view.* As Saburo scanned the surrounding jungle, he knew that Obasi wasn't far. He could sense that Obasi was watching him, and as he led Tomas north, he prayed that Dak was right. He prayed that Tomas would regain enough of his memory to lead him to the valley but not enough that he would see Saburo for who he was.

Serena flew through the trees as she headed toward the place where she'd last sensed Tomas. She loved the freedom that she had as a wisp. However, her sights were set so much higher. She wouldn't be happy until she could permanently take human form. The puppeteer had other plans . . . plans that only benefited the puppeteer . . . not Serena. Serena giggled to herself. She and the puppeteer had planned everything out to the very last detail. Well, almost . . . Serena's version of how the plan played out, in the end, was entirely different from the puppeteer's plan.

It didn't take long for Serena to reach the tree where Tomas was taken captive. She landed on a branch and waited, confident in the knowledge that Tomas was coming to her. An hour later, Tomas and another man emerged from the jungle and stood beneath the tree. Serena looked on as the two men conversed. Tomas kept referring to the man as his Lord. *Oh, this is too easy.* It was time to put everything into motion. Serena flew out of the tree and playfully danced around the heads of the two men. As soon as Tomas started to speak, Serena flew in through his parted lips and took over his mind. She couldn't believe how damaged his mind was—how damaged he was. Softly she spoke to him, and Tomas answered.

Tomas, I am here to help you.

Help me? Can you help me remember? I must take my Lord home.

Yes, Tomas, and you will, for this man is your Lord. When you look upon him, you will only see the face of the Lion People.

The Lion People.

Yes, Tomas, the Lion People. That is who this man is. And now you will remember the way home.

Home? Where is home?

See my thoughts, Tomas. See the great mountain. Your home is on top of this mountain.

Yes, my home. I remember.

Good, Tomas. Now take your Lord home.

Can you take my pain away?

Yes. Serena chanted softly, whispering to Tomas' mind. The mind was powerful, and it could do wondrous things. And what Serena told it to do was to hide the pain from Tomas. Burry it deep within the safe place that Tomas had called home since his capture. Serena knew that it would only be a temporary fix. Once Tomas regained control of his mind . . . well, the pain would be excruciating. But Serena didn't care, she just needed Tomas to lead the man he was with to the village. After that, she would no longer need Tomas. When Serena was finished, she left Tomas and flew toward the village, where Travis was waiting for her.

Saburo watched on in disbelief as a bright blue wisp flew out of Tomas' mouth and then headed south through the jungle. "What the hell was that?" Saburo never believed in the supernatural or in ghosts and spirits. But how would he explain what he just saw? *Obasi's going to have a field day with this.* Saburo turned his attention to Tomas. *Was he harmed by the wisp? Is he still going to be able to help me?* As Saburo studied Tomas, he couldn't believe what he was seeing. It was as if his eyes were playing tricks on him. Tomas appeared to be transforming right in front of him. He stood straight and stretched his arms above his head. When he brought his arms down, he stretched out his fingers on both of his hands. It was as if he was waking from a long sleep and needed to stretch the kinks out of his body. Then he turned to Saburo, smiled and bowed without flinching or grimacing in pain.

"I am honored to serve you, my Lord."

"Are you feeling okay?"

"Of course, my Lord. Why would I not?"

"You don't remember a blue wisp rattling around in your body?"

Tomas looked confused at Saburo. "Blue wisp? I know nothing of a blue wisp."

"You don't remember it flying around our heads and then entering your body?"

"I know nothing of what you speak. I did not see a blue wisp."

Saburo sighed. He knew that he hadn't imagined it. Tomas obviously didn't have a firm grip on reality, a fact that would work well in Saburo's favor. "Well, then I guess we should leave. Did you want any pain medication before we head out?"

"Why would I need pain medication? I am fine, my Lord."

Saburo just gently shook his head and sighed. "All right. Then I guess we should head out."

Tomas looked around the area where they were standing as if he were searching for something. With a look of complete puzzlement, he returned his gaze to Saburo. "I seem to have misplaced my machete. May I borrow yours?" Tomas pointed to the machete that Saburo had sheaved to his belt.

Saburo slowly reached for his machete. *What the hell! What machete? What the hell is he talking about? Did the wisp do this to him? Should I trust him?* Saburo handed the machete over to Tomas. "Do you know where you're going? Do you want to take the lead?"

"Of course, my Lord." Tomas turned and headed south, hacking at the vegetation with the machete firmly grasped in his broken hand. Saburo simply stood, utterly astonished at what he was witnessing. It was as if Tomas had no injuries — as if he were pain-free. Saburo followed, keeping an arm's length away from Tomas. Saburo knew that if Obasi were here, he'd swear that Tomas was possessed and that the blue wisp was controlling his every move.

Serena was pleased with herself. Her job, for now, was to make sure that Tomas led the man called Saburo to the village, and so he would, though Serena knew the puppeteer was more interested in the men that would be following Tomas. A mighty army to do with as the puppeteer pleased. Daylight was fading, and Serena had one more job to do before she could return to her host. She entered the village where Travis and his men were camped. She had time, so she hid among the crates and listened to what the men had to say. They were anxious . . . they were waiting for her return. Serena giggled as her plan played out in her mind. She was just about to leave her hiding place when the puppeteer's thoughts filled her mind.

Do not be overconfident. That is what got you into this mess in the first place. Just remember, it is by my graciousness that you are here. It was my will that allowed you to walk the grounds of our home. You will do my bidding or suffer by my hand. Now leave these men and return to your host.

Serena wanted to lash out and put the puppeteer in its place. But if there was one thing she had learned during her imprisonment, it was patience. Her time would come. *I have to join with the one named Travis. Then I will return to my host.*

Why is it so important that you feel the need to protect those that betrayed you? You must know that soon I will take human form, and when that happens no one in the Valley of the Lion People will be safe. These men have no chance against the force that I will be unleashing against the Jelani Tribe.

True. But will it not be fun to watch them try?

The puppeteer went quiet for just a moment. *I know you as well as I know myself. Play your games, but keep in mind that I will not hesitate to destroy you in order to accomplish what I have come here to do.*

Oh, I know. We are kindred spirits. Loyalty, family, means nothing to either one of us. It never has. You need me, and I need you . . . for now. And when the time comes, know that I will do everything in my power to survive.

I would expect nothing less.

The aura dissipated as Serena smirked to herself. There was once a time when she would, and did, do everything in her power for the sake of her family. And what did she get for her troubles? Imprisonment in a dark, empty hole. She learned her lesson. The only thing that was important was her survival, and she was going to get it at any cost. Serena focused on the group of men sitting around the fire pit. It didn't take her long to find Travis. She flew toward the men, having her fun as she danced around their heads. Only this time they didn't swat at her. They simply watched her, and they watched Travis. She hovered just in front of him, staring deep into his eyes.

He was the perfect candidate. She entered him through his slightly parted lips and became one with his mind.

You did well. You found the village.

I knew the way as if I had been here before.

It is time for you to meet the tribe that you need to protect.

Protect from who?

More of a what. An evil so sinister that mere mortals tremble before it. But you will not fear it. You will stand tall and protect the tribe.

Protect the tribe.

Yes. Tomorrow a woman will come to you and show you the way. You will protect her and the tribe with your life.

With my life.

You will not falter. You will be strong. You will use your weapons to destroy those that would harm the tribe.

Protect the woman . . . protect the tribe.

Yes . . . protect . . . protect. Serena left, yet she made sure her words remained, echoing in Travis' mind.

Authia, Tamara, and Sensay sat staring at one another. Authia let go of Tamara and Sensay's hands and looked up at Nathen. "Did you hear any of that?"

Nathen shook his head. "You three were deep in your trance. I couldn't hear anything. What was said?"

Authia returned her gaze toward Tamara. "What did you make of that? Who or what is *The Destroyer*?"

Tamara stood and looked down at her Mistress. "I am not certain. I am confused as to what I witnessed. I must speak with my mother."

Nathen shifted Joshawa to his left arm and extended his right hand toward Authia to help her to her feet. "*The Destroyer*? Is that what the aura is?"

"No, my Lord. The aura waits for *The Destroyer*. I believe it wants to join with *The Destroyer* and become whole. I had heard stories when I was a child. I must speak to my mother. She will know what this *Destroyer* is."

Authia looked over to Sensay, who was still sitting on the ground. "Sensay, I got the impression that *The Destroyer* is coming from outside of our valley. Have you ever heard of such a person?"

Sensay did not look up at Authia but instead stared straight ahead, oblivious to her surroundings. "*The Destroyer* is not a person. It is the evil that resides in a body of its choosing."

"Then you have heard of it?"

This time Sensay did look up to Authia. "Heard of it . . . yes. But in my lifetime, I have never witnessed it."

"I want you to come with us, Sensay. Maybe if we put what

you know and what Casandra knows together, we'll have an idea of what we're facing." Authia didn't wait for a response. She walked over to Nathen, took her sleeping child from him, then motioned toward Sensay. "Help her, please."

Nathen did as he was told and helped Sensay to her feet. He gently wrapped her arm around his, and the four made their way to the priestess' hut. As Authia left Sensay's hut, she was surprised to see that the sun was already starting its descent in the western sky. She turned to Nathen. "How long were we in there?"

"Quite a while. Long enough for Joshawa to feed twice and nap."

"Wow! It felt like minutes." Authia was nervous. The aura had penetrated her to her very core. She could feel its anger, its desire to inflict harm on those that it considered its enemy — on the people that, to the aura, had betrayed it. And there was something else. Something familiar, but Authia couldn't quite make it out. When they reached the priestess' hut, they found Sam shirtless as Casandra examined his wounds.

She looked up at the group as they entered the hut. "You've been gone a while." She turned to Sam and handed his shirt back to him. "You no longer require my services. You are healed."

Sam bowed to Casandra. "Thank you." He turned his attention to Authia and Nathen. "I will take my leave, allow you some privacy."

Authia smiled at Sam. "Thank you, but I think maybe you should stay. We're expecting Serena back shortly, and she may have news on Tomas." The expression on Sam's face told Authia that he wasn't sure as to whether or not he wanted to hear news of Tomas. "Please stay. We all need to know what has happened to Tomas."

Reluctantly, Sam sat on the ground next to the firepit.

Authia focused on Casandra. "Is Serena with you?"

"No, my Mistress, but I do expect her back shortly. The sun is setting, and Serena, for whatever reason, doesn't like to be out in the dark."

"Good. When she returns, you must tell us when the aura is with her."

"Of course. I assume that you were able to meld with it?"

"Yes, we were." Tamara approached her mother. "Please take my hands." Tamara gently took her mother's hands in hers. "I want you to see what I saw. Feel what I felt. Confirm my suspicions."

Casandra did not say a word. She stood facing her daughter, looking deep into her eyes. She could feel Tamara's energy passing through her hands and into her body. Casandra saw past Tamara's eyes and deep within the recesses of Tamara's mind. Tamara's thoughts came alive and danced wildly before Casandra. Casandra projected her thoughts onto Tamara's, then focused on only one thought. Tamara's meld with the aura separated from the other thoughts, and as it became clearer, the other thoughts dissipated from view. Casandra could see and feel what Tamara had experienced in the meld. The only difference was that Casandra knew what the aura was. And she knew of *The Destroyer*. She couldn't believe it. *How, why, would our Ancestors allow this? The tribe was at peace. There was no need for punishment.* She let go of Tamara's hands but did not look away.

"What is it, mother? What did you see?"

"Death. Death to the Jelani Tribe."

CHAPTER SEVENTEEN

Nathen stared in disbelief at what Casandra had just revealed. "What do you mean, death to the Jelani Tribe?"

Casandra took a deep breath and closed her eyes. Softly she spoke an incantation, and as she did, she placed her palms together, held them in front of her face, then gently blew on them. As her breath warmed her hands, a pure white light emanated from the center of her palms. Slowly she opened her eyes, at the same time pressing her palms tight against the other. A minute later, she separated her hands, and the light diminished. Casandra walked over to the table at the back of the hut. Underneath the table was a collection of parchments. She opened her left hand, and with the palm of her hand facing the parchments, she slowly scanned each one individually. Nathen watched on as Casandra's hand actually started to glow when it passed over one of the parchments. She continued on, and as she did, her hand returned to normal. Casandra stopped, reached over, and removed the parchment that had caused the reaction. She looked ominous as she turned to face everyone.

"Many centuries ago, a new Lord was appointed to rule the tribe. His mind was sick, and he turned our people into heathens that did not respect our Ancestors. Instead, they honored and paid homage to the new Lord. They treated him as if he were a God. Our Ancestors looked down upon us with shame and sadness. They decided to purge our tribe and spare only those few that still honored and respected them." Casandra unrolled the parchment and held it out for everyone to see. "They unleashed *The Destroyer,* an aura that possesses a human body and through this body, reeks unspeakable pain, suffering, and death." The drawing was crude. It depicted a shapeless form taking control of one of the men from the tribe. That man became twice as large as the rest of the men in the tribe. His eyes glowed red, his breath was fire, and he attacked the Jelani Tribe with a vengeance like none other. Only a select few remained alive.

Nathen looked up from the parchment and directed his question to Tamara. "I thought you said the aura was not *The Destroyer*?"

"I did not sense evil of that magnitude contained within the aura." Tamara looked over at her mother. "Why would I not sense an evil such as *The Destroyer*?"

"I don't know. *The Destroyer* has always been an aura that is dark and evil and only knows one thing, and that is to destroy . . . to kill."

Nathen was still in shock from what he'd just seen sketched on the parchment. "How do we fight such evil?"

Casandra started to roll up the parchment carefully. "We don't, my Lord. I can't even begin to fathom why our Ancestors would release *The Destroyer* at this time. We've been at peace since you took over as our Lord. You would think that it would have been during my family's rule that our Ancestors would have found a need to release *The Destroyer*." Casandra returned the parchment to its resting place. Then she turned to face the group. "If the aura in the village is *The Destroyer*, then Tamara should have sensed that. The fact that she didn't concerns me. Maybe *The Destroyer* is not the aura at the village. Maybe *The Destroyer* is hiding in the aura that I sense when Serena is with me."

Everyone in the hut held their breath and stared wide-eyed at Casandra. Nathen knew, without a doubt, what she was inferring. Authia passed Joshawa over to Nathen. "Please take him to Tammy and Hansen." Authia turned to face Casandra. "I think it's time to speak with your Ancestors."

"But, my Mistress, Serena will be returning soon. I don't

think we should chance her finding out what we are up to."

"True, but we have to discover who or what this *Destroyer* is." Authia looked back at Nathen, who was just leaving the hut. "Nathen."

Nathen stopped and turned to face Authia. "Yes, my Love."

"After you drop off Joshawa, could you come back here and stand guard outside of the hut? If Serena returns, you could engage her in conversation and at the same time warn us that she's back."

"Of course, I'll be right back."

Authia sat on the ground in front of the fire pit, crossed her legs and looked up at everyone who was standing and staring at her. "Well, come on. Let's get this done."

Casandra went to retrieve the clay pot that contained the leaf packets which would open the doorway between their world and the world of their ancestors. As she carefully placed them within the confines of the fire pit, Sensay and Tamara joined Authia, taking their place around the fire pit. Sam stood by the entrance, his back pushed firmly against the wall of the hut. To Authia, it looked as though he wished he could disappear altogether. When Casandra was finished, she too took her place sitting with them. The women were an equal distance from one another. Casandra held out her hands. "Join hands with me, my sisters. Let us be as one."

Authia took Sensay and Tamara's hands within hers. "So how does this work Casandra?"

"I will open the doorway to the land of our ancestors. You must speak to them. Keep them focused on you while I try to read them."

"Me? Why would they speak to me? I'm an outsider. Why don't they speak to Tamara?"

"You, my Mistress, are gifted, and you're the mate to our Lord. They'll want to speak with you. And besides, you're the best person to play on their, what did you call it, vanity?"

Authia chuckled. "Yes, vanity, and you're right, I would be the best person. So, how do I address them?"

Casandra smiled at Authia. "Listen to what I say, follow my lead." Casandra closed her eyes, looked up to the heavens, and addressed her Ancestors. To Authia's amazement, Casandra spoke in English and not the language of the priestesses. "Hear me, Ancestors of our past. We seek an audience with you. The Mistress of the Jelani Tribe wishes to speak with you. Hear me, Ancestors of our past. Join with us so that we may speak with you, become one with you."

Authia watched as the packets in the firepit started to vibrate. They raised a couple of inches off the ground, then began swirling within the confines of the pit. Faster and faster they flew, forming a cylinder as they did. Yet as they moved, they made no sound and did not disturb the air surrounding them. To Authia, the quiet was surreal and unnerving. She wondered if it was the calm before the storm. She continued to stare at the packets, watching them come together and then flatten out, forming a circular platform approximately twelve inches above the pit.

Casandra continued. "We are ready to receive you, Ancestors of our past. Honor us with your presence. Come and hear what our Mistress has to say."

A yellow glow appeared above the platform. It became thick, similar to a dense fog, something that Authia had seen before. Only this time the fog took shape and within minutes, standing before Authia were three Lion People, two men and a woman. From what Authia could see, their features were more pronounced than the Lion People she was familiar with. They were dressed in ceremonial gowns. Elaborate masks were covering the upper half of their face.

Princess Imani, who stood between the two Lords, addressed her companions as she looked upon the group sitting around the fire pit with intrigue and concern. She melded with the Lords to prevent her thoughts from being overheard. *So, these are the faces of the saviors of the Lion People.* She turned to her right so that she was facing Lord Adeeowale. *There is much strength here, Lord Adeeowale.*

Lord Adeeowale shook his head and looked at Lord Chike, uncertainty clearly evident in his expression. *And you, Lord Chike, do you see the salvation of the Jelani Tribe within the souls of these people?*

Lord Chike smiled as he looked at the people sitting around the fire pit. *I see much more.* He returned his gaze toward his companions. *There is an evil surrounding the valley of our home. An evil that we allowed to slip by us unchecked. And now this evil threatens all that we cherish. All that we are destined to protect. These people were chosen not by us but by all the Lords and Priestesses that watch over this valley. We are here to give them the tools that they need to fight this evil.*

Authia's voice penetrated the depths of the Ancestor's minds. *Lords and Priestess, I hear your voice, I feel your concern, your fear. I ask you to help us protect the Jelani Tribe."*

Priestess Imani focused her thoughts on those of the Mistress of the Jelani Tribe. An outsider, but an outsider who loved and cared for the Lion People. *We have presented you with protection in the form of a great priestess.*

Meaning no disrespect but do you honestly believe that Serena will be our savior? You are all-powerful, and you know of the evil that waits to harm us.

Priestess Imani was surprised by Authia's comment. *Your ability is stronger than we were aware of. You were able to hear our thoughts, were you not?*

Authia respectfully bowed her head. *I apologize, my Lords*

and Priestess. *If I have offended you or disrespected you, it was totally unintentional. Your thoughts came alive in my mind as if you wanted me to hear you.*

Priestess Imani continued to listen to Authia with respect as she witnessed this outsider stand her ground.

As Mistress of the Jelani Tribe, I implore you to help us. You have been chosen to look after us because of your compassion and your great strength. Strength that you can use to protect your people. Serena was a great gift, but you know of the evil that is waiting to attack us. Do you believe that Serena is the answer? Do you not think that we need yourselves to confront and destroy the evil that waits for us?

Princess Imani addressed Authia. *You may not be a priestess as I am, but you are strong, and you have earned your place as Mistress of the Jelani Tribe. We have sensed the turmoil that comes your way. There is more than one enemy at your doorstep. One is driven by greed and hatred, and the other is driven by retribution and the desire to destroy the Jelani Tribe. What we have sent you is all you need. Harness her powers, remind her of what it means to be a Priestess of the Jelani Tribe. Achieve this, and you will have an ally stronger than anything that comes your way.*

As Authia melded with the Ancestors of the Jelani Tribe, effectively distracting them, Casandra went to seek out what they had hidden deep within the recesses of their minds. She was confused, for she didn't sense malice or contempt. There was only sadness and concern. Casandra was certain the aura that was contained within the Ancestors wasn't that of the aura from the village. She was about to end the meld when Lord Adeeowale came to her. *Did you find what you were looking for?*

My Lord, no I didn't. Why, my Lord? Why would our Ancestors unleash The Destroyer *on our village when it is at peace?*

Why do you think it was us?

Who else could release such a travesty?

The answer is in the question, for we did not release The Destroyer.

I don't understand, my Lord.

We have given you the answer the only way we could. Because of our laws, we cannot reveal any more than we already have. The answer is with Serena.

Casandra watched as the Ancestors faded away. When the smoke had cleared, she looked at everyone that sat around the pit. Her gaze fell upon Authia. "Did you hear the interaction between the Ancestors and myself?"

"No, I was speaking with the priestess. She, and apparently the other two Ancestors, feel that Serena is our best hope to win this battle. She told me to harness her powers, to remind her of who she was."

"I spoke to Lord Adeeowale. He felt my presence, but he wasn't angered by it. He too revealed that Serena is the answer. Our Ancestors are honor-bound to protect the Jelani Tribe, but they are also bound by the laws of our people. They can't inflict harm on another Ancestor. If I understood him correctly, then he is telling me that *The Destroyer* is one of our Ancestors."

Authia gaped at Casandra. "How could that be? Why would an Ancestor want to destroy their own people?"

Casandra slowly shook her head at the same time shrugging her shoulders. "I don't know. But it appears that Serena plays a more integral part of our survival than we originally thought." Casandra closed her eyes and melded with Nathen, who stood guard outside the hut. *Can you hear me, my Lord?*

Yes, Casandra.

Please join us. I am in need of your services.

Nathen entered the hut and went to stand just behind Authia. "What can I do for you?"

"The Ancestors are not the ones that are planning to

unleash *The Destroyer*. However, I believe they know who *The Destroyer* is. Unfortunately, they can't reveal that information to us without breaking the laws of our people. So what they did was send us Serena."

"How does sending Serena help us?"

"I believe that she knows who *The Destroyer* is or at least who the aura is. When she returns, I want you to engage her in conversation. I need you to push her so that she fully concentrates on you and nothing else. If the aura is part of her and senses her anger, it just might show itself. At least to her. I will stay in the background and watch. Hopefully, I will learn who or what the aura is." Casandra went quiet as she stared past Nathen, past the village and deep into the jungle. She could sense that Serena was returning. "Serena is on her way. Quickly, all of you leave. But not you, my Mistress, or my Lord."

Tamara, Sensay, and Sam left the hut while Nathen joined Authia and Casandra around the fire pit. Just a few minutes later Serena entered the hut, teasing the occupants as she flittered around them. Casandra closed her eyes and opened her mouth ever so slightly. Immediately Serena flew in, joining with Casandra's mind and being. Casandra allowed Serena to take over while she remained in the background, fully aware of all that would transpire.

Nathen addressed Serena. "What did you learn."

"No hello, how are you? Your manners leave much to be desired, my Lord."

"Let's get one thing perfectly clear. I don't care how you are. You are here to serve one purpose, and that is to serve me. To do my bidding. You are merely a puppet under my control."

Serena looked at Nathen in utter disbelief. Did he know?

Why would he use the word puppet? "So, you are not the gracious Lord that you make yourself out to be."

"Until you have proven yourself and earned my respect, I will treat you as if you were the enemy. You are a traitor to our people, to my family."

"And how am I to earn your respect if you do not trust me?"

"I'll never trust you. And I could care less if you end up back where you came from. The Ancestors may have faith that you'll atone for your past behavior. However, I have the luxury of knowing who you are, and you, Serena, have no heart, no compassion. You think only of yourself. You'll never risk your life, your existence for the betterment of the tribe."

Serena had no comeback. All she could think of was that black hole she had lived in since Nathen defeated her. She didn't want to go back, and the thought that there just might be a chance that she would frightened her to her very core. She wanted to be whole, a living being, and she wanted to live once more among her people. The puppeteer had promised her just that, but Serena knew the puppeteer only too well. And the puppeteer would not hesitate to sacrifice her if it meant the survival of the puppeteer. Serena was playing a dangerous game, and she had to decide if and when she was going to put her plan into action. Just as she was about to speak with Nathen, the puppeteer came to her.

It would be unwise to betray me. You owe me, and I intend to collect. Do as I have instructed, or I will destroy you.

Serena thought for just a second. A sinister smile crossed her lips. *You may have control of me now. But try to renege on your promise, and you will be sorry.* Before the puppeteer could respond, Serena addressed Nathen.

"Okay, I will agree that, in the past, I have not given you any reason to trust me. I was angry and hurt. I loved your father with all my heart, and I felt as though he betrayed me. But it was I who betrayed him. I am here to make up for all the pain and suffering I caused, not only to you but also to my people." Serena paused and glanced over to Authia. "And also, to you." She took a deep breath, then addressed Nathen. "But if I help you, what are you prepared to give me in return?"

"I thought you were supposed to help us so that you wouldn't return to the prison that has been your home."

"True. But you, as Lord of the Jelani Tribe, are in a position to offer much more. Like my freedom, for instance."

"Your freedom?"

"I want to join the living and once more be part of the Jelani Tribe."

Nathen looked at Authia with a blank expression on his face.

Authia shook her head and shrugged her shoulders.,.

"Serena, how am I supposed to do that? I have no powers. I have no influence with the Ancestors of our past."

Serena smiled . . . should she reveal to Nathen what she knew? Was the puppeteer still listening? Serena made a decision that could possibly affect her future, and not for the better. "If there is one thing I learned about you, it is that you are an honorable man. I will promise to help you, to help our people. You, in turn, will speak to our Ancestors on my behalf. Do we have a deal?"

"We have a deal. But I warn you, Serena, cross me, and I'll personally see to your destruction."

Serena smiled, then withdrew inside of Casandra.

Casandra listened as Serena conversed with the aura. *What is she up to?* But at least Cassandra had new information. She patiently waited until Serena was secure within the deepest recesses of her mind. She opened her eyes to find both Nathen and Authia staring at her in anticipation of what she was to reveal. "Well, one thing is for certain, the two auras are one and the same. It's weak and apparently depending on Serena to accomplish what it needs until it regains all its strength."

Nathen looked apprehensively at Casandra. "So, Serena was lying to us. She is not here to help us."

"I'm not certain about that, my Lord. Serena and the aura communicated for just a couple of minutes. I got the distinct impression that Serena isn't totally confident that she'll be safe with the aura. There was a great struggle going on in Serena's mind."

"Then you believe that she might help us."

"Oh, she'll help us all right. I just don't know how far she intends to take that help."

Authia stood, walked over to the table that held the clay pots, and leaned against it. She crossed her arms over her chest. "I guess we're just going to have to wait and see how things play out. Casandra, do you know who the aura is?"

"Unfortunately, yes I do. At least, *what* she is."

Nathen and Authia responded in unison. "She?"

"Yes, the aura is an Ancestor. She used to be a priestess."

Authia stood away from the counter and walked over to Casandra. "You are contradicting yourself. How can she be an Ancestor and not be a priestess?"

"She is powerless, therefore not a true priestess. For some reason, her powers were taken away from her. A priestess stripped of her powers would be banished to the same place Serena would have been sent. Somehow, she escaped and has found a way to regain her powers. That is why our Ancestors cannot reveal to us who she is. It is against our laws."

Nathen queried. "Does Serena know who she is?"

"I'm certain she does. Though I don't think she will share that information anytime soon."

"So, we have to play along until she decides to tell us what we need to know?"

"Unfortunately, yes."

"Can you bring her back? I need to talk to her about Tomas."

"Of course, my Lord." Casandra closed her eyes and opened the pathway to Serena. When she opened her eyes not a minute later, it was Serena addressing Nathen.

Serena knew that she was walking a fine line and she was going to have to decide on which side she would stand. "You wanted to see me, my Lord?"

"What information do you have on Tomas?"

"He is broken both physically and in his mind. I have convinced his mind that he is fine. He leads a man to our village. The man is followed by a great army."

"Is this the army that is meant to destroy us?"

Serena thought for a second before she answered. "Actually, it is not the army that you need to fear. It is *The Destroyer*, and he is on his way."

"Who is *The Destroyer*?"

"I am not certain. But he is close. And if the aura is allowed to join with *The Destroyer* there will be little the tribe can do to defend itself."

CHAPTER EIGHTEEN

Saburo followed Tomas for only twenty minutes, then Tomas stopped and glanced about the jungle as if he had lost something.

"Why have we stopped, Tomas?"

Tomas gazed upon him. "We forgot Sam. He is still in the tree. We must go back and get him."

Tomas turned and started walking back toward the tree. Saburo had to think fast. "Tomas, Sam's not there. He . . ." Saburo hesitated for just a second. "He left ahead of us. He said he'll meet us at the valley." Saburo watched as Tomas slowly turned to face him. He had a puzzled look of concern and appeared as though he was staring off into the distance and not directly at Saburo.

"Are you sure, my Lord? I have no memory of this."

Saburo walked over to face Tomas and placed his right hand on Tomas' left shoulder. "I reached out to him. I told him to clear the way for us."

"Really? You did this?"

Saburo smiled at Tomas. "Yes, Tomas. Shall we continue?"

Tomas also smiled, nodded his head, then once again he raised his machete and struck down at the dense vegetation that blocked their path.

Saburo closed his eyes and heaved a heavy sigh. *That was close.* He opened his eyes and watched as Tomas cut through the vegetation as if he were on a mission of great importance. Saburo continued to follow Tomas, knowing full well that, in Tomas' mind, he *was* on a great mission sanctioned by the Gods.

Tomas led Saburo to the encampment at the hut. When Tomas entered the clearing, he lowered the machete to his side and scanned the area in confusion. It wasn't as he remembered. Tomas left his Lord standing on the outskirts of the clearing as he walked over to one of the fire pits. This was where he and Sam made their dinner. But where did these other fire pits come from? Tomas knelt on his haunches and placed his hand in the ash of the pit. Slowly he lifted his hand, which was balled into a fist, to almost eye level. Then he spread out the bottom two fingers that had formed his fist and allowed the ash that was contained inside his fist to disperse in the wind.

Tomas continued to gaze about the clearing, ignoring the fire pits, and focusing only on the hut. Slowly he stood up, tilted his head slightly to one side, and scrutinized the structure that stood before him. Something was familiar about the hut, something evil. He looked back at his Lord then returned his gaze toward the hut. He was hesitant about entering the hut, but why? Cautiously he made his way over, and with much reservation, entered, only to find it empty. There should have been wooden boxes and metal sticks, but all that was left was the impression of where they once lay. Tomas moved to the center of the hut, and in the dirt was a dried pool of what looked like blood. He knelt and ran the fingers from his left hand through the dirt. Tomas froze in place as memories of the hut flooded his mind. Someone had lain here, hurt, in incredible pain. Was it Sam? The memories were incoherent, as if they didn't belong to him. As if he remembered something from someone else's past. He turned to see his Lord standing at the entrance to the hut, and instead of the confident man he knew his Lord to be, standing there was a man filled with fear.

The sun slowly descended, cloaking the Jelani Tribe into

darkness. Nathen stood outside his hut, watching as the women of the tribe went about lighting the lanterns that surrounded the communal fire pit. Remnants of their dinner hung loosely on the spit that was positioned over the pit. However, the flames that once licked the carcass of the eland, an African antelope, now were just red-hot coals. Nathen was so lost in his thoughts that he didn't notice when Hansen joined him.

"Penny for your thoughts."

Nathen turned to face Hansen, smiled and ever so slightly, then shook his head. "They're not worth a penny." He returned his gaze to the fire pit. "I have all these little scraps of information, and somehow, I must put them all together and figure out how to save these people."

"Did you notice that you seldom refer to them as *your* people."

Nathen looked back at Hansen. "No, I didn't. Hansen, these are my people, but at the same time, they're not. I came from this tribe, I resemble them, I am one of them, but it just doesn't feel right. I don't know how to explain it other than I feel like an outsider. I haven't earned the right to lead these people."

"From what I've heard, no one from your family actually earns the right to lead the tribe. It's handed down from one Lord to the next. If Serena hadn't of interfered, you would have been the next in line after your father to rule these people."

"You're right . . . I guess no one in my family actually does earn the right to rule."

"Yeah, but if you think about it, Nathen, out of all of your family, you are probably the only one that truly earned his place. You didn't just take over the rule from your father as all your ancestors have done. You had to fight for it. You had to save your people from Casandra. Your tribe was a mess, and you brought order, the feeling of security to these people. They look up to you. Why can't you accept that?"

"I don't know. It just doesn't feel right."

"You're one complicated Lord," Hansen smirked as he shook his head. "So, are we heading to the village tomorrow morning?"

"You and I are, Hansen. Nathen gets to sit this one out." Authia walked up to Nathen and kissed him ever so tenderly on his cheek.

Before Nathen could respond, he felt the presence of someone standing right behind him. He turned to find Casandra, dressed in her animal skins, a smug look of satisfaction gracing her lips.

"Good evening, my Lord."

"Why do I have the feeling that I'm addressing Serena?"

"Probably because you are."

"I thought you didn't like the dark?"

"Not as a wisp, but in Casandra's body, I am safe."

"Let me speak with Casandra."

Serena sighed. "If you must." She closed her eyes, retreating deep inside of Casandra. Nathen watched as Casandra opened her eyes, took a deep breath, and slowly let it out.

"I assume I am addressing Casandra now?"

"Yes, my Lord?"

"What is Serena up to?"

"I'm not sure, my Lord. She has news for you. I sense that she's anxious about the path she has chosen to follow."

"And what path is that?"

"A path that could be her undoing. As I said before, she's conflicted. She came here with a purpose, one that I feel involves the aura from the village. Our Ancestors told us that Serena is the key to our survival. They can't harm the aura, which tells me that the aura is, or was, a priestess in her own time. A priestess that Serena knows."

Nathen thought back to how the Ancestors had imprisoned Serena, how they'd sent *The Destroyer* to purge the tribe. "How is it that these Ancestors that look over us can't harm the aura, yet they imprisoned Serena, they destroyed their own tribe?"

"If you recall, my Lord, Serena caused your family great harm. She all but wiped your line from existence. And our Ancestors did nothing to stop her."

"Yes, why is that?"

"As evil as she was, she was still a priestess, a very powerful priestess. Our ancestors swore an oath centuries ago that they would bring no harm to any Lord or Priestess while they still draw breath. I believe that when this blood oath was consummated, none of our ancestors ever dreamt that one of their own would cause such misery to our tribe."

Authia interjected. "Yes, but they did eventually imprison her. Why then, and not when all the trouble started?"

"When she was a spirit, she was technically dead, but still had her powers. Therefore, in the eyes of our Ancestors, she was still a priestess, only in spirit form. When our Lord destroyed her, she lost everything that made her who she was. It was then that the Ancestors were in a position to punish her, and they did just that."

Again, Authia questioned Casandra. "What about *The Destroyer*? They sent him to wipe out pretty much the entire tribe?"

"The Ancestors themselves can't harm a Lord or Priestess. However, that being said, they can arrange for someone or something to do it for them. They released *The Destroyer* in the body of a tribesman that was not a Lord or Priestess. By doing so, they gave the ruling Lord of the time a chance to defeat *The Destroyer*. If the Lord and the priestesses could not defeat *The Destroyer*, then it would be *The Destroyer* that eradicated them from existence. Not the Ancestors."

"So, they were interpreting the rules to suit their needs?"

Casandra thought for a second. "Yes, I guess they were. And they're doing it again. They can't touch the aura or stop *The Destroyer*. However, they can give us the tools to defeat them."

Nathen's head was pounding with all the information he was trying to digest. It was a game, a sick, senseless game. Pitting his resources against the resources of a priestess and an evil so dark that, to Nathen, only the sorcery of a great priestess would have a chance of defeating it. "And the Ancestors, in their great wisdom, sent us Serena . . ." Nathen's voice trailed off.

Casandra continued for him. "To combat the evil that is at our doorstep. And if they sent us Serena, then they must have believed that she could win this battle for us."

Nathen didn't share the same belief as the Ancestors. Trust was not one of his stronger suits, especially when it came to Serena. "So, we have the aura who is supposedly an Ancestor. Who is *The Destroyer*?"

"Only the aura, and possibly even Serena, knows the answer to that."

Tomas looked upon his Lord, surprised by the mask of fear that he wore upon his face. "My Lord. What troubles you so?"

Saburo's eyes went wide. "Why do you feel that I'm troubled?"

"It is as clear as the sky above us. Does this place trouble you? Do you sense something, my Lord?"

"Yes . . . yes, I do sense a great evil here. Maybe we should leave?"

Tomas looked back down on the area of the ground that was soaked in blood, then returned his gaze to his Lord. "I agree, there was a great evil here. Maybe we should leave before the evil returns."

"I think that would be wise. Come, Tomas, we'll find shelter in the jungle."

Tomas watched as his Lord left the hut. Something was nagging at him. He scanned the hut one last time, his gaze falling on the bloodied dirt. There was something familiar about this place. The hairs on the back of his neck tingled, sending shivers down his spine. Yes, this place was evil—it was time to leave. Tomas left the hut to find his Lord patiently waiting for him. Machete in hand, Tomas pointed in a southerly direction. "We will go this way. That is where we will find the road where we once camped. It will be dark by the time we get there, so we should hurry." Tomas walked into the jungle, allowing it to envelop him. Then, with the ease of a skilled tribesman, he hacked at the vegetation as he cleared a path for him and his Lord.

Serena waited somewhat impatiently for Nathen to be finished with his conversation with Casandra. If only she could hear what they were saying. It would give her the insight she needed to make her decision. But in reality, hadn't she already decided? The puppeteer had promised her that she would be human again. The issue was that the puppeteer couldn't be trusted. If the puppeteer's plans didn't go as she wanted, then she would have no problem sending Serena back where she came from. However, even though Serena's hatred for Nathen's bloodline still lingered, she knew that Nathen was an honorable man and he would keep his promise.

You are treading on grounds that should never be walked on. The puppeteer's voice echoed within the confines of Serena's mind.

I told you that I would do everything in my power to accomplish my dream of being human once more. You are going to be challenged, and I do not believe that you will come away unscathed.

You are a fool! By our laws, I cannot be touched. Even in my weakened state, I am more powerful than any priestess that walks the grounds of our valley.

You greatly underestimate the current High Priestess and my host. You underestimate me. The Ancestors that watch over the Jelani Tribe may not be able to touch you, but I can! And I can give the Jelani Tribe what they need to destroy you.

You do as you see fit, but I warn you. Do or say anything to harm me, and I will crush you. Mention my name, and I promise you that you will never see daylight again!

Serena giggled—the puppeteer had just made her decision for her. *You can threaten me all you want, but inside this body, you cannot touch me. Outside of this body I will have the protection of the Ancestors . . . you will lose . . . Mother!*

CHAPTER NINETEEN

Celest's anger was more intense than anything she had ever felt. Her daughter had betrayed her, turned her back on her. Celest blanketed the outsider's village in a darkness that was so black, not even the outsider's torches could penetrate its depths. She focused her anger on the huts of the village, and one by one they crumbled to the ground. After several minutes of destruction, she calmed herself. What was she doing? Wasting what little strength she possessed, and for what? She knew her daughter was not to be trusted. She knew that Serena would do anything in order to become human once again. Celest retreated inside the one hut she had left standing. It was the hut of a sorceress, and it would serve her well. The aura of the hut was strong, and Celest took full advantage as she fed off its energy. She didn't need her daughter. She didn't need anybody. *The Destroyer* was on his way, and when he arrived, she would have her revenge on the Jelani Tribe.

Rick and his men had finished their meal and were engaged in friendly banter as they sat around the firepit. Rick watched as the last rays of the sun disappeared behind the western horizon. It was then that the village fell into darkness. Rick scanned the area but could see nothing. He knew Travis was less than an arm's length away, but he couldn't see him. He couldn't even make out his silhouette. Tentatively Rick stood and reached out in the direction that he had last seen Travis. He groped in the darkness till his hand bumped against Travis' arm. "Travis? Is that you?"

"Yeah . . . what the hell . . . I can't see a thing."

"Me neither." Rick was about to call out to his men when the wind started to swirl around them. It grew in intensity, which caused Rick to lose his balance. He was thrown into Travis, and the two hit the ground so hard it knocked the wind out of both of them. Rick tried to get up, but Travis held him back. He shouted as loud as he could to be heard over the roar of the wind. "We're safer on the ground. Can you hear it?"

Rick shouted back at Travis. "Hear what? All I hear is that damn wind."

"No, listen."

Rick strained to hear whatever it was that Travis could hear. Then it came to him, the sound of destruction. "What's that?"

"It's the huts. They're being pulled apart."

The wind grew in intensity, pelting Rick with stones and branches. He curled into a ball, hoping to protect himself from the wrath of the storm. Then, as suddenly as it had appeared, it was gone. Slowly Rick stood, surveying the village as he did. The soft rays of the moon revealed the aftermath, and it was devastating. "What the hell just happened?" Rick immediately sought out his men. With the exception of some cuts and bruises, they seemed to be fine. The same could not be said of the village. All but one hut was destroyed. Rick walked over to Travis, who was standing a few feet away from the last remaining hut. "What do you make of that?"

Travis didn't take his focus off the hut. "It's like a tornado. Destroying everything in its path. But if you are just outside of the funnel, you remain unscathed, just like this hut." Rick started to walk toward the hut, but Travis grabbed his arm and held him back. "Not a good idea."

Rick looked questioningly at Travis. "What? I was just going to get a closer look."

Travis slowly shook his head. "There's something very

wrong inside that hut. It's not safe." Travis turned to face Rick. "Don't ask me how I know, I just do. No one can enter that hut. I'm serious, Rick." Travis turned back to face the hut. "There's something, alive, inside that hut, and it means to harm us."

Rick didn't know what to say. Had Travis lost it? Had the wisp done something to him? "Okay Travis, the hut is off limits. Tell the men to keep their distance." He watched as Travis turned around and went to speak to the men. They listened to him, and Rick could tell that they took what he said as fact. They were frightened, and for that matter, so was he.

Serena could feel the turmoil building inside of her mother. She was out of control—which could be a good thing. She just might exhaust her energy and have nothing left when it came time to join with *The Destroyer*. But to Serena's dismay, her mother stopped herself and regained her composure. Then there was nothing. Serena could no longer feel, sense, or hear her mother. She smirked to herself . . . *and, so it begins*. Her mother was blocking her, but that was of no consequence. Priestesses as powerful as Tamara, Casandra, and herself could easily break down her mother's defenses, especially in her weakened state. It was time—she needed to speak to Nathen.

Serena focused on Casandra, and as she did, she could feel the gateway to the outside world open. She could smell the jungle, she could feel the breeze of the night air brush delicately against her face. When she opened her eyes, her Lord stood before her. Serena bowed before him, and for the first time in his existence, she gazed upon him with respect and admiration.

Nathen appeared perplexed. "Is this Serena? Or am I still addressing Casandra?"

"It is Serena, my Lord."

"You usually look upon me with contempt and aberrance. Why the sudden change?"

"What I desire more than anything is to be human once more. I want to walk barefoot on the ground that is our valley. I want to experience the sweet taste of freedom. In order to accomplish this, I must decide which of the two — you or the aura — as you refer to her, will honor their promise to make me whole."

"I already told you, I can't promise you your freedom, and especially not your existence."

"Maybe not, but you can promise me that if I help you defeat *The Destroyer*, you will speak to our Ancestors on my behalf. That you will do everything in your power to free me."

"And you believe that I'm the one you should side with? According to the Ancestors, the aura is a priestess, and as a priestess, she would have the ability to give you what you desire."

"Yes, if she could be trusted. And is that not what it is all about . . . trust?"

"You don't trust the aura?"

Serena went quiet. She was about to incur the wrath of her mother. And if her mother was successful and joined with *The Destroyer*, then Serena was as good as dead. "If there is one thing I learned after two centuries of watching you grow into a man, die, and be reborn again, it is that each and every time, when you became an adult, you were always an honorable man. A man that could be trusted. The aura only looks out for herself, and she would not hesitate to sacrifice me if it meant her existence. I know her as well as I know myself. The aura is my mother."

Casandra was listening to everything Serena had to say. Her

heart almost stopped when she heard who the aura was. Without warning, Casandra closed the gateway, forcing Serena to return deep inside of her. Frantically she opened her eyes and stared at her Lord. "This revelation isn't good. If Serena is truthful and the aura is her mother, then we have a bigger problem than we originally thought. We must gather everyone . . . immediately!" Casandra didn't wait for a reply from Nathen. She headed straight for the gathering hut. Fear and uncertainty enveloped her as she melded with the others. Her message had been short, but she could feel that the nervousness in the tone of the message did not go unnoticed by anyone.

Casandra entered the gathering hut and made her way over to the raised platform at the back of the hut. Gingerly she touched it as she closed her eyes. She focused on a time long ago when the tribe was first led by the priestesses alone. In particular, a High Priestess named Celest. She was the first and the cruelest. Her mastery of the dark arts was unsurpassed. And that was what filled Casandra's heart and soul with fear.

I wish I could say that if I had known how my mother was going to lead our people, that I would have never destroyed Joshawa's bloodline. Casandra could hear Serena speaking to her. She could feel her emotions as if they were her own. Serena was sincerely saddened, though Casandra was not sure what exactly made her sad.

But you did know. You knew what your mother was capable of, and you still destroyed the only family that could have stopped her.

I knew what my mother was capable of. How could I not? She taught me everything she knew. I was so blinded by my anger and my desire for revenge that I chose not to see what was standing right in front of me. And now my mother plans to use her sorcery to destroy our village, our people.

Well, we're not going to let that happen. If we work together, we'll have the strength needed to defeat your mother. Question is, are you going to be able to do whatever it takes to destroy her? To wipe her from our existence?

There was no hesitation from Serena. *I have, I am, swearing my allegiance to my Lord and Mistress. I am prepared to help in any way I can.*

Casandra could sense Serena's sadness lifting as it was replaced with the attitude she was known so well for.

My mother is strong. Her sorcery is consumed by evil and darkness. However, she is also under the misguided impression that she is all-powerful and that we are of no consequence to her. I will be happy to prove her wrong.

Casandra smiled to herself. There was no deceit in Serena's heart — she was going to help them. And as Casandra turned to face the entrance to the gathering hut, she felt a wave of confidence rush through her body.

Obasi lay on the jungle floor, his arms raised above his shoulders, his head resting in the palms of his hands. He stared up at the evening sky. The stars shone brightly, and the moon was a beacon, basking the jungle in its soft rays of light. As he lay there, he became aware of someone standing a few feet to his right. "You have news for me."

The nervous man cleared his throat. "Yes, Obasi. Saburo and the prisoner made it back to where that lone hut stood. But they didn't stay."

"Where did they go?"

"They headed south, deeper into the jungle."

Obasi smiled to himself. South was where they would find the valley of the Gods. And he was sure that the prisoner was leading Saburo straight to it. "How far ahead of us are they?"

"A day, day and a half. Just as you requested."

"I want them no more than half a day away. I want to know where they are and what they are doing every couple of hours."

"That would require more manpower. I thought you were trying not to be seen?"

Obasi turned his head and glared at the man that stood before him. He didn't need to say a word. "Yes, Obasi. I'll take care of it immediately." The man left as Obasi chuckled to himself. He loved having so much control over his men. He gazed up at the evening sky. There was one man that he had to make entirely sure that he was in total control of. He had given Saburo too much rope—it was time to rein him in.

CHAPTER TWENTY

Nathen stood in the center of the gathering hut, his arms folded across his chest, his biceps accentuated by the sleeveless animal skin vest he wore. His loincloth covered his thighs to just above his knees. He could feel the anger welling up inside of him. He watched as Authia, Tamara, Sensay, Tammy, and Hansen entered the hut. Nathen's and Authia's eyes met, and he allowed his frustration to fill her mind. She walked over to him, placing her hand tenderly on his forearm.

"What's wrong, Nathen? You look as though you want to strangle someone."

"I know who the aura is." He looked away from Authia and toward the small group that was gathered at the hut's entrance. He shook his head in disbelief. "We fought Serena, and it wasn't easy." Nathen returned his gaze toward Authia. "We barely won that battle, and now we are pitted against her mother. A High Priestess who is more powerful than Serena ever could be."

Authia looked wide-eyed at Nathen. "Her mother! Are you serious? Is that why Casandra sounded so upset when she melded with me?"

"Oh, come on now. I would have hoped that you would have more faith in me and my powers."

Nathen and Authia turned around to find Casandra standing just next to them. Nathen unfolded his arms and took Authia's hand in his. "Serena, I have no doubt that you're a very powerful priestess. But we both know that your mother is highly skilled in the dark arts, and she has no conscience, no moral guidance, which makes her a very dangerous foe."

"True enough. Come, Casandra and I have a plan."

The group sat on the ground, forming a circle in the middle of the gathering hut. Serena sat across from Nathen, Authia at his side. Serena began. "We have an advantage, in that we know who the aura is and what she is capable of."

Nathen was skeptical. "I wouldn't call it an advantage."

"My Lord, it is. We know what to expect, and if we know that, we can prepare for it."

Authia interjected. "Okay, so we know how to prepare for her. We also have a group of very dangerous men heading this way. How are we going to deal with them? How are we going to know who *The Destroyer* is? And most importantly, how do we keep your mother from joining with him, or for that matter, with her? We don't even know if *The Destroyer* is male or female."

Serena giggled. "You are always so full of questions. The first thing we have to do is agree that we need to use every bit of sorcery at our disposal to combat my mother."

Nathen nodded in agreement. "We always knew that. And it's especially true now that we know Celest is the aura."

"Exactly. In Casandra's body, I can enhance her abilities. However, if I were to choose another host and become the dominant entity, then I could join with Casandra and the other priestesses, and we would be a force to be reckoned with. Just Casandra and I would give my mother a worthy challenge."

Flashbacks of dealing with Serena in the past flooded Nathen's mind. He was having difficulty trusting her, and for a good reason. After everything she had put him through, put Authia through, she hadn't earned the right to be trusted. However, that being said, what choice did he have? He needed her and her sorcery if he was going to stand any chance of defeating Celest. "What do you mean by another host?"

"Simply that. Another host, one who is gifted, someone

who is prepared to offer herself to me willingly. Then Casandra and I can work together with you and the others. The sorcery that we will have at our disposal will be greater than anything we can conjure now."

The plan was tempting. Nathen knew that the power that would be at his disposal would be immense. But the question was, would it honestly be at his disposal? Or, once Serena had a host she could dominate, would she betray him and the tribe? As if she could read his thoughts, Serena's voice came alive in Nathen's mind. *I do not blame you. I would not trust myself either. But you have to believe. Let go of the past. I want nothing more than to see my tribe survive this evil. My mother used my ego, my hatred for your father, to her advantage. It took me over two hundred years to recognize the truth. Tell me, my Lord, what can I do to earn your trust?*

It takes time to earn someone's trust. Time that we don't have. I want to trust you. I want to believe that you're here to help us, not destroy us. But it's your mother that we — you — have to kill. Can you do that, Serena? Can you kill your own mother?

My mother was lost to me years before my death. Her need for power, her desire to be the most powerful priestess known to our tribe took precedence over me. I will not be killing my mother. I will be killing the monster that she became. So what can I do to earn your trust?

Let me speak with Casandra. Nathen could feel Serena's presence leave him, and as quickly as she was gone, Casandra took her place. *Casandra, I need your wisdom.*

How can I help you, my Lord?

Should we trust Serena to take another host? One that she'll control.

My Lord, I've known Serena for a very long time. As long as I was High Priestess, I watched her. Her mind was consumed with revenge and hatred. She knew nothing else. The Serena that I am host to now is a very different Serena.

How so?

181

She no longer craves revenge. Hatred doesn't rule her heart. She understands what her mother was, what she is now. You took a chance and trusted me. Now I ask that you trust Serena.

The group silently sat and observed Nathen as he stared blankly past them to a place only he knew of. He was aware of them, though, to him, they were apparitions floating around him. He had to decide and choose what he believed was the lesser of two evils. *If you trust her to take another host and behave, then I'll trust her as well. I'm putting all my faith in you.*

And we'll not disappoint you. It is time for Serena and you to join the others.

Nathen focused on his surroundings and found Authia sitting facing him, her hands in his. "I knew you were with me."

Authia smiled at Nathen. "Just to keep you focused. I think, no, I know you made the right decision." Authia took her place at Nathen's side. "All right, Serena, what's next."

Serena moved to the middle of the circle. "Please, close the circle around me." Everyone moved closer together, completely encircling Serena. "I need a willing host. One who is gifted. One who will allow me to dominate and take control of their body, their mind, their very soul. Is there one among you who would be willing to do so."

"You have little to choose from, Priestess of the Lion People." Sensay spoke with confidence. "Your new host must be gifted, which leaves you with only the priestesses, the Mistress of the Lion People, and me."

Serena turned to face Sensay. "Your gift is great for one who is not a priestess."

Sensay smirked at Serena. "The Mistress is with child, it would not be safe for her or the baby. I am old, ready to join my ancestors. And if I join them while protecting the Lion People, then I will be able to join my ancestors with honor. I willingly offer myself as host to you, my Priestess Serena."

Sensay bowed her head to Serena then looked up, gazing deep into her eyes. "Take me. I am ready."

"You are brave. However, you do understand that once I take control of your body, your essence, everything you are Sensay, will cease to exist. I cannot promise that I will be able to return you to your body."

Sensay slowly shook her head as she smiled. "As I said, I am ready. I do not expect to return. You may have my body and do with it as you see fit. My soul, my very being, will be with my ancestors, and that is where I wish to remain."

Saburo remained several feet behind Tomas, watching as he skillfully sliced through the vegetation that lay before him. Saburo couldn't believe the ease with which Tomas moved. He should be in excruciating pain, unable to walk, never mind able to push through the jungle brandishing a machete. What frustrated Saburo the most was that the entire time, Tomas kept mumbling to himself. Saburo asked on more than one occasion who he was talking to, but Tomas just stared at him blankly, seemingly totally unaware that he was speaking to himself. They trekked through the jungle for hours, not saying a word to each other. Daylight became night, and as the stars shone high above them, Saburo called out to Tomas. "It's getting pretty dark. We should call it a night."

Tomas turned to face Saburo. "But, my Lord, we are so close. Do you not recognize where we are?"

Saburo scanned the jungle as if he were familiarizing himself with it. But instead, he was trying desperately to figure out what to say that wouldn't give him away. "You're right, Tomas. We are close. I'm having difficulty getting my bearings in the dark. That's why I need you. I need you to show me the way."

"Of course, my Lord." Tomas bowed to Saburo, then

turned to continue hacking at the vegetation. Not twenty minutes later they broke through onto an old dirt road. The moon shone down on them, revealing to both Saburo and Tomas not one but three fire pits. Tomas stared at them, obviously confused by what he saw. "I do not understand, my Lord."

"What don't you understand?"

Tomas walked over to the closest fire pit. "There should be only one fire pit. The one we made." Tomas turned to face Saburo. "Where did these other two come from? It is like the place we just left. Too many fire pits." Tomas turned to face the fire pits. "We are not safe here. Too many fire pits. There are others in the jungle." Frantically Tomas headed to the other side of the road. "We must leave. Come, my Lord."

Saburo ran up to Tomas and placed his right hand on Tomas' left shoulder, forcing him to turn and face him. "Tomas, calm down. These fires are old. Whoever used them is long gone. Don't you think that it would be safer for us to spend the night here?" Saburo gestured toward the dirt road. "Rather than in the jungle where we can't see our enemy coming?"

Tomas looked upon Saburo as if he was trying to remember something.

"Are you okay, Tomas?"

"I feel as though I have heard those words before." Tomas frowned as he gave his head a shake. "I apologize, my Lord. My mind is playing games with me. Let me start a fire, and I will watch over you as you sleep."

"But first we should eat. You start the fire. I'll find us some food."

Tomas made himself busy starting the fire while Saburo entered the jungle in search of dinner. He was kneeling on the ground focused on a piglet rooting in the ground a few feet away from him when he heard someone approach him from behind. Saburo firmly grasped the machete in his right hand. In one fluid motion, he stood, swung around, and had the blade of the machete at the man's throat. He was taken aback, because standing before him was one of Obasi's men. Slowly he lowered his machete. "What the hell are you doing here?"

The man was obviously nervous. Not once did he divert his attention off the machete as he spoke to Saburo. "Obasi wants to keep a closer watch on you."

"What the hell! He knows he can't do that. Tomas can't see you, and especially not Obasi."

The man finally looked away from the machete and stared directly at Saburo. "All I know is that I'm to keep you in sight and report every few hours."

Saburo took a step closer to the man with his anger displayed openly on his face. He raised his machete and pressed it against the man's chest. "You do what you have to, but tell Obasi this. I can't do my job if Tomas sees any one of you and starts to remember. If I have to, I'll kill anyone who comes between me and finding out what that little man knows. Do I make myself clear?"

The man looked down at the machete, its tip penetrating his flesh. His gaze fell back to Saburo. "Look, I'm only following orders, just like you."

Saburo stood back lowering the machete to his side. "Fine, follow his orders, but stay out of my view. I'll not hesitate to kill you . . . you can take that message back to Obasi." Saburo checked over his shoulder, only to find that his dinner was long gone. He looked back at the man. "Great, you scared my dinner away."

The man just smiled, picked up a large, tattered, canvas bag that was at his feet, and handed it to Saburo. "Enjoy." Then he disappeared into the jungle. Saburo opened the bag to find a smallish dead python snake. Snake wasn't his favorite food, but it was better than nothing. He gazed back into the jungle. Obasi was closing in, and that only meant one thing. He had to be getting close to this valley that Obasi wanted so badly. And Saburo knew that once he did reach it, he was as good as dead.

Authia sat in the circle that was formed around Serena. "So how do we transfer you to Sensay? It was quite an elaborate ceremony when you joined with Casandra."

"That was because I had to travel from the afterlife, from my containment, to the world as you know it. Now, it's just a matter of moving from one host to another."

"Like how you possessed me while I was pregnant with Joshawa?"

"Similar, only this time I will not be hiding in the recesses of Sensay's mind, as I did with you. I will become Sensay."

Nathen inquired. "Which form will you take? Yours or Sensay's?"

"If it pleases my Lord." Serena looked directly at Nathen. "I would prefer to appear as myself."

Nathen questioned Serena. "You can do that? Take on any appearance that you wish?"

"Not any appearance. I can only choose between myself and the host. I would like to choose myself."

Nathen turned his attention to Authia. "What do you think, my Love?"

"I don't see the harm. If Sensay is willing to move on, to be with her ancestors, then why shouldn't Serena appear as herself?"

Sensay smiled at Authia. "I am ready. I would prefer that Serena appear as she is. When I leave this earth, I want all of me to leave. I do not want to linger on as the shell for another person."

Authia shrugged her shoulders. "Well then I guess Serena,

you'll be as yourself. What do we do now?"

Serena faced Sensay and gently took her hands. Tamara stood next to them, placing a hand on the top of each of their heads. She glanced over at her Lord and Authia. "As High Priestess, I ask my Lord and Mistress permission to join the Priestess Serena with the body of Sensay."

Authia and Nathen nodded their approval, and Tamara began.

"Close your eyes, Sensay. Seek out your Ancestors. Open your mind, your soul, to me. Casandra, open the gateway, allow our sister to flow through you. Serena, search for the light. Use my body to find your new home."

Authia watched in fascination as Tamara began to chant in the language of the priestesses. Her eyes were closed as she swayed back and forth. Then the body of Casandra started to glow a brilliant blue. The color swirled around inside of her, then, as if suddenly shown the way, it shot up and into Tamara's hand. Authia watched as the blue light traveled up Tamara's right arm, across her chest, down her left arm, and into Sensay. Tamara stood back with her arms stretched out in front of her. The palms of her hands were facing Sensay. She continued to chant as the blue light enveloped Sensay, swirling around her, lifting her from the ground that she sat on. Her body hovered a few feet off the ground, wildly jerking as though it were being shocked. The entire process lasted only minutes. The body, still hovering above the ground, became quiet. The brilliant blue light grew dimmer as the body was slowly lowered to the ground.

Authia grabbed Nathen's hand as she held her breath. The blue light diminished, revealing a body lying on the ground. Her head was turned to the side, her long red hair covering her face, concealing it to those around her. She wore a gown unlike anything that the Jelani Tribe had ever seen. It was light blue and almost sheer. The skirt of the gown fell in delicate layers to just below her knees. Authia knelt by the body, placing her left hand gently on its shoulder. "Serena, is that you? Can you hear me? Are you all right?"

Slowly the body began to move—pushing itself up to a sitting position. Her red hair fell away from her face, revealing dazzling green eyes. Authia knew this face for she had seen it before, many times. "How are you, Serena?"

Serena bowed to her. "I am well, my Mistress, and ready to do your bidding."

CHAPTER TWENTY-ONE

R ick woke to the sounds of the jungle. He opened his eyes to see the sun rising on the horizon, bathing the village with its warmth and light. His men, including Travis, were sitting by the fire enjoying their morning coffee. Hanging over the fire pit was a small bush pig. The scent of roasted meat filled the campsite. Slowly Rick climbed out of his sleeping bag, rolled it up, then went to join his men. "Coffee getting any better?"

Travis handed Rick a tin mug filled with steaming coffee. He chuckled at Rick. "Yeah, I think we've finally got this figured out. Next time our platoon gets separated in battle, I'm going to make sure the cook is with us."

Rick sat on the ground next to Travis. "So, when is this woman supposed to be coming?"

"No idea." Travis took a sip of his coffee and stared deep into the coals of the fire.

"You got something on your mind?"

Travis focused his attention on Rick. "I don't know what that wisp did to me, but I know things. I look at something, and it's like I can see the glimmer of something else. Like the hut. I know there's evil there. When I look into the hut through the entrance, I keep seeing a glimmer like an apparition. As if it's constantly walking back and forth past the entrance."

"An apparition? Like a ghost?"

"No, not a ghost. I don't know what it is. But I saw the same thing at the falls. In the bedrock, close to the edge of the falls. There was a glimmer, as if something wasn't right."

"Do you think that it has something to do with the people we are supposed to help?"

"It has everything to do with them. They need our protection."

"What are we protecting them from? The apparition, or Obasi?"

A voice came from behind them. "Obasi."

Both Travis and Rick turned to find Taylor standing behind them. "Is there more of that coffee?" Taylor sat next to Rick and accepted the cup of coffee from Travis.

Rick couldn't believe what he heard. The one man they were trying to avoid. "What do you mean *Obasi?*"

Taylor took a swig of the coffee. "There are two men heading this way. One is Saburo, we all know who he is. The other, I have no idea. He's bruised up pretty bad, but I don't think it was by Saburo's hand."

"Why do you say that?" Rick knew what Saburo was capable of. His and Obasi's cruelty was well known in the Congo.

"Because the second man doesn't appear to be afraid of him. He actually bows to him. And judging from Saburo's reaction, I don't think he's all that comfortable with all the attention."

Rick continued. "Where are they? How far away from us?"

"They're heading to the camp with the pond. Probably spend the night there which means that they'll be here mid-afternoon tomorrow."

Travis put his mug down on the edge of the fire. He looked directly at Taylor. "And what about Obasi?"

"Obasi is following Saburo. Greg caught up with me before I headed here. Obasi was keeping a good day, day and a half between him and Saburo. But now, he's ramped things up. He's only half a day behind Saburo. Which means he could be here as early as tomorrow night. Greg's gone back to keep watch on Saburo."

Rick was not pleased. Was Obasi the person the village

needed protecting from? "Why is he following Saburo?"

"No idea."

"Who's with Obasi?"

Taylor took a deep breath. "Everyone. His entire platoon."

Serena opened her eyes and surveyed her surroundings. The hut she was in was tiny and filled with memories. Sensay occupied this hut as well as Authia. This was the first day of Serena's new life. She sat up and held her hands in front of her. She examined them as she turned them over. Then she glanced down at her legs, her body. She was human and looked exactly as she had when she became a spirit two hundred years ago. She could barely contain her excitement. She wanted to jump up and scream to the world — *I am human again!* Serena knew that this was only a temporary fix. Once she completed the job the Ancestors sent her to do, she could very well lose this body and join the afterlife. She now placed all her hope, her trust with Nathen.

Serena stood and walked out of her hut. The village was alive, with her people going about their morning chores. Breakfast was cooking over the communal fire pit, and Serena realized that she was actually hungry. But satisfying her hunger would have to wait. She had to find Authia. It was time to meet the village's protectors. As Serena walked through the village toward Nathen and Authia's hut, she was very much aware of the attention she was drawing. Everyone knew who and what she was. The fact that her dress was unlike anything the tribe had ever seen before pleased Serena. She knew that the stunning blue bodice that clung to her figure and the skirt that delicately flowed in the slight breeze was provocative. Serena enjoyed standing out in a crowd. As she continued toward Nathen and Authia's hut, she held her head high, and with a smirk of satisfaction, she made her way past all the onlookers.

Nathen lay on his sleeping mat, Authia cradled in his arms. He glanced over at his son, sleeping peacefully on his bed of pillows. Authia stirred in her sleep, which brought Nathen's attention back to her. He couldn't keep his eyes off her — she was so beautiful, and she was all his. Tenderly he kissed her forehead, then pulled her closer to him. All he could think of was how much he wanted her. His body pulsated with desire, with the need to make love to her.

"You always want to play." Authia smiled at Nathen as she gazed up into his emerald eyes.

"Can you blame me? I have this beautiful, sexy woman lying naked next to me. What else could I think of?"

Authia wrapped her arms around Nathen's neck, bringing his lips a breath away from hers. "Well, Joshawa isn't awake yet. We have some time."

Nathen needed no further prodding. He passionately kissed her while he gently laid her on her back. He was just about to start exploring her body with his lips when he heard someone approaching their hut.

"My Lord and Mistress, are you awake?"

Nathen groaned as he reluctantly rolled over onto his back. "Yes, but you may not enter."

"Of course, my Lord. However, we do need to discuss my Mistress' meeting with the outsiders. They are expecting her this morning."

Nathen sat up and glanced over at Authia, who was trying very hard not to laugh. "Very well. We'll meet you at the pit in ten minutes. Make sure Hansen is there, and please send Tammy here to watch Joshawa."

"Yes, my Lord."

Nathen could hear Serena leave. He returned his attention

to Authia. "So, what does a man have to do to get some privacy with his wife?"

Authia sat up, allowing the blanket to fall to her hips, exposing her ample breasts. Nathen playfully rolled his eyes at her. "Now you're just teasing."

Authia stood and went over to where her animal skin skirt and top were lying. She wrapped the skirt around her waist while Nathen watched. "I enjoy teasing you." She tied the top around her neck, then slowly brought it down, purposely taking her time to cover her breasts. "Maybe we could play later after Joshawa falls asleep for the night?"

Nathen stood, leaving the blanket on the sleeping mat. He was naked, revealing his engorged manhood for Authia to see. He walked over to her, drew her into his arms, and passionately kissed her. "No *maybes* about it, we are definitely playing tonight." He kissed her one more time, then got dressed in his animal skins. Not five minutes later, Tammy came to the hut.

"You guys decent? Can I come in?"

Authia pulled the flap to the entrance of the hut to one side. "For sure. Come on in." She tied the flap, securing it to the side allowing the morning breeze to flow into the hut. "Nathen and I are meeting Serena at the pit. Then I'm heading to Sensay's village. Can you watch Joshawa until I return?"

"Not a problem." Tammy went over to Joshawa and sat beside him. She glanced over at Nathen, grinning and chuckling as she did. "You may want to wait a couple of minutes before you head out."

"Why? What do you find so amusing?"

Authia followed Tammy's gaze and laughed. "Your playfulness hasn't worn off yet."

Nathen glanced down at the noticeable bulge in his loincloth. He looked over to Authia. "This is all your fault."

Authia laughed. "My fault? You're the one who wanted to

play."

Nathen studied the two women, and the thought of them enjoying his predicament significantly reduced the size of his bulge. "I'm good." Nathen extended his hand for Authia to take. "Let's go and find out what Serena needs of us." Nathen knew exactly what Serena had promised the man called Travis. Authia was to meet him and convince him and the men that accompanied him to come to the valley and help protect the village. The one problem with the plan was that Nathen couldn't be there to protect his wife. And that one problem did not sit well with Nathen.

Serena patiently waited by the communal fire pit for her Lord and Mistress to arrive. She stood alone, not speaking with anyone, for none of the inhabitants of the village would approach her. Serena could see the fear in their eyes. They remembered her, or more to the point, the stories of her. If she was going to make this village hers, then she was going to have to win the hearts of the people. Not an easy task, especially since she'd been labeled.

"Interesting choice for your garment. Do you think it is wise to draw so much attention to yourself?"

Serena turned to see Casandra standing before her. "I came with the garment. However, if you feel I would blend in better dressed in animal skins, then I will defer to your judgment."

Casandra smiled at Serena. "You dress as you see fit." Casandra walked over to the pit, picked up a wooden bowl, and filled it with fresh fruit and bread. She turned to face Serena as she offered her the bowl. "Hungry?"

Serena accepted the bowl, smiling at Casandra. "Actually, yes, I am." Serena chose a piece of pineapple. She bit into it, savoring the sweet juices that exploded in her mouth. "I had forgotten how sweet and succulent this fruit is. It has been a long time since I tasted food of any kind."

"I'm pleased that you are here. The tribe needs you. You have a great opportunity to atone for . . . shall we say, your indiscretions."

"That would be putting it mildly. I destroyed an entire family, a family of Lords. I can only imagine what I will have to do to atone for that indiscretion."

Casandra bent down to fill a bowl of fruit and bread for herself. She turned to face Serena, smiling as if she knew something Serena didn't. "You never know . . . miracles do happen." Serena watched as Casandra popped a piece of pineapple into her mouth. At the same time, she appeared amused by Serena's look of complete bewilderment.

Authia and Nathen walked hand in hand to the communal fire pit. They were joined by Hansen, who was shirtless and had cut his jeans off just above the knee. They walked in silence, and as they approached the pit, Nathen's people moved to one side, giving their Lord a wide birth. Authia smirked, gazing up at Nathen. "It's as if you were parting the sea."

Nathen frowned. "I don't know if I'll ever get used to all this attention."

Serena approached them, bowing to Nathen and Authia. After what was considered a respectful duration for her bow, she righted herself and spoke to Authia. "My Mistress, you must ready yourself. The one called Travis is waiting for you. I have already planted the seed in Travis' mind. He will follow you. However, I cannot guarantee that the rest of his men will."

Nathen let go of Authia's hand. He stepped closer to Serena. Authia knew that he was trying to intimidate her. "And who's going to protect Authia on this little adventure?"

Hansen stepped forward. "I'll go with her, Nathen. I'll keep her safe."

"Thank you but, no offense, that's not good enough. I want to go. She's my wife, my responsibility."

Authia placed her hand on Nathen's arm, gazing up into his eyes. "I love that you want to be my knight in shining armor, but the whole purpose of the deception spell is so that these men will see you as they see themselves. The spell will not work outside of our valley. You know that. You also know that you wouldn't remain hidden if you thought for one minute that I was in trouble."

"That's irrelevant. These men are armed and could easily overpower Hansen. You're not going without proper protection. That's the last I'm saying on the matter."

Authia pushed in front of Serena, standing a breath away from Nathen. She looked at him with all the feelings of frustration that bubbled up inside her. "I'm not one of your people that you can control. Are you ever going to learn that? I'm the person best suited for this . . . mission, and I'm confident that with Hansen at my side and a little intimidation, I'll control the situation. However, I'll not downplay the possibility that these men could be dangerous. That being said, how about we have Tuval and Arman hide in the trees? They can watch over me, and if I'm threatened, then they can bombard the men with arrows while Hansen and I escape."

Authia could feel everyone staring at her. And there was something else. Tuval and Arman's names were echoing in her mind. As if they were being repeated over and over. She gave her head a gentle shake and returned her attention to the people who surrounded her. She had spoken out to the Lord of the village. Even being the Mistress, what she did would be considered disrespectful.

However, Nathen came to her rescue. He gently cupped

her chin as he smiled lovingly at her. "As usual, my wife speaks with wisdom. I'd prefer that I hide in the trees, but I think you and I both know that I wouldn't be able to stay there if I thought for one minute that you were in danger. So, I agree. Tuval and Arman will accompany you." Nathen lowered his hand and directed his attention to Hansen. "You'll wear a machete at your side. Even though you don't know how to use it, you'll carry a bow drawn back with an arrow in place and ready to use. You'll carry a sheath of arrows on your back." Nathen turned to Authia. "You'll also carry a machete."

Authia smirked to herself. She'd won, as she knew she would. She turned to Serena. "I apologize for cutting you off."

"No apology needed, my Mistress. I greatly respect your tenacity."

Tamara joined the group. She had been at the birthing hut welcoming a new addition to the tribe. "Tuval and Arman wait for you at the falls. They are ready to protect our Mistress with their lives."

"So, that was you rattling around in my mind. You were listing to our conversation."

"Yes, my Mistress. It is good that I can be in two places at once. Do you not think so?"

"Yes, most definitely. Your ability to meld with me, even without my knowledge, is amazing."

Tamara smiled at Authia as she slightly bowed her head. "Thank you. Now I do believe that the men are waiting for you. You should leave, my Mistress."

"Not dressed like that, you're not. Go back to our hut and change into a t-shirt and jeans."

Authia playfully bowed to Nathen placing her arm across her belly as she did. "Yes, my Lord." She headed back toward the hut, but not before Nathen gave her buttocks a gentle slap. When she was about halfway, she stopped and looked back at the group of people surrounding the pit. She blocked her thoughts from Nathen. *Tamara, can you hear me?*

Yes, my Mistress.

Do me a favor.

Certainly.

I don't know how this is going to turn out. No matter what happens, I need you to keep Nathen in the village. Keep him safe.

My Mistress, you do not have faith in the outcome of this meeting?

Not really.

There is much to fear, for The Destroyer *is close. However, the men that wait for you are not evil. They also fear, fear for the evil that approaches them.*

How do you know?

I know because Serena knows. You, my Mistress, as always, are the key.

The key to what?

The key to our survival.

CHAPTER TWENTY-TWO

Obasi stood, leaning against a large Kapok tree. His arms were folded across his chest. His body glistened with sweat, and he knew his expression did not indicate as to his present mood. His men surrounded him, hiding in the jungle, keeping out of sight, as Obasi had instructed. He didn't fear the openness of the area surrounding the Kapok tree. His men were loyal, or more to the poin,t feared him, feared his temper. They would protect him to their death. Having that much power, that much control over his men pleased Obasi, and he grinned ever so wickedly as he stared off into the depths of the jungle. Several minutes later, one of the men he had sent to watch Saburo approached him. Obasi pushed off the tree and placed his left arm at his side while his right hand rested on the handle of his machete. The man was obviously intimidated by Obasi's stance. "What news do you have?"

The man stopped a few feet away from Obasi. "Saburo and the little man made it to a road. Actually, it looks like it may have been a migrating trail, a very old one. The men we follow also stopped there."

"Is this their destination?"

"No. There is evidence that the men headed further south. Will Saburo follow them?"

"That is yet to be seen. Did Saburo see you?"

The man was quiet, cleared his throat, then continued, "Yes, we spoke."

"And what did he have to say for himself?"

"He's not pleased that you are following closer than what was originally planned."

Obasi felt his expression change to that of anger. The man backed up, visibly fearful of what Obasi might do. "I'm not here to please Saburo. Keep a close watch on him. I want to know every move he makes."

The man nodded, then left to join the rest of his comrades. Obasi just stared straight ahead. Saburo was a fool if he thought he was going to reach the valley and plunder its riches without him. Obasi left the protection of his men and headed in the direction Saburo would be found.

Authia and Nathen reached the falls where Tuval and Arman were waiting for them. Authia had changed clothes, as Nathen requested, though her jeans were slightly tight around the waist with the small baby bump that formed her belly. Tammy, Hansen, Serena, and Tamara joined them minutes later. "All right Serena, what do I need to know?"

Serena walked up to Authia and offered her hands to her. "Join with me, my Mistress, and I will show you all there is to know of the man named Travis."

Authia took Serena's hands in hers as she closed her eyes, allowing her mind to become one with Serena. Serena showed her the mind of Travis. He was a good man—someone whose intentions were to protect the weak. To protect those that couldn't protect themselves. She also learned that the men he was with were of the same mind. Fourteen men carrying weapons that could even the odds. Authia opened her eyes and smiled at Serena. "How did you know to choose this man?"

Serena smiled back. "He has an aura about him. I knew the minute I laid eyes on him that he was the one. Now go, my Mistress. Bring back our protectors."

Authia let go of Serena's hands and turned to Nathen. "I'm going to be fine. There's no need to worry." She leaned up and kissed him on his cheek. "Go back with Tamara and wait at the gathering hut. I will bring the men there. Send a couple of our warriors to wait for us on our side of the falls. Tuval, Arman, enter the falls after us in case any of Travis' men are by the pond. Then when we return with them, wait till we enter our valley before you leave the protection of the trees." Authia turned her attention to Hansen. "Ready?"

"As I'll ever be." Hansen turned to Tammy taking her hand in his. "I'll be back before you know it."

"You better be . . . and in one piece."

Tamara walked up to Authia. "Here, take these." She handed Authia two leaf-covered packets. "As you are about to enter the falls, hold one of these in the palm of your hand. Face it toward the falls, then meld with me."

"I thought these packets only worked for the priestess whose essence it holds?"

"True. But you are a powerful melder. I will be one with my packet through you. Now go, my Mistress. Bring back our saviors."

Travis stood at the edge of the jungle separating the village from the falls. He could just barely see the falls through the thick vegetation. According to the wisp, a woman was going to present herself to Travis sometime in the morning. And for reasons that Travis couldn't understand, he knew she would be coming from the direction of the falls. As he was about to rejoin the men who were still by the fire pit enjoying their breakfast, he caught a glimpse of a yellow glow coming from behind the falls. The glow became brighter as it expanded toward the edge of the bedrock. It was then that Travis saw what appeared to be two people emerging from within what could only be described as a giant, almost transparent, yellow globe. As they stepped onto the valley floor, the glow disappeared, revealing a man and woman. Travis stared at the couple, then ran back to the group to get Rick.

Authia slowly closed her hand around the packet and watched as the glow dissipated around her and Hansen. She walked over to the pond, scrutinizing the area, making sure no one was there. After she was confident that the coast was clear, Authia melded with Nathen. *We're here, and there's no one by the pond. You can send Tuval and Arman. And don't worry sweetheart, I'm going to be fine.*

I'll continue to worry until you're by my side, safe and sound. That's my prerogative.

Authia smiled and gently shook her head. *Yes, it is, and I love you for it. I'll see you soon.*

Authia looked over to Hansen. "Okay, Tuval and Arman are on their way. Let's get this done."

Hansen stepped in front of Authia. "I'll lead, you follow right behind me. If there is any trouble, I want to be first on the firing line."

"There won't be any trouble. That's why Serena chose Travis."

"Doesn't matter. Nathen will kill me if anything happens to you. Get behind me." Hansen's expression was more scolding than angry. Authia smiled and gestured for him to lead the way. They walked toward the village, Authia directly behind Hansen. She glanced over her shoulder to see Tuval and Arman scaling two trees, positioning themselves to protect her. When Authia and Hansen walked into the clearing surrounding the village, they were greeted by fourteen men, armed, though they appeared to be more curious than defensive. Leading the group were two men, one of whom had to be Travis. The group of men stopped while the two men in front approached. Authia moved next to Hansen, squared her shoulders, and addressed the men. One had his right hand resting on the butt of his gun. Authia gestured toward him. "If I were you, I would carefully remove your hand from your gun."

The man smiled at Authia. "And why would I want to do that?"

"Because, if you even make the slightest movement, the men I have hiding in the jungle will interpret that as a threat against me. You'll be dead before your gun leaves its holster."

The man scanned the area. "What men?"

"Trust me, they're there, and their weapons are aimed at you. I'm here to meet Travis. I'm here to seek your help. I'm not here to cause trouble."

The man slowly fanned his fingers and withdrew his hand from his gun. "I'm Rick." He nodded to the man next to him. "This is Travis. Did the wisp send you?"

Authia had been so focused on the men in front of her that she didn't notice the havoc that had been wreaked upon Sensay's village until now. She gazed upon it in horror. "What happened here?" She started to walk toward the village, but Hansen held her back. She looked at the hand securely grasping her forearm then looked up to meet his gaze. "Why are you stopping me?"

Hansen removed his hand, then gestured toward Rick and Travis. "I'm not totally convinced that you're safe." He directed his attention to Rick. "So, what happened to the village?"

"Your guess is as good as mine. One minute it was standing, the next, every hut was blown to pieces. All except that one hut." Rick nodded toward Sensay's hut.

Authia moved closer to the two men, Hansen right at her side. "Let's just say you probably angered the aura that has taken up residence in the village."

Rick looked questioningly at Authia. "Aura? What aura? Does it have anything to do with that wisp?"

"There's a lot that needs explaining, on both our parts. But not here. I'd be more comfortable discussing this in our own village."

"Okay, but you still haven't answered my question. Did the wisp send you?"

"You can say that. I'm Authia, Mistress of my village, and this is Hansen." Hansen nodded to the men. "I understand that you are peacemakers. That your only desire is to protect those that can't protect themselves."

Rick gazed upon Authia in bewilderment. "How do you know what we are? What our desires are?"

Authia smiled at the men. "I know because Travis told Serena . . . the wisp. We're in need of your help . . . your protection. There are men coming that could be a threat to our village. We can protect ourselves from the men but not against their weaponry."

Travis casually glanced over to the stockpile of weapons and explosives. Then he turned his attention back to Authia. "So, you not only need us, you need our weapons. You're right. Men are coming, and a lot of them. And they're very dangerous, with or without weapons. That being said, every man here has agreed to help you. This Serena person is right. We are here to protect, to defend those that can't defend themselves. I can't guarantee that we'll win this battle, but I promise you, we'll give it our best shot."

"That's all I can ask for. I need you to follow me. I'm going to take you to a special place, hidden from the outside world."

"You're referring to going behind the waterfall. I saw you. It appeared as if you came out of the bedrock. And there was a glow surrounding you."

"Yes, you're right. We're going behind the waterfall. And that glow you saw, let's just say it's a little bit of magic."

Rick raised an eyebrow. "Magic? Magic is simply an illusion. And if it's our weapons you want, you're going to be out of luck. We can't get the explosives wet."

"And you won't. Trust me. We'll go to our village where

you can speak to my husband." Authia hesitated for just a second. "You're going to witness things that are beyond anything you've seen before. Wisps and walking out of bedrock are just the beginning. I need you to trust me, but I'm also going to have to trust you. So, I'm going to give you a friendly warning. If you or any of your men do anything to disrupt or harm our people or our village, you'll be punished, and the punishment is death."

Rick and Travis' eyes went wide as they gaped at Authia in utter disbelief. Then she continued, "If you are honestly here to protect us, then there'll be no issues. However, if you or any of your men have any other ideas, then you should stop your journey here." Authia paused just long enough for her words to sink in. "I'll leave and meet you at the pond in ten minutes. Speak to your men. Make sure those that cross into our valley are, shall we say, pure of heart." Authia smiled then turned to leave, Hansen right behind her.

Nathen nervously paced the confines of the gathering hut. Tamara sat on the raised platform, watching him. "Is it your intention, my Lord, to lessen your fear for my Mistress by creating a furrow in the ground?"

Nathen glanced down to find a noticeable depression in the ground where he'd been walking. He looked over at Tamara and sighed. "My fear can't be lessened by just walking." He headed over to the platform and took his place next to Tamara, though he didn't look at her. Instead, he just stared off into the distance, seeing past the gathering hut and to the falls where four of his warriors patiently waited for Authia to return. "I should be there to protect her. I should be the one confronting these men."

"Your love for my Mistress is as deep as the love your father had for your mother. He was with her when she died, and with all his strength, he could not protect her."

Nathen quickly turned to face Tamara. "What are you saying? Do you know something that you're not telling me?"

Tamara placed her hand on Nathen's arm. "No, my Lord. I know nothing more than what I have already shared with you. You have to know that even with your love as deep as it is and your great strength, if it is time for my Mistress to die, then there is nothing you can do." Tamara tenderly smiled at Nathen. "Our lives, the lives of all that live in this valley, precariously rests on the edge of a great ravine. On one side is certain death, on the other, peace and contentment. You will not know which is your fate until you take that last step."

"And what if I choose not to travel to this ravine?"

Tamara crooked her head slightly and appeared surprised at Nathen's comment. "But, my Lord, you are already there, as we all are." Before Nathen could respond, Tamara sat straight up and closed her eyes. "They are returning. *The Destroyer* is not among them. However, he is close."

The sounds of birds and monkeys chatting in among the trees woke Saburo. He lay still, his eyes closed, contemplating his day and wondering how much longer he was going to be able to keep up the façade. As he took a deep breath of the morning air, he could smell the aroma of freshly made coffee. He opened his eyes to find Tomas staring down at him, a mug of coffee in his left hand.

"You are awake, my Lord. I made you coffee." Tomas waited till Saburo was standing before him, then handed him the coffee. "You must eat, then we'll head out."

"Where are we going today?" Saburo took a sip of the steaming coffee.

"To the place we camped at the last time I led you to your home. Do you not remember? There is a pond where you can bathe."

"Yes. Of course, Tomas. I'm beginning to remember." Saburo took a stab in the dark. "My home is close, isn't it?"

Tomas gave Saburo a troubled look. "My village is half a day walk from there. Your home is beyond that. How is it that you remember so little?"

"There are gaps in my memory. Someone doesn't want me to find my way home. But you'll take me there, won't you, Tomas?"

"Of course, my Lord." Tomas surveyed his surroundings. "Evil lives in the jungle. It follows us." Tomas returned his gaze to Saburo. "Our time is running out. Eat quickly, my Lord. We must continue our journey." Tomas turned and went back to the firepit. He knelt by the fire, flattened a large palm leaf, then piled fruit on the leaf along with a few pieces of meat that he had ripped from the small animal roasting above the fire. Saburo approached him and watched as Tomas dutifully prepared his meal. Time was running out, and apparently, they still had another day to go. Saburo gazed deep into the jungle. Obasi was near, and Saburo knew that Obasi would be closing the gap. Obasi was focused on the valley that was protected by the Gods. There was something he wanted in the valley, and Obasi was not one to share. Saburo sat next to Tomas and accepted the palm leaf. As he ate his breakfast, his mind was racing, thinking of some way he could appease Obasi and hopefully stay alive.

Obasi was motivated, and it didn't take long for him to catch up to the two men he had sent to watch Saburo earlier. The men were startled when Obasi walked out onto the path in front of them. He stood facing the men, his hand resting on the handle of his machete, his expression sinister to the point of being unnerving. He looked over his shoulder at the obvious path his men were following. Slowly he returned his gaze to his men. "Is this the path Saburo made?"

Nervously the shorter of the two men addressed Obasi, "Yes, Sir. There is another path over there." The man pointed to the left of the path they were on. "It leads to the same road that Saburo is at now. It was probably made by the group of men that were camped at the hut we found."

Obasi grinned, aware he was revealing the large gap where his two front teeth used to be. "How far?"

"Close. A couple of hours, if you hurry."

"Return to the other men. Stay half a day behind me. I will follow Saburo myself."

The two men looked at each other in disbelief.

"You've a problem with that?"

Again, the shorter man replied, "No, Sir." Both men turned on their heels and headed back.

Obasi smiled. The valley that was protected by the Gods was close, he knew it. A heinous plan formed in his mind as he stared down the path. He would dispose of the group of men that carried the weapons. Then he would set a trap that would kill his men. He wanted none alive to share in the wealth. All that would be left at that point was Saburo and the little man. Obasi started to double-time it down the path. He would use Saburo until the valley was revealed to him. When it was, the valley floor would glisten with Saburo's blood.

CHAPTER TWENTY-THREE

The sun was directly above the falls, basking the calm waters with its warmth. Travis stood at its edge, allowing the mist from the falls to gently spray over his body, a welcome reprieve from the heat. Several minutes later, the rest of his companions, laden with backpacks and litters, stood alongside Rick. Travis turned to Hansen who protectively stood at Authia's side. "Now what?"

Hansen climbed a large, flat rock that served as the entrance to the falls and addressed the group of men. "Authia will lead the way. She'll conjure a large yellow globe. Don't be afraid. Stay inside the globe at all times. Believe it or not, while you're in the globe, you'll remain dry. The rocks behind the falls are slimy, and the path is narrow, so watch your step." Hansen faced Authia and nodded his head. "Whenever you're ready."

Travis watched as Authia turned to face the falls. She raised her hand in front of her, opening it to reveal some sort of leaf covered packet resting in the palm of her hand. Within seconds the packet started to glow, and as Travis looked on in disbelief, an immense, yellow globe formed around them. Authia nodded to Hansen who called out to the men. "Okay, we're heading in. Remember, stay within the globe."

Travis stood to one side as the men walked past him, disappearing behind the falls. When the last man entered, Travis followed. The path was narrow and slimy as Hansen had forewarned. But what was truly amazing was that the spray from the falls seemed to splash against the globe and run down its sides. Travis remained perfectly dry. It only took a few moments for him to pass behind the falls and walk into a valley which was lush and green beyond anything he had seen before.

Travis stood at the entrance to the valley with his mouth gaped open at the sheer size of the plants and trees that surrounded the clearing. It wasn't until Rick called out to him that he noticed the four men waiting to greet his platoon. They were tall, well over six feet, and were wearing loincloths made of what appeared to be animal skins. Their hair was dark, almost black, and fell past their shoulders. They were intimidating with their piercing dark eyes, high cheekbones, and facial expressions that shouted, *don't mess with us*. Their bodies were rippled with muscle, their biceps twice the size of his own. If the rest of Authia's tribe looked like these guys, then she'd be right. They could easily defend themselves in a fight of strength.

Rick instructed his men to lower the litters but to keep their backpacks on. He and Travis made their way over to Authia and Hansen. Travis sized up the four men standing behind Authia. "I see what you mean."

Authia appeared confused. "I'm sorry?"

"Being able to defend yourself against the men heading this way. Do the rest of your tribe look like these guys?"

Authia chuckled. "For the majority, yes. Our women are quite tall, as well."

"You're not that tall."

"I wasn't born to the tribe. I'm what they consider as an outsider. Now if you'll follow me." Authia turned and headed into the jungle, two of her warriors and Hansen following close behind. The remaining two warriors took their positions behind the group.

Authia's mind was racing. So far, the spell they had cast was working. Travis and his men obviously saw the warriors as they saw themselves. Then a frightening thought came to

Authia. *What about Serena? She wasn't present when they performed the spell.* Quickly Authia melded with Nathen.

Sweetheart, is Serena with you?

Yes, my Love. She wishes to meet Travis.

Is Tammy there?

No, she's watching Joshawa by the pond. Is everything all right?

I'm not sure. We need to find out if the spell worked on Serena. Otherwise, she's going to have to hide and remain out of sight.

How far away are you?

We're close.

I'll take care of it.

Authia ended the meld then checked over her shoulder for Hansen. She nodded her head for him to join her. "I need you to run ahead. Go to the gathering hut."

"Why? What's going on?"

Authia lowered her voice. "You and Tammy are the only way we know that the spell we cast on the village worked. I need you to go ahead and make sure that the spell worked on Serena. If it didn't, then meet me on the outskirts of the village, and we'll keep the men there until Nathen has time to hide her."

"You got it." Hansen broke into a run and disappeared into the jungle.

Rick started to approach Authia, which resulted in a spearhead being pressed against his neck. He stopped short, as did the rest of his men. "Whoa!" He lifted his hands up shoulder height as if he were surrendering.

Authia gazed up to her protector, then placed her right hand on the spear and gently lowered it. "He's not a threat. None of these men are. Treat them accordingly."

The warrior bowed to Authia and placed his spear back at his side. Authia turned to Rick and smiled. "I apologize. My warriors are very protective of me, especially against strangers. That being said, I would caution your men against any movement or words that could be misinterpreted as a threat. I might not be there the next time."

Rick looked wide-eyed at Authia. "How are we to protect you if these Neanderthals are shoving spears in our face every time we appear threatening? If we're going to protect you, we'll be carrying guns."

Authia continued to walk toward the village chuckling at Rick's choice of words. "Neanderthals?" She glanced over at Rick. "You think my warriors resemble cavemen?" Authia returned her gaze toward the jungle.

"They're huge, and they carry primitive weapons."

"True. But they're much more civilized."

"That's yet to be seen."

Authia gently shook her head. "In answer to your question, this evening we'll hold a ceremony introducing you to our village. That will put my warriors at ease. However, they do not trust outsiders. Your job won't be easy."

"Great. So, we'll be fighting on two fronts."

"No. You just need to earn their trust."

"And how about you? Do you trust us?"

"Yes. But I have the advantage of seeing inside of Travis. And through him, I learned what you and your men are about." Authia said a silent prayer as she approached the village. Thank God they had performed the spell. She could only imagine these men's reaction if they saw the Jelani Tribe in their true form.

In the gathering hut, Nathen was waiting for Authia along with Tamara, Serena, and Casandra. After melding with Authia, Nathen went over to Serena, who was standing by the entrance looking out into the jungle. "We may have a problem."

Serena turned to face Nathen. "What kind of problem?"

"As you know, we cast a spell on the village so that the men that are coming see us as they would see themselves."

"I'm aware of that, my Lord." Serena thought for a second then smiled. "You are afraid that the spell did not include me."

"Yes, and I don't see anything amusing about that. If the spell didn't work on you, then you'll have to remain hidden at the birthing hut until this is all over."

"I am an integral part of this plan. You must not banish me, my Lord."

"I'm not banishing you. I'm protecting the village."

Casandra approached Nathen and Serena. "What's wrong, my Lord? I sense that you're troubled."

"Serena wasn't present when we performed the spell that changed our appearance. Authia has sent Hansen ahead. We need to find out how these men are going to perceive Serena."

Casandra shrugged her shoulders. "That's simple, my Lord. She was joined with me. Therefore, the spell would affect her as it had affected me."

Nathen shook his head. "No. She didn't join with you till after the ceremony."

"A fact that I'm well aware of. However, when I became her host, she became a part of me. Trust me . . . she's under the influence of the spell."

Before Nathen could respond, Hansen came out of the jungle. He approached them, noticeably studying the two women. "Hey, Nathen."

"Hansen. How's my wife?"

Hansen grinned at Nathen. "In control, as she always is." As he spoke, he turned his attention to Casandra. "You, I know. You, however, are too tall to be Tamara. And judging from that smug look on your face and the way you're dressed, I'd say you're Serena." Hansen turned to face Nathen. "No worries. The spell worked. I'm going to head back and let Authia know."

Nathen was relieved—he knew Serena was right, he was going to need her when he went up against Celest. "I'm coming with you. I want to see these men for myself . . . before they enter the village. Casandra, please wait here with Tamara and Serena."

Casandra bowed to Nathen. "Yes, my Lord."

Nathen and Hansen walked toward the edge of the village, closely followed by two of Nathen's warriors. There they stopped and waited for Authia and the men that were to be their protectors to arrive. Several minutes later, Nathen could hear the sound of men pushing their way through the jungle. Shortly after, Authia came into view. Nathen drew a breath of relief, happy to have her back and in one piece. The group of men stopped, and only two of them followed Authia to meet Nathen.

Nathen watched their approach, sizing them up. They were obviously nervous—Nathen knew even in his altered state, he was still an imposing figure. "Glad to have you back, my Love." Nathen reached out and took Authia's hand in his as she stood beside him.

"Nathen, this is Rick." Rick extended his hand which Nathen accepted. "And this is Travis, the one Serena spoke of."

Nathen accepted his hand but didn't quite let go immediately. "So, you're here to save us?"

Travis stood still, his hand in Nathen's, sweat starting to bead on his forehead. "Yes, at least we are going to give it our best shot."

Nathen let go of Travis' hand. "Your best shot is more than we have right now. Thank you for coming." He looked over Travis' shoulder at the men standing a few feet away. "Your men will stay here. I'll have food and water brought to them. You two will come with me. We have a lot to discuss."

Authia interjected. "I told them that we'd have a ceremony tonight to welcome them and to let the tribe know they're not dangerous."

"My wife thinks of everything, and she's right. Your men will remain here until after the ceremony. I don't want to upset the people of this village. Your men will be guarded, strictly precautionary."

Rick nodded his head. "Of course. Strictly precautionary." There was obvious sarcasm in the tone of Rick's voice. "I'd like Taylor to accompany us. He might have information that could be useful."

"By all means."

Rick turned to face his men. "Taylor, front and center." As Taylor joined them, Rick turned back to Nathen. "My men are tired. I trust that they'll have better sleeping accommodations than the jungle floor?"

Nathen snorted. "The people of this tribe sleep on the jungle floor every night. You and your men will be allowed to sleep in the gathering hut. It's the only hut we have that will accommodate your numbers. You'll be given sleeping mats, but that is as luxurious as it gets."

Nathen's attention was diverted as Tuval and Arman joined them. "Good, you're here. See that these men are fed and have warriors guard them, for their own protection."

Tuval and Arman bowed to Nathen then carried out his orders. Nathen, still holding Authia's hand, turned and headed toward the gathering hut. He casually glanced over his shoulder to make sure his three guests were following. This was the beginning. Now that these men were here, it was becoming real. As Nathen and Authia entered the gathering hut, a wave of uncertainty crashed into the wall of strength at Nathen's very core.

With determined strides, Obasi closed the distance between him and Saburo. He knew that Saburo was getting close. He knew that there was a purpose to Saburo's insistence that he stay out of sight. Saburo wanted the plunder for himself. Anger grew inside of Obasi, poisoning his mind — his very thoughts. The merciless sun beat down on him, and with no food or water, and the fact that he was pushing himself to the very brink of exhaustion, delirium had started to possess his every thought. He didn't see the jungle or the birds or animals. All that lay in front of him was a valley, lush, green, and laden with gold.

Saburo trudged through the dense vegetation, and he continued to be amazed at how Tomas was able to keep up the pace with his injuries as extensive as they were. They had been walking since morning, and now the sun rose high above their heads, which caused the heat to soar to temperatures that far exceeded Saburo's tolerance level. He'd lived in the jungle all his life, yet he had never experienced conditions as harsh as what he was being subjected to now. All he could think about was the pond that Tomas promised would be at their next camp. Then, according to Tomas, they still had another half day to go. The jungle became denser the further they went, and all the time Saburo had the unnerving feeling that he was being watched. Would Obasi be so foolish as to take a chance that Tomas would see him? Tomas seemed to be firmly planted in the role he was playing, but with his mind so damaged, there was no way of telling what would push him over the edge. Saburo had to confront Obasi and tell him to back off. Unfortunately, a confrontation like that could get him killed.

As they traveled further south, the fact that someone was

close, watching, ate at Saburo's nerves. It was time to confront Obasi. Saburo was a skilled tracker, but then, so was Obasi. Hopefully, Obasi was unaware that Saburo was on to him, and he could use that to his advantage. Obasi was to his right, a few hundred yards away at most. Saburo widened the gap between him and Tomas, at the same time shifting ever so slightly to his right. When the jungle swallowed Tomas, and he was no longer in sight, Saburo whirled around and focused in the direction he knew Obasi would be. "I know you're there. You might as well come out." The jungle lay quiet as Saburo scanned the dense vegetation. "Why are you hiding? Come out, face me, tell me what you want."

Still, the jungle remained quiet. "I'm doing what you told me to do, Obasi." Saburo drew his machete at the sound of someone crashing through the jungle. Then he realized that Obasi was running away from him, which made absolutely no sense. Without even thinking, he took off after his stalker. The heat no longer affected him, because he was in survivor mode. Within minutes he caught up with the person he pursued. He tackled him to the ground, sending the man's gun flying. Saburo straddled him and placed the blade of his machete tight against the man's throat. It wasn't Obasi that lay on the ground, but rather a man who resembled the platoon of men that had been heading south ahead of him.

"Who are you?" Saburo pressed the blade of the machete even tighter against the man's neck, causing the skin to tear. Blood trickled down the sides of his neck. "Answer me."

"Get off me, and maybe I will."

"You're in no position to make demands. Who are you?"

"You're looking for Obasi? He's close, and he's on his own. At the rate he's closing the gap between you and him, I'd say he's on a mission."

Saburo gazed at the man, confused by his revelation. "What do you know of Obasi?"

"Get off me, and I'll tell you." The man stared at Saburo, showing no fear, no pain.

Saburo slowly withdrew the machete from the man's neck. He gazed upon him suspiciously. He was the enemy, why should he trust him? "I'll get off, but you make one move that I don't like, and I'll gut you like a pig."

"I'd expect nothing else from you, Saburo."

Saburo's eyes went wide as he gazed at the man in shock. "How do you know my name?"

"Like I said. Get off me, and I'll tell you."

Saburo moved aside, removed the man's machete from his belt, stood and looked down at the man. "You can stay on the ground. Now, who are you? How do you know Obasi? How do you know me?"

"I'm a peacemaker, or at least that's what I came here to be. Name's Greg, and it's my job to know who you are, who Obasi is, and what you're capable of."

"You're part of the platoon that's heading south."

"Is that a question or a statement?"

"It's a statement. I know exactly where your men are. Why aren't you with them?"

"'Cause it's my job to keep an eye on you and Obasi and your men."

"Was getting caught part of your job?"

"No, as a matter of fact, it's quite embarrassing. But then you're one of the best." Greg snickered. "In so many areas. Who's the pygmy that you're following?"

"That's none of your business. Now, you mentioned Obasi was close?"

"Did I?"

Saburo aimed his machete at Greg. "You're not in a position to be stupid. Answer my question."

Saburo could see that there was no fear in this man. As a matter of fact, he looked upon Saburo with contempt. "What does it matter if I answer your questions or not? I know you, I know what you do. You're going to kill me whether I talk or not. So why should I give you anything?"

Saburo nodded his head in agreement. "Yeah, you're right. Killing you would give me great pleasure. However, I'm fighting a different, more complicated, battle right now. I'll guarantee your safety if you tell me what I need to know."

Greg laughed. "Guarantee my safety. What a joke. You can't guarantee anything. If you don't kill me, Obasi surely will."

Saburo thought for a second as he stood over Greg. Slowly he fastened his machete to his belt then, using Greg's machete, cut a length of a low hanging vine. "Stand up and turn around." Greg did as he was told and Saburo bond his hands behind his back. "I have two choices. Leave you here to die, or bring you with me. If I choose to bring you with me, you can't say one word to the man I am following. You follow my lead, or I promise you, I will kill you where you stand."

Chapter Twenty-four

Rick, Travis, and Taylor followed Nathen and Authia to the gathering hut. Rick was astonished by what he witnessed. An entire tribe of primitive people dressed in animal skins. They carried bowls made of clay and baskets made of palm leaves. He felt like he was in one of those articles featured in the *National Geographic* magazine. When he entered the gathering hut, he was overwhelmed by its size. Nathen was right . . . it could easily accommodate his men. The hut was circular and bare, with the exception of a raised platform at the very back. The platform was covered with a bright red blanket and had clay pots on the ground that completely encircled the platform. He casually walked over and examined the intricate design on the blanket. There was one marking that was out of place. A large stain, reddish-orange in color.

"That is a marking of a great warrior that gave his life for our Mistress. It is a reminder of a time when our tribe was not as it should be."

Rick turned around to find a beautiful woman standing before him. She was dressed in what appeared to be a ceremonial gown. Her appearance was similar to the other women he had seen, but there was something different about her. She was just a little taller than Authia, and she had a look of innocence about her. Rick couldn't take his eyes off her.

"Is there something wrong?" she asked.

"No. Sorry. You just startled me."

She tilted her head slightly and appeared as if she was trying to understand his response. "You do not look as though you are startled. I am the High Priestess Tamara. It would please my Lord if you would join us." Tamara gestured toward the group in the center of the hut.

"Ladies first." Rick followed Tamara over to the group and went to stand next to Travis. He met Travis' gaze and immediately knew what he was thinking. "Oh, shut up."

Travis chuckled and leaned over to Rick. "I didn't say anything. She is cute, though."

Nathen sat cross-legged on the ground, motioning for everyone to join him. They formed a small circle, and while Nathen waited for them to settle, he gazed upon his guests. They had brought with them a handful of men, weaponry that the tribe had never seen, and the slightest glimmer of hope. Serena positioned herself across from Travis. At the same time, she had a clear line of sight to Nathen. Nathen watched her as she stared openly at Travis. A small smile graced her lips, and to Nathen, her eyes spoke volumes. Nathen could easily tell that she wanted to speak to Travis, to let him know that it was she who'd spoken soft whispers inside his mind. Travis stared back, but he was apparently uncomfortable with the attention. Nathen turned his gaze back toward Serena. "Are you done?"

"My Lord?"

"Don't pretend that you don't know what I'm talking about. Do you have something to say to Travis?"

"If it pleases my Lord, then yes, I do."

Nathen smiled and nodded.

"It is good to finally meet you face to face."

"Last I saw of you, you were a tiny blue wisp flittering around our camp."

"And now I am human, with only the color of my garment to remind me of what I once was."

"So why me?"

"Because of your aura. When I first saw you, I knew that

your mind would be open to suggestion. And your aura was that of kindness. You are what we call pure of heart."

Authia interjected. "Yes, but Serena, in the beginning, you weren't looking to save us. You were trying to destroy us. Why would you send us help?"

"Travis was my plan B. I never truly trusted my mother. And I wanted to have an escape route in case she reneged on her promise. It would take an army to fight *The Destroyer*. I wanted to make sure that one was available to me. To us."

Rick looked at Serena and Authia in complete bewilderment. "Woah. Your mother? Who's your mother? And who the hell is *The Destroyer*?"

Nathen took a deep breath and slowly let it out. "It's time you learned the history of the Jelani Tribe. I've been told that the Jelani Tribe is as old as the dirt we walk on. It has existed in this valley hidden from the outside world for centuries. Our people are special in ways that you can never understand. Our priestesses are gifted. They can conjure spells and spirits, meld minds, feel and see auras. Our tribe is protected and watched over by the Lords and Priestesses that once ruled this valley."

Rick interrupted, "Are you saying that the priestesses are witches?" He glanced over to Tamara, who smiled at him.

"No, we are not witches. We do not worship pagan Gods or devils. Though, sadly, some of our priestesses have dabbled in the dark arts." Tamara casually looked over to Casandra and Serena. "But that was another time, long ago. Our people do not worship, but rather respect our Lord and Mistress. Not only the ones that rule today, but also those that have ruled before."

Authia continued the conversation. "I'm sure you've heard of empaths . . . telepathy?"

"I've heard of them, haven't necessarily believed in them or telepathy for that matter," Rick responded. "However, after watching what Travis went through, it does give some credence to what you are claiming."

"It's not a claim. It's a fact, and you'd better start believing, because these gifts are going to help keep us, including you and your men, alive."

Nathen took over the conversation. "You are in the presence of three of the most powerful priestesses of our time. As we are going to trust in you, you will have to trust in their abilities. Serena's mother, Celest, was a dangerous, cruel, and very powerful priestess. She lived two centuries ago and ruled the tribe after my father and mother died."

Rick, Travis, and Taylor looked at Nathen as if he had just grown horns. Travis spoke, "Your father and mother? Shouldn't you be putting a *grand* and a few *greats* in front of that?"

"Not really. I was born two hundred years ago. Serena was married to my father, but it didn't work out, and my father took an outsider as his new wife. For two hundred years, Serena lived in the spirit world dictating my life. She had placed a curse on me so that I would only live for twenty-nine years . . . then I would die only to be born again. If it wasn't for Authia and her gifts, I'd probably be still living the curse."

Rick shook his head. "I call bullshit. You say you're not witches, but you place curses on people. You're trying to tell me that you're two hundred-years-old?"

"Technically, I'm thirty. But my mother gave birth to me two hundred years ago. Look, I know this all sounds ludicrous, and it's going to sound a whole lot more implausible as I reveal more of what we're up against. But if we're going to win this, you're going to have to start opening your mind to unbelievable possibilities. The aura living in the village that you just came from is Celest, Serena's mother. And she's bent on destroying the Jelani Tribe. She is the one who destroyed the village."

Travis interjected, "Is she the glimmer I saw in the hut? If she's part of the tribe, why would she want to destroy it?"

Serena chuckled, "Because of who she is. And yes, she is the glimmer. My mother was punished by our Ancestors and was banished to a place that can only be described as a black hole, consuming everything around you so that there is no light. No companionship. Just loneliness and darkness." Serena's expression was that of sadness, and Nathen knew she was remembering her time in that dark place. "My mother was angry that she was sent there and somehow she managed to escape. And in that very second where she was between plains, between the dark hole and reality, she managed to meld with me. Unknown to our Ancestors, she imparted to me her plan to gain her revenge. She relied on the fact that I would be as angry as her, that I would crave revenge on those that imprisoned me into that dark hole. And somehow, she knew that the Ancestors would send me to help our tribe. What she did not count on was that my desire to never return to that place again was greater than my anger and my hatred."

Nathen continued, "Celest is waiting for a human host. Someone who is as cruel and brutal as she is."

Rick commented, "Well, that's got Obasi written all over it."

"Who's Obasi?"

"He's one mean son of a bitch. He kills for pure pleasure. He has no conscience or moral guidance."

"And he's headed this way?"

Taylor responded, "In a big way. He's on a mission, and that mission is leading him straight to your doorstep."

"How could he possibly know to come here? Why would he be coming here?"

Taylor glanced over at Rick then back to Nathen. "Anyone in Obasi's wake dies. He leaves no survivors unless he believes that they're useful to him somehow. Then he keeps you alive, beating and torturing you until the will to live no longer exists. When he gets what he wants, he puts you out of your misery. He managed to separate our platoon, trapping our greater numbers to the north of us. The jungle floor is littered with their dead bodies. Fourteen of us headed south, away from the fighting. Problem is with all the crates and gear we're carrying we've left a trail that a baby could follow. Obasi and his men were following our trail for no other reason than to kill us."

Nathen listened to what Taylor had to say, and one word jumped out at him. "*Were* following? They no longer follow you?"

"As a matter of fact, no. They're not following our trail at all. Obasi's second in command, Saburo, separated from the group and is following this little man. Obasi is following Saburo. He was a good day and a half behind Saburo, but now he's ramped things up. Greg is out there trying to find out what he's up to."

Nathen and Authia looked at each other then back at Taylor. Nathen questioned Taylor. "What little man?"

"No idea who he is. What I can tell you is that he's been beaten, severely. I'm surprised he can stand never mind push through the jungle. He continuously bows to Saburo. Calls him my Lord."

Authia's eyes went wide. "Oh my God, it's Tomas. It has to be. But why would he be calling this man Lord? That doesn't make sense."

As Authia spoke, Nathen kept his attention focused on the group, especially Serena. Her eyes were fixated on the ground, she was biting at her lower lip, and when she realized Nathen was watching her, she only glanced at him through the corner of her eyes. "You have something you want to share, Serena?"

Serena glanced over at Nathen. She appeared as though she was giving it considerable thought. "Not really."

"Wrong answer. Let me put it this way. What did you do?"

Casandra placed her hand on Serena's knee. "You won't be in any trouble. You must tell us what you know."

Serena glanced down at the hand resting on her knee. She looked up at Casandra then over to Nathen. "You told me to go find Tomas. Which is exactly what I did."

"Why is he calling the man he is with Lord?"

"When I first went looking for Tomas, I was still under the belief that my mother would give me my greatest wish. All I had to do was, basically, everything she asked of me."

"And what did she ask of you?"

"She wanted me to lead a group of men to the village. She is looking for a host."

"Where does Tomas play in all this?"

"The first time I went to the place he was captured, I was able to lock onto his aura. And believe me, it was not easy. There was so much death, so many lost souls. I followed the aura to where it was the strongest. That is where I found a large pool of blood-his blood. Through that blood, I learned that he knew where to find the Jelani Tribe. I shared that information with my mother."

Nathen didn't like the direction the conversation was going. It was bad enough that Celest knew how to find them. But she wasn't a threat until she joined with her host—something they could possibly prevent. But with these men having Tomas, that changed everything. What if he had already told them about the tribe and where to find the hidden valley? "And what else did you share with your mother?"

"I told her how many men were in the camp." She looked over to Travis. "Yours, as well as the group of men that are following you."

"So, back to my original question, why is Tomas calling the man he's with Lord?"

"You have to understand, my Lord, all this I did before I decided to side with you. I want you to know Tomas is a good and loyal man. He would not willingly give you up."

"Get to the point Serena."

Serena stared at Nathen, and for the first time, Nathen actually saw fear in her eyes. "Whatever you did, Serena happened in the past. How you act now, and in the future, will decide your fate."

Serena smirked at Nathen. "Are you referring to all my past ill deeds or just my recent ones?"

"If you help us defeat your mother and save the tribe, save our valley, then it would be all your past ill deeds, including the ones that involve my parents and me."

Serena let out a heavy sigh. "Good to hear. My job was to get the men that captured Tomas to the village. My mother wanted their numbers. She was not particularly interested in Travis' men. She wanted to use Tomas' knowledge of the tribe for her benefit. However, he was broken. His mind, his body, his spirit. He was not Tomas. The only way I could use him to my mother's benefit was to join with his mind and convince him that he was whole."

Travis spoke up, "Like you joined with me?"

"Not exactly. With you, I just whispered suggestions, planted a seed, so to speak. With Tomas, I had to rebuild his mind, make him forget all he suffered. When he and the man you call Saburo came to the tree, I joined with Tomas. I saw and felt his pain. I saw the beatings, and I also saw a way to have Tomas do as I wanted. He was hiding deep inside his subconscious. However, a part of him was searching, looking for who he was. In a brief moment, he saw you, my Lord. That was my way in. This is the part that I am not particularly proud of. Tomas' body was badly broken. He would never be able to make the journey in his current state. I took over his mind and convinced him that there was no pain. I blocked all memory of his imprisonment. When he looked upon himself, he would only see himself as he was before his capture. When he looked upon Saburo, he would only see you, my Lord. As far as Tomas is concerned, he is leading the Lord of the Lion People home."

"Why would he believe that I wouldn't know how to find our valley?"

"I do not know, my Lord. Somehow Saburo has been able to convince Tomas to show him the way home."

Nathen glanced over to Casandra. She appeared troubled. "Casandra? What's wrong?"

Casandra addressed Serena. "What happens if Tomas regains his memory?"

"I believe you know the answer to that as well as I do."

Nathen spoke up, "Well, I don't know the answer, so why don't you enlighten me."

Serena continued. "The memories of all his beatings will flood his mind. He will not be able to retreat to his safe place. And the pain of his injuries will attack him ten-fold. He will suffer, horrifically, and his only salvation will be to die."

An eerie silence filled the hut. Authia, tears running freely down her cheeks, gazed upon Nathen as she tried to speak, but no words came forth. Her thoughts filled Nathen's mind. *We have to protect Tomas.*

I know my Love. There must be some way. "Serena, how can we prevent him from regaining his memory?"

"Short of keeping him isolated from reality, I do not see how we can. If he sees you and Saburo together, he will regain his memory. If he sees the man who beat him, he could regain his memory. I am sorry, my Lord. There is nothing we can do for Tomas. His fate was sealed the day they captured him."

Obasi felt weak, almost to the point of exhaustion. He had been pushing himself for hours, closing the gap between him and Saburo. His body screamed at him to rest, to nourish himself. But his mind, overtaken by greed, distrust, and hate, won out. The afternoon slipped into evening, and as the sun made its final appearance in the western sky, Obasi finally slowed his pace to a walk. He scrutinized the trail he had been following. It lay before him like a beacon to his innermost desires. Saburo had not bothered to conceal the path he and Tomas made. Obasi knew that he wouldn't dare incur his wrath. The ferns, vines and jungle floor that had been disturbed by Tomas' machete were fresh. They were close. Tomorrow Obasi would no longer be following a path—he would be following Saburo himself.

Saburo had a firm grip on Greg's forearm as he roughly pulled him toward the area where he'd last seen Tomas. How he was going to explain Greg to Tomas, he had no idea. He was flying by the seat of his pants. The path Tomas cut was beginning to close in around them till it disappeared altogether. Saburo stopped as he listened to the sounds that surrounded him. He scanned the area desperately trying to find any sign of Tomas. "Shit!"

"Lose someone?" Greg snickered at Saburo.

Saburo let go of Greg's arm, grabbed the front of his shirt, and brought his face within inches of his own. "Keep your god damn mouth shut, or I will shut it for you." He let go of Greg's shirt and pushed him away.

Greg stumbled but managed to keep standing and smiling.

Saburo's emotions were running high. He was angry—the last thing he needed was a prisoner. By rights, he should kill him, but something deep inside was nagging at him. He needed to keep him alive. He was also frightened, mostly for himself. What if he'd lost Tomas? Obasi would not hesitate to kill him. He needed to find Tomas. However, in Tomas' current state of mind, he could be anywhere. He looked around again, but there was no sign of Tomas anywhere. Where would he go? He was loyal to this person he called his Lord. Why would he desert him? Saburo's mind was racing. Then he realized that Tomas would never desert him. He had sworn to protect him. So, where was he? Slowly Saburo looked up, into the trees and there, sitting on a branch several feet off the ground was Tomas. Of course, he would hide in the trees. That was what he'd done before. "Tomas, what are you doing up there?"

Tomas stared down at Saburo, his machete firmly grasped in his right hand. "Waiting for you, my Lord. Are you all right? Who is that with you?"

"I am fine, Tomas. Please come down."

Tomas scaled down the tree with the agility of a monkey. He stood in front of Saburo, not taking his gaze off the man standing next to him. "Is he a threat?" Tomas pointed his machete at the man. "Should I take care of him, my Lord?"

"No, Tomas. He's not a threat." Saburo turned and glared at Greg. "You're not going to be trouble, right?" Greg just shook his head. "See, Tomas. We'll keep him with us until I decide what to do with him."

Tomas shrugged his shoulders, turned, and started hacking at the foliage, clearing a path to his destination. For hours they made their way through the jungle, and as the sun was about to set, Tomas broke through into a clearing. It was a reasonably large area with apparent signs of people bedding down around the fire pit. At the edge of the clearing was an area packed down by what appeared to be large, narrow crates.

Tomas turned to face Saburo. "This is the place, my Lord. There is the path to the pond." Tomas pointed with his machete to the left of the clearing. "Will you be taking that man to the pond? Will you be removing his bonds?" Tomas stared at the man as if he were deep in thought. "Will he be punished?"

"Why would we punish him, Tomas?"

Tomas continued to stare at the man. "Is that not what we do to prisoners? We hurt them."

Saburo realized that Tomas could be starting to remember, and if he did, the outcome would surely end in Suburo's demise. "No, Tomas. He's not a prisoner. I tied his hands for his own protection. See, I'm removing them now." Saburo stood behind Greg and removed his bindings. Greg rubbed his wrists as Saburo purposely stood between Tomas and Greg. "No one is getting hurt. Will you be okay if I go to the pond with this man?"

"Of course, my Lord. I will find us dinner." Tomas turned and disappeared into the jungle.

Saburo turned to face Greg. "You know this place?" Greg remained quiet. "I asked you a question."

"I thought you wanted me to shut up?"

"Don't play games with me. This place shows all the signs that your men were here. Am I right?"

"Yeah, you'd be right. What are you going to do about it?"

"Where are they headed?"

"South."

"And what is to the south of us?"

"Why are you following this little man?"

"Look, I'm between a rock and a hard place right now. Obasi is close, and if I don't give him what he wants, he's going to kill me. I've got to level the playing field."

"And how are you going to do that?"

Saburo was quiet for a moment, just staring at Greg. What he was about to do could get him killed whether he found this valley of the Gods or not. "I'm going to let you go."

Greg appeared stunned by Saburo's decision. "You're going to let me go? Why? So you can hunt me down?"

"No. I want you to find your men and warn them. Obasi is coming, and he's heavily armed. He wants whatever is to the south. I'm supposed to find it for him. However, I don't think that any scenario Obasi has in mind is going to work in my favor."

"So, that's it. You're just going to let me go so I can warn the very people that you've tried to kill."

"You're going to warn them and tell them that for your life, I want their protection. They seem to be headed in the direction Tomas is taking me, so I'm sure I'm going to run into them sooner or later. I can help. I can give you Obasi. I *will* give you Obasi."

CHAPTER TWENTY-FIVE

Tammy stood by the communal firepit, Joshawa sitting at her feet. He had a bowl of meat and bread in his lap. Joshawa was oblivious to Tammy as he devoured his supper. Tammy gazed down at Joshawa and smiled as she watched Joshawa shove another handful of meat into his mouth with the palm of his hand. She looked back up and stared off in the direction of the gathering hut. Hansen and the others had been in the hut for hours. The sun was already disappearing behind the tall trees that lined the western sky. She sighed as she sat next to Joshawa, placing another piece of meat in his bowl. "I guess they'll come out when they're ready."

Nathen was exhausted. They had spent the last few hours bringing their guests up to speed on who and what the Jelani Tribe was. And their guests had brought them up to speed on what they were up against. Now, all they needed was a plan. If only it were that simple. Nathen had patiently listened as the group bantered back and forth on how they could protect the tribe. Unfortunately, all they'd accomplished was giving him a colossal headache. Nathen raised his hands in front of him, his palms facing out, and he also raised his voice so that he could be heard over everyone else. "Okay, enough!"

One of the warriors that were standing guard outside the hut entered. "Is everything all right, my Lord?"

Everyone stopped speaking and looked over to Nathen. "Yes, it's fine." The warrior bowed and left the hut. "We're tired, and we're not accomplishing anything. It's late, and I, for one, am ready to call it a night. We'll perform the welcome ceremony tomorrow morning. Is that all right with you,

Casandra?"

"Of course, my Lord."

Nathen stood and extended his hand to help Authia up. "Use everything you've learned today to come up with a plan to defend the tribe. I want ideas from everyone." Nathen glanced over to his guests. "Keep in mind that our gifts, for the most part, do not extend past this valley. The priestesses can only meld with individuals that have the same gift. With the exception of Authia and Hansen, no one from this tribe can venture past the falls."

Rick spoke up. "But didn't a couple of your warriors leave your valley to protect Authia when she came to meet us?"

"Yes, and they did so at great peril. I will not permit anyone from the tribe to leave this valley. Keep that in mind when you're formulating your plan."

"That's all well and fine, but I have a man on the other side of those falls, and he has no idea where we are. I have to send someone back, tonight."

"Not tonight. There are many dangers in the jungle beside the two-legged variety. I'll have one of my men escort one of your men to the falls first thing in the morning. He'll wait there until your man returns and then escort them back." Nathen and Authia left the hut, and following close behind them were the two warriors that were standing guard outside. Nathen stopped and turned to face them. "Why are you following us?"

The larger of the two warriors spoke. "There are strangers in our village. We will stay by your side and see to your protection."

"We don't need protecting from these men. Lead the men waiting on the edge of our village to the gathering hut, then bring them sleeping mats, water, and food. They are not to leave the hut unless they have to relieve themselves. If they do, only one man at a time, and have two warriors guarding him."

The two warriors appeared puzzled at Nathen's request. Nathen, not impressed by having to explain himself, gave the two men a look of pure frustration. "I'm protecting them from us, and from the animals that lie await outside of our village." Nathen started to leave but then changed his mind. "And have Tuval meet me at my hut first thing in the morning." With that, Nathen turned, and he and Authia headed toward the communal firepit.

Authia looked up at him and giggled. "Are we a little cranky?"

Nathen looked down at Authia and smiled. "I'm tired, and I'm hungry. I'm not cranky."

"Says you. Look, Tammy's by the firepit. I don't see Joshawa, though. Maybe he's napping. Let's go and get you something to eat. Then maybe I can help brighten your spirits."

"My spirits don't . . ." Nathen looked back down to Authia who seductively smiled back at him.

"Maybe my spirits do need brightening." Nathen wore an ear to ear grin as he approached Tammy.

"Well, don't you look happy. What's going on?"

"Apparently my spirits need brightening. Something Authia is very skilled in accomplishing."

"Ahhh . . ." Tammy smirked at Nathen and Authia as she handed them each a bowl that contained meat, fruit, and bread. "Maybe you don't want these?"

Nathen took the bowl from Tammy. "I most certainly do."

As he was eating, Hansen joined the group. Tammy passed him a bowl as well. "Thanks, sweetheart. So, Nathen, what do you think of our guests?"

"Not sure. They brought some powerful weaponry, but they admitted that they're not skilled soldiers."

"Don't need to be skilled, just smart. With the right plan in place, I think that we may just have a shot. However, I don't know how you're going to fight Celest without at least one priestess leaving this valley."

"I know." Nathen placed his bowl on the ground. "Somehow we have to get Serena and Casandra to the village without anyone seeing them. But that is a problem for tomorrow." Nathen took Authia's bowl from her and placed it on the ground next to his.

"Hey, I wasn't finished."

"I promise to bring you as much food as you want . . . later. Tammy, is Joshawa asleep?"

"Yes, and conveniently in my hut. Go, have your fun. Aunty Tammy and Uncle Bill will take care of Joshawa tonight."

"Hansen . . . it's Uncle Hansen."

Tammy frowned as she slightly shook her head. "That sounds weird."

"Well, so does Uncle Bill. What do you think, Nathen?"

"I think I'm going to take my wife to bed."

Authia giggled as she wrapped her arms around Nathen's bicep. "Goodnight, you two."

Rick and Travis made sure all their men were fed and settled for the night. The gathering hut was the only hut in the village that didn't have a fire pit, and because of the lack of ventilation, one was not permitted. Rick thought of going to the large fire pit in the center of the village to warm up the coffee, but then decided not to. It was quite unnerving being outside of the hut and having the entire village watch every move he made. Instead, he unfastened his sleeping bag from his backpack and laid it out next to Travis. "Village life ends early." Rick crawled into the sleeping bag, lay on his back, and laced his fingers behind his head as he stared up at the ceiling of the hut. "I hate that we're all confined to this hut."

Travis removed his shirt and sat cross-legged on top of his sleeping bag. "I think it's just for our benefit. It's easier to keep an eye on us if we're all in one place."

"True enough. I don't like leaving Greg alone out there."

"It's just for tonight. He's smart. He'll know to wait. Besides. I don't think we'd get two feet past this hut without a spear in our face."

"Yeah, you're right Travis. There's no sense upsetting the locals. What do you think this *welcoming ceremony* is all about?"

"I don't know. But as long as it doesn't involve blood or a human sacrifice, it should be all right."

Rick chuckled. "Thanks for that visual. Have you given much thought to a plan to beat Obasi?"

Travis glanced over at Rick. "He has forty plus men. We have fourteen."

"I wouldn't discount the locals. They may not know how to use a firearm, but that doesn't make them any less dangerous."

"True, but we still need to even the odds. And if we can't use the warriors or the priestess' gifts to our advantage, then we have to come up with a plan that doesn't involve them."

"We can't use them on the other side of the falls, but we should be able to use them here. We just need to find out exactly what they can do and how we can use it to our benefit."

"I agree, Rick, but I think we need to formulate a plan that doesn't rely on sorcery. We have to break up Obasi's men like he did ours. After we get Greg, we should mine the hell out of the village on the other side of the falls. Then place some of our men in the trees to fire on any of Obasi's men that make it through the minefield. Then we'll need a second wave of attack. If this Tomas guy is showing Saburo the way here, then we have to assume that Obasi also knows how to get here. If any of his men make it past the falls, we should have a second wave waiting for them there. The clearing that you walk into when you leave the falls is surrounded by jungle. Nathen's warriors could easily hide there, then once Obasi's men clear the falls, just hammer them with everything these locals have. And for good measure, we should have one last line of defense at the village itself. That will be mostly our men. There must be someplace we can hide the women and children. Then, with the help of Nathen's warriors and priestesses, we form a barricade that completely encircles the village. We may not have grenades, but we do have dynamite and plenty of rifles."

Rick glanced over at Travis. He grinned to let Travis know that he was pleased with his plan. "I knew there was a reason I kept you around. We'll present this plan to Nathen in the morning. Any ideas on how to handle Serena's mother?"

"That's totally up to Nathen. Sorcery and evil spirits are beyond my realm of experience." Travis climbed into his sleeping bag, rolled onto his left side, his back facing Rick, and closed his eyes. "Rick, you do know that this is more or less a suicide mission?"

"Unfortunately, yes, I do."

The moon shone brightly above Saburo's campsite. He had to pretend he was sleeping in order for Tomas to fall asleep. He watched Tomas, curled into a ball, sleeping peacefully. He was an incredibly loyal little man. He would defend who he thought was the Lord of a mysterious valley to his death. And ask nothing in return. Loyalty such as his was scarce, pretty much nonexistent in the men who followed Obasi. Obasi's men didn't respect him, they feared him. Saburo threw another log on the fire. He gazed around at his surroundings.

He knew if Obasi was close, he would see the fire. He would know where Saburo was, and that was fine with him. Wherever Tomas was taking him, it was close, half a day away. He thought of the man he had captured and realized that he was taking a huge risk letting him go. But deep down, Saburo knew his days were numbered with Obasi. Once again, he glanced over to Tomas. He wasn't a threat to Obasi. He wasn't in a position physically or mentally to defend himself against Obasi, and Obasi knew that, but still, he'd beaten him. He knew that Tomas couldn't provide a military advantage, but still, he beat him almost to death. This was the man that Saburo had sworn loyalty to. However, both he and Obasi knew that Saburo's loyalty wasn't for the protection of Obasi but for something much more precious to Saburo. Slowly Saburo shook his head. Ever since Obasi heard Tomas speak of the valley that the Gods protected, he had become even more ruthless, more dangerous. If Saburo was going to have any chance of survival, he had to switch sides. And he had to do that before he found the valley. His life rested solely on the hope that Greg would do as Saburo asked and convince a group of men that most likely hated him to protect him. Saburo stood, took one last glance at Tomas, then headed toward the pond.

Tomas lay quiet on the jungle floor. He was curled up into a ball, close to the fire. He could feel its warmth, and even though the night had only cooled slightly from the heat of the day, he welcomed the warmth, for it made him feel safe, as if a warm blanket had been wrapped around him. From the corner of his eye, he watched the Lord of the Lion People. Tomas knew the Lord hadn't fallen asleep. He knew that something was different, though he couldn't quite put his finger on it. That other man, it was as if Tomas had seen him before. But no matter how much he searched his mind, he couldn't remember when he would have seen him. Once the Lord had disappeared down the path to the pond, Tomas got up, picked up his machete, and followed him. All he could think of was to protect the Lord, nothing else mattered.

Obasi finally called it a night. He climbed a nearby Kapok tree and sat on one of its larger branches. He'd be protected from most of the predators of the night. However, snakes were always an issue, whether you were in a tree or on the ground. He pulled out his bush knife from its protective sleeve that was attached to his belt. He cut a piece of vine, then proceeded to bind the butt of the knife to the palm of his hand. He knew that when he fell asleep, he wouldn't drop the knife, and it could very well save his life if a python came his way. Obasi settled on his tree branch as he rested his back against the trunk of the tree. The branch easily supported his weight, and its sheer girth would make it almost impossible to see Obasi from the ground. He would sit there, facing south. In the distance, he could see the glow from a campfire. A small smile graced his lips — he was so close. He looked behind him to the north and could see the glow from the fires his men had made. They were less than a day away. Obasi made himself comfortable, and as he succumbed to sleep, he dreamt of a valley rich with gold, a valley drenched in the blood of his enemy, and he was at peace.

CHAPTER TWENTY-SIX

Nathen sat by Authia, watching her every move. Slowly she woke up and stretched her arms above her head. "Good morning, my Love."

Nathen lay down next to Authia, wrapping her in his arms, pulling her tight against his naked body. "You feel so good. Thank you for last night."

Authia looked up and smiled at Nathen. "You were pretty amazing yourself."

Nathen leaned in and softly kissed Authia. "I wish I could express to you what it feels like to have you in my life. To have someone love me. Physically, emotionally, sexually. Before I met you, I was nothing. I belonged nowhere. I never considered myself a man, but rather some sort of beast. Then you came along and gave me your love. You gave me a reason to live. And I thank the heavens every day for that gift. For Tanya sending you my way." Nathen ran his hand along Authia's belly. She was just starting to show, and Nathen could sense the child that lay secure within her belly. He felt the baby's heartbeat, and he felt every move the baby made. "And to make my life even more special, you are gifting me with a second child."

"You had something to do with that. Nathen, you are the most wonderful man I have ever met. Loving you is easy." Authia reached up and tenderly kissed Nathen. "Now maybe we should get up and go get our son. Plus, I have to get ready."

Nathen looked dumbfounded at Authia as she stood up and started getting dressed in her jean shorts and t-shirt. "Ready for what, and why are you putting on your shorts?"

Authia smirked at Nathen. "Well, I'm not crossing the falls

in my animal skins. Your rules . . . remember?"

Nathen sat up and reached over for his loincloth. "Who said you were crossing the falls?"

Authia pulled her t-shirt over her head. "I have to go. How are we going to know what's going on over there if I don't go?"

Nathen stood and wrapped his loincloth around his waist. "I don't think so. We can find out what's happening when the men get back."

"Okay, now you're just being stupid."

Nathen shot Authia a shocked look.

"What if something's going on over there and the men don't come back?"

"All the more reason for you not to go."

"You know as well as I do that I have to go. I'll have Rick send two of his men with me, and they will be heavily armed. I won't leave the safety of the jungle until I know the village is safe. Besides, I want to see if I can find out anything more about Celest."

Nathen's mind ran wild with all the different scenarios that could happen on the other side of the falls — and none of them were good. "I don't like you putting yourself in danger." He walked over to Authia and placed his right hand on the side of her face. "I don't know what I would do if I lost you."

"You're not going to lose me. Now let's go get Joshawa, then head for the gathering hut."

Nathen watched as Authia left the hut. His gut was churning, and he felt as though he was going to be sick.

Rick woke to the aroma of pork and coffee that had wafted into the hut from what he assumed was the large firepit in the center of the village. He climbed out of his sleeping bag to discover that most of his men were still asleep. Gently he kicked at Travis' feet. "Okay sleeping beauty, time to get up."

Travis opened his eyes and looked around. "Right, the hut. What time is it?"

"No idea. Haven't been outside of the hut yet. Get up, and we'll go find Nathen."

Travis grabbed his t-shirt, kicked off his sleeping bag, and got up. He was pulling the t-shirt over his head as he and Rick tried to leave the hut. However, the minute they stepped outside, two warriors, spears in hand, blocked their path. Rick glared at them trying, without much success, to appear intimidating. "What the hell? We need to see your Lord." The warriors didn't move. "Now!" Still, they didn't move. Rick glanced past them toward the fire pit. From where he stood, he could see Authia. "All right, you Neanderthals, I have to see Authia, and she's right there." Rick pointed toward the firepit, but the warriors didn't budge. Rick yelled, trying to capture Authia's attention. He watched as she turned to face the gathering hut. "Can you call your watchdogs off?"

Authia smiled and spoke to one of the warriors standing next to her. He picked up his spear and headed toward Rick and Travis. "Follow me." The two warriors blocking their path moved to one side, and Rick and Travis followed their new bodyguard to the firepit. "What the hell, Authia. We can't even leave the hut?"

"Trust me, it's for your own protection. It will all be fine once we welcome you to the tribe. But before we do that, I think we should go find your man."

Travis spoke up. "We need to speak with Nathen first. We have a plan that just might work."

"You do? That's great. He'll be here right away . . . he just went to get our son."

Seconds later Rick saw Nathen heading toward them with his son and accompanied by Hansen. Nathen didn't appear happy. If looks could kill, he and Travis would be dead where they stood. Nathen joined them, handing Joshawa over to Authia. "Great news, sweetheart. Rick and Travis have a plan, and if you wipe that scowl off your face, they just might share it with you."

Nathen gave Authia a dirty look, then turned his attention to Travis and Rick. "You came up with a plan?"

Travis nodded. "Yes. When we head out to find Greg, which we should do sooner than later, we'll bring the crate of mines with us and let's say four of our men. We'll plant mines all over the village then leave four of our men in the trees. When either Saburo or Obasi come, the minute they enter the village, they will start setting off the mines. The men that don't get blown up by the mines will be picked off by our men in the trees."

Nathen asked, "And what if they get past your men?"

"That's when your warriors come in. Have as many as you can spare in the jungle by the falls. If anyone enters the valley, your warriors will wait till the last man clears the falls and then hit them with everything they have. As an added precaution we'll set up a defense on the outskirts of the village. Any voodoo your priestesses can offer will help. Is there any place the women and children can hide?"

"My Lord." Everyone turned to find Casandra and Serena standing behind them. "We can send the women, elderly, and children to the birthing hut."

Nathen shook his head. "I don't think that's far enough. If we fail, it will only be a matter of time before they find the hut."

Serena smirked at Nathen. "You of little faith."

"You have a way to protect the birthing hut?"

"Yes, my Lord, and possibly the village as well."

"Enlighten me."

Authia watched the interaction between Nathen and Serena. Serena always enjoyed baiting Nathen, but now there was far more respect in her tone.

"As long as this tree stands, I will protect you. Do you remember those words?"

Nathen went quiet as he stared blankly at the group.

Authia could tell he was recalling a memory. She was about to meld with him when he spoke. "You know I do. And I see where you are going with this. The tree still stands, and if it stands, my father will be there to help protect the birthing hut."

"Exactly. Between your father and let's say two of our priestesses, the enemy will never see the birthing hut. They'll only see the jungle."

Rick spoke up, "Okay, not sure what you two are talking about, but if we are going to plant those mines, we had better leave now. I'll pick out four of my men, and we're going to need that yellow globe to get through the falls."

Authia spoke up, "I'll take care of that, and if your men are going to hide in the jungle, you're going to need some camouflage. Meet me at the priestess' hut in five minutes." Authia watched as Rick and Travis headed for the gathering hut then she melded with Tamara.

Tamara, I need some of that green mud. Enough for six people.

Yes, my Mistress. Where do you need me to be?

I'll meet you at the Priestess' hut. Oh, and I'm going to need another couple of packets for the falls.

Of course.

Thank you, Tamara.

Authia scanned the group that stood before her. "Okay, I'm going with Rick and Travis. If there is anything wrong, I'll meld with Tamara."

"You'll meld with me."

"Not a good idea, Nathen. You're too emotionally attached. I need someone with a clear head."

Nathen didn't respond, which evoked a smile from Authia.

She knew he understood. "So, we have the human threat covered, how about the supernatural one?" Authia directed her question to Serena and Casandra.

Casandra responded, "You'll have to leave that one to Serena and me. In order for us to defeat Celest, we will have to leave our valley and wait at the village."

"But you could be seen. And won't Celest know that you're there and suspect something?"

"That's the least of our problems. By the time we make ourselves known, no one is going to care what we look like. And as far as Celest is concerned, yes, she'll know we are there. But in her present state, there's nothing she can do."

"But if she knows you're there, then won't she be ready for you when she can do something about it?"

"The best time to confront Celest is after she has chosen her host. Then we make our move."

Authia was stunned. "You want her to join with *The Destroyer*?"

Serena laughed. "The host is not *The Destroyer* until Celest becomes one with him. We have to make our move when she is at her most vulnerable, which will be when she is in the process of joining with her chosen host. Even knowing that we are there, she will still have to focus all her energy on the host. Those few minutes will be our opportunity to destroy her."

"So, you're going to wait until this Obasi person shows up?"

Casandra and Serena looked at each other then smiled at Authia, answering in unison. "Yes."

Ten minutes later, the priestesses hut was full to capacity. Four of Rick's men, as well as Rick, had shown up as requested. Authia, Nathen, Hansen, and Tamara were there as well. Authia searched the room for Travis, but he was nowhere to be seen. "Rick, where's Travis?"

"We can't both go. He's going to stay behind and help organize our second line of defense as well as start helping move everyone to the birthing hut."

"You think we need to move everyone now?"

"Better sooner than later. If we move them now, we can make sure they're settled and protected. So, what's this camouflage you were speaking of?"

"It's the best. You can hide in the trees, and no one will be the wiser." Authia went to the table at the back of the hut and collected two of the four bowls. She gave one to Tamara and one to the group of men. "Apply it to any exposed skin."

Tamara walked over to Rick and scooped some of the mud with her fingertips. Gently she applied it to Rick's forehead. "Do not be afraid to apply it generously." She ran her fingers down his nose and over his left cheek. Authia watched the interaction between Rick and Tamara. Tamara was lost in her endeavor to make sure Rick's face and neck were completely covered, while Rick just stared at her. Authia smirked, for she'd seen that look before when Hansen first met Tammy. And then her smile faded. At some point, Tamara's true features would return, and that could just lead to heartache. She was so lost in her thoughts that she didn't hear Hansen approach her.

"Penny for your thoughts."

Authia turned to find Hansen standing there with a bowl of green mud in his hands. "What are you doing?"

"Going with you."

"No. There's no need. I have plenty of protection."

"Yes, you do." Hansen glanced over at Nathen. "But I know Nathen would feel better if I was at your side."

Nathen smiled as he nodded his head in agreement. "Yes, I would. Thank you, Hansen."

"You're very welcome. Now, Authia, how about applying

some of this mud to your face and arms."

Twenty minutes later, the entire group, including Tammy, Travis, Tamara, and Nathen, were at the falls. Rick called for everyone's attention. "Okay, everyone, here's how it's going to play out. We have no idea who or what is waiting for us on the other side. Our main objective is to find Greg, keep Authia safe, and plant these mines. John, Ed, you head in first. If the coast is clear, then Ed, you come back and get us." John and Ed each carried two pistols on their belt as well as a large hunting knife. They both carried rifles and had enough ammo to stand their ground for some time.

Authia spoke up, "I'm going to have to go with them. These packets will only work for me. I'll follow the men through the falls, and then I'll come back to get the rest of you."

"Fine. When Authia comes back, I'll lead my men with the litter. Hansen, you follow next. Authia, you take up the rear. If there's any trouble, Hansen, I want you to get Authia back on this side. If the coast is clear, then we'll head to the village, and hopefully, Greg will be there waiting for us. Okay, if everyone is clear, let's get this done."

Tammy walked over to Hansen. He was covered in green mud, carrying a machete, and had a large hunting knife secured to his belt. "I hate it when you do this."

"Sweetheart, I can't just stand by and watch. You know that."

"I know. Doesn't mean I have to like it. Can't even kiss you with all that muck on you."

Hansen smiled at Tammy. "You can kiss me when I get back."

Authia smiled at Nathen, who was standing next to Tammy. "You, too. Don't worry. Just take care of Joshawa. I'll be back before you know it." Authia turned to Ed and John. "All right, guys, you're up." She walked over to the falls, took one last glance over her shoulder, then raised her hand in front of her. She opened her palm, revealing the leaf cover packet. As before, it started glowing, and then a large yellow globe started to form. Ed and John walked past her, and the three entered the falls.

Greg had spent the better part of the night following the trail Taylor had left for him. Not that it mattered, because the trail Rick and the men had left was as blatant as a neon sign. Now, in the early hours of the morning, Greg looked at the mountain he had to climb. According to Travis, that was where they would be waiting. Waiting for a blue wisp. Greg shook his head in annoyance, since he didn't believe in ghosts and goblins, or wisps for that matter. And if he hadn't seen it for himself, he would have thought his entire platoon was going nuts. For the next couple of hours, Greg followed the trail. The air was getting thin, his head ached, and no matter how much water he consumed, he still felt light-headed. There was one thing he was grateful for. Traveling so early in the morning meant it was still relatively cool, and the bugs had only just begun to swarm. He had kept alert, checking behind him constantly, expecting to find Saburo hot on his heels.

After what felt like forever, Greg had reached his objective. But it wasn't what he was expecting—the village was trashed. There was debris scattered throughout the clearing. Only one hut remained standing, and as he approached it, a cold shiver ran down his spine. He stopped, not taking his focus off the hut. Something told him to stay clear, that it wasn't safe. Greg scrutinized his surroundings, looking for some sign of his companions. The footprints were chaotic, heading in all directions. Cautiously he walked over to the far edge of the clearing, and through the jungle he could see what appeared to be a waterfall and a pond. He looked back over his shoulder at the destruction that was once a village. If his companions had survived whatever happened here, they would have sought out a water source. Greg entered the jungle and headed toward the falls. He was desperate as he searched for a sign, any sign, that his friends were still alive.

CHAPTER TWENTY-SEVEN

Ed led the way along the path behind the falls, keeping as close to the wall as he could. Even though he'd already experienced walking in the yellow globe, he was still mesmerized by the sheer power one little green leaf packet held. And he was also impressed by the power contained within Authia which allowed her to project something that defied everything he believed in. They made their way to the edge of the opening, then Ed raised his hand shoulder height and balled his fist, indicating he wanted the group to stop. He scanned the area surrounding the falls and the pond but saw nothing. Without taking his focus off the opening, he reached behind him and pulled a set of binoculars from a pouch attached to the back of his belt. He raised them to his eyes and focused them on the jungle itself. Besides some birds and monkeys, the jungle appeared to be quiet. He was about to lower his arms when he caught a glimpse of something that had moved in the jungle. Something that was heading toward them. He adjusted the binoculars bringing into focus what he believed would be Obasi. Seconds later, Greg came into view. Ed smile broadly. *Thank God.* He put the binoculars away and signaled everyone to move ahead.

Greg slowly made his way through the jungle, acutely aware of his surroundings. Anything, anyone, could be waiting for him when he exited the jungle. He stood at the very edge, just a step away from being totally exposed, and that was when he saw it. A yellow light was coming from behind the falls. Greg stared in utter disbelief at what appeared to be a large globe emerging from the falls. He tilted his head slightly as he tried to make out what was inside the globe. Then, as suddenly as it appeared, it was gone, and standing in its place were three people. Greg couldn't believe what he was seeing — the two men were from his platoon. Greg walked out into the clearing not caring who the woman was. All he hoped was that Ed and John were not the only survivors. He waved at the group as he walked toward them. "Am I glad to see you. Where's everyone else? And what the hell are you covered in?"

Ed laughed as he extended his hand. "Glad to see you too. I want you to meet the people we're going to be protecting. Or at least their Mistress."

Authia stepped forward. "My name is Authia. It's good to meet you. As for the rest of your men, they're safe in my village." Authia focused her attention on Ed. "I'm going to head back and get the others." She left the group and once again, Greg watched as a yellow globe encased her and then she was gone.

Greg shook his head in disbelief. "What the hell is that all about?"

Ed spoke up, "Long story. We'll explain when we get back to the village. In the meantime, we're going to be planting a few mines in the village. Want to help?" Greg was about to answer when the men were distracted as once again, a yellow globe appeared from behind the falls.

Rick, leading the group, approached Greg. "Man, it's good to see you." He extended his right hand to Greg at the same time placing his left hand on Greg's shoulder. "I was afraid we might have lost you."

"It was touch and go for a bit. Is Taylor with you?"

"Yeah, he's back at the village. I want you to meet Hansen. He's Authia's bodyguard."

Greg nodded at Hansen then looked over at the litter that was laying on the ground. "I thought you said a few mines.

You brought the whole damn crate."

Rick responded, "I want the entire clearing in the village littered with these mines. When Obasi and his men come, I want to blow them to kingdom come."

"Sounds good to me. However, you may want to hold off for a bit."

Authia gave Greg a look of disapproval. "And why would we want to do that?"

"Cause Saburo is right behind me, and he wants to change sides."

Ed laughed. "Yeah, right. And I'm going to grow horns."

"Seriously. He captured me yesterday. Told me that he doesn't see a favorable future for himself when it comes to Obasi. He let me go so I could tell you, Rick, that he wants our protection."

John spoke up, "He wants our protection against Obasi? And why should we do that?"

"He says he'll give us Obasi. Look, I think he's serious. At no time did he try to hurt me, and he had plenty of opportunities. And he's very protective of the pygmy that's leading him here."

Authia gasped. "What pygmy?"

"I don't know. Some man he calls Tomas."

Authia stood there with her mouth gaping open. "Tomas is still with Saburo, and he's still alive?" She looked at Hansen then back at Rick. "We can't mine the area until Tomas is safe. Greg, how close are they?"

"If they left before sunrise, I'd say very close. A good half-day ahead of Obasi."

"Well, that settles it. We'll wait for Saburo and Tomas. Then we'll mine the clearing. Hansen, you're with me."

Greg glanced over at Rick. "Is she calling the shots?"

Rick watched as Authia and Hansen disappeared into the jungle. "Sure in hell looks that way."

Authia made her way into the clearing and straight for Sensay's hut. Celest's aura hung like a heavy veil cloaking the hut in darkness and evil. Authia stopped a few feet away and stared inside. She didn't see the apparition that Travis had spoken of, but what she did see frightened her to her very core. Celest's aura was beginning to take shape. There was a dense fog that encompassed the entire hut. As Authia concentrated on the fog, it appeared as if it were taking on the shape of a person. However, it was fazing in and out of focus. Nervously, Authia melded with Casandra.

Casandra, can you hear me?

Yes, my Mistress. Is everything all right?

It's Celest. She's starting to take shape. Authia waited for a reply, but none came. *Casandra? Are you still there?*

What shape is she taking?

It's like a dense fog in the shape of a person, but it doesn't look as though she can maintain the shape. It keeps dispersing and almost fills the entire hut.

She's preparing. She's getting stronger. The host she has chosen must be close.

He's about half a day away.

It may be time for Serena and me to make our way to the village. It's imperative that we are there when Celest's host arrives.

You might be right. But be careful. Rick and his men are going to be mining the entire village.

Authia was about to continue, but something behind her distracted her. Slowly she turned to see Tomas standing at the edge of the jungle. Behind him was a man who Authia assumed was Saburo. She was about to call out to Tomas when she heard a high-pitched cry coming from the hut. It was deafening, and as Authia turned to face the hut, the fog that once filled the hut burst free. Its cry echoed throughout the jungle, and before Authia could move, it crashed through her. Authia's body jerked from the sheer force that collided with her body. It tore through her compressing her chest so that she couldn't take a breath. Authia desperately clawed at her throat, trying to breathe, but it was if she was in a vacuum. Seconds later, everything went dark, and Authia crumbled to the ground.

Nathen, Arman, Tuval and four warriors were waiting in the clearing at the falls. Nathen was pacing, impatiently waiting for Authia's return. Suddenly he stopped and faced the falls. The feeling of apprehension was starting to build inside of him like a volcano ready to erupt.

Arman went to stand next to Nathen. "What troubles you, my Lord?"

"She's been gone too long."

"She was here only moments ago, my Lord. I'm sure she's fine."

"I'm not so con . . ." Nathen stopped midsentence. He felt Authia's fear, her pain. And then there was nothing. Desperately he tried to meld with her, but there was no response. Nathen had started to head for the falls only to have Tuval and Arman hold him back.

"You can't go there, my Lord. You must stay on this side." Arman and Tuval each had a firm grip on Nathen's forearms. He glared at them, the anger welling up deep inside of him. He tore free with ease and started to run toward the opening. He had only made it a couple of feet when Arman and Tuval tackled him. With the help of the other warriors, they were able to pin him to the ground. "You can't go, my Lord. You know that."

Nathen roared at the men. "Let me go! Authia's in trouble. I have to save her."

"My Mistress was very adamant that no one follows her to

the other side."

Nathen struggled with everything he had, but he couldn't shake the men off him. "Don't you understand? She's in danger. I have to go to her." Tears started running down Nathen's cheeks. "I have to save her."

Hansen stood at the edge of the clearing watching Authia as she approached Sensay's hut. She stood there for just a minute, then turned around. Hansen followed her gaze and saw Tomas and another man standing just a few feet away from him. Hansen was about to walk over to Tomas when a deafening, high-pitched sound came from the hut. He covered his ears as he watched a large fog-like mass fly from the hut. It traveled right through Authia and crashed against what appeared to be an invisible barrier that separated it from Tomas. Over and over the wall of fog crashed against the barrier as it tried to get at Tomas. Its shrill screams echoed throughout the village and sounded much like a wounded animal. Finally, it stopped and flew back into the hut. Hansen ran to Authia's side. She lay on the ground, motionless, and she wasn't breathing. Quickly Hansen tilted Authia's head ever so slightly then proceeded to give her CPR. Rick joined him, compressing her chest as Hansen pinched her nose and breathed into her mouth. After what felt like several minutes but in reality, was seconds, Authia started chocking. Hansen helped her sit up as she struggled to breathe. "Are you okay?"

Authia took a couple of deep breaths. "I'm fine, Hansen. Thank you. How long was I out?"

"Not long. What the hell happened? What was in that fog? It looked like it had a mind of its own."

"Believe me, it does." Authia took another deep breath

then realized that Nathen would know that she was hurt. "Oh my God, Nathen."

"What about him?"

"He'll know something happened." Authia immediately melded with Nathen. *Nathen, are you there?*

Yes, what happened? Are you all right? I tried to come to you, but they wouldn't let me.

I'm fine. I'll explain later. I have to go, but I'll be back soon. Authia stood up and glanced over in Tomas' direction. "Tomas, you're back." Authia walked over to Tomas who respectfully bowed.

"It is good to see you, my Mistress. Are you all right? I have your husband with me." Tomas gazed past Authia to the men that were approaching.

Authia knew what he meant, and she was also aware of the importance of keeping up the charade. "I am fine, Tomas. Thank you for bringing Nathen back to me."

At that point, Saburo walked out from his hiding place behind a Kapok tree. Rick and his men immediately drew their guns only to have Greg step between them. "Okay, put those away. I told you, he's here to help."

Everyone reluctantly holstered their guns while Tomas looked on. Authia kept her attention on Tomas. She knew his mental state was fragile, and he appeared very confused. "Tomas, it's so good to see you. Are you okay?"

Tomas glanced over to Saburo and then back at Authia. "Are you not happy to see your husband?"

"Yes, Tomas, I am. But a lot has gone on. Can we go to the waterfall and talk there?"

"Of course, my Mistress." Tomas took a step forward then stopped. He was looking at Rick as if he knew him. Then he just shook his head, retreated into the jungle, and walked toward the pond, totally ignoring the destruction of his village. Nor did he offer any comment on what had just transpired.

Authia followed Tomas with Hansen at her side. "I don't know, Authia, it's as if he's in his own little world."

"Technically, he is. A world that Serena created for him. So, what happened after I blacked out?"

"That wall of fog went straight for Tomas. But the craziest thing happened. It was as if there was an invisible wall protecting Tomas. The fog just crashed into it over and over, then it finally gave up and went back into the hut."

Authia looked over to Hansen. "It went after Tomas?"

"That's what it looked like. He was the only one there."

"Not true. Saburo was there as well."

"Yeah, but you couldn't see him. He was hidden behind that huge tree."

"That doesn't make sense. Tomas couldn't be the host. He's too good-natured. His resolve to protect the Lion People would make him an unlikely candidate."

"Well, maybe she senses that Obasi is close?"

"Perhaps." Authia watched as Saburo waded into the cool waters of the pond. He went as far as his thighs then dove in. Tomas, however, had stopped short and was staring at the crate of mines. Authia walked over to him and placed her right hand on his shoulder. "What is it, Tomas?"

Tomas didn't take his gaze off the crate. "That should not be here."

"What? The crate?"

"Something is not right." He closed his eyes as if he was trying to recall a memory. "There should be many crates. But not here." Slowly he opened his eyes and gazed up at Authia. "I am not feeling well. I would like to go rest, but not near that crate."

"Of course, Tomas. Why don't you go over to that shaded spot by the pond? I'll come get you when we're leaving." Tomas bowed to Authia and headed off to where he was told to go. Hansen observed him leave. "What do you think that's about? Do you think he's starting to remember?"

Authia just sighed. "I hope not. For his sake." Rick and his men joined Authia and Hansen. A couple of minutes later, Saburo, dripping wet, joined them as well. Authia glared at him. "Are you responsible for his injuries?"

"No. Well, not really."

"What is it? No or yes?"

"He was beaten at Obasi's hand... I just didn't do anything to stop it. That's why this whole façade is working. Because he doesn't fear me."

"What façade?"

"When he was delirious, he spoke of a valley protected by the Gods. Obasi believes that there is treasure in this valley, and he'll do anything to get it. Which includes letting Tomas believe that I am his Lord, and he's showing me the way home."

"My husband knows his way home. Why would Tomas believe that he wouldn't?"

"Because I was able to convince him that I didn't remember. Look, I don't know what's going on in his head. I watched him blaze a trail through the thickest jungle I've ever been through. And he did it with a broken hand, jaw and multiple injuries that should have had him on the ground withering in pain. There's something at work here that's bigger than you, me or anything else for that matter."

"You didn't by chance see a wisp enter Tomas?"

Saburo stared at Authia with his mouth gaping open. "Yes. A blue wisp. What do you know of that?"

"Well let's just say she's the reason he's capable of what you've seen him do." Authia addressed the rest of the group. "Okay, we've got about half a day before Obasi gets here. We have to plant the mines, but most importantly, we have to keep Tomas from seeing the crates or seeing Saburo and Nathen together. I think, by his reaction to you, Rick, that we should keep him clear of you and your men as well."

Saburo interjected, "It would probably be a good idea if he didn't see Obasi, either. Those are memories that I don't think he wants back."

Hansen spoke up, "So what are we going to do with him? He can't come back to the village, and he can't stay here."

Authia smiled. "Actually, he can come back to our village. We just have to make sure he doesn't see Nathen or your men, Rick. I'll have Nathen clear everyone away from the path to the village. Then I'll take him to Sam's hut. If I tell him that he has to stay in the hut, then he will. When this is all over, I'll have Casandra and Serena see what they can do for him." Authia glanced over to where Tomas was resting. A small smile graced her lips. "He's sleeping, so let's get this crate to the village and start planting the mines. Once the mines are planted, everyone here, including you Saburo, can hide in the trees and wait for Obasi and his men. Whoever survives the minefield, pick them off one by one."

Saburo interjected, "Obasi won't enter the clearing himself. He'll probably climb one of the bigger trees that gives him a clear line of sight to the entire village. Then he'll send his men in first. Once the mines start going off, he won't leave the tree. Then, when he starts seeing you firing from the trees, he'll try to pinpoint your location then figure out a way around you. Your best bet is for me to hide close to where he'll be. He's an expert when it comes to blending in, but I'll know. I'll find him, and I'll be happy to put a bullet right between his eyes."

Rick chuckled. "Like I'm going to give you a weapon."

"Why not? I know Obasi. I'm your best chance to kill him."

Rick and his men started arguing with Saburo until Authia raised her voice to get their attention. "Shut up!" She glanced over to Tomas who remained sleeping. "This is not helping." Authia extended her hands to Saburo. "Give me your hands. I should have done this when I first met you."

Saburo looked at Authia then down at her hands. "Done what? Why do you want my hands?"

"Just give them to me."

Reluctantly Saburo took Authia's hands. She closed her eyes then searched deep within Saburo. She witnessed Tomas' beatings, and as she watched Obasi's fist repeatedly slammed into Tomas' face, tears began to run down her cheeks. She witnessed Saburo's cruelty. However, he never laid a hand on Tomas. His emotions, his thoughts were crashing into Authia's mind, which revealed to her his hatred for Obasi and everything he stood for. Authia opened her eyes and let go of Saburo's hands. "Give him a rifle." Rick and his men gawked at Authia. She just sighed and shook her head. "Now! Hansen, stay with Tomas. Make sure he doesn't leave the pond."

"You got it."

Authia stood there until Rick unwillingly handed Saburo his rifle and two clips. "Good, now let's get those mines planted. Saburo, Rick, you're with me." Authia headed into the jungle, Saburo at her side, Rick taking up the rear.

"So, you trust me now?"

"Yes, I do. However, that doesn't forgive your past."

"How can you decide to trust me just by holding my hands?"

"Let's just say it's a gift." Authia glanced over to Saburo as they headed toward the village. "Why the change of mind? Why the sudden compassion for Tomas?"

"Hell, lady, he was of no tactical advantage to Obasi, but yet Obasi still beat him almost to death. That didn't sit well with me, but I couldn't say anything. Obasi would have had me shot if I challenged him. And with all the talk of a valley protected by the Gods, of treasure, Obasi ordered me to use Tomas to find this valley. He doesn't give a shit about Tomas, or me for that matter. He just cares about himself."

"So, are you protecting yourself or Tomas?"

"As I see it, the death of Obasi protects not only Tomas and me but also you and your people. If Obasi finds your village, your people are as good as dead." Saburo and Authia had reached the edge of the jungle. They were about to take a step into the clearing when, once again, the village was filled with high-pitched screams. The fog shot free of the hut and screamed as it flew toward them. Both Saburo and Authia took a step back, and they were about to run when the fog slammed against the invisible barrier that Hansen had spoken of. Saburo immediately put his arm out in front of Authia and took another step back, forcing Authia to step back as well. He was about to grab his rifle, but Authia stopped him. She shook her head as she concentrated on the fog. It had gone quiet and just floated at the edge of the clearing. Authia looked over to Saburo, then back at the fog. With her left hand, she took hold of the back of Saburo's belt and gently nudged him forward. When he stood at the edge of the jungle, the fog went wild. Its screams deafened them. Over and over it crashed against the barrier. Authia pulled Saburo back, and the fog stopped, once again floating at the edge of the clearing. Authia looked back up at Saburo. "I have an experiment I want to do. Come with me." She looked over at Rick. "Stay here. Don't try to go any closer."

Rick, not taking his focus off the fog, answered. "No worries there."

Authia and Saburo headed back to the pond. She went over to Tomas and gently nudged him awake. "Tomas, I need your help."

Tomas sat up and reached for his machete. "Anything, my Mistress."

"Come with me. You too, Hansen." They made their way back into the jungle, but Authia led them to a spot in the clearing where they couldn't see Rick and his men. She positioned Saburo and Tomas just a couple of steps from the edge of the jungle. She watched as the fog shifted away from where Rick and his men were and slowly crept toward them. Authia stood behind Saburo and Tomas. When the fog settled in front of them, she stood behind Tomas, put her hands on his shoulders, and gently moved him closer. The fog remained quiet, just floating in place. She guided Tomas back then did the same with Saburo. The second Saburo stepped at the edge of the jungle, the fog went wild. It screamed at them as it crashed wildly at the barrier. Authia quickly pulled Saburo back, and the fog went quiet. Authia stepped in front of Saburo and Tomas, took a couple of steps forward, but didn't enter the clearing. She closed her eyes and tried to meld with the fog.

I know you can hear me, Celest. I have something you want. Something you need. Authia waited for a response, but none came. She opened her eyes and glanced over to Saburo. "Well, it appears that you're going to play a larger part of our survival than you thought."

"What are you talking about? And what the hell is that?" Saburo pointed toward the fog.

"That is Celest, a very powerful High Priestess. And she has chosen you."

"Chosen me for what?"

"To be *The Destroyer*."

CHAPTER TWENTY-EIGHT

Obasi was tired and hungry, but most of all, he was driven by his desire to find the treasure that he knew was waiting for him in the valley protected by the Gods. It was mid-morning when he entered the camp. He scanned the area and could tell without a doubt that Saburo had spent the night here. He was close, so close. He wanted nothing more than to push on, shorten the distance between him and Saburo. But he also knew that if he was going to be victorious, he needed his strength. Obasi followed the trail that Saburo and Tomas made as they headed toward the mountain. Within ten minutes, Obasi knew where they were going. He gazed up at the top of the mountain that towered before him. Of course, the valley he sought out would be in the heavens with the Gods. He smiled to himself and headed back toward the camp. He would wait until his men reached him. Why put himself in danger when he had an army of men at his disposal? Obasi went into the jungle and found his dinner. He also came across a pond of freshwater. As his meal cooked, Obasi stripped down, then plunged into the refreshing waters of the pond. An hour later, after his belly was full, Obasi chose the most massive tree he could find. He climbed high within its canopy, settling on one of the large branches that stretched out over the camp. From there, he would wait and watch. As soon as his men made it to the camp, he would reveal himself, then let them lead the way to his final destination.

Authia led Saburo and Tomas back to the pond where Hansen was waiting. "You guys wait here. I'll be right back."

Saburo went to join Authia. "I'm coming with you."

"No, you're not. You're staying right here."

"But you need me when Obasi gets here."

Authia smiled at Saburo. "You're right." Then she turned and walked back into the jungle toward Rick and his men. A couple of minutes later, she approached Rick, scanning the village as she spoke to him. "I want you to leave the crate here, then all of us are going to walk into the clearing."

"Are you crazy? What about that fog?"

"She's not in the clearing. Besides she doesn't want you, she wants Saburo."

"Saburo?"

"It's not Obasi that Celest is looking for. For whatever reason, she's chosen Saburo as her host. Now come on, I want to see if there is any reaction when we enter the clearing." Authia walked ahead, not waiting for a reply. She casually strolled to the center of the clearing while keeping her entire focus on the hut. Celest didn't make a sound. Authia glanced over her shoulder and grinned as the men approached her. They were obviously nervous about what could possibly happen. "I think we're okay. She won't bother us . . . she's saving her energy for Saburo. Rick, get your men and start burying the mines. I'm going to take Tomas and Saburo to the village."

Rick looked at Authia in disbelief. "You're taking Saburo? Aren't we going to need him?"

"Yes, but it's too dangerous to have him anywhere near Celest. So you're going to have to face Obasi on your own. I'll send Hansen to join you, and then when I have Tomas and Saburo settled, I'll come back."

"Maybe you should stay at the village. It'll be safer if you do."

"Thanks, but you'll need me to communicate with my village so they'll know what's happening here."

"We have the best walkie talkies you can buy. I'll get you

one. There's no need for you to be here."

"Sorry, Rick, but no matter how good your walkie talkies are, their transmission won't be heard on the other side of the falls."

"And your method will?"

"Most definitely. I'll be back as soon as I can."

"Fine, but what if hurricane Celest decides to make another appearance?"

"Then, if I were you, I'd run." Authia chuckled to herself as she headed back to the pond. She knew very well that Celest wasn't going to leave her hut until Saburo returned.

Nathen stood in front of the falls, his arms crossed over his chest, waiting for Authia. His men kept their distance. Nathen had settled down after he heard from Authia, but he still let it be known that he was upset with them. After what seemed to be an eternity, Authia melded with him. He relaxed his body as he listened to what she had to say.

Nathen, are you still at the falls?

Of course, I am. I will remain here until you return.

That's sweet, but I need you to do something for me. I have Tomas, and I want to take him to the village, but he can't see you or Rick's men. Authia stopped talking for a second. *Actually, he shouldn't get a glimpse of the tribe either. He knows what they look like, and their new appearance might confuse him.*

Where do you want to take him?

To Sam's hut. I'll have him stay there until this is all over. Then maybe Casandra and Serena can help him in some way.

Not a problem, my Love. I'll send Arman to clear a path to Sam's hut. In the meantime, I'll hide in the jungle until you pass by.

No, I need you, Casandra and Serena at the gathering hut.

Why?

Because I'm bringing The Destroyer *with me.*

What!

I'll explain when I see you. We're heading over.

What do you mean you have The Destroyer? *Obasi is with you?*

Patience sweetheart. I'll see you soon. Authia ended the meld, leaving Nathen thoroughly bewildered.

He glanced over at his men and called Arman over. "I need you to clear a path to Sam's hut. Authia is bringing Tomas, and he can't see anyone."

Arman bowed to Nathen and headed back to the village. Nathen then sought out Tuval. He motioned for him to approach. "I have to head back to the gathering hut. Authia is on her way with Tomas and apparently *The Destroyer*."

"*The Destroyer*, my Lord?"

"I have no idea. Just stay out of sight, but at the same time protect her. Follow her to the village. Have our men stay out of sight as well, but they can remain here."

"Yes, my Lord." Tuval signaled his men and they all disappeared into the jungle. Nathen took one last look at the entrance to the falls. *I hope you know what you're doing, Authia.*

Authia made her way back to the pond. As she approached, Tomas bowed to her. "What are we going to do, my Mistress?"

"I'm taking you to see Sam."

Tomas' eyes went wide. "Sam? He is here?"

"Yes, Tomas, and he's waiting for you. He's at my village."

"When can we leave?"

"Right now, if you would like."

"Yes, I would like that." Tomas picked up his machete that was lying on the ground. "I am ready when you are, my Mistress."

"Great. Hansen, would you go and help Rick and his men? I'll be back as soon as I get Tomas settled."

"You got it." Hansen started to head for the village with Saburo right behind him.

Authia stepped into Saburo's path. "Where do you think you're going?"

Hansen joined Authia, folding his arms in front of him.

"To the village. They'll need my help."

Authia crooked her finger at Saburo and motioned him to follow her. When they were a few feet away from Tomas, she continued. "Really? And how do you plan to help them?"

"I may not be able to enter the village, but I can hide in the trees, and I'm one hell of a shot."

"Sorry, not happening. I don't want you anywhere near the village. You're coming back with Tomas and me." Authia held out her hand. "And you won't be needing that rifle."

Saburo shot Authia a dirty look of as if to say *who the hell do you think you are.* "You may be the Mistress of your village, and you may have him" —Saburo gestured toward Hansen.— "on a tight leash, but you're not in charge of me. I want Obasi, and I'm going to be the one to kill him. I'm not giving up my rifle."

Authia smirked at Saburo. "You have no idea what you're up against. However, I do. And if you want to stay alive, you'll listen to me. I'm taking you to my village, and my warriors don't know you. You make one move they don't like while you're carrying that rifle, and they will shoot first, ask questions later. Now hand over your rifle."

Hansen added his opinion. "I'd listen, if I were you. Her warriors will give their life for her, and they have no problem taking one."

Saburo didn't look pleased. "Why do I think that your warriors are not the issue?" He handed the rifle to Authia, who passed it on to Hansen. Then she nodded to Hansen, who slung the rifle onto his back, then left to join the others.

Authia focused her attention on Saburo. She stood close to him and lowered her voice. "This is not the place or time to discuss this. Besides keeping you and Celest apart, my main objective is to keep Tomas safe, and right now you are confusing him. You're supposed to be my husband, and my husband listens to me. So right now, I want you to smile and say, *of course, my Love.* Make him believe that you're sorry for doubting me, or you will see first-hand the wrath of my true husband. And believe me, you don't want to do that. Understood?"

Saburo glanced over to Tomas, who was apparently upset by what was going on. "I don't like being in the dark. If I don't get to Obasi first, I'm a dead man."

"It will all be explained at my village. But trust me, Obasi is the least of your worries. Now, do as I say and make Tomas happy."

Authia stood her ground. Deep down, she was terrified, but she couldn't let Saburo know that. She had to gain the upper hand, and the only way she could think of doing that was by showing no fear. So she stood still, waiting for him to comply. "Well?"

Saburo glanced over to Tomas, then smiled at Authia. "Sorry, my Love. I shouldn't be arguing with you. After all, you do know best." He leaned over and kissed her on her cheek. Without taking his gaze off Authia, he spoke to Tomas. "So, Tomas, shall we follow my wife?"

Authia took a couple of steps back, then turned to face Tomas. He was smiling and seemed relieved by what he witnessed. "Yes, follow me." Authia sarcastically smiled at Saburo, then headed toward the falls.

Hansen made his way back to Rick and his men. He found them gingerly handling the mines as they strategically placed them around the village. Hansen walked over to Rick who was overseeing the placement of the mines. "What can I do?"

"As soon as the mines are placed, we'll start burying them.

You can help with that, but keep in mind that these mines have hair triggers." Rick continued to watch his men, although his thoughts were clearly somewhere else.

"You got something on your mind besides mines with hair triggers?"

Rick smiled, appearing slightly embarrassed. "I was wondering. The High Priestess Tamara, is she married?"

Hansen chuckled. "No, she's not. Look, Rick, she's adorable, she's sweet, but I wouldn't be pursuing anything romantic till after this is all finished and the village is safe."

"Oh, of course. I was just asking." Rick, making an obvious attempt to change the subject, scanned the trees surrounding the clearing. "Come with me." He headed for a tree that was just a few feet from the clearing. Both he and Hansen climbed till they were a good twenty feet up. Rick straddled a thick branch while Hansen stood on a branch that was a foot away. He placed his left hand on the trunk to balance himself as he looked down on the men placing the mines. Rick pointed in the direction of the path that led to the village. "They'll come that way. I'm going to place one man on either side of the path about twenty feet before the entrance to the village. The rest of us are going to position ourselves along this side of the village, about thirty feet from the clearing." Rick pointed down to the mines. "I'm positioning the mines so that most of Obasi's men will enter the clearing before they start setting them off. The mines will be heavily concentrated to the left of the path and in front of it. That way it will force Obasi's men to either run back down the path where the two men I have there can pick them off, or they're going to run toward us. Either way, we are going to nail them with everything we have. By the time all this is said and done, I'm hoping that all of Obasi's men, including him, will be dead. And if there are any still alive, it won't be many."

"Do you think we have enough men?"

"We could always use more. But if Obasi shows up later today, what we have will have to do." Rick turned to face Hansen. "We have the element of surprise, and that gives us a huge advantage. Now let's go bury some mines."

Authia was grateful that the walk back to the village was in silence. Saburo made it quite evident that he was unhappy with her decision to bring him back to the village, whereas Tomas was clearly elated at the thought of being reunited with Sam. As soon as the huts came into view, Authia steered Saburo and Tomas to the far left, keeping them on the far side of the huts and out of view of the village itself. After they passed a few of the smaller huts, the gathering hut came into view. Authia stopped and addressed Tomas. "My husband is needed at the gathering hut. He will go there, and I will take you to Sam. Okay?"

Authia smiled at Tomas as he nodded in agreement. Then she motioned for Saburo to follow her. She took him out of earshot of Tomas. "My husband, Nathen, is waiting for you at that large hut." Authia pointed to the gathering hut. "Go there and get comfortable. That's going to be your home until we figure out how to deal with Celest."

"So, I'm a prisoner."

"No. Consider yourself under protective custody." Authia continued to watch Saburo as he reluctantly headed toward the gathering hut. After Tuval joined him, she focused on Tomas. "Sam is just over here." Authia led Tomas to a small hut at the very edge of the village. Standing outside of the hut was Sam. Authia was delighted when she saw Sam's look of immense joy at seeing his friend. But that was quickly replaced with concern when Sam got a closer look at Tomas' face and body.

"Tomas, I can't believe I'm seeing you. I was so afraid that you had died."

Tomas appeared confused. "Why would I be dead? I was not in any danger. And besides, I had the Lord of the Lion People with me."

Sam glanced over at Authia, obviously perplexed at Tomas' comment. Authia leaned over as she wrapped her arms around him, giving Tomas the impression that she was hugging Sam. Quietly she whispered into his ear, "Just play along." Authia straightened up and addressed Sam. "I think Tomas would like to rest. He's been on a long journey."

Tomas smiled at Authia. "Yes, do you have room for me in your hut, Sam?"

"Of course, I do. Come with me."

Tomas and Authia followed Sam into his hut. The hut was only nine feet in diameter and bare of any personal belongings. Alongside the small fire pit located in the center of the hut were a couple of clay bowls containing fruit, meat, and bread. There were also two sleeping mats placed close to the fire pit, and blankets folded neatly beside each one. Sam smiled tenderly at his friend. "Take your choice, Tomas."

Tomas glanced down at the mats, chose the one closest to him, and laid down. He curled up into a ball, closed his eyes, and immediately fell asleep. Sam reached down and tried to remove the machete that was clasped tightly in Tomas' right hand. He looked up at Authia. "He won't let go."

"I think it's a matter of he can't let go rather than he won't. Let's talk outside the hut."

Sam nodded, covered Tomas with a blanket then followed Authia outside the hut. "Why can't he let go? Why does he look like he does?"

"He's been badly beaten, Sam. By rights, he shouldn't be able to walk, talk, or hold a machete. Right now, his mind has been altered by Serena, one of our priestesses. It's very important that he remains in the hut until I say it's safe for him to leave."

"What do you mean by altered?"

"It's a long story. One I'll be happy to tell you later. For now, if you want Tomas to survive, you have to do exactly as I say."

"Of course, my Mistress."

"Don't leave his side. I'll post a warrior outside of your hut. He'll get you anything you need. When Tomas wakes up, just play along with his fantasy. Tell him that the Lord of the Lion People has requested that you both remain in the hut. Can you do that for me, for Tomas?"

"Yes, My Mistress."

"Good. I have to go now. Nathen is waiting for me." As Authia headed toward the gathering hut, tears ran down her cheeks. She couldn't get the image out of her mind of Tomas' badly beaten body curled up into a ball, his broken hand locked into place around the butt of the machete.

CHAPTER TWENTY-NINE

Saburo headed toward the gathering hut cursing Authia under his breath. *Who the hell does she think she is? She's making a big mistake taking me out of the picture. Obasi is going to bury her!* Saburo was so focused on his thoughts that he didn't notice when someone stepped out onto the path until he almost collided with him. Saburo looked up at the very large man that stood in front of him. "What the hell? Who are you?"

"I'm here to take you to my Lord. He's right over there." The man pointed to the entrance of the gathering hut then stood perfectly still, staring at Saburo, patiently waiting for him to lead the way.

Saburo glanced over to the hut then back to the man towering over him. "I guess you want me to go first." The man didn't answer Saburo. He just stood there, continuing to stare. Saburo muttered *asshole* under his breath then turned and headed toward the hut.

When he entered, there were two more men, one standing on either side of the entrance. They stared straight ahead, a spear in their right hand, a machete at their waist. Saburo sized up both men. They were just as tall and big as the one who'd brought him there. The hut itself was massive and was filled with sleeping mats, crates, and backpacks. It was probably where Rick and his men were staying. In the center of the hut were three people—two women, one, older, dressed in what appeared to be a ceremonial gown and the other, who appeared much younger, in a blue, almost transparent gown that flowed to her knees. She was absolutely beautiful. The third person was a man dressed in animal skins. His thighs were like tree trunks, his biceps twice the size of Saburo. Saburo assumed that he was Authia's husband, and if he was, then Authia was right, he didn't want to mess with him.

The man approached Saburo, extending his hand to him. "I'm guessing you're Saburo."

Saburo shook the man's hand. "You'd be guessing right. And you must be Nathen. Wouldn't mind having a few of you guys watching my back."

Nathen snickered. "My wife told me you were coming, and she also told me about the incident at the other village."

Saburo quickly glanced around the hut. "That's strange, 'cause I didn't see her come this way."

"She didn't have to. What do you know of Celest?"

"You mean that crazy patch of fog that sounds like a wild banshee?"

"Yes, that's exactly who I mean."

"You got me. I walked out of the jungle and whatever that was came at me as if I was something it wanted to destroy."

"What that was, was my mother." The woman in the blue gown approached Saburo and Nathen.

"This is Serena, a priestess of our village."

Saburo gawked at Serena in disbelief. "Your mother? Funny, I don't see a family resemblance."

"Well, she is. Not that I am proud of it."

"What do you mean, it came at you?"

Nathen gestured toward Casandra. "And this is Casandra, priestess, and healer of our village."

"Priestess and healer? Are you two witches, witch doctors, whatever you want to call it?"

"They are gifted in sight, potions and spells, and no, they're not witches." The group turned to find Authia standing at the entrance.

Nathen's face lit up. "My Love, I am so happy to see you

unharmed." He walked over to Authia, took her in his arms, and tenderly kissed her. As he gently pulled away from the kiss, he frowned at her. "I don't want you going back. It's too dangerous. I'm sick with worry for you."

"We'll discuss that later. Where's Joshawa?"

"With Tammy at the birthing hut. You probably noticed that the village is pretty empty. Only the warriors are left."

"Good. At least that's one less thing we have to worry about." Authia focused on Casandra. "I don't even know how to explain it. Celest is no longer just an aura. When I saw her in the hut, she was trying to take form, but it was as if she couldn't hold it. Then when Saburo showed up, she went wild. Looking at her is like seeing a heavy fog roll in off the water. Just wilder. Rick referred to her like a hurricane, which is pretty accurate."

"So, she went after Saburo, but she didn't get to him? How did you stop her?"

"I didn't. She couldn't go past the clearing. It was like there was an invisible barrier preventing her from leaving the village. She slammed against it over and over, but she couldn't penetrate it."

"Strange! I don't understand."

Authia glanced over to Serena, who appeared deep in thought. "You know something?"

"I might. As you know, our Ancestors cannot harm a High Priestess or Lord. The best they can do is imprison the Lord or High Priestess when they lose their essence, what makes them who they are."

"Which is what they did to you and your mother."

"Yes. According to my mother, all she could think of during her imprisonment was revenge. She hated the Ancestors and the tribe. However, no one ever escapes, so she never thought past her hatred. Then, by some miracle, she was given an opening. She had no time to plan . . . she could only act, which is exactly what she did."

Authia mulled over everything she knew about the Ancestors and *The Destroyer*. "I don't get it. If she's looking for revenge by setting *The Destroyer* loose on the village, why wouldn't she come to our village and seek out a warrior? Why would she go to the other village?"

Serena glanced over at Casandra, who smiled at her.

Authia could tell that they knew what was going on. "Well?"

Serena continued, "That is just it. She would not have gone to the outsider's village. And if she did, why would she limit herself to just the village?"

Authia replied, "It didn't look like she was expecting that barrier to be there. The way she attacked it, she was pissed."

"When I was imprisoned, the Ancestors made it quite clear that there was no escape. They monitored that dark hole all the time."

Nathen was confused. "Well, then how did your mother escape?"

"Honestly, I do not know. But she did not get away as easily as she thought she did. They knew, but they could not stop her without hurting her, which is strictly forbidden. So, they tricked her."

Authia was witnessing a side of Serena she had never seen before. Serena was practically giddy. It was as if she finally realized why the Ancestors had chosen her to be the tribe's protector. "She thought she was going to the village, and she did, just the wrong village. They imprisoned her in that village. They sent me to help you, knowing that I would be in contact with my mother. Knowing that I would be forced to make a choice."

Authia spoke up, "Do you think the Ancestors knew what your choice was going to be?"

"I do not see how they could, especially since I did not

know that I would even be in a position to make a choice."

Saburo was growing impatient. What these people were focused on was irrelevant. Obasi was the one they had to be prepared for. Saburo had no doubt that Obasi was *The Destroyer,* and if he got to this village, these idiots would find out the hard way. "You guys are fixated on the wrong person. I don't know who this Celest person is, or what she wants with me, but if you don't prepare for Obasi, he will wipe you off the face of this earth. It'll be as if your tribe never existed."

Nathen took his attention off Authia and onto Saburo, who almost wished he kept his mouth shut. As Saburo stared down Nathen, he realized that the man didn't appear overly upset with his outburst. "Seriously, Obasi is wacked in the head. He takes pleasure out of killing people. If you don't prepare for him, he'll win."

Nathen took a step closer to Saburo. "And how do we prepare for him?"

"The mines will help, but they're not the answer. Obasi will send his men in first. He'll watch his men die from high in the trees, and he'll know where the mines are and where your men are hiding. Obasi's scary smart. He'll wait until he has an opening, and while you're killing his men, he'll slip by unscathed."

Authia interjected, "If that's the case, then we get an eye on Obasi. I'm sure Rick knows what he looks like."

Saburo just shook his head. "Are you kidding me? You're not going to see Obasi until he wants you to see him."

"Then what are we supposed to do?"

"Send me in. I can get close to him. I have something he wants."

Casandra took a step forward. "Out of the question." She focused her attention on Nathen. "He can't go in without

Serena and myself, and that's not going to happen until we know for sure he is *The Destroyer* and we discover a way to defeat Celest."

Nathen continued, "I agree with Casandra. There must be another way."

"Obasi's committed to finding your valley. As far as he knows, only Tomas and I can lead him there. If you want him to expose himself, then you need bait. And if you won't let me go in, then there is only one other person."

Authia appeared horrified. "No, we can't use Tomas as bait."

"It's the only way," Saburo insisted. "Look, Obasi will find a way around the mines and to the waterfall. Rick and his men will be occupied with Obasi's men. Have Tomas at the waterfall. When Obasi comes into the clearing, you have him."

Authia glanced over at Nathen. "If Tomas sees Obasi, he could start remembering. It could kill him."

Nathen thought for a minute. "I'm not totally convinced that using bait is the way to go. However, Saburo, you know Obasi best, so we may have to defer to your judgment. That being said, what about Sam? He looks like Tomas. Maybe Obasi won't notice the difference."

"Oh, he'll notice," Saburo said. "Believe me . . . he knows every bruise, every broken bone. If this guy Sam shows up, Obasi will know right away."

Serena spoke up. "What if we send Tomas, but we block his mind, prevent him from seeing Obasi for who he is."

Nathen glanced over to Serena. "And how do you plan to accomplish that?"

"If I were still a wisp, I could do it easily. However, that option is no longer available to us. Someone, a priestess, will have to be in direct contact with him, project her thoughts over Tomas'. He will see what she sees."

Saburo rolled his eyes. "More voodoo. She'll see Obasi. How's that going to help Tomas?"

"We do not know who Obasi is. So, when we see him, he may appear as a threat, but there will be no memory of him. To Tomas, he will just be another intruder."

Saburo actually saw the logic in the plan. "This could work. We could place Tomas and the priestess close to the falls. As soon as Obasi sees Tomas, he'll head right for him. We could have one of Rick's men hide close to the pond so that he'll be behind Obasi. The minute he has a close shot, Obasi's dead. Your problem and mine solved in one shot." Saburo was excited—a plan that could actually work. A plan that would keep him alive.

Nathen listened to the banter, but he didn't hear what was being said. His gaze fell on Authia, who was already looking in his direction. He knew what she was thinking, what she was planning on doing. He closed his eyes and melded with her. *You can't do what I know you're planning.*

We have no other choice.

There has to be another choice.

Only a priestess can project her thoughts. A priestess or me. Nathen, you know that none of the priestesses can cross the waterfall. If they do, we'll be dealing with an entirely different, bigger problem. I have to go. I have to protect Tomas. You know that.

Nathen opened his eyes and sought out Saburo. "Are you sure that Obasi will not harm Tomas or the priestess that goes with him?"

"Obasi's hell-bent on finding the valley. If he sees Tomas, he'll try to get to him. If Tomas is out in the open, then Obasi has to go into the open. You'd have to be the worse shot on the planet not to hit him. The plan will work."

"All right. We'll deal with the Obasi threat first. Then,

when that's over, and providing we're all still alive, we'll deal with Celest. Saburo, I'm glad you like to use bait. You're going to be Celest's."

Authia walked over to Nathen and wrapped her arms around his forearm. She gazed up at him and smiled, then turned her attention to Saburo. "When do you think Obasi will come?"

Saburo thought for a second. "Just a minute." He started to leave the hut, but the two warriors blocked his path. Saburo looked up at them then over his shoulder at Nathen. Nathen nodded his head, and the two warriors stepped aside. Saburo looked outside at the evening sky. He returned to the group and addressed Nathen. "It won't be long before the jungle is enveloped in darkness. Obasi's highly superstitious. He'll not travel at night. I'm guessing he's at the camp at the base of the mountain. He'll leave at first light, and he'll be motivated. He'll push his men. You can call Rick and his men back for the night, but I'd have them in place by sunrise tomorrow."

Nathen glanced over to Authia then back to the group. "As I said before, no one from the village can cross the falls. Authia will go with Tomas." As Nathen left, Authia at his side, he glared at Saburo. "Your plan better work. If Authia is harmed in any way . . . Obasi will be the least of your worries."

CHAPTER THIRTY

Authia made her way back to the other village. The sun was setting, casting an eerie shadow on the only remaining hut. It was so quiet that even the jungle spoke in whispers. Authia stopped several feet from the edge of the clearing. She scanned the trees for some indication that either Rick, Hansen or any of the other men were there. The silence was all that greeted her, and as she continued to scan the village and surrounding trees, panic started to well up inside of her. What if Obasi was already there? What if Saburo was wrong? Fear enveloped her, causing her heart to beat so fast, she thought for sure it was going to explode from her chest. Then, out of the corner of her eye, she caught some movement. She whirled around to find Hansen standing there. "Oh, my God! You scared me. Where is everybody?"

Rick dropped out of the tree just two feet from where Authia was standing, startling her. "Sorry, my bad. Wanted to see how this muck worked. You really couldn't see us?"

"No. I told you it would work. Tell your men to come back. According to Saburo, Obasi won't be here until late tomorrow morning."

"And we are trusting him why?"

"He wants Obasi dead as much as you do." Authia started to head back to the falls, Hansen at her side.

The moon shone brightly above the village. Rick stood at the entrance of the gathering hut waiting for his men to clean up and eat. He was still covered in the green muck, and since his return to the village, he hadn't eaten anything. He was lost in his thoughts of Tamara. When he first arrived back at the village, he had watched her help fill the clay bowls with food for his men. She was wearing her animal skins, and Rick found himself jealous of the fact that her top barely covered her breasts and his men were obviously taking notice. Rick slowly shook his head. Who was he kidding? She was the High Priestess, and he was, technically, a warrior and an outsider. Far beneath her station in life.

He buried his thoughts of Tamara and concentrated on the village itself. With Nathen evacuating the village, they'd never had the opportunity to perform the welcoming ceremony that Authia spoke of. It turned out that it wasn't necessary. With only the warriors left in the village, Rick assumed that he and his men weren't perceived as a real threat anymore. He guessed they'd finally realized that he was here to help. Rick's men had returned to the hut bathed, fed and ready to call it a night. As he stood there, staring out at nothing, Travis came and stood by his side.

"You planning on taking that muck off anytime soon? Or are you going to leave it on for tomorrow?"

Rick chuckled. "No, I'm going to clean up. How's Saburo getting along?"

"He's keeping his distance. The men are a little leery of him. Anyway, I came to say goodnight."

"Okay. I won't be much longer." Travis went back into the hut, and Rick headed for the pond. When he arrived, he found it deserted. The pond itself was still, and the only sounds were those of the jungle. The rays of the moon danced on the water as if they were playfully teasing it. Rick marveled at the tranquility. It was so peaceful, it was a place where he could easily relax and be himself. Rick stripped naked and waded into the water until it was as high as his hips, then dove in. He surfaced a few feet away, his back to the shore, and started scrubbing at the muck on his arms and face. As he did, he recalled Tamara as she'd tenderly applied the muck to his body. As the memory came alive in his mind, so did the emotions, and immediately, his heart began to beat faster, his manhood throbbed with desire.

"Did you need me to help you? Is that why you are thinking of me?"

Rick whirled around to find Tamara standing at the edge of the water, still wearing her animal skins. She had a clay pot in her hands. "I brought you some food."

"How did you know I was thinking of you?"

"I am sorry. I can sometimes hear thoughts. However, yours are more of a feeling of what you are thinking. Are you displeased with me?"

"Oh, God, no. Do you know what I was feeling?"

"You were recalling a memory, and it pleased you. Would you like me to help you remove the muck? Water alone will not work." Before Rick could answer, Tamara placed the clay pot on the ground, walked over to a nearby palm tree, and pulled off a couple of palm leaves. "These will do nicely." Without removing her animal skins, she waded into the water to join Rick. He couldn't believe what was happening. She was standing so close to him. She dampened one of the palm leaves and started to gently wipe his face clean. She gazed at him with such a look of innocence. He stood still, arms at his side, desperately wanting to wrap them around her and pull her close. Tamara stopped wiping his face and pulled her hand away. She stared at him as if she was trying to understand something. "Am I hurting you?"

"No, you're not hurting me."

"I do not understand." Tamara appeared confused as she stared at Rick, her eyes focused on his eyes. To Rick, it was as if she were searching his mind for an answer.

"Are you hearing my feelings now?"

"I can normally hear another priestess' thoughts or my Mistress'. I have never been able to hear an outsider's thoughts. But your thoughts come alive in my mind. However, they do so in the form of emotions. What were you thinking that pleases you so much?"

Rick chuckled. "That could get me slapped."

"Why would I slap you?"

Rick drew a deep breath. This woman had such power over him. Should he tell her what he was thinking? Or should he wait? Wait until tomorrow night, which held no guarantees that he'd even survive to see it? Rick threw caution to the wind. "You're one hell of an amazing, beautiful woman. As far as my thoughts go . . . may I show you?"

"Yes, you may."

Rick placed his fingers under her chin, tilted her head slightly up, and then tenderly kissed her. He pulled away, bracing himself for the slap, which never came.

"You wanted to kiss me? Why?"

"Why did you let me?"

Tamara stepped closer to Rick. "I do not know. I only know it feels right." Tamara looked at Rick as if she'd discovered some deep secret. "I now understand my Lord and his father. We do not choose who we give our heart to. Nor do our Ancestors choose for us. It just happens."

"Are you saying you love me?"

Tamara leaned up and tenderly kissed Rick. Then she took a couple of steps back. "I am saying that you hold my heart. Unfortunately, there will come a time when you may not want it."

Rick took Tamara's hand in his and gently pulled her toward him. He wrapped his arms around her, leaned in, and passionately kissed her. Tamara pulled away from the kiss and placed her fingers against his lips. "I must go. Do not waste your love on me. There will come a time you will regret it." Tamara turned and walked out of the pond and into the jungle.

Rick just stood frozen in place watching her. *Too late Tamara, and I will never regret it.*

Tamara walked toward the village, her tears running freely down her cheeks. She stopped for only a second, looking back at the pond. She wiped her tears and then headed to the priestess' family hut. He loved what he saw, and even though her Lord proved that an outsider could love someone from her tribe, she believed that something as wonderous as unconditional love would never happen to her. The minute he saw her for who and what she truly was, she would lose him. Fate was cruel, for no man in her village made her feel as Rick did. And probably none never would.

Obasi sat in the massive Kapok tree waiting for his men. A few hours later, they started emerging from the jungle. They arrived in small groups, but as the last man arrived, their numbers grew to thirty-nine men strong. Obasi climbed down from his perch, then silently made his way to the far edge of the camp. It was slightly higher, giving Obasi the sense of towering over his men. As he stood there, not one man uttered a sound. He slowly scanned the group of men, taking his time, allowing the tension to build. To him, this was power, the power to instill fear in the very hearts of the men he commanded. "Saburo has shown me the way to what we desire. He has shown me where the men we hunt have gone. They've found sanctuary in a valley that is not theirs to occupy. We'll hunt these men. We'll kill these men and take the valley back!" Obasi raised his right arm, hand balled into a fist, high above his head and his men cheered him. "When the first rays of the new day reveal themselves to us, we'll head to the valley concealed high in the mountain that rises before us. We will be victorious, and we will be rewarded!"

Obasi smiled as his men cheered and hollered. Little did they know that they were celebrating their own death, a fact that pleased Obasi. For he alone would enter the valley. He alone would reap the bounty that waited for him.

Nathen sat by the fire pit in his hut watching Authia prepare for the next day. He sighed, which didn't go unnoticed by Authia. "Nathen, you know this is the only way."

"You shouldn't be putting yourself or our child in a situation that's so dangerous."

"What choice do I have? As it is, I should be in the trees where I can let you know what's happening out there. But if Saburo is right, using Tomas as bait may be the only way we can kill Obasi. And the only way we can use him as bait is if someone—me—blocks his memories. No one else can do it without exposing the tribe for who they are. You know that. So unless you have a better idea, then stop brooding and maybe give me a little encouragement. Help me believe that I'm going to survive the day."

Nathen stared into the fire, not saying a word. He had an ominous feeling about the outcome of the battle that was to be fought for the protection of the Jelani Tribe. A battle he should be leading, not sitting back waiting to hear of the outcome, praying it all goes well. He looked up at Authia, who was standing by his side. He held out his hand to her, which she accepted, then gently pulled her down beside him. He placed his hand on the side of her face, gazing deep into her eyes. "Do you have any idea what it's like to watch someone you love fight a battle that you yourself should be fighting? I'm helpless. I can't protect the people of this tribe or the woman I love without jeopardizing everything we've put into place. I should be out there, and to hell with shocking Rick's men. Maybe if I expose myself and my warriors, then the enemy that's at our doorstep will think twice about challenging us."

"Or maybe they'll be so scared that they will, as Tammy put it, shoot first, ask questions later. On our own, we've no defense against their weapons. But with Rick's men, Hansen and myself, we have a chance to win this." Authia knelt before Nathen and placed her hands on either side of his face. "You know in your heart that this is the only way. This is our only chance to survive. Saburo's plan is sound. Obasi will be dead before he gets anywhere near me. And between Rick and his men and all those mines they planted, Obasi's men don't stand a chance."

"I'm not so convinced. I almost lost you once because I wasn't there to protect you. I can't . . . I won't let it happen again."

"I'll tell you what. If at any time I sense that I'm in danger, I'll not hesitate. I'll come back and leave the fighting to our first wave of defense. Agreed?"

"Agreed." Nathen gathered Authia into his arms and held her close against him. He knew Authia only too well, and her idea of being in danger was completely different from his. At that moment, Nathen made a promise to himself. And that promise was to protect Authia at all costs, even if it meant exposing himself and the tribe for who they were.

CHAPTER THIRTY-ONE

Obasi sat in his tree, focused on the eastern sky. He knew that in a matter of moments the first rays of the sun would poke their head above the horizon. He glanced down at his men, who were dressed, armed, and ready for the anticipated battle. Again, he checked the horizon to witness the darkness fade to light as the sun made its appearance. His men needed no prompting—they immediately set off in the direction they were instructed to go. Obasi waited for the majority of his men to start up the trail, then he climbed out of the tree and followed them, keeping hidden from view. His men knew he was there, but they just couldn't see him. Obasi preferred it that way. It kept his men on their toes, for they knew if they said one word, made one comment that Obasi didn't like, he would come out of hiding, walk up behind them and slit their throat.

Nathen stood at the entrance of his hut observing the village and the camaraderie between outsider and warrior. They gathered around the communal fire pit sharing their morning meal. For the first time in the vast history of the Jelani Tribe, a bond had been formed so outsider and warrior would fight side by side in defense of the tribe. The only women left in the village were Authia, Tamara, and two priestesses. Nathen had sent Casandra and Serena to the birthing hut, much to their displeasure. However, in the end, they had to agree with Nathen. They were too important in the demise of Celest to risk their lives in the battle against Obasi.

Nathen waited till the men had their fill of the boar roasting over the fire before he went to address them, preparing them for the pending battle. He had faith in the plan, at least up to the part of Authia being used for bait. That part didn't sit well with him at all. As he made his way over to Rick, he formulated his own plan, which was to be close to the falls in case Authia needed him. He would not let her be hurt again. Not like before. He walked up to Rick, his expression solemn. "It's time to address the men."

"You address the men like that, and they're going to think that you're sending them to die. The least you can do is make it look like you think we have a chance."

"Sorry. I know you have a good chance, a very good chance. It's Authia that I'm worried about."

"Hey, I don't blame you. But she's going to be fine. I've asked Ed to hide by the pond. He's an expert with a rifle, and he's the best we have. All Obasi has to do is make an appearance anywhere by the pond, and he's a dead man." Rick patted Nathen on the back. "Now let's get these men motivated."

A couple of the warriors had put together a makeshift platform for Nathen and Rick to stand on so everyone could see them. They climbed onto it together, and as they stood facing their men, Nathen scanned the group looking for Authia. He found her standing with Tamara and Hansen at the very back of the gathering. They made eye contact, and Authia's smile revealed to Nathen how much love, how much trust she had in him. Her smile gave him the confidence he needed to do what had to be done. He took a deep breath, put on a smile, and addressed the men that stood before him.

"Today is a day that will go down in the history of our tribe as proof that outsiders can be a welcome addition to our lineage. To our way of life. We stand together to fight a common foe. To protect the families of the Jelani Tribe. To protect our way of life. To protect our right to live. These outsiders" — Nathen gestured to the crowd — "they have asked for nothing from us. They are putting their lives on the line to protect a people that up to a couple of days ago, they didn't even know existed. And how do we repay them? Simple, we take up arms and fight by their side. Now, we aren't skilled in the weaponry that these men have, nor can we venture past the falls. But we are damn good and lethal with the weapons we do have. We'll protect our borders on this side of the falls. If by some miracle, Obasi and his men make it into our valley, then we will make damn sure that it will be in this valley that they take their last breath." The entire group of men cheered, raising their arms, shouting out their belief that they would be victorious.

Rick raised his hands to silence the crowd. "All right, this is how it is going to go down. According to Saburo, Obasi isn't going to put himself in the line of fire. He'll send his men in, and while we pick them off, Obasi is going to be looking for a way around the fighting. I've already assigned nine men to hide in the trees between the falls and the village. Two men are going to hide in the trees on either side of the path that leads into the village."

"Not a good idea." The comment had come from Saburo, who now headed toward the platform.

"And why is that not a good idea?" Rick asked.

"Have you heard nothing that I've said? You're not dealing with your average GI Joe. Obasi stays alive for one reason. He's crazy smart, and he can assess any situation and turn it around in his favor. When he gets to the village, he won't be on the ground. He'll be in the trees watching, waiting for you to make a move. I promise you. He'll see the two men, sneak up behind them, and slit their throats. They'll never see him coming."

"The priestesses have made up a camouflage that will blend us into the trees. It works pretty damn well. He won't see us."

"Obasi doesn't just look for men hiding in the trees or on the ground. He looks for telltale signs, like the leaves of a tree not lying the way they should. Have you ever heard of or seen a chameleon?"

"Yeah. It's a ten-inch lizard that can change colors. I think I've only seen one in the whole entire time I've been here."

"Obasi plays a game with me. See who can find the most chameleons. Even when they are camouflaged, and you can't really see them, he finds them. It's amazing to watch him in action. Believe me . . . he'll find your men."

"Then what do you suggest we do?"

"Forget about Obasi. The best opportunity you'll have to kill him will be at the pond. You need to focus on his men. Lessen the numbers. Keep all your men in the trees that are between the village and the pond. Arrange them into the shape of a horseshoe. Let whatever men that aren't killed by the mines pool into this horseshoe. If you have to, shoot at them to corral them where you want them to be, then nail them from all sides."

Nathen chuckled. "And why would they be stupid enough to allow themselves to be corralled into an obvious trap?"

"Obasi doesn't choose men to follow him because they have a mind of their own. He chooses men that are easily manipulated. Men that will fear him, not stand up to him and basically not have an original thought of their own. They follow him like sheep to the slaughter. Believe me, they'll walk, or rather run, into your trap without giving it a second thought. However, know that these men are ruthless killers. If Obasi wants you dead, then they will see that it happens."

Rick spoke up, "And how do you fit into all of this? You don't seem to be the *follow no questions asked* kind of guy."

"Obasi doesn't like to have direct contact with his men. How did he put it? *Don't get close to them. That way, when they die or if you have to kill them, there will be no remorse.* He needed a go-between, someone strong who the men would follow and someone that he had something on. Something he could use as leverage."

Rick continued, "And what was his leverage over you?"

"My two sisters. They're in one of the villages that he controls. They remain under his protection as long as I serve him. I piss him off, and they're as good as dead."

Rick shook his head. "I'm so sorry."

"Nothing to be sorry about. Just kill that bastard, and then I can go to free my sisters."

"Okay, while we're killing Obasi's men, what will Obasi do?"

"He'll watch. Keep to the trees. He'll find a way around the fighting. As soon as you open fire, he will know that you are protecting whatever is behind you. That's where he will head. Don't worry about him. But at the same time, don't underestimate him." Saburo turned to face Ed, who was standing next to him. "Find someplace to hide where you can lie flat on the ground. Make sure there is a lot of foliage to conceal you from above. And not just you, your rifle as well. Don't make a sound. Any sound you make he *will* hear, and then you're as good as dead. The minute you have a shot, take it and make it count, because you won't get a second chance."

Nathen spoke up, "I've arranged for a dozen warriors to be waiting, hidden in the jungle, on our side of the falls. Now, if by some miracle, some of Obasi's men get past your men as well as mine, then the warriors that are not protecting the birthing hut will be at the village with the last couple of your men. It will be our last line of defense. In all honesty, I strongly believe that this battle ends on the other side of the falls." Nathen glanced over to the priestess' hut to see two priestesses as well as Tamara heading his way, carrying clay bowls. "Our priestesses are coming with more of the green muck. Get it applied, then we'll meet at the falls in thirty minutes." Nathen jumped off the platform and made his way over to Authia. As he walked past Saburo, he motioned for him to follow.

Authia watched as Nathen and Saburo approached her. She glanced at Hansen, who nodded his head that he understood, then she glanced over to Tuval, and he and Arman joined the group. Authia smiled at Nathen, walked up to him, throwing her arms around his neck and passionately kissing him. Nathen wrapped his arms around her waist and pulled her tight against him. Seductively she nibbled on his lower lip as she slowly pulled away.

"Wow! What did I do to deserve that?"

"It's not what you did, but rather what I'm going to do."

Nathen looked at Authia in complete bewilderment. "And what are you going to do?"

Authia reached into the front pocket of her jeans and withdrew a green leaf packet. She opened it up to reveal a white powder. "I know you as well as I know myself." Authia tenderly smiled at Nathen. "You'll never stay on this side of the falls. When Obasi approaches Tomas and me, I will be nervous, possibly even scared, and you'll sense that. I know that you plan to wait by the falls and not in the village as we discussed."

Nathen seemed shocked.

"Your blocking abilities need some work."

Nathen glanced at the powder then back up at Authia. "And what do you suggest I do? Sit back here while I know you're in danger?"

"Yes, that's exactly what I want you to do. There's too much at stake. I love that you want to be my protector, my savior, but not this time."

"Sorry, my Love. But I will not sit back and allow you to be hurt."

"I know. And that's why I have to do this." Authia raised her hand that contained the packet and blew its contents into Nathen's face.

He shook his head and used his hands to wipe the powder from his eyes.

"I'm sorry, sweetheart, but it was the only thing I could think of." She watched on as Nathen tried to speak.

He started to sway, then fell to the ground, unconscious.

Saburo, visibly shocked by what he just witnessed, glanced down at Nathen then back up to Authia. "What the hell did you just do?"

"He's sleeping. He'll be fine. Probably really upset with me when he wakes up, but he'll get over it. You're going to the birthing hut with Arman, Tuval, and Hansen. Help protect the warrior's families." Authia glanced over to Hansen. "Before Nathen wakes, place him on top of the roots of the great tree. His father will make sure he stays put. Stay by his side, Hansen. He'll be easier to deal with if you're there."

"Don't worry Authia . . . I'll take care of him."

Saburo interjected, "Ahhh . . . what does his father and a tree got to do with anything?"

Authia chuckled. "Watch and learn. You'd better leave now. I have no idea how long he'll be out." Arman and Tuval placed Nathen onto a litter then each took an end and lifted him up. Authia walked over to Nathen and ran her hand alongside his face. "I'm so sorry, my Love. But I had no other choice." She leaned over and tenderly kissed him. Then she stood back, not taking her focus off Nathen. "Okay, go. I'm going to get Tomas." Authia didn't move. Instead, she just stood watching until they were swallowed up by the jungle. When she started to leave, her mind came alive with Tamara's voice.

Rick watched on as his men prepared themselves for the upcoming battle. He scanned the area for Tamara but couldn't find her. He felt disappointed, because he genuinely wanted to see her one last time before he left.

Travis, covered in the muck, rifle slung onto his back, joined Rick. "We're almost ready."

Rick glanced over at Travis. "Sorry, what did you say?"

Travis laughed. "Get your mind in the game. She went into that hut over there." Travis motioned toward the priestess' hut. "Go say what you have to say, then meet us at the falls." Travis' expression went from lighthearted to very serious. "We need you focused, Rick. A hundred and ten percent. If you can't, then stay back."

Rick placed his right hand on Travis' shoulder. "You're right, and I *will* be focused. You can trust me. I'll say what I have to say to Tamara, then I'm all in."

"Good to hear, 'cause we could really use you." Rick watched as Travis left to join the other men. Travis was right, he had to be focused, but he also had to deal with his feelings for Tamara and her apparent feelings for him. With determined strides, he headed toward the priestess' hut.

Tamara, dressed in her ceremonial gown, sat on the ground of the hut staring into the lifeless coals of the fire pit. She needed advice, so she melded with her Mistress and requested her help. She only had to wait a few minutes before Authia joined her. When Authia entered the hut, Tamara glanced up, revealing to her Mistress her tear-stained cheeks and the sadness that overwhelmed her.

Authia sat by her side and took her hand in hers. "Tamara, what's wrong?"

"I am in need of your guidance."

"Of course. What do you need?"

"You told me the story of how you met my Lord. That you fell in love with him before you saw him. Am I correct?"

"Yes."

"Did you ever imagine what he would look like?"

"Many times. I even dreamt about him, but now that I think about it, in the dreams I never saw his face."

"When you did see his face for the first time, did it displease you?"

Authia had a look of puzzlement, and then she smiled at Tamara. "Do you have feelings for one of the outsiders?"

Tamara looked down at the ground then slowly she raised her head, tears in her eyes. "Yes. Is that wrong?"

"Oh my God, Tamara, no, not at all. Does he feel the same way toward you?"

"Yes, I believe so. You did not answer my question. Did it displease you when you saw my Lord's face for the first time?"

"I knew all along that Nathen was hiding something about his face. But I never really gave it much thought. When he finally did reveal his face to me, I saw the Nathen I loved."

Tamara looked puzzled. "I do not understand."

"I was head over heels in love with Nathen for who he was on the inside. It didn't matter what he looked like. Your physical appearance doesn't dictate who you are. You're afraid that when the spell is lifted that he won't love you anymore?"

"Yes. And that is why we can never be together."

Authia sighed. "I don't know what to tell you, Tamara. A lot depends on what kind of person he is. You see, I, myself, do not hold a lot of value in what a person looks like. I care about who the person is. If your guy feels the same way, then you have nothing to fear."

"How do I know if he feels the same way?"

Rick interrupted. "You can try asking."

Tamara's head shot up. She looked at Rick, then at Authia who was smiling at her. "I think I'm going to leave the two of you alone." Authia got up to leave, then stopped at Rick and whispered something to him.

When she left the hut, Rick came to sit next to Tamara.

"What did my Mistress speak to you?"

"A friendly warning."

"I do not understand."

"Well let's say she made it clear that I was not to hurt you. So, are you going to ask me?"

"No. It is hard to ask a question when you are not aware of the meaning behind the question."

"Well, that's not cryptic. Tamara, I heard part of your conversation. Why does appearance mean so much to you?"

"It does not. But it may mean a lot to you. In order to protect the tribe, we have hidden ourselves behind a veil of deception. When that veil is lifted, you will not be happy with the reality of what we are."

"Not quite sure what that means, but it kind of reminds me of a story I once heard."

"A story?"

"It was about an entire town of people that had been horribly disfigured because of a government experiment that went terribly wrong. They found a way to hide their disfigurement so that other people would see them as if they were normal. In order for the *spell* to work, they couldn't leave their town. Just like you can't leave your village. Tamara, I'm no different than Authia. I don't judge a person by their appearance. I don't know what you are hiding, and frankly, I don't give a damn. I love you. Your innocence, your devotion, who you are." Rick took Tamara's hands in hers. "I'm going out there not to fight for your village. I'm fighting for you. Please trust me. I would never hurt you."

Tamara sat quietly holding Rick's hands. Should she trust him? Could he love her for who she truly was? "My Lord took a chance. He revealed himself to my Mistress, not knowing for sure what her reaction would be. There are no guarantees in life. Yes, I will trust you on one condition."

"Name it."

"When this battle is over, and we are as we should be, you must be honest with me, and yourself."

"Done." Rick smiled at Tamara. "Would I be out of line if I asked for a good luck kiss?"

Tamara put her arms around Rick and pulled him close to her. The kiss was tender, passionate, and warmed her to her very soul. "You must leave. I will ask our Ancestors to watch over you."

"You're not coming to see me off?"

"No. We cannot be seen in public as a couple until you have received the permission of my Lord."

Rick stood and pulled Tamara to her feet. He gathered her into his arms. "That's first on my list when I get back." He kissed her one last time and left the hut.

Tamara remained standing, overwhelmed by what had just transpired. Could there be a chance that he would accept her for who she was? She smiled at the prospect, but her joy was short-lived. A feeling of dread and death surged through her body. It was playing with her, taunting her. Then a voice, distant, barely discernable came to her. *You are such a fool.*

Who are you? Tamara crooked her head ever so slightly. She sensed the aura behind the voice. *Celest. I thought you would be saving your energy.*

Oh, you are good. I was told that you are gifted in sensing auras. Why are you here?

I have a proposition for you.

I do not understand. You have nothing that I want.

You want that young man that just walked out of your hut.

Tamara had to be careful. She couldn't reveal any

emotions, for Celest would surely feed off them. Calmly she addressed Celest. *I am listening.*

I have something you want, and you have something I want.

And what is it that you want?

Energy, strength, power!

And why would you need me?

Join with me. Help me right a terrible injustice, and I will see to it that your man survives the battle that is yet to come.

I do not sense that his life is in danger. Therefore, you have nothing to offer me.

Do not be so sure of yourself. There is more than one battle that needs to be fought.

I am aware of that. He will not be a participant in the second battle.

Are you sure of that?

CHAPTER THIRTY-TWO

Obasi watched his men as they hacked at the vegetation, widening the trail that Tomas had made before them. He was beginning to lose patience with them. The heat, insects, and thin air were slowing them down. Obasi, unaffected by the conditions, double-timed it until he was ahead of them. Then he walked out onto the path. His stance was rigid and extremely intimidating. His left hand was resting on the handle of his machete, and concealed in his right hand, was his hunting knife. The men were walking two abreast, and when the first two saw him, they stopped dead in their tracks. Obasi could see the fear in their eyes, and he could smell the fear that oozed from their pores. And even though he gave the appearance of being extremely angry, deep inside, he was reveling in their discomfort.

He waited until he knew he had their undivided attention. "I made it very clear that we are to reach the top of the mountain before noon." Obasi gazed up at the morning sky and took note of where the sun was. He turned his attention back to his men, glaring at them. "You walk like women. Slow! Maybe you need motivation. Those of you that don't reach the top of the mountain by noon today will die by my hand."

One of the two men at the head of the group nervously spoke up, "We will Obasi, but we could use a break. We need water. We need to rest."

Obasi didn't say a word, and he didn't take one second to think. With the skill of a marksman, he threw his hunting knife at the man who spoke out. The knife embedded deep into the man's chest. He tried to speak, but the only sound that came forth was a gurgling sound as the blood pooled in his mouth and trickled down the sides of his lips. He fell to his knees, then onto his back. He was dead before he hit the ground. Obasi calmly walked up to him, withdrew his knife from the man's chest, wiped the blood off on his pants, then turned to face his men. "Does anyone else need to rest?" There was no response. The men continued their hike, stepping over the body of their comrade. As they walked past Obasi, not one man made eye contact. They had picked up their pace, and Obasi smiled as he retreated back into the jungle.

Rick, covered in green muck, rifle slung onto his back, and enough ammunition to last the entire day, made his way to the falls. His men were waiting as well as one of the priestesses. However, Nathen and Hansen were nowhere to be seen. Rick sought out Travis, who was standing at the entrance to the falls. "Where are Nathen and Hansen?"

"Apparently Authia has them at the birthing hut. Did you have your talk? Are you good?"

Rick smiled at Travis. "Better than good. So if we're all here, let's head out and get into position."

Travis nodded his head and glanced over at the priestess who stood a couple of feet away from him. "Ready when you are."

The priestess opened the palm of her hand, revealing a green leaf packet. As she entered the falls, the yellow globe that the men knew to expect surrounded her as well as those that followed her. She only ventured halfway behind the falls. The men had to inch past her as they continued to the other side. When the last man exited the falls, Rick watched as the yellow globe disappeared from view.

Travis approached Rick. "What the hell? Why didn't she come through? I almost wiped out twice trying to get past her."

Rick smiled at Travis. He knew perfectly well why she didn't venture any further. "She had her reasons. I want you to get the men in the trees. I'll get Ed tucked away." Rick searched his men until his gaze fell on Taylor. "Taylor, front and center." Taylor made his way through the men and stood before Rick. "We need to communicate with Authia. I want you to stay here. I'll radio you when we are in position then I want you to go back, let Authia know we are ready, then double-time it back here."

Taylor nodded that he understood and went to stand by the entrance to the falls. Rick glanced down at his watch. "If Saburo's right, we should be seeing Obasi, or at least his men, within the next couple of hours."

"We'll be ready. I got a good feeling about this, Rick." Travis grinned as he glanced over toward the jungle. "Obasi is as good as dead." He looked back at Rick and extended his hand. "Here's to the end of Obasi's tyranny."

Rick accepted Travis' hand. "And to new beginnings." Rick watched as Travis led the men into the jungle, all except Ed. "You're with me." Rick led Ed to the very edge of the clearing right next to the pond. "Obasi has no reason to come this way." Rick handed Ed a walkie-talkie. "Keep this thing off. Once you've killed Obasi, radio me. Then I want you to take Authia and Tomas back to the village."

"You got one of those packets?"

Rick smiled. "Nope. You're going to get wet. Now find yourself a spot to lie down, and I'll make sure you're well covered." Rick spent the next thirty minutes making sure Ed was settled in. His rifle was in place resting on a couple of small logs that they had brought with them. Rick was taking no chances that Ed would get tired while holding the rifle, and by repositioning his grip, give himself away to Obasi. Remembering what Saburo had said, Rick made sure that the vegetation covering Ed looked as natural as possible. When he was finished, he climbed a nearby tree and looked down at the ground. He smiled, nodding his head. Ed totally blended in—he couldn't see him at all. Rick climbed back out of the tree and headed toward Travis, taking his position at the front of the horseshoe, closest to the path that led out of the jungle. Once he was settled, he radioed Taylor.

Authia left the priestess' hut and headed toward Sam and Tomas' hut. She was conflicted about her feelings concerning Tamara's love interest. On the one hand, she was happy for Tamara, for she knew that Tamara had not found anyone to give her heart to. She also knew that Tamara was saddened that she would end up with a mate of Nathen's choosing, not hers. But on the other hand, Rick was an outsider who had no idea of who or what the Jelani Tribe was. Would he still love her when her true appearance was revealed to him? Nobody, including Rick, knew the answer to that. However, Authia made it perfectly clear of what would happen if he hurt Tamara. Authia smiled to herself. There was a time when Tamara had protected her, so now she was returning the favor.

Authia reached the hut to find the warrior she had placed there, standing in front of the entrance, guarding the hut. As soon as he saw her, he bowed, then stood to one side. Authia called out before she entered. "Sam, its Authia, may I enter?"

"Of course, my Mistress." Sam pulled the flap covering the entrance to one side, allowing Authia to enter.

She found Tomas sitting on his sleeping mat, the machete still firmly grasped in his right hand. He stood and bowed before Authia. "How are you, Tomas?"

"I am fine, my Mistress."

"Please sit. I need to talk to you. Both of you."

Sam and Tomas sat cross-legged by the fire pit that was still warm from their morning meal. Tomas spoke first. "Do you know how long the Lord wishes us to stay here? I would very much like to go home."

"And you will, Tomas, very soon. Nathen, our Lord, has a favor to ask of you."

"Anything, my Mistress."

"I have to go to your village, and Nathen would feel better if you came with me. To protect me. Would you do that for me?"

Sam looked at Authia, obviously unsettled by her request. But Tomas smiled and appeared delighted. "It would be my honor. When do we leave?"

"Shortly. I just need to speak with Sam outside of the hut. Can you wait here?"

"Yes." Tomas rested his hands on his knees with no indication that he was in any pain.

Authia stood and left the hut followed by Sam. "I don't understand, my Mistress. I thought it was too dangerous for Tomas to leave the hut."

"It is, but we need his help. I'm taking every precaution to protect him."

"What do you need him to do?"

"There's a very bad man coming this way. And, unfortunately, Tomas is the only one who can draw this person out into the open so that we can kill him."

"It sounds as if you're using Tomas as bait."

"Not just Tomas, myself as well. I'll be by his side the entire time." Authia heard someone approaching and turned to find Taylor. "Is it time?"

"Yes, we're ready."

"I'm on my way. You head back. I'll be right behind you." Authia glanced over at Sam. "Trust me, if there was any other way to do this, I would. But there isn't, and we haven't much time."

"All right. I trust that you'll take good care of Tomas. I'll go get him."

Sam disappeared into the hut while Authia sent the warrior away. A minute later, Tomas emerged from the hut. "Ready, my Mistress."

"Thank you, Tomas. I have one other favor."

"Anything."

Authia tried to appear nervous. "Would you mind holding my hand? I'm very nervous about going to your village."

It was obvious to Authia that Tomas didn't understand her request. She had to come up with a lie that he would believe. "You see, Tomas, I'm usually with Nathen, and he always holds my hand to make me feel safe." Authia held her breath as she waited for a reaction from Tomas.

Tomas appeared to be giving her comment a great deal of thought. Finally, he smiled and shook his head in agreement. "I would be honored to hold your hand. Only, I do not know if it will be enough to make you feel safe. I am not a Lord."

Authia smiled as she took a breath. "Oh, it will, Tomas. I'll tell you what. How about I close my eyes and pretend for just a moment that you are Nathen."

Tomas appeared as though he was giving Authia's suggestion of holding her hand serious thought. "If you think that would help. Though I do not see how."

"Can't hurt to try." Authia extended her right hand to Tomas, who grasped it firmly in his left hand. Authia closed her eyes, concentrating on Tomas. She saw into his mind— she saw his memories that had been buried deep within the furthest recesses of his mind. And she wept, for she had never seen one person suffer such atrocities. Authia gave her head a shake then focused her memories onto Tomas'. She flooded his mind with thoughts of his village, her village, and the people that he called family and friends. Slowly she opened her eyes and glanced over to Tomas. He was smiling as he looked up at her. She read Tomas, and all she could see were her own thoughts. It had worked, and as long as they held hands, Tomas would be safe.

Nathen started to stir. He felt like he was swimming in a pool of fog. He tried to open his eyes, but they wouldn't cooperate. His eyelids felt heavy with sleep, and his head throbbed. Nathen fought to gain control of his body. He forced his eyes to open and then tried to focus on what was in front of him-but everything was blurred. He tried to move his legs, but they wouldn't budge.

As he concentrated on his surroundings, a silhouette of someone sitting beside him came into view. The person was speaking to him, but Nathen couldn't make out what the person was saying. He felt something cool being placed against his lips. The person sitting next to him was trying to get him to drink. Nathen welcomed the water and gulped as much as he could. His head started to clear as well as his vision just in time to see a bucket of water being poured over his head. Nathen cursed as he shook his head. He tried to raise his hands to wipe the water from his face, but they were secured tight against the sides of his body. With a clear head, he looked up at the person that was holding the bucket.

"What the hell Hansen. What did you do to me?" Nathen was sitting on the ground, his back against his father's tree. He looked down at his legs only to find them held in place with the roots of the tree. These roots were also responsible for securing his arms in place.

"Not me." Hansen knelt on his haunches, the bucket at his side. "Did you actually think you could hide your thoughts from Authia?"

"Authia did this?"

"Well, yes. Her and your father."

"My father?"

Yes, my son. You are to remain here until Authia has completed her task.

Her task is going to get her killed!

There is no guarantee for any outcome. Authia is confident that neither she nor Tomas is in any immediate danger. She read Tomas, and she did not see death. However, in your current state of mind, you could do more harm than good.

How can you possibly say that?

If you enter the outside world, they will see you for who you are. The people who came to protect you will be distracted. And distraction could kill them.

Nathen sat very still thinking hard about what his father said. *I admit, I never thought of that.*

Exactly. You only think of the one person, not the entire tribe. As Lord, you must do what is in the best interest for all concerned. Not just Authia.

She's everything to me. I couldn't live with myself if anything should happen to her.

I know, my son. I felt the same about your mother. I put her ahead of everything, and look what it got me. I lost on all fronts. I will continue to hold onto you until I am certain that your head is clear. That you will make the right decision.

And what is the right decision, Father?

Only you know the answer to that.

Nathen closed his mind to his father and opened it to Authia. *You've been busy, my Love.*

Are you angry with me?

Yes. But I understand the reasoning.

Really?

Well, let's say I'm beginning to. Where are you?

I'm just entering the falls. I'm with Tomas. I promise I won't endanger myself. If I think for one second that I'm not in control of the situation, I'll come back. I have to go. I love you, but I'm not sorry for what I did.

There's nothing to be sorry about. You made the right decision for the tribe. Something I was unable to do.

Nathen closed his eyes. He knew Authia was scared, and in his present situation, there was nothing he could do. Visions of her lying on the ground, beaten and bloodied danced in his mind, taunting him. Nathen roared in frustration, sending the nearby birds and animals scurrying in all directions. When he was finished, he looked over to Hansen. "I need your help. Authia needs your help."

CHAPTER THIRTY-THREE

Authia made her way to the outcrop of rocks where she and Tomas were to remain in order to flush out Obasi. Tomas tried to continue walking, but Authia held him back. He glanced up at Authia. "Are we not going to my village?"

"Actually, Nathen wants us to wait here. Let's just sit on these rocks until he arrives." Tomas sat next to Authia, checking out his surroundings, entirely oblivious to what was coming his way. Authia, on the other hand, was totally aware and made sure that from whatever direction Obasi approached them, his back would be to Ed.

Rick sat in his tree, straddling a branch, with his rifle resting across his lap. He was listening, waiting for any indication that Obasi and his men were approaching. He was thinking of maybe climbing a little higher when he realized that the jungle had become quiet—a little too quiet. The absence of any animal noises told Rick that the enemy was close. He signaled to his men, and they raised their rifles, getting ready to fire. A few minutes later, they could hear the sound of machetes hacking at the vegetation, then the sounds of men approaching. From Rick's vantage point, he could see where the path entered the clearing. First two men came into view, then four, then ten. However, they stopped at the edge of the clearing. Rick watched the men, wondering what the hell they were doing. Did they somehow see the mines? One of the lead men glanced back over his shoulder, looking into the trees. Rick followed his gaze but could see nothing. The man signaled to his men, and they continued to walk further into the clearing. They held their rifles, ready to fire as they scrutinized the village.

Rick held his breath as they approached the mines. The majority of Obasi's men were in the clearing when the first mine went off. Then another and another. The screams of men echoed throughout the jungle. Obasi's men were running in all directions, all directions except for the path they just came from, the path they knew was safe. And Rick knew it was because Obasi was there. He strained to see into the trees, but then he remembered Saburo's words. *Don't worry about Obasi. Focus on his men. Lessen the numbers.* Rick raised his rifle and concentrated on the men below. Every one of Obasi's men had started to run into the jungle right into the middle of the horseshoe. Then they stopped as they stood there looking everywhere but in the trees. It was Rick that was to take the first shot that would signal the rest of his men to start firing. He aimed his rifle at the group of men, put his finger on the trigger, but he didn't fire. He just stared at the men below. It would be like shooting fish in a barrel, they had no chance. But wasn't that the way it was supposed to be? It was either them or him. No, it was either them or Tamara. Rick aimed his rifle, pulled the trigger, and fired the first shot.

Obasi sat in his tree, high above the ground, watching his men as they approached the village. For some reason, they suddenly stopped. Obasi glared down at them as he reached for his hunting knife. He pulled it from its sheaf and was about to throw it when one of his men looked up at him. He knew they couldn't see him, but just the threat that he was there would be enough, and it was. His men pushed forward, and he returned the knife to its resting place. Obasi leaned his back against the tree, folded his arms across his chest, and watched.

His men were cautious, too cautious. *Get on with it!* Obasi scanned the village. It had been destroyed, leaving only one hut standing. The debris from the destruction of the other huts littered the village. Something caught Obasi's attention. It was the way the debris was scattered. There was a definite pattern that was void of any debris. He sat up and took a closer look then realized that the ground appeared too neat, as if it had been swept with palm leaves. Obasi chuckled to himself. He leaned back against the tree and waited for the show. Sure enough, not a moment later, the first mine went off, and Obasi smiled as he watched his men being blown to kingdom come. They scattered like rats on a sinking ship, but not one of them would dare come down the path toward Obasi. They knew if they did, they were dead.

Obasi continued to watch as his men ran into the jungle. He wanted a better vantage point, so he leaped from one tree to another with the skill and agility of a monkey. He stopped about halfway into the jungle and listened to the quiet. He could just make out his men through the thick vegetation. They were standing all together, rifles raised, ready to shoot at anything that moved. Then the first shot rang out, followed by so much gunfire that it deafened Obasi. His men didn't have a chance. But that was fine with Obasi, because their death gave him what he needed, what he wanted.

He focused on the gunfire but couldn't make out who was firing. He concentrated solely on the trees, and that was where he saw the slightest glimmer of a rifle. He followed down the rifle's barrel in the attempt to find the hand that held it but could see nothing. He was the best, and nothing could hide from him. Yet the men that wielded these weapons blended into the trees as if they were one with the tree. For a minute, his mind wandered, fearful that some sort of sorcery was concealing these men, that maybe the Gods themselves were protecting these men. He sat very still, watching the path of the bullets until it was clear to Obasi what these men were protecting. Gods or no Gods, he knew where he had to go.

Ed lay perfectly still as he monitored the area surrounding the pond. He could see Authia and Tomas sitting on an outcrop of rocks. Not seconds later, the mines started going off. He could hear men screaming, and he could hear them crashing through the jungle. Then it went quiet. He waited for the first shot, but it didn't come. What was Rick waiting for? He glanced over in the direction of the jungle, half expecting Obasi's men to come running out. But no one came, and then the silence was filled with the sounds of gunfire. The gunfire was so loud, Ed didn't hear the sound of the man moving from one tree to another. At first, he ignored the leaves that fell from the tree above him. He was focused on the matter at hand, which was to kill Obasi. It wasn't until a small branch fell and hit him on the back of his head that Ed made a fatal mistake—he looked up. The next thing he knew a large man was straddling him, his knee pressed firmly on Ed's back. Ed could feel his head being pulled back, and before he could make a sound, the cold steel blade of a knife sliced across his throat.

Hansen made it back to the village in record time. Nathen was adamant that Authia was in danger, and Hansen believed him. He also knew he was the only one that could cross the falls without risking the tribes secret. He ran up to one of Rick's men. "I need your rifle."

The man looked at Hansen as if he were crazy. "There are plenty in the crate. Go help yourself."

"They're dismantled, yours isn't." Hansen held out his hand. "Now give me your rifle, or I'll take it from you. Unless of course, you want to explain to Nathen why I couldn't go to protect his wife?"

The man looked at Hansen wide-eyed. "Here, take it."

"That's better." Hansen examined the trigger area of the rifle. "Is the safety on?"

"Are you kidding me?"

"Look, it's a simple question."

"No, it's not. Just aim and pull the trigger. Do you know how to load it?"

"Won't be necessary. I'm only going to get one shot."

Hansen slung the gun onto his back and ran toward the falls.

Authia sat on the rock next to Tomas. She held his hand on her lap, cradling it ever so tenderly. When the first mine went off, both Tomas and Authia jumped to their feet. Tomas tried to let go of Authia's hand, but she held on. She could feel his fear, she could see it in his eyes when he glanced up at her. "It's all right, Tomas. We'll be safe here."

"Safe from what? What is going on?" The sound of exploding mines and men's screams stopped, and the jungle became quiet. "We should leave. This place is no longer safe." Tomas tried to pull Authia back toward the falls, but she wouldn't budge.

"It's going to be okay, Tomas. You must trust me." It was then that the shooting started. The sound of gunfire and chaos filled the jungle. Authia tried desperately to calm herself. She didn't want Nathen sensing that she was scared, especially since he couldn't do anything about it. She scanned the perimeter of the clearing waiting for the inevitable, waiting for Obasi. The gunfire seemed to be going on forever, and it was obviously affecting Tomas. He squeezed her hand to the point of being painful. He tugged at her again only this time he was trying to pull her toward the jungle. "What are you doing, Tomas?"

"The trees. We must hide in the trees."

Authia pulled back, stopping Tomas in his tracks. "No! We have to stay here. It's too dangerous in the jungle." Authia was about to pull Tomas against her and wrap her arms around him when she saw a man emerge from the jungle. He was African, filthy, and wearing only camouflage pants. He walked toward them, a smile on his face. Authia knew immediately that he was Obasi. She glanced over to Tomas who was staring at the man as if he were in a trance. She returned her gaze to the man, wondering why Ed had not fired, Obasi was completely exposed, Ed had his opportunity. Total fear enveloped Authia when she realized that the man came from the exact spot where Ed was hiding. As he grew closer, Authia could see the knife he was carrying in his right hand. He had it down at his side, and the blade was covered in what appeared to be blood. Red droplets fell to the ground, staining the dirt. She pulled Tomas, who was still transfixed on the man, closer to her. Authia knew that even though she promised Nathen that she wouldn't put herself in harm's way, it was too late to run.

The man stopped less than three feet away from her. Authia gathered all the courage she had and spoke to him. "I assume you're Obasi."

He smiled at her, revealing the large gap in his teeth. "You know me?"

"Everyone knows you. Your reputation has spread to the furthest corners of Africa." Authia had no idea what she was doing. Her only hope was that playing on his ego would buy her time. The gunfire was diminishing, which hopefully meant that Rick and his men would be coming back very soon.

Obasi glanced over to Tomas. "You have my guide."

"Your guide?"

Obasi chuckled. "Don't play with me, woman. I want the little man."

"Why? What's he to you?"

"That's none of your concern."

"Maybe I can help you."

Obasi looked at Authia as if he were weighing his options. "You mean nothing to me. You have no value." Obasi ran his knife from Authia's throat to just between her breasts. "Normally I would take you, have you, but there are far more desirable pleasures that await me. I'll take this little man, and he'll show me the way."

Authia was about to speak, but Obasi placed his left index finger on her lips. She could taste him—she could smell him. He took a step closer, and through his touch Authia, for the first time ever, saw what the future held for her. Tears started running down her cheeks, and then she gasped as she felt the blade of his knife slowly being pushed into her belly. Her body trembled. She took one breath, then another, then she crumpled to the ground letting go of Tomas' hand.

CHAPTER THIRTY-FOUR

Hansen ran as fast as his legs would allow him. When he reached the falls, he tucked the rifle close to his body in his attempt to keep it as dry as possible. He made his way over the slimy rocks, walked out into the clearing only to see Authia fall to the ground. There was a man standing over her, laughing, and standing next to him was Tomas. Tomas just stood there, his eyes wide, machete at his side, entirely focused on the man. Hansen raised his rifle, took aim through the scope, but before he could pull the trigger, what he witnessed made him lower his rifle as he watched on in horror.

Nathen's father still hadn't released him, and for a good reason. Nathen knew his father was one with his mind. He knew that his father could feel Authia's emotions as he could. Nathen sat on the ground, angry, staring ahead, not conversing with anyone, including his father. Suddenly, the roots that bound him became tighter. Nathen was about to call out to his father when Authia's emotions bombarded him. She was scared, Obasi was near. Her fear escalated, and for a brief moment, Nathen could see what Authia saw. He saw her future, he saw her lying on the ground, bloodied. Nathen screamed out to his father. "Release me! Now!"

I am sorry, my son. It is too late for Authia, but it is not too late for the tribe. The battle is not yet over. If I release you and you go to Authia, all will be lost.

I don't give a damn about the village, about the tribe. Don't you understand? I have nothing if I don't have her.

Nathen's father didn't respond. Nathen tried to reach out

to Authia, but there was only darkness. Tears filled his eyes as he hung his head and cried uncontrollably.

Tomas watched as the strange man approached. Something flickered in his mind. A memory buried deep within him. The man stood an arm's length away from him. His voice, his smell was all familiar. But how? He was speaking to Authia, and she called him Obasi. Something wasn't right. Tomas looked at Authia then back to Obasi. He saw the knife in Obasi's hand. Tomas remained fixated on the hand that held the knife. He knew it—he just couldn't place it. He watched as Obasi buried the blade of the knife deep into Authia's belly, and he did nothing. Authia fell to the ground, letting go of his hand.

The floodgates to Tomas' mind flew open, and as he listened to Obasi's laughter, all his memories of Obasi came to the surface.

Tomas' anger welled up inside of him. He glanced down to Authia then back up to Obasi. "You have killed my Mistress."

Obasi sneered at Tomas, stepped over Authia's body, then focused his attention in the direction of the falls. Obasi had his back to Tomas, and even though Tomas had a clear view of the falls, it didn't register to him who the man standing by the falls was. Nor did it register to him that he was holding a rifle. All he could hear was Obasi's laughter, all he could feel was Obasi's fist pummeling his body, his face. Even though the pain grew more intense with every memory, Tomas didn't care. He took a couple of steps back, raised the machete high in the air then ran toward Obasi, jumping at the last minute so that he would land on Obasi's back. He wrapped his legs tight around Obasi's rib cage. With his left arm, he put Obasi in a stranglehold, pulling as hard as he could to cut off Obasi's air. Then he took his machete and drove it deep into Obasi's chest. Obasi fought hard to pull Tomas off, but Tomas had too firm of a grip. Obasi dropped to his knees, his arms at his side. In one fluid movement, Tomas released his hold on Obasi's neck, and as he jumped off, he sliced at Obasi's neck with his machete. Tomas landed on his feet, and on the ground before him lay Obasi's headless body.

Tomas looked up at the man running toward him. He looked familiar. Tomas turned away and went over to Authia, lay on the ground next to her, and allowed the pain to consume his body.

Nathen sat on the ground, defeated. Wishing that it was him lying on the ground in a pool of his own blood. His father had released some of the pressure of the roots, but not enough for Nathen to escape. At this point, he didn't care. The last image he had of Authia was one he didn't want to keep, but one that he knew would haunt him for the rest of his life.

Minutes later, Tammy and Casandra approached him. They appeared to be in a hurry. Casandra knelt at Nathen's side, placing one hand on Nathen's shoulder, the other on the roots. "Please release my Lord. My Mistress needs him." The roots that bound him retreated into the ground. "Come with me, my Lord."

Nathen didn't budge. "Why? It's all over."

"No, my Lord, it isn't."

Nathen glanced up at the two women. Tammy was smiling at him. "You take pleasure in Authia's death?"

"Nathen, the tribe remains concealed."

Nathen straightened up. "What are you talking about?"

"I see you as I see me. If Authia was dead, you'd be back to normal."

"I saw her die, I felt it."

Casandra stood, looking down at Nathen. "You felt something, my Lord, but it was not her death. Now come quickly, she may not be dead now, but her life force is fading."

Hansen ran up to Authia, dropping to his knees when he reached her. She was on her side with her hair covering her face, the knife still embedded in her belly. Delicately he moved the hair from her face, then checked her neck for a pulse. He found one, but it was very weak. She was so pale, as if all the blood had been drained from her yet the pool of blood that she lay in was not that great. Hansen was conflicted as to whether or not he should move her. He glanced over to Tomas, who was curled up into a ball moaning in pain. He listened for the sounds of fighting but could hear none. Hansen took a chance and started yelling for help.

Rick raised his rifle so that the barrel was aimed at the canopy above him. He signaled to his men to stop firing. Sadly, Rick surveyed the human carnage that lay on the jungle floor. So much death. He climbed out of the tree, followed by his men. John was the first to approach him. "I didn't see any stragglers. I think all Obasi's men are here."

Rick didn't take his focus off the bodies piled one on top of the other. "Check them. See if any are alive and if they are, treat them for their injuries."

John looked at Rick in disbelief. "You want us to help them?"

Rick glared back at John. "I'm not lowering myself to Obasi's level. This" — Rick gestured toward Obasi's men — "doesn't please me or make me happy. Now take care of the wounded. We'll bury the dead."

John was about to argue with Rick when both men heard the cries for help. Rick signaled to his men. "That's Hansen. Keep your head on a swivel, Obasi may still be out there. This could be a trap." Rick cautiously led his men to the edge of the jungle. At first, he only saw Hansen leaning over a body with Tomas curled up next to it. There was one other body lying just off to the side. Rick entered the clearing trying to determine who the bodies were. However, when he realized that the body Hansen was leaning over was Authia, he broke into a full run, dropping to his knees when he was at her side. She was so pale, and there was a knife protruding from her belly. The headless body of Obasi was less than two feet away from her. "What the hell happened here? And what are you doing here?"

Hansen continued to stare at Authia. "Nathen sent me. He told me Authia was in danger, so I came here to protect her." He glanced up at Rick, his expression forlorn. "I didn't do a very good job. She has a pulse, but it's not very strong."

"What happened to Obasi? Did you kill him?"

"No. Tomas did. I can't even begin to explain what I witnessed. By the time I crossed through the falls, it was already too late. Authia was on the ground. I went to take a shot, but Tomas jumped on Obasi's back and did that to him." Hansen motioned in the direction of Obasi.

Rick looked in the direction that Ed was supposed to be. "Why didn't Ed take the shot?" Rick glanced over to Travis, who was already heading over to where Ed had been hidden. When he arrived, he just looked over at Rick and slowly shook his head. Rick felt sick. He's the one who hand-picked Ed, and instead of giving him the opportunity to kill one of the cruelest men on the face of the earth, he'd sent him to his death. He looked back over to Authia just as Hansen was about to pull the knife from her belly. "No! Don't remove it."

Hansen let go of the handle. "Why? We can't leave it in

her."

"If we remove it, she could bleed out. We've got to get her back to the village. Go get the litter that we hid. We'll take her back on that."

Hansen got up and headed into the jungle. Rick called Travis and John over. "Travis, take Tomas and head back to the village. Let them know we're coming with Authia." Travis didn't say a word. He bent down and scooped Tomas into his arms. Tomas cried in pain as Travis stood back up. "Make sure they know that she's on the brink of death." Travis nodded, then headed for the falls. John stood by waiting for his orders. "As soon as we get Authia on the litter, I want you and the rest of our men to check for wounded."

"You still want us to tend to the injured?"

"Yes. Nothing's changed. Let those that survived know that Obasi is dead."

Hansen returned with the litter. It took four men to lift Authia onto the litter so that the knife would not be disturbed. Then Rick and Hansen picked up the litter and headed for the falls.

With every ounce of strength he had, Nathen propelled himself through the jungle heading toward the falls. He had sent Casandra and Serena to the priestess' hut to make ready for Authia. Tammy remained behind with Joshawa. Nathen arrived just as Rick and Hansen were exiting the falls. He ran up to Authia, placing his hand on the side of her face. She was so pale, and her chest barely moved as she breathed. Her belly and the litter were covered in blood. Nathen placed his hand on her belly searching for any sign that their child was still alive. But he felt no heartbeat, no movement. All he felt was emptiness, and he knew that their child was dead.

Nathen went to pick up Authia, but Rick spoke out, "No,

Nathen. We have to keep her still. We don't want the blade to cause any more damage."

"I understand, but I can make it back to the village a lot quicker than you. And right now, every minute counts." Nathen gently scooped Authia into his arms. He held her as flat as he could, even though all he wanted was to pull her tight against him. "See you back at the village, and thank you." Nathen ran toward the village, his powerful legs closing the distance. He constantly attempted to meld with Authia, but there was nothing. Like her womb, he only felt emptiness. However, that didn't deter him. While there was still a spark, a minute chance for survival, Nathen would not give up. With a clear head and purpose in his heart, he entered the priestess' hut and laid Authia down on the mat that was next to Tomas.

Serena knelt by Authia's side. She placed her hands on Authia's chest, closed her eyes, and started chanting in the language of the priestesses. A faint glow encompassed Authia, lingering for only a few seconds. Serena opened her eyes and glanced over to Casandra and Tamara. "She is beyond potions and healing spirits. We must summon all the priestesses and pray to our Ancestors. It is the only chance she has."

Casandra nodded her head in agreement. "My Lord. Please return to the birthing hut and bring back our priestesses and your child. Waste no time."

Nathen left the hut, not saying a word.

Casandra turned to Tamara. "Go to our family hut and bring back as many packets as you can. These packets must represent all of the priestesses."

"Yes, mother." Tamara left, returning only moments later with two clay pots brimming over with packets. "Shall I place them around our Mistress?"

Serena interjected, "No, only on top of her. Make sure that she is completely covered from her neck to her toes. Place extra packets around the knife." Tamara went to work, having to return to the priestess' hut two times in order to have enough packets. When she was finished, Hansen and Rick had returned as well as Nathen, Tammy, and the priestesses. Cradled in Nathen's arms was his son. Nathen glanced over to Authia, then to Serena. "Now what?"

"Now it is up to the Ancestors and Authia. She has to want to live. May I have your son?"

Nathen gathered Joshawa a little closer to him. "What do you want with Joshawa?"

"As I said, my Lord, my Mistress must also fight to live. She will need encouragement. I will place Joshawa at her side. She will see him, and if she wants to hold him, then she will have to fight for that pleasure."

Nathen held Joshawa out to Serena who took him tenderly in her arms. She gazed into his eyes and smiled. "You are named after a great man. A man I loved with all my heart. He fought for your father and your grandmother's life. I was a different person back then, and I stopped him. Now it's your turn to fight for your mother, and I promise to do everything in my power to help you." Serena placed Joshawa at Authia's side.

Joshawa looked at his mother, placing a chubby hand on her head. Then he lay down at her side and placed his arm across her neck.

Serena smiled and turned to the others. "We are ready. Come join me, my sisters. Form a circle around our Mistress." Serena glanced over at the bystanders. "You may watch, but under no circumstance can you interfere. Will you see to that, my Lord?"

"Of course." Nathen turned to face Hansen, Rick, and

Tammy. "Rick, you're the only one here who hasn't already witnessed one of our ceremonies. Tamara will never be in danger. You mustn't interfere, or I'll remove you any way I have to."

Rick shrugged his shoulders. "Hey, I'm not saying or doing anything. If you swear that Tamara's not in any danger, then I'll believe you."

Nathen turned back around and nodded to Serena. "Whenever you're ready."

Serena sat on the ground, motioning her sisters to join her. They joined hands, closed their eyes, and then Serena began to chant. She called out to her Ancestors, only she did so in English so that her Mistress would hear them and understand. "We call out to the High Priestess Imani, to Lord Adeeowale and Lord Chike. Hear our pleas. Our Mistress lies before you and she is injured, near death. She is here in this state because she was trying to protect your people. The people of the Jelani Tribe. We ask that you show her mercy and give back to her the life she was so willing to lose in our protection. Oh Ancestors, hear our pleas, help our Mistress."

The priestesses all bowed their heads, and as they did, the packets started to glow. Each packed joined with the packets next to it until they formed one large packet. Joshawa barely stirred, as if he knew his job was to hold on to his mother. Authia's body lifted ever so slightly from the mat, allowing the packets to surround her completely. It was as if they had a mind of their own.

Serena, her head still bowed, continued her chanting while the other priestesses remained quiet. "Thank you, Ancestors of the past. I feel that you are near. Please show yourself. Tell me what needs to be done to save the life of our Mistress." Serena gazed up to see an apparition appear above Authia's body, and she knew exactly who it was. "High Priestess Imani, you honor us with your presence."

"Priestess Serena. I see you have found your way. Tell me, why is the life of this outsider so important to you?"

"My Priestess Imani, she is an outsider only in appearance. Her heart is pure and devoted to the Jelani Tribe. She has earned your help."

"It is not our way to save the life of an outsider."

Serena was becoming frustrated with the Ancestor who'd chosen to show herself. "How can you say that when she has saved the tribe not once but on two occasions This time from outsiders, and once before, when she threw down the tyranny that ruled our tribe."

"This is true. However, her life force is too weak. She is beyond even what we can do."

"Then join her with another life force."

The High Priestess Imani smiled. "You have someone in mind?"

"Yes, take me. I will offer my life force so that my Mistress will live."

Chapter Thirty-Five

Nathen and the others were given the privilege of not only seeing what was transpiring but also hearing. Authia needed a life force. Otherwise, she would die. Nathen was ready to offer his when Serena spoke up. Nathen couldn't believe what he was hearing. Of all people, it was Serena who would offer her life force to save Authia. He'd been told not to interfere, but he couldn't just stand by without confronting Serena and finding out her motive behind her generous offer. He was about to step forward, but Rick held him back. Nathen turned and glared at him. "What do you think you're doing?"

"Your rules. No interference."

"You don't understand what's happening."

"Someone has offered herself to save Authia's life. What's not to understand?"

"That someone is Serena, and you don't know our history."

"Maybe not. But are you willing to risk undoing whatever's going on here? As I see it, Authia needs a life force. Who cares where it comes from."

Nathen turned his attention from Rick to Authia and his son. What would he give, what would he do to save the life of the woman he loved? Rick was right . . . he couldn't interfere. Nathen shook loose of Rick's grasp, folded his arms across his chest and glared at the back of Serena's head.

"My, Serena, you have come a long way. Are you sure that you want this? Your decision goes against everything that you desire."

"What I desired was to be human, which, as you can see, I am. Now my only desire is to make amends and to save the life of my Mistress. I took the life of someone she loved. Can you think of a better way to ask for forgiveness?"

"I always had faith in you. And you have not let me down. Know that with this sacrifice you have earned your place with the Ancestors, High Priestess Serena."

Serena was overjoyed. Not only could she possibly make up for the life she had taken, but she would also have a place with the Ancestors. She was about to step forward when Casandra intervened. She appeared to be upset with Serena's decision.

"Serena, you can't do this. Let one of the other priestesses offer their life force. We need you to fight Celest."

"You do not need me. You have all the power you need sitting right next to you."

Casandra glanced over to Tamara, then back to Serena. "She's too young, too inexperienced."

"I will let you in on a little secret. Out of the three of us, my mother fears Tamara the most. Trust me . . . she will be the driving force behind my mother's demise." Serena smiled as she gazed down at Authia. "I am ready."

The High Priestess Imani raised her arms in front of her, her palms facing out. "Then it shall be done."

Serena left the circle and went over to pick up Joshawa. She placed him on Authia's chest, then lay down next to her so that their bodies were touching. The packets grew brighter as they started shifting, reaching out until they completely covered Authia, Joshawa, and Serena with only the handle of the knife being exposed. The cocoon became brighter as it tightened around them. High Priestess Imani waved her hands over the cocoon, causing it to spin almost out of control. In a flash of light, the cocoon disappeared, and the knife fell to the ground.

Authia was in a dark place. She tried to focus on her surroundings, but she couldn't see past the darkness. She felt weak, as if she was completely drained of all her energy. She couldn't see so she, concentrated on what she could hear and what she could smell. She could smell Nathen, and she knew he was close. She tried to smile but didn't have the strength. She could hear people speaking but couldn't make out what they were saying. Then she felt her son. She tried to reach out to him, but her arms wouldn't cooperate. She was becoming weaker, and the desire to live was fading. *So, this is death. I will never see my son or Nathen again.*

You are going to have to do better than that. Where is the fighter, the person who does not give up?

Serena?

Yes, my Mistress.

Where am I?

You and I are in the realm between reality and the afterlife. If you want to go back to your son and Nathen, then fight for it. Reach out to your son. Take hold of him.

I can't. I haven't the energy.

Then perhaps I can help. I offer you my life force. It is yours for the taking. All you have to do is to want to live. Take your son, prove that you are worthy of my gift.

I don't understand.

What is there to understand? Either you want to live, or you do not. The choice is yours.

Authia could feel her son laying on her chest. He was reaching up to her. She could hear him cry out for her. Authia tried to reach up to him, but her arms remained at her side. Authia closed her eyes and dug deep inside of herself. She thought of her mother and all that she had done to protect her. She thought of what it had cost her mother. She thought of those who believed in her, gave their lives for her. *I'm not throwing away what was given to me. Help me, Serena, help me find my way home.*

You are ready. Take your son, and I will give you my life force.

Authia focused everything she had on her son. Her arms didn't feel so heavy. They raised toward her chest, wrapping themselves around Joshawa. She held on tight, tears forming in her eyes. *I want to live, Serena.*

And so you shall. Serena once more became a wisp and entered Authia. Only this time she didn't possess her. She joined her life force with that of Authia's. Serena could feel Authia's heart grow stronger with every beat. She could feel the blood that nourished Authia flow through her veins. She could feel the wound caused by the knife slowly closing, as if it had never been there. And Serena was at peace. It was time for Serena to join her Ancestors, but before she left, she spoke one last time to Authia. *I am sorry, my Mistress, but your child, the one you carried in your belly, did not survive. If I could have saved her, I would have.*

Her?

Yes, her. You will live to see your son grow into a man, but he will be your only child. Serena smiled at Authia. *And you will be your own person. Know that nothing of me will remain. Well, almost nothing.*

Serena left Authia's body and stood next to her Ancestor, watching on as Authia's body was gently lowered onto her sleeping mat.

The High Priestess Imani smiled at Serena. *Welcome, High Priestess Serena. Come with me. We must prepare you for your next battle.*

Nathen watched in horror as the cocoon that contained Authia and his son disappeared. Only the knife remained behind. It lay on the ground, stained in Authia's blood. Nathen walked over to her sleeping mat, slowly shaking his head. He turned to face Casandra. "What just happened? Where are Authia and my son?"

"Calm yourself, my Lord. They're with Serena, and they're in a place that is safe. However, my Mistress must choose to live, or she and your son will be lost to us forever."

"Of course, she wants to live. Authia is a fighter."

"Then there is nothing to be concerned about. We just have to wait."

"How long?"

"Not long, my Lord. They can't remain where they are for any length of time."

Nathen sat on the ground next to Authia's sleeping mat. He focused solely on the mat, hoping that maybe, just maybe, if he concentrated hard enough, she would reappear. The minutes dragged on for what seemed like an eternity. Nathen could tell that everyone in the hut was watching him. Not a word was said. Even Tomas managed to fall into a deep sleep, oblivious to his pain.

The shimmer of light started ever so slightly. Nathen didn't even notice it at first. What he felt was a surge of warmth coming from the sleeping mat. He gazed up from the mat and saw the light. It was taking shape as it was slowly being lowered onto the mat. Nathen held his breath as the light diminished and Authia and his son appeared.

Authia opened her eyes and smiled at Nathen. "Hello, my husband."

Nathen gathered her and Joshawa into his arms. He held them so tight that Joshawa began to cry. Nathen pulled away from the embrace and gazed at Authia, tears in his eyes. "I thought I lost you, both of you."

"I'm so sorry. I shouldn't have stayed. I knew something was wrong, but I was afraid that if I ran back to the falls, Obasi would follow me."

"Shhh, my Love. There is nothing to be sorry about. Are

you all right?"

"Yes, I'm fine. Though my chest hurts."

Nathen delicately pulled Authia's shirt to one side. Just above her left breast was a small tattoo of a blue wisp.

Authia started to laugh.

"What's so funny, my Love?"

"Serena mentioned that she left something of herself behind."

Tammy scanned the small group that was hovering over Authia, thrilled that she was alive. However, in their exuberance, she could see that they were completely missing what was staring them right in the face. At least everyone but Rick. "Umm . . . Casandra . . . wasn't Serena part of the circle that created the concealment spell?"

Casandra turned to face Tammy. "Yes, she was."

Tammy watched as Casandra's face went from joy to fear. "And our sister is now dead."

Everyone turned to face Rick—everyone except Tamara. She stood frozen in place, totally aware of the consequences of Serena's death. The Jelani Tribe appeared as they should be. Rick and his men would see the tribe in their true form. Rick would see *her* in her true form. Tears started running down her cheeks, for she was sure that Rick would no longer want her. She felt a hand on her shoulder, and slowly, she turned to face the man who held her heart. She wiped the tears from her face, squared her shoulders, and looked upon Rick to show him that she had accepted what she knew would come to pass.

He smiled at her as he reached up and held a couple of strands of her shocking red hair between his fingers. "I like redheads."

"You find my appearance amusing?"

"I find you amusing. Why would you think that I would love you any less?"

"Do you not see what stands before you?"

"I see you, Tamara. I see a beautiful, caring, loving person. How could I see anything else?"

Tamara was confused. She wanted to see what he saw. Did her appearance not change? She glanced over at Tammy. "How do you see me?"

"Like I did when I first came here. The spell's broken."

She returned her gaze to Rick. "You see me as I truly am, and you still want to give your heart to me?"

"Yes, I do." Rick went to lean closer to Tamara, obviously in an attempt to kiss her, but suddenly stopped. "I'm forgetting one thing." He turned to face Nathen. "Lord Nathen, do I have your permission to give my heart to Tamara?"

Nathen smiled. "Tamara, do you wish to give your heart to this man?"

"Yes, my Lord, it would please me greatly."

"Then you have my permission."

Rick pulled Tamara close to him and tenderly kissed her. As he pulled away, he appeared to be troubled as if he had forgotten something. "Shit! Sorry sweetheart, I just realized that my men are outside with your people. They're probably wondering what the hell just happened. I have to go to them."

Tamara took his hand. "I will go with you. Stand by your side."

Authia looked at Nathen. "You should go too."

"I'm not leaving your side."

"I'm fine. Help Rick explain who we are."

Hansen walked over to Authia. "Go on Nathen. Tammy and I will stay with Authia."

Nathen, Tamara, and Rick left the hut. Authia handed Joshawa to Tammy and was about to stand up when she noticed Tomas. "How is he?" Her eyes got wide. "Oh my God, what about Obasi? Did Ed kill him?"

Authia knew right away that something was wrong. Everyone had a look of dread on their face. "What happened?"

Hansen knelt in front of Authia. "Obasi is dead, but it wasn't Ed that killed him. Obasi actually killed Ed."

Authia was overtaken with grief. Their plan was perfect. Why didn't it work? "Then who killed Obasi?"

Hansen motioned toward Tomas.

Authia looked over to Tomas then back at Hansen. "I don't understand. How?"

"I don't know, Authia. I was watching it from the falls. You fell to the ground, and it was as if something snapped in Tomas. He jumped on Obasi's back, and . . . well, he killed him."

Authia knew precisely what had happened to Tomas—he'd remembered. She moved closer to Tomas and took his hand in hers. Slowly he opened his eyes, smiling when he saw Authia.

"You are alive, my Mistress. I am so happy to see you."

"I owe you my life, Tomas. The tribe owes you a great debt."

"It is my job, my honor to protect the Valley of the Lion People." Tomas closed his eyes as Authia moved closer to him. Delicately she ran her hand along the side of his face. Through their touch, Authia could feel his energy slowly leaving him.

She looked up to Casandra. "What is going to happen to Tomas? Can we help him?"

"I can't see how my Mistress. There's too much damage. There is nothing we can do for him."

"You can give me back my life, but you can't help him?"

"You were easy. You had a knife wound. Your mind was sound. His isn't."

Authia fought back the tears. She could feel Tomas gently squeeze her hand. She gazed down at him. "What can I do for you, Tomas?"

"It would honor me if you would bury me with your people."

"Now, don't talk like that."

"Please, my Mistress."

Authia tried to maintain her composure. "Yes, I promise, but there is no need to talk about that now."

"My Mistress, I remember everything. I am broken in body and mind, but I am whole in spirit. I go to my ancestors as a proud warrior. Do not be sad for me, be happy. Celebrate my life, not my death." Tomas took one last breath as he closed his eyes. Authia sobbed as she felt Tomas slip away. Then there was nothing. Just an empty shell.

Rick and Tamara led Nathen to the communal fire pit. Rick's men had returned, and they were all gathered with Nathen's people at the pit. However, they stood divided, Rick's men and Saburo on one side of the pit, the tribe on the other. Nothing was being said, just awkward silence as Rick's men gawked at the warriors. Rick sought out Travis, then went to join him. "Guess I got some explaining to do."

"Hell, yeah. What happened? One minute they were normal, and now they look like this."

"This is normal, Travis. Normal for them. They're still the same people. Were there any survivors?"

Travis shook his head. "No. We have a lot of bodies to

bury."

"Okay, we'll figure that out later. Right now, Nathen and I are going to try to make some sense out of this for the men."

"What about Tamara?"

"What about her?"

"Well, she's a little different now."

"Not to me."

Travis chuckled. "How am I not surprised."

Rick went to join Nathen on the makeshift platform. Tamara remained on the ground at Rick's side. Rick looked over to Nathen. "Mind if I lead?"

"Be my guest."

Rick looked at his men, then at Nathen's. "I'm not sure where to begin."

One of his men shouted out. "You can start with why they look the way they do."

"What you're seeing is the true form of these people. Nothing has changed. They're still the same people you shared breakfast with this morning. There's no reason to treat them any differently than before. They had changed their appearance so we would accept them, so we would help them. What I'm trying to tell you is that it doesn't matter what they look like, these are still the people that needed our help. They call this the Valley of the Lion People. Tomas and his people have protected the entrance to this valley for as long as they can remember. Tomas put his life on the line to protect these people. Our job here is done. The threat is gone. It's time to celebrate, but not just our victory. Today we celebrate the joining of two worlds. We'll show this tribe that they don't have to hide. At least not from us." Rick focused his attention on the Jelani warriors. "I'm proud to know you, proud to be a part of your history." He looked over to his men. "Who here is ready to embrace the Jelani Tribe for who and what they are?"

Travis walked over to Tuval and offered him his hand, which Tuval willingly accepted. "I can't speak for the rest of the men, but If you ever need me, I would gladly fight alongside you. I hope we can be friends."

Nathen answered Travis. "We are friends, Travis. And I know I speak for the entire tribe when I say that you and any of your men will always be welcome in this valley." Rick stood next to Nathen as they watched on as an outsider and warrior came together as friends.

Chapter Thirty-six

The day was coming to an end, and as the sun slipped behind the trees, two great warriors were being put to rest. Nathen and Authia stood side by side watching as the last shovel full of dirt filled Tomas' grave. Tomas and Ed were buried alongside the warriors of the Jelani Tribe. Once the people that were hiding at the birthing hut returned, a special ceremony would be held honoring both men. Nathen had decided that it was still not safe for his people to return to the village. They still had one more battle, and it could prove to be even more dangerous than the first.

Sam walked over to Tomas' grave and laid the machete that won the battle on top of the fresh dirt. Nathen came to stand next to him. "How are you, Sam?"

Sam didn't take his eyes off the grave. "I'm fine, my Lord. My friend is gone, but he died protecting the Valley of the Lion People." Sam looked up at Nathen. "He would want it no other way."

"What are you planning to do now?"

"I don't know. Sensay sent our people away. I don't know where they went. Perhaps I can track them."

"Sam, you are more than welcome to stay with us. Call this valley your home."

Sam's face lit up. "Really, my Lord. I can stay with you?"

"Yes. We would be happy if you made your home here."

"Thank you, my Lord."

"We're going to head back. Are you coming?"

"No, I'd like to stay with Tomas a little longer."

Nathen patted Sam on his shoulder, then went to join Authia. They walked hand in hand to their hut. Nathen could tell that Authia's mind was restless. "What troubles you, my

Love?"

"It's been quite a day." Authia stopped and looked up at Nathen. "I actually saw my death. All my life, I have only ever been afforded glimpses into what lies ahead for me. But when Obasi put his finger to my lips, I saw everything. I was so scared, Nathen."

"I know. I saw it too."

"That had to be so hard for you. I hope you understand why I had your father restrain you."

"Yes, to a point. The outcome could have been very different if I'd been allowed to save you. We just don't know if it would have been a good thing or a bad thing. And we never will."

"There's something else. When I was with Serena, she told me that I would never be able to have any more children. I'm so sorry."

Nathen gathered Authia into his arms. "There's nothing to be sorry for. I have you, and I have Joshawa. That's all I need." He pulled Authia away just enough so he could see her face. "Let's get back to our hut before Joshawa wakes up. It's going to be a difficult day tomorrow, and you're going to need your sleep." Nathen and Authia continued on to their hut, knowing full well that if Celest were to win, then there would be a force unleashed that would be far more devastating than Obasi ever could have been.

Tammy lay on her sleeping mat as she examined her exposed belly. She ran her hands over the slight baby bump. "I'm not really keen on clothing made of animal skins, but when our baby gets bigger, I just might have to suck it up and wear them anyway."

Hansen came to sit next to her. "I need to talk to you."

Tammy looked over at Hansen, then sat up and lowered

her t-shirt over her belly. "You look serious. Is everything okay?"

"Yes. I love you so much."

Tammy leaned over and kissed Hansen. "And I love you."

Hansen sighed, dragging out the silence. "I'm not sure how to put this."

"Just spit it out. I'm not going to bite."

Hansen grinned at Tammy. "Well, I don't know about that. Tammy, I don't want to raise our baby here."

Tammy was shocked. "You want to leave the valley?"

"Yes, I do. Look, I want you and the baby to have everything you need. Like your clothing. It may be a small thing, but it means the world to me. And also, I don't see a future for our daughter here."

Tammy threw her arms around Hansen's neck. "Oh my God, I was thinking the same thing." She let go of Hansen and sat back, absolutely giddy with relief. "I love Authia and Nathen, but now with the baby . . . I want to have this baby in a hospital. I want a crib and a playpen and everything else that goes with having a baby."

Hansen took Tammy's hands in his. "Then it is settled. After I help Nathen with this whole Celest thing, we'll leave. I'm sure Rick's men are going to want to leave, and they'll probably head to Cabinda. We'll go with them."

"Where are we going to live? I don't want to live on a freighter."

"Neither do I. Not with a baby. Do you have any suggestions?"

"Well, actually, I wouldn't mind going back to Burwood."

"Burwood? After everything you've told me about this place, I wouldn't mind living there as well. Burwood it is."

Tammy squealed with delight. She placed her hands on either side of Hansen's face. "I love you so much." She leaned over and kissed Hansen almost sending both of them off balance. They both laughed, then Tammy thought of something. Her expression of joy was replaced with one of concern. "When are we going to tell Nathen and Authia?"

"After we deal with Celest. I don't know if I'm going to play a part in the battle with her, but I have to be here in case Nathen needs me."

Tammy nodded her head. "Okay. One more battle, and we're out of here."

Tamara and Rick sat on the lush jungle floor at the edge of the pond. The water was so still, the jungle quiet. Even the sound of the falls seemed softer than usual. Tamara, dressed in her animal skins, had a question for Rick. A question that she was dreading to ask, because the answer could be devastating to her.

"You look like you are miles away."

Tamara turned to Rick. "I am sorry. My mind is occupied."

"And what occupies that beautiful mind of yours?"

"A question."

"Okay, I'll bite. What's the question?"

Tamara was quiet. She really didn't want to ask. "Are you helping my Lord with his battle with Celest?"

"I'm not sure yet. Nathen hasn't revealed any plan of attack. But yes, my men and I have decided to stick around in case Nathen needs us."

"And what if he does not need you?"

Rick shrugged his shoulders. "Well, then I guess the men will head to Cabinda. That was our original plan."

"Your men?"

Rick smiled at Tamara. "Okay, I get where this is going now. You think I'm going to leave."

"It has crossed my mind."

Rick pulled Tamara closer to him, wrapping his arms

around her. "You silly girl. Do you actually think that I'd leave without you?"

"Well, I cannot leave the valley. I have heard stories of how my Lord was treated when he lived in the outside world."

"Who's asking you to leave the valley?"

"I do not understand."

Rick smiled as he shook his head at Tamara. "You leaving the valley is only one option. The other is me staying here with you."

Tamara's eyes went wide with excitement, and she smiled broadly. "You would do that for me?"

"I would die for you. But yes, I always intended to stay here with you."

Tamara threw her arms around Rick hugging him with everything she had. "You truly do love me."

"Yes, and when this whole thing with Celest is over, you and I are going to be spending a lot more time together."

Saburo sat cross-legged on the ground outside of the gathering hut watching the group of men—outsiders and warriors—sharing in an evening meal. The scent of the bush pig roasting over the open fire was enticing, but Saburo had no desire to mingle with anyone. Nathen had left two warriors to guard Saburo, not to protect him, but rather to make sure he didn't take off. They needed him in their battle with Celest. He was going to be the bait. Well, that hadn't worked out too well for Tomas, and Saburo had no misconceptions that it would work out any better for him. A half-hour later Travis came over to join Saburo, bringing him a bowl of food.

He sat next to Saburo, handing him the clay bowl. "You should eat something."

"Yeah, I need my energy to bait that crazy banshee at the

village."

"You were the one who thought baiting Obasi with Tomas and Authia was fine. What's the difference?"

Saburo looked over at Travis, shocked by his comment. "Are you kidding me? Authia and Tomas just had to stand there. I have to let that thing possess me."

"Do you really think Nathen would endanger your life?"

"Actually, yes. He made it very clear that if anything were to happen to Authia, he would kill me. Well, something happened."

"Don't worry, Nathen needs you. He's not going to kill you." Travis smiled at Saburo. "At least not until after Celest is dead."

"That's comforting."

"So, what are your plans after all this is said and done?"

"If I live, then that's easy. Free my sisters. Then maybe try to free the villages that Obasi had control of." Saburo's mind wandered off to the village where his sisters were held captive. It wasn't going to be easy to free them, at least not on his own. "What are your plans?"

"I was thinking. Saving this village from Obasi reminded me why I was here. I don't really have anything or anyone to go home to. Don't suppose you want some help?"

"You'd join with me?"

"Sure. Why not? As long as you are serious about helping those that can't help themselves."

"I am. Nothing would make me happier than destroying everything Obasi built. There are a lot of villages out there that live in fear." Saburo glanced over at Travis. Was he serious? Enemies working together — who knew. He extended his hand to Travis. "Shake on it?"

Travis took Saburo's hand. "I guess I've got to keep you alive now."

"That would be nice." Saburo stared out into the jungle. So

much had happened in the past few days. A week ago, he would have killed Travis where he stood. Now, they were going to work as a team. Saburo smiled to himself. It was as if an enormous weight had been lifted from his shoulders. He was finally a free man.

Casandra was in the priestess' hut standing at the back table. She was sorting her herbs for no particular reason. She sighed as she stared down at the table. Tamara was with someone she loved, and Serena was gone. Casandra had never felt so alone. And now everyone was looking at her to figure out how to deal with Celest. The problem was, without Serena, she had no idea. Casandra didn't have as much faith in Tamara as Serena did.

You of little faith.

Casandra's head shot up. *Serena? Is that really you?*

Who else would it be?

How are you doing this?

Saving Authia's life has given me certain privileges. Now, get your head straight. Our plan to defeat my mother will still work. Tamara is the answer.

CHAPTER THIRTY-SEVEN

The morning was full of promise, a promise of a future that would re-write the story of the Jelani Tribe. Tamara had risen early, long before any of her family or the tribe, for that matter. She dressed in her ceremonial gown and headed for the gathering hut. She knew her mother feared for her safety, and if Tamara could sense that, then so would Celest. Celest would feed off her mother's fear, and that would result in her being victorious. That was why Tamara was heading to the village on her own. Well, not exactly on her own. Tamara approached the warriors that were guarding the gathering hut.

The warriors looked at her, obviously perplexed.

Tamara just smiled at them as she unfolded a large palm leaf that contained a greyish powder. Carefully she blew the powder into their faces. They stood staring straight ahead in a drug-induced trance. They would remain that way for thirty minutes, and when they came out of it, they would have no memory of Tamara or anything else that transpired in that thirty minutes. She carefully brushed away all evidence of the powder, then entered the gathering hut. Cautiously she maneuvered between the men who were sleeping soundly on their sleeping mats until she came across Saburo. Gently she nudged him awake, placing her finger to her lips, indicating that she wanted him to be silent. She motioned him to follow her, then quietly headed out of the hut.

Saburo sat up, allowing his eyes to adjust to the darkness of the hut. Tamara wanted him to follow her. He gazed around the hut to find everyone else sleeping. Saburo grabbed his t-shirt and boots and headed out. He found Tamara standing just outside of the hut. The two guards appeared to be completely oblivious to Saburo's presence. He tried to speak to Tamara, but she only shook her head, then once again motioned him to follow her. Saburo quickly pulled his t-shirt over his head, pulled on his boots, then followed Tamara. She led him out of the village, heading in the direction of the falls. Once there, Tamara faced the entrance to the falls and pulled a packet out of the folds of her gown. Saburo reached out and grabbed her arm. "Whoa . . . what's going on here?"

Tamara looked at Saburo as if he should know. "We are going to confront Celest. Is that not what you are here for?"

"Well, yeah, but where's everybody else?"

"Who else were you expecting?"

"I don't know. An army. You can't seriously believe that just you and I alone can go toe to toe with that . . . whatever or whoever you want to call it?"

"She is called Celest, and I most certainly do." Tamara turned back to face the falls, raising her hand as she did, but Saburo once again gently pulled her back.

"You wouldn't happen to have a plan on how just the two of us are going to defeat her?"

"We are going to challenge her."

"Challenger her how?"

"In order for her to control your body, she must first control your mind. I will simply prevent her from accomplishing that."

"Simply?"

"I prevent her from controlling your mind, and she has to willingly surrender herself to the Ancestors who watch over us."

"And if you lose?"

"Then I will be faced with dealing with *The Destroyer*."

"So, in other words, you lose, and she gets me."

"Yes. Does this plan suit you?"

"No! Don't you have a plan where I'm not the guinea pig?"

"I do not understand. What do pigs have to do with the plan? And what is a guinea pig?"

"Never mind. Okay, so we win. What's stopping her from sticking around?"

"The Ancestors will be present, and they will take her if she loses."

"Why don't they just take her now?"

"It is against our laws. However, if a deal is struck, then she will be honor-bound to comply with it. And we do have one Ancestor that can make sure Celest does comply. Shall we leave?"

Saburo glanced back toward the village. "What the hell, I wasn't planning to live long anyway."

Tamara and Saburo exited the falls, expecting to see the pristine jungle floor that lay between the pond and the jungle. But that was not to be. Rick's orders had been to check for survivors and to bury the dead. In preparation of burying the dead, Rick's men had carried the bodies out of the jungle and lined them up on the ground next to Obasi's body. No one had survived, so a decision was made that due to the sheer number of bodies, burning them would be their best course of action. They had burned the bodies for the remainder of the day and well into the night. All that was left was ash and bone. At some point, a large grave would be dug, and the remains would be buried together. Saburo looked at what was left of the men he had fought side by side with. He was saddened by what had become of them. However, he knew that there was no other way. He made the sign of the cross, then continued to follow Tamara into the jungle.

Tamara and Saburo made their way through the jungle, only

stopping when they reached the edge of the clearing of the village. Tamara focused on the one remaining hut. She could feel Celest's aura. It hung like a heavy veil cloaking the entire village. She turned her attention to Saburo. "You will wait here. Do not come closer unless I call for you." Not waiting for a response, Tamara turned and headed into the village. She could sense that Celest was aware of her presence, but for whatever reason, she wasn't making an appearance. Tamara positioned herself about ten feet from the edge of the clearing, putting herself between Saburo and Celest. She stood tall and proud, her hands linked together resting in front of her. She had been planning to meld with Celest, but then thought better of it. Saburo should hear all that transpired between her and Celest.

"I know you are aware of my presence. Why do you not show yourself?" There was no response, so Tamara continued, "You know me, and I know you. By now you must realize that you have no chance of victory. Do you remain here because you fear the alternative?"

Tamara waited, expecting a fog-like apparition to appear, but instead, the shape of an actual person approached her. She appeared similar to a ghost, almost transparent, but Tamara could tell that she was from the tribe. As she drew closer, Tamara could make out that she was smiling, almost to the point of being condescending.

"And what makes you so certain that I will not be victorious?" Celest stopped only a couple of feet from Tamara.

"Because only an Ancestor or a great priestess can bring about *The Destroyer*. You are neither."

Tamara could not only see the displeasure on Celest's face, but she could sense it. Celest was becoming angry, which was precisely what Tamara was hoping for. "Did you not realize your failure when you discovered that you were trapped in this village?"

"I have not failed. You are here, which is what I wanted. And you have brought me my host. Trust me, you will feel my wrath, and the Jelani Tribe will suffer by my hand."

"I do not believe so. As I said, you are trapped here. Your host is out of your reach. Without a host, you are nothing."

"You can keep this host from me, but that will not stop others from coming here."

"I am aware of that possibility, hence the reason I am here. As you put it, I have a proposition for you."

"I am listening."

"I wish to challenge you."

Celest snorted at Tamara. "Challenge me? You cannot be serious."

"But I am. You do not wish to accept my challenge?"

"You are too young, too inexperienced to challenge me."

"I do not understand. Did you not ask for me to join with you?"

"Yes, but only because you are weak, and I could easily control you."

Tamara could feel the tension in Celest's voice. She knew Celest was leery of her. "Well, then the challenge should not be a problem. Or is there another reason why you do not wish to accept?"

"You have no idea who you are playing with."

"I am not playing. I am very serious. So, will you accept?"

Celest remained quiet as if she was sizing up the situation. "Exactly what is the challenge?"

"Simple. In order for you to control your host, you must first control his mind. I intend to stop you. If I succeed, you must willingly surrender yourself to our Ancestors."

"And when I win?"

"Then I must defeat *The Destroyer*."

"And what if I choose not to surrender myself?"

"That is why I have asked them to join us." Tamara pointed upward, where the three Ancestors who had imprisoned Celest floated above them as apparitions.

Celest slowly gazed up.

"They will make sure that you honor the challenge."

"I do not fear them or you. I accept."

Casandra lay on her sleeping mat, staring at the roof of the hut. She felt unusually groggy, and she was having trouble focusing. She closed her eyes, fighting the urge to fall back to sleep. She needed to wake up, and most importantly, she needed a clear head. After the morning meal, her Lord was going to want to hear her plan to defeat Celest. Unfortunately, she had no plan. At least not one that didn't involve Serena. She sighed as she turned to face Tamara, only to find her sleeping mat empty. At first, Tamara's unoccupied sleeping mat meant nothing. She was, and always had been, and early riser. But as Casandra glanced around the hut to find the rest of her family still asleep, warning bells started ringing in her head. She'd never had an issue waking up, no matter how little sleep she got. But here she was groggy, unable to shake the cobwebs from her mind. Then the realization of what happened became abundantly clear. Tamara had made her a broth before bed last night and insisted that she drink it all. Casandra sat up, holding her head in her hands. How stupid could she be? Tamara had drugged her, again. And she'd allowed it. Casandra knew exactly what Tamara was up to. She got up and staggered to the entrance of the hut, where a bucket of freshwater was waiting for her and the other priestesses. She grabbed the bucket and dumped its entire contents over her head.

Tamara slightly bowed her head to Celest. "Then shall we begin?"

Celest sneered at Tamara. "I think I will save you to the last."

Tamara appeared puzzled by the comment. "I do not understand."

"When I control my host and become *The Destroyer*, I will kill you last. I want you to live to witness the destruction, the death of the Jelani Tribe."

"You are confident. Perhaps overconfident. You greatly underestimate me, and our people."

"We will see. Bring him to me."

Tamara left the clearing and walked toward Saburo. "It has begun. It is important that you empty your mind and hear only my thoughts."

"Is it that easy?"

"No, it is not. You must be strong. You must fight Celest. Not physically, but rather mentally. Now take my hands and allow me to become one with your mind."

Tamara took Saburo's hands in hers. She closed her eyes, searching his mind, projecting her thoughts over his. Her thoughts would become the barricade that would prevent Celest from controlling Saburo's mind. It was, at best, a plan based solely on hope and determination. There was no room for error — she had to succeed. Her life, Saburo's life, and the life of her people depended on her being victorious. Once she was firmly planted within Saburo's mind, she melded with him.

Can you hear me, Saburo?

Yes. This is amazing. It's as if you are part of me. As if you were me.

Technically, I am. You and I are as one, and together we will defeat Celest.

What do you need me to do?

Do not interfere. Do not speak with Celest. If you do, then she will find a pathway to control you. You must focus on me. Listen to me. Follow my lead. And most importantly, you must not break the bond between us. Do you understand?

What bond?

The connection. When we enter the village, you will kneel in front of me, facing me. I will place my hands on either side of your head. That is our bond. We are one through my touch. You must not break that bond, for if you do, we will lose. Do you understand?

Yeah, I think I do.

Tamara slightly crooked her head as if she was trying to understand the meaning of his comment. *You think so? You must be aware of precisely what is expected of you. If not, then Celest wins. I will ask again. Do you understand?*

Yes, I understand. Now let's get this over with.

Casandra headed toward the communal fire pit to find Nathen. He was there with Authia, Joshawa, Tammy, Hansen, and Rick. She approached Rick, obviously taking him by surprise. "Where is Tamara?"

Rick shrugged his shoulders. "I don't know, I thought she was with you. Why are you all wet?"

"I needed to wake up, and no, she isn't with me. But I know exactly where she is. Do you know where Saburo is?"

"Never thought to look for him. Nathen has two warriors watching over him."

Casandra glanced over in the direction of the gathering hut. One warrior stood on either side of the entrance. With determined strides, she headed toward them with the others close behind. She confronted them, glaring at them as she did. "Did Saburo leave this hut?"

Both warriors looked at each other then back to Casandra. The taller of the two slightly shook his head. "No, my Priestess. He has not left the hut."

Cassandra barged into the hut, searched for Saburo, then

when she couldn't find him, she confronted the warriors again. "If he has not left the hut, then explain to me why he's not there."

The guards appeared dumbfounded. Again, the taller of the two spoke. "I don't understand, my Priestess. We didn't see him leave."

Nathen approached Casandra. "Do you want to tell me what's going on?"

"That foolish girl. She knew that I had no faith in her. She knew that without Serena, I felt that we had no chance of defeating Celest."

Rick spoke up. "Where is she?"

"She and Saburo are at the village. She's taking Celest on by herself."

Tamara led Saburo into the village just a few feet away from Celest. She could feel the excitement building in Celest. It was like a storm brewing to hurricane levels, waiting to explode all around them. Tamara melded with Saburo. *We have no time. You must kneel before me now.*

Saburo quickly kneeled before Tamara raising his head so that he could see her face. Tamara placed her hands on either side of his head as she stared deep into his eyes. *Have faith in me, and we will win.* Celest wasted no time. She morphed into a gaseous state, then viciously crashed into Saburo, causing his body to jerk uncontrollably. Tamara held on with everything she had. *Calm yourself, Saburo. Look into my eyes. See nothing but my thoughts.*

Saburo could feel Celest penetrate his very being. He felt her slamming against the walls that Tamara had built around his mind. He felt the pain of her invasion.

Then Tamara's voice came to him, soothing him. *Calm*

yourself, Saburo. Focus on me, look deep within me.

Saburo did as he was instructed. He locked onto Tamara seeing only her eyes, and within those eyes, he found his strength. He not only saw Tamara's thoughts, but he also felt what she felt. He knew Celest was there, but it was as if she were a dream. Saburo could feel the pain that surged through Tamara's body as Celest continued her attempt to break down the walls that protected his mind. However, Tamara managed to maintain her composure, hiding her emotions, revealing nothing to Celest.

Celest's anger and hatred consumed her as she desperately tried to penetrate the walls surrounding Saburo's mind. She had underestimated Tamara, and the reality that she might lose loomed over her like a black cloud, void of any light, any promise of victory. She had to rethink her strategy. She had to strengthen the odds in her favor, and there was only one way she knew to do that. She quieted herself, gazing up at the Ancestors that watched over her like vultures waiting for their prey to die. *Not today!* In order for Celest to bond with her host, she must first control his mind — his basic instinct for survival must be quashed. Then she could control his body and become *The Destroyer*. That was, if she followed the rules, and Celest was never one to follow the rules.

Casandra ran back to the family hut, where she procured two packets from their hiding place — one belonging to herself and one to Tamara. These were their original packets containing their essence, their life force. When she left the hut, Nathen, Authia, Hansen, and Rick were waiting for her. Rick had a gun holstered to his belt. "There is no reason for you to come with me. There is absolutely nothing any of you can do to help."

Rick shook his head. "There is no way that I'm not going. If Tamara is in danger, then I have to go."

Nathen added his opinion. "Sorry, Casandra, I'm coming with you." Nathen turned to face Authia. "You, however, are staying behind."

"What? How can you not include me?"

Nathen just glared at Authia.

"Okay. I guess dying once in a week is enough. I'll stay behind with Joshawa."

Nathen turned to address Hansen. "Would you mind staying behind to make sure she doesn't leave the village?"

Hansen smiled at Nathen, whereas Authia glared at him. "Sure, no problem."

Casandra was becoming impatient. She didn't have time for debates. "I'm leaving now. If you want to come, then come." Casandra secured the packets in her waistband, then ran as fast as she could toward the falls.

Tamara was blocking Saburo's mind with everything she had. She incorporated every trick that she had learned, and it appeared as though it was working. She could feel Celest's anger, her frustration as she tried, unsuccessfully, to break down the barricade. The downside was that each and every time Celest attacked the barricade, it would cause Tamara intense pain. Up to now, she had been able to conceal the pain she felt from Celest, but there was no way of knowing how long she could keep that up. She was about to meld with Celest, tell her it was time to give up, when everything went quiet. Celest was no longer attacking the barricade, she no longer possessed Saburo. Tamara opened her eyes to see Celest in her gaseous form hovering just above Saburo. "Are you admitting defeat?" Tamara continued to hold on to Saburo, maintaining the bond.

"Who says I am defeated?"

"You have left your host's body. You no longer try to control his mind. You have failed. You were unable to break through to Saburo's mind. Shall I invite the Ancestors, or will you?"

Celest laughed at Tamara. "I told you that you were too young, too naive. Look up at the Ancestors. They know what is going on, and they can do nothing."

Tamara glanced up to the Ancestors and saw in them fear and sadness. She looked back at Celest just in time to see her envelop Saburo. She controlled his body, and before Tamara could meld with Saburo, his hands came up encircling her neck, squeezing tighter and tighter. Tamara was having difficulty breathing. *Saburo stop!* She gasped for air. *Take back control of your body.* She could feel Saburo fighting to control his body, but the more he fought, the tighter the grip around her neck became. She was beginning to feel light-headed, so she let go of Saburo, broke the bond, and started clawing at his hands, trying to pull them away.

Casandra, Nathen, and Rick arrived at the outskirts of the village just as Saburo was placing his hands around Tamara's neck. Rick reached for his gun and was about to head into the village when Casandra stepped into his path. "You can't go to her."

Rick pointed toward Saburo. "Can't you see? He's killing her!"

"Yes. And if you—either one of you—enter the village, you'll just be giving Celest more bodies to feed off. I'm going in. No matter what you see, you must stay here."

Casandra ran up to Tamara. She intended to help strengthen the bond, maybe even distract Celest so that Saburo would let go. But just as she was about to join with

Tamara, Tamara let go of Saburo and grabbed his hands, trying to pull them away from her neck. Casandra immediately placed her hands on either side of Saburo's head. *Hear me, Saburo. You must let go. You are killing Tamara.* Casandra could sense the conflict that consumed Saburo. And each time he tried to control his hands, Celest just squeezed tighter. There was no getting through to Saburo, and if Casandra didn't do something soon, she would lose her daughter. She closed her eyes and melded with Saburo. *Forgive me, but I must save Tamara.* While still holding onto Saburo, Casandra shouted to Rick. "Shoot him! Shoot him now!"

Casandra watched as Rick drew his gun, aimed in her direction, then hesitated. She glanced over to Tamara, whose arms were now limp at her side. She turned back to face Rick. "Now, please, shoot him!" There was a loud noise, then Saburo fell to the ground.

Chapter Thirty-eight

Nathen watched on as Saburo fell to the ground. Tamara was on her knees, her hands on her chest, free of Saburo's grip, but still gasping for breath. Rick tried to go to her, but Nathen stopped him.

"Stay here. Tamara's okay, but Celest is still there, and she's minus a host."

Rick holstered his gun, not taking his attention off Tamara. "She can't use a host if he's injured?"

"Not if the host is dead. I don't know about injured. Why?"

Rick glanced over at Nathen. "She didn't tell me to kill him. She told me to shoot him. Which is exactly what I did, in his shoulder." Rick glanced back at Tamara. "I don't know why he isn't getting up, but he should be okay."

Nathen smiled at Rick. "My respect for you just grew ten-fold. You're a good man."

Rick watched as Casandra helped Tamara to her feet. "Good enough to marry Tamara?"

"We'll talk."

Casandra helped Tamara to her feet. Her neck was severely bruised and swollen, but she appeared to be breathing easier. When she was sure Tamara was all right, she turned to face Celest. Celest was back in her human form, appearing very smug. "You're done, Celest."

"Done? I have not even begun to start. My host may be injured, but he is still there for my taking."

"I would think twice before making any attempt to possess him." Tamara, her voice raspy, squared her shoulders and confronted Celest. "You failed. As per our agreement, you must surrender yourself to our Ancestors."

"Agreements mean nothing to me. Especially when our Ancestors cannot touch me. I am no longer in spirit form. I have transformed into a living, breathing entity. And as such, they" — Celest pointed to the Ancestors that still hovered above them — "cannot touch me. Now I will take my host and have my vengeance on the Jelani Tribe and our Ancestors."

A voice coming from behind Celest spoke. "You think you are so smart."

Casandra smiled as she witnessed Celest's smug look of satisfaction turn to that of concern. Casandra spoke to the newcomer. "It's nice of you to join us, sister."

Celest whirled around as the apparition took on human form.

"I would not miss this for the world. Hello, mother."

Serena took pleasure in watching her mother gawk at her, speechless. "Are you not pleased to see me?"

"How is this possible? You cannot be here."

"And yet, here I am."

"How are you doing this?"

"I am an Ancestor now."

"An Ancestor? No, there is no way. You betrayed your people."

"Yes, I did. However, unlike yourself, I saw the light. I embraced the light, and through it, I was able to atone for my betrayal."

"Well, that is irrelevant. As an Ancestor, you have no power over me."

"Really? Are you sure of that?"

Celest was quiet, and Serena could see by her reaction that she was second-guessing herself. "You see, mother, I am an Ancestor, but I am also your daughter. Did you know that there has never been an Ancestor who had a direct descendant living during their reign? Or in your case, a direct entity."

"What does that have to do with anything?"

"It has everything to do with what is happening right here, right now. As an Ancestor, our laws are clear. I cannot touch you. However, as your daughter . . . and you in the form of an entity . . . I can do anything I please. Apparently our laws do allow for an Ancestor to punish a direct relative such as their child or their mother. You see, as a High Priestess or Lord, we are expected to act as such. Failure to do so is looked upon with great disdain."

"You are making this up. There is no such law."

Serena took a step closer, forcing her mother to step back, right into the arms of the Ancestors. The two Lords grabbed onto her arms as the High Priestess stood behind her. "If there was no such law, how could our Ancestors restrain you?"

"I demand that you let go of me!"

Serena could feel her mother's fear, and she could see it etched deeply in her expression. "I think not, mother." Serena glanced over to Tamara and Casandra. "Will you join me, my sisters?"

Tamara and Casandra went to stand on either side of Serena, facing Celest. Cassandra reached into her waistband and handed Tamara her packet. Serena retrieved a packet from the folds of her dress. "Do you recognize this, mother?"

"It is a packet. Most likely yours."

"Now mother, you know exactly whose packet this is. I know you can sense your own essence."

"That is not possible. My packets were all destroyed."

"Not all. Thankfully, I had the foresight to hide one of your packets. And not just any packet. Your original packet."

Celest knew that what her daughter was holding was her original packet. What she didn't know was whether it could still be used against her. She tried to fight the grasp that the Lords had on her, but it was of no use. She watched as her daughter slowly unfolded the packet, revealing what was left of her original essence.

"All right, you have my essence. What do you plan to do with it?"

"I have spoken to the Ancestors, and it is our decision that you are too dangerous to be imprisoned. That a more permanent solution must be inflicted on you. It is by the ruling of the Ancestors, including myself, that you be put to death."

Celest laughed. "To death. There is no such thing as death for a priestess. You and the Ancestors are well aware of that."

"You are right, but it has been brought to our attention— thank you, Tamara—that there is one way. It has never been put into action because it requires the essence of two living High Priestesses."

Celest looked at her daughter, then at Casandra and Tamara. Was this true? She stood before two living High Priestesses. Was it possible that she could be put to death?

Serena began speaking in the language of her people. "Ancestors, give me the power that will banish the evil that stands before you."

Serena turned slightly to face Tamara. "My sister, will you willingly give up a portion of your essence so that it will enable us to destroy the High Priestess Celest?" Tamara didn't say a word. She opened her packet and gently shook a portion of her essence onto Celest's.

Serena then turned to face Casandra. "My sister, will you willingly give up a portion of your essence so that it will enable us to destroy the High Priestess Celest?" Casandra also added her essence to that of Celest's.

Serena placed her hand over the packet, then closed her eyes. "Ancestors, take the essence of these High Priestesses and combine them as one. See the essence that belongs to the High Priestess Celest. See her evil, see the darkness that surrounds her. Ancestors, I ask that you create a poison that will consume the High Priestess Celest and scatter her to the four winds."

The packet trembled ever so slightly. Its green leaves turned black as if they were rotting.

Serena opened her eyes and stared directly at her mother. Tears streamed down Celest's cheeks as she fought to free herself, but it was too late. Serena raised her hand that contained the packet toward the heavens. "Let it be done." The contents of the packet swirled out into the open, then flew toward Celest.

Serena watched as the essences of three High Priestesses encircled her mother. The Lords let go of their grip on Celest and stood back. Celest's cries could be heard echoing throughout the village. Then, in a flash of white light, she was gone, her dust carried by the winds to the furthest corners of the valley. As Serena witnessed her mother's death, a profound sense of peace, of closure, washed over her, and at that moment she knew what it meant to be a High Priestess of the Jelani Tribe.

CHAPTER THIRTY-NINE

Nathen stood at the edge of the crowd watching as the people of the Jelani Tribe celebrated their victory side by side with the outsiders. Everyone that had been hidden at the birthing hut returned in time for the evening meal and to join in with the festivities. Saburo, his arm in a sling, was resting comfortably in the priestess' hut. Tamara had been treated for her injuries and was helping to serve the meal.

Rick joined Nathen, watching Tamara as she filled clay bowls with fruit. "Congrats. You won."

"There was no way I could have saved this tribe without you and your men." Nathen glanced over at Rick. "I owe you a great debt."

"Consider it paid. My reward was being able to accomplish what I came here to do."

"And what was that?"

Rick turned to face Nathen. "To protect a people that could not protect themselves. I was thinking, Nathen. You won this battle. But who's to say that other outsiders won't find their way to your doorstep? You have to think about your future and how to prevent this from happening again."

"You have any suggestions?"

"Well, actually, I do. Your people never leave this valley. So why not eliminate your one weak spot? The entrance to your valley."

"I'm not following you. How do we eliminate the falls?"

"I still have a crate of dynamite. We don't eliminate the falls. We blow up the entrance to your valley."

"That could work. The tribe would be safe. However, the outsiders that stay here could never leave. You had mentioned something about marrying Tamara?"

"Yes, I'm very serious. But I understand that I need your permission."

"Technically, you do. But like I said, you're a good man, and if Tamara wants to marry you then its fine with me. That being said, you do realize that if we blow up the entrance to this valley, you would never be able to leave. There will be no changing your mind."

"I have no intention of changing my mind. So, when do you want to blow up the entrance?"

"It's not that easy. I have to present the option to the entire tribe, and they have to agree."

"When do you want to do that?"

Nathen glanced over to the communal fire pit. "Let them celebrate. I'll call a meeting for first thing in the morning."

Authia had just laid Joshawa down for the evening. She sat next to him, watching him sleep. He was on his back with his little arms resting above his head. He had such a look of innocence as he slept. He was just a child, oblivious to the outside world and to those that would harm him. Authia was distracted as Nathen entered the hut. "You're home late." She stood, walked over to him, and placed her arms around his neck. "It sounds like quite a party out there."

Nathen wrapped his arms around Authia's waist. "There's a lot to celebrate." He leaned in and kissed her ever so tenderly. "We need to talk."

Authia glanced up to Nathen. He appeared so serious but at the same time, sad. "What's going on?"

"Come sit with me." Nathen led her to their sleeping mat, and they sat sitting across from each other. "I was speaking to Rick. He has come up with an idea to keep the tribe safe forever."

"Really? How does he plan to accomplish that?"

"By blowing up the entrance to our valley."

"What? But if we blow up the entrance . . ."

Nathen finished Authia's sentence. "No one would ever be able to leave."

Authia knew Nathen better than he did himself, and she knew that blowing up some rocks wasn't his primary concern. "Let me guess. You don't know on which side of the falls you want to be."

Nathen smiled at Authia. "You can always read between the lines. And no, I don't."

"You know, Nathen, whatever you decide I'm behind you one hundred percent."

"I spent my life wanting to know who I was. Where I belonged. I know now, but there's still something missing. I have the answers to my questions, but I'm still not whole."

Authia took Nathen's hands in hers. "It's obvious. These are your people. They're not your family. You have never referred to the tribe as your tribe, as your Family. Your heart is still in Burwood."

"You're right. And if it was just the two of us, I'd have no problem going back to Burwood."

"What do you mean, just the two of us?"

"Joshawa." Nathen glanced over at his son. "If we remain here, then he has a chance at being happy. At finding love, having a family. If I take him back to Burwood, then I'm sentencing him to a life of loneliness. Of never knowing true love."

"You don't know that. You found me."

"But it took two centuries to find you. Joshawa doesn't have that kind of time."

"Okay. I'll tell you what. I think Joshawa is going to be just fine whether he grows up here or at Burwood. I'm content to be wherever you are. So, you have to decide. Be true to your heart. It knows where you need to be. You don't have to decide now. Sleep on it." Authia reached up and kissed Nathen. "When are you going to tell everyone?"

"Tomorrow morning. Tuval is letting everyone know that there's a meeting."

"All right. Let's go to bed." Authia lay in Nathen's arms, unable to fall asleep. She could sense the conflict brewing inside of him. It was as if he were in a tug-of-war, and between the two sides was a bottomless pit of uncertainty.

The sun had just risen in the eastern sky. Tamara stood outside the priestess' hut, dressed in her animal skins, watching the brilliant colors fill the morning sky. She smiled as she recalled Rick telling her that Nathen had given his permission for her to marry him. Nothing could have made her happier. She was lost in her thoughts until one of the warriors passed by her and wished her a good morning. She smiled at him, then entered the hut to tend to Saburo.

She found him sitting by the fire pit, slowly rotating his injured shoulder. "How do you feel this morning?"

"Still a little sore, but I have more movement."

Tamara knelt by his side and removed the bandage to inspect the wound. "It is healing nicely. I will ask my mother, but I think you can go back to the gathering hut."

"Is the patient going to live?"

Tamara turned to see Travis standing at the entrance to the hut. "Why would he not?"

Travis chuckled. "No reason." He went over to sit next to Saburo while Tamara applied fresh herbs to the wound. "How are you feeling?"

"Great, considering I got shot by your boss."

Travis laughed. "Well, be thankful he's a good shot. Do you think you'll be strong enough to go back to the outside world?"

"Sure. When?"

"Sooner than later. Rick wants to blow up the entrance to the valley."

Tamara's head shot up. "What?"

"Yeah, he and Nathen think it's the only way to protect the tribe."

Nathen had awakened early, leaving Authia and Joshawa asleep in their hut. He needed to think, so he headed to the pond where he thought he would be alone, especially at this time in the morning. However, he was greeted by Hansen, who had gone to the pond for an early morning swim. Nathen sat at the edge of the pond just staring off into the distance, not at anything in particular.

Hansen, dressed in his shorts, soaking wet, sat next to him. "Care to share? Or would you rather be alone?"

"I'm not sure what I want."

"Okay, spill. What's going on? You and Authia have a fight?"

Nathen glanced over to Hansen with a *you got to be kidding* look on his face.

Hansen just smiled. "Thought that would get your attention."

"I was talking to Rick. We're going to blow up the entrance to the valley. I've called a meeting this morning to tell the tribe."

"You're serious? You're really going to blow it up?"

"It's the best way to ensure the safety of the tribe."

"So, when are you planning to do this?"

"Not sure. The sooner, the better."

"You should know, Nathen. Tammy and I have decided to leave the valley. She wants to go back to Burwood."

Nathen nodded. It was a simple decision, and yet he

couldn't make it. Neither choice sat well with him, and mostly because of Joshawa. "Authia and I are having the same discussion. Authia says it's up to me, but I can't figure out which is the right answer."

Hansen shrugged his shoulders. "Is there ever really a right answer?"

"I'd like to think there is."

Hansen stood up and patted Nathen on the back. "I'll leave you to your thoughts. See you at the meeting."

Nathen didn't acknowledge Hansen leaving. He just sat there, frustrated, mostly with himself. The right answer for him was not the right answer for his son.

The gathering hut was filled to overcapacity. Rick's men had cleared out all of their belongings, and they were ready to continue on with their lives. Nathen was told that several of Rick's men had decided to join Travis and Saburo in their fight to free other tribes. The remaining men were heading home. Nathen had requested that Rick's men wait by the communal fire pit for the tribe's decision. If necessary, they would help plant the dynamite before they left the valley.

Nathen was sitting on the raised platform, Tamara at his side. Rick and Authia had joined them, standing just behind them. Once everyone was in attendance, Nathen and Tamara stood up. Nathen raised his hand to quieten the crowd. "We all know why I've called this meeting. Our tribe was attacked on two fronts. We were victorious, but at a cost. Many lives were lost. And even though most of the lives were that of our enemy, it's still a tragedy. Rick has come up with a plan to ensure that our valley will never be threatened again. It's a good plan. One that I believe should be implemented today. It involves sealing the entrance to our valley so that no outsider will ever find it again." The tribe was quiet, and for the first time, they bowed, showing their acceptance before it was asked of them.

Nathen looked over at Rick and motioned for him to stand between himself and Tamara. He turned to address the tribe. "Some of us have a decision to make. A decision as to whether or not we wish to remain in the valley." Nathen gestured toward Hansen and Tammy, who were standing in front of the platform. "Hansen and Tammy have decided to go back home, which I believe is the right thing for them to do. They are having a child, and the child should be raised among her own people. I also have an announcement. Rick has asked for Tamara's hand in marriage, and I have granted that request. Rick has proven, beyond a doubt, his loyalty to this tribe. In my mind, he has earned the right to marry Tamara. Bow if you accept this marriage, or stand and be heard." Nathen was pleased and relieved when his entire tribe bowed to him, their Lord.

And now Nathen had to broach a subject that he himself didn't know the answer to. But if he was to decide to return to Burwood, then the tribe needed a leader. A strong, just, and compassionate leader. He looked at the people that trusted him, respected him, the people that chose him to be their leader. "Sealing the entrance to the valley is the right thing to do. I must be honest with you. I am seriously considering returning to my home at Burwood." The tribe went so quiet you could hear a pin drop.

Arman stood to be heard. "But, my Lord, you have done so much for us. For this tribe. How could you think of leaving? We need you."

"Arman, you have been a true and loyal friend. Yes, I think of you more as a friend than a warrior. But you and the tribe have to understand that I have an entire family back at Burwood who love Authia and me. They would embrace Joshawa and love him as they have loved me. They raised me to be the person I am today. That being said, I also have to think of my son. His home is here. He belongs here. Bringing him to Burwood would not be in his best interest. As his father, it is my responsibility to do what is best for him. This is one of the most difficult decisions I have ever had to make. If I do decide to leave, then you'll need someone to take my place. As there are no others in my bloodline, then I must choose a successor. According to our Ancestors, no priestess shall ever rule the tribe again. It is not their place. I have given it serious consideration, and there is only one person I can think of that would lead this tribe as I would. One person that would be a symbol of how our two worlds can be united. I choose Rick as my successor."

Anyone could have knocked Rick over with a feather. He stood with his mouth gaped open, not believing what he just heard. Nathen wanted him to lead the tribe? Nathen was still speaking to the tribe. Rick, in complete bewilderment, focused on Nathen.

"We have been shown that not all outsiders are bad. That they will come to our aid. Rick has chosen to remain here with all of you. He has already proven to the Jelani Tribe that he is a compassionate, strong, caring individual. My father chose an outsider for a wife, and if she had been allowed to live, she would have proven that an outsider can be one with the Jelani Tribe. I say that we follow in my father's footsteps and allow an outsider, who has gone above and beyond protecting this tribe, to rule this tribe. That his children be afforded the same lineage that my children would have been given." Nathen turned to face Rick. "If the tribe chooses you, will you accept this appointment and agree to rule this tribe as I would?"

Rick was in shock. Did he really want to rule an entire tribe of people? He wasn't comfortable when he had led his platoon. But then he had been leading his platoon to situations that could mean their death. Here he would be offering guidance, and he would be here to keep the peace. Which was precisely what he had set out to do in the first place. "If the tribe accepts me, then yes, I will accept the appointment. I will rule this tribe in your honor, as you would want me to. All I ask is that the entire tribe accept me. I don't want to force myself on anyone who doesn't want me as their Lord."

Nathen turned back to face the tribe. "It's up to you. Bow if you accept Rick as your Lord should I leave, or stand and be heard."

A sense of pride and admiration filled Rick's heart as he watched every person of the Jelani Tribe bow and accept him as their new Lord.

Nathen and Authia returned to their hut. The decision to blow up the entrance sooner rather than later had been made, and Rick's men were already at the falls planting the dynamite. Now another more crucial decision had to be made. Nathen watched as Joshawa played with his blanket. He was putting it over his head, then pulling it off, giggling with delight. Authia came to sit next to Nathen. She wrapped her arms around his bicep and laid her head on his shoulder.

"I think you made the right choice leaving Rick in charge."

Nathen continued to watch Joshawa. "That was one of my easier decisions. Did you know that Tammy and Hansen are going back to Burwood?"

"Yes. Tammy told me."

"Did she tell you why?"

"Not really. I never thought to ask."

"It's because of their child. They want to raise her where she has the best chance to be happy. They never gave it a second thought. They did what was in their child's best interest, not theirs. If we stay here, then Joshawa will be guaranteed to have a normal life."

"It sounds as though you've made up your mind."

"I can't help but think of Burwood. The people there have always loved me, treated me no differently than themselves. Charles was an amazing father. He didn't have to raise me . . . he chose to. The main reason I was unhappy was because I didn't know who or what I was. Joshawa would know that. He would know his heritage."

"I sense a *but* coming."

"But he would never know the love of a woman. Do I have the right to take that from him?"

Authia sat back and took Nathen's hands in hers. "Sounds like we're staying."

"Would you be all right with that?"

"I told you, Nathen. As long as I'm with you, then I don't care where I am."

It was late afternoon, and after hours of strategic planning, the dynamite had been placed and was ready to be ignited. Travis, Saburo, and the other men were already on the other side of the falls. The only ones who remained were Rick and Tamara, Tammy and Hansen, Nathen, Authia, and Joshawa. They stood in silence, all staring at the mountain of rock that was to be used to seal the entrance to the valley forever. Nathen watched and listened to his friends as they said their final good-byes. Tammy had just finished hugging Authia for what seemed to be the fiftieth time. Nathen smiled as he approached her. "Do you have any hugs left for me?"

Tammy jumped up and threw her arms around Nathen's neck. "I'm going to miss you the most." Tears started filling her eyes. "When I came to Burwood, I was a mess. You, Charles, and Edward saved my life. But it was mostly you. You carried me to those caves. You taught me how to be content with myself for who I was. You helped me, and so many other people. Morris, the captain of the freighter, told me that you saved him as well. You have left your mark on so many people. If you do nothing else with your life, teach your son how to be like you."

Tammy hugged Nathen again. She stood back, wiping the tears from her eyes. "I'll give Charles a hug for you. Is there anything you want me to tell him?"

Nathen was overrun with emotion. It had never occurred to him how many lives he had touched or how much good he had done. He always dwelt on the negative, never the positive that came from living in Burwood. "Tell him that I love him and that I miss him. Tell him that I will tell Joshawa all about his grandfather. But most importantly, explain to him why I made this decision."

"Of course, Nathen. I'll tell him how important you are to the tribe. How important it is for Joshawa to grow up with his own people." Tammy looked over her shoulder to Hansen. "I guess it's time to leave." She reached up, kissed Nathen's cheek, then went to join the others.

Nathen walked up to Hansen, who extended his hand to him. "A handshake isn't going to cut it." Nathen wrapped his arms around Hansen, and when he pulled away, both men had tears in their eyes. "I can't thank you enough, Hansen, for everything. You will be a welcome addition to Burwood. Now get out of here. You have to make camp before you lose the light."

Everyone watched as Tammy and Hansen left the valley. Rick walked over to Nathen. "I'm going to lite the fuse. We should all stand back a bit." The fuse ran almost the entire length of the clearing, working its way into an intricate web of fuses leading to dozens of sticks of dynamite.

Nathen kept hearing Tammy's words. *You left your mark on so many people. You saved my life. Teach your son to be like you.* He watched as Rick lit the fuse, but it was as if he was in a trance. Nothing going on around him was registering. What had Authia said? *These are your people. Burwood is your family.* He was a fool. He didn't belong here, and neither did his son. Nathen glanced over to the fuse. It was already halfway to the entrance. He looked for Authia, who was standing at the edge of the clearing holding Joshawa. He ran up to her and scooped her and his son into his arms.

Rick grabbed at Nathen's arm. "What are you doing?"

"I almost made a terrible mistake. Take care of the tribe."

"Where are you going?"

"Home." Nathen turned and ran to the entrance with Rick yelling after him.

"Nathen, you don't have time."

The words barely left Rick's lips when the dynamite started to explode. One stick after another, shattering the rock until the entrance was a solid wall of stone.

Hansen and Tammy were standing by the pond when the explosions started. It was deafening, sending plums of dust and debris flying out of the passageway. When the explosions finally stopped and everything went quiet, Hansen cautiously approached the passageway trying to see through the dust. It was so thick that he was having difficulty breathing, he could taste the dirt. He was about to turn around when he heard something, very faint. He strained to listen to what sounded like a baby crying. The rock and debris that lay before him started to move. He could just make out a patch of golden-red hair. Suddenly, he realized what he was seeing.

"Tammy, get over here." Hansen and Tammy started digging at the debris frantically trying to get to Nathen. It took ten minutes, but they were finally able to free Nathen. It appeared that he had turned his back to the force of the explosion in order to protect Authia and Joshawa. They were fine, and it was evident that Nathen was only unconscious.

Authia helped Hansen drag Nathen toward the pond. She sat next to him as she cleaned his cuts, all the while trying to meld with him.

Can you hear me, Nathen? Please tell me that you're okay. There was only silence. Authia sat on the ground and lifted Nathen's head into her lap. Joshawa sat next to Nathen snuggling as close as he could get. Again, Authia tried to meld with Nathen. *You can't check out on me. Wake up, Nathen. You have a family to take care of.*

Nathen started to stir. He opened his eyes and smiled when he saw Authia gazing down at him. "Are you okay, my Love? Is Joshawa okay?"

"Yes, we're both okay. What happened, Nathen? Why did we leave the valley?"

Nathen sat up. His head was pounding, and his body ached. "Because we belong at Burwood. That is our home, and it will be Joshawa's home as well."

Nathen gathered Joshawa up in his arms. "We're going home, Joshawa. Where we belong. You'll be happy there. You'll have so many people to love you." Nathen drew Joshawa close, gazing out to the jungle as he did. They were going to begin the last leg of their journey, their journey home. Nathen had finally come to terms with who and what he was. He had finally understood what Burwood meant to him.

The lone Ancestor watched Nathen from the edge of the realm of spirits, and he did so with profound sadness. Nathen's choice had consequences that were beyond Nathen's vision. Consequences that he, as an Ancestor, would have to deal with. The Ancestor knew that Joshawa's journey was not as

Nathen would want or plan for. The cruelty of mankind would rear its ugly face and once again put Nathen and Joshawa to the test.

The End

You may also enjoy the following from eXtasy Books Inc:

Taming the Beast
Christine Frances

Excerpt

Tanya briskly walked toward the pier. It was eleven fifteen. She had fifteen minutes to reach the Hangman's Den and meet William. Just enough time. The last thing she wanted was to remain anywhere near that place for any length of time. Tanya and Nathen had slept the day away, waking only an hour before her prearranged meeting with William. Frantically she had run around preparing Nathen for his journey to freedom and her evening on the pier.

Tanya had been warned about how dangerous the pier could be at night and especially around the Hangman's Den. It was a haven for prostitutes, drug dealers, and smugglers—not a place someone like Tanya would wish to frequent. That was why she'd taken extra care when she dressed for the night. A dark grey heavy woollen jacket that had belonged to Mrs. Gibbons's late husband and a pair of baggy jeans concealed her figure. She'd also borrowed a large, tattered shawl from Mrs. Gibbons. It was yellowed with age and smelled of moth balls. She draped it over her head, concealing her face. Because the shawl was so long and wide, she was also able to crisscross it in front of her and then drape it back over her shoulders, effectively concealing Nathen. The way she had positioned Nathen under the shawl made it appear as if she were a heavy-set person rather than a woman cradling a child. From a distance, she looked like an old bag lady bundled up to keep the night chill away.

Tanya turned the corner of an old freight office and cautiously made her way down the pier toward the Hangman's Den. The full moon was hidden behind a blanket of thick cloud, making the pier seem even more sinister than it actually was. Rows of freighters lined the docks, all cast in their own eerie shadows. Crates had been piled next to a few of the freighters waiting to be loaded in the morning. Tanya kept to the shadows, carefully walking past each freighter till she at last reached her destination.

Loud music filtered through the doors of the bar along with the drunken sounds of laughter. As William had promised, a pile of crates was positioned not ten feet away. Tanya quietly slipped in behind them, then checked her watch. Exactly eleven thirty. William should be there any minute. Nathen restlessly stirred under the shawl, making a slight gurgling sound. Tanya quickly wrapped her arms around him and began to pace her confined area. God help her if Nathen woke up and decided he was hungry again. He'd eaten well before they left and fallen back to sleep, for which Tanya was grateful. But Nathen had a healthy appetite, and it would not be unusual for him to want another feeding in such a short time. To Tanya's relief the gentle rocking lulled him back to sleep, and once again he was quiet. Another glance at her watch revealed that it was eleven forty-five. "Come on William. What's keeping you?"

As each minute ticked by, Tanya's imagination tormented her, playing with her fears. Another burst of laughter from the bar broke the eerie silence that surrounded her. Cautiously Tanya drew her shawl closer around Nathen. Her fear began to take over her common sense as the laughter grew louder. Silently Tanya stepped further back into the shadows of the crates. She wished that the darkness of the night would totally encase her and make her invisible to those who would harm her or Nathen.

Tenderly Tanya pulled the shawl back from Nathen's face. As she did, Nathen stirred in her arms, snuggling closer to the warmth of Tanya's body. When he reached his goal, a small smile graced his tiny lips, and once more he fell into a content slumber. Tears escaped from Tanya's eyes and slowly trickled down her cheeks as she gazed into the peaceful sleeping face of the unsuspecting child. Her lower lip trembled as she closed her eyes tight trying to fight back the anguish she felt deep in her heart. Could Laura ever understand what she was about to do? That it was the best for Nathen. She took a deep breath, then another in the hope that the cool, brisk, night air might clear her head. That it just might bring reason back to her thoughts.

It was twelve thirty, and Tanya knew that soon the bar would be emptying its contents of unsavoury patrons onto the pier. She had to be gone by then. She found herself constantly scanning the dimly lit pier for any sign of William. He was never that late before. What if he'd changed his mind? What if he wasn't coming? Sheer panic began to form an angry knot in the pit of Tanya's stomach. Nervously Tanya bit her lower lip as she strained to hear a sound, any sound that would assure her that William was on his way. But no sound came, and after another half hour, Tanya faced the painful realization that Nathen had not found a safe sanctuary, that she had misread her vision and everything that had been done for Nathen was in vain.

Tanya took a deep breath, squared her shoulders and was about to leave the safety of the crates when she heard it. The rhythmic slap of oars against the water. A few minutes later, after the pier was quiet again, Tanya carefully stepped out from behind the crates. A few yards away she could see William emerging from behind an old freighter. Quickly he approached her, clutching in his massive hand a wicker bassinet lined with blankets.

"Sorry I'm late. I couldn't get away any sooner." William

gently reached up with his free hand and wiped away Tanya's tears. "Are you all right? I can tell you've been crying."

"I'm fine, just take him." Tanya gently laid Nathen in the bassinet, then leaned over and kissed him on his forehead. "Goodbye, sweetheart."

"Are you sure you want to do this? Maybe you should come with us. I'd take good care of you, Tanya. We could raise this baby together."

Tanya looked up at William and smiled. She reached up to gently caress the side of his scarred face. A calloused hand came up to cover hers.

"I know you would, William, but it wouldn't work. It wouldn't be fair to you."

"You still haven't gotten over Charles, have you?"

"No. Not even close."

She took her hand away, then leaned over to kiss Nathen one last time. Unnoticed to William, Tanya slipped a note under the pillow, then quickly walked away.

Her tears ran freely down her cheeks as she gazed into the emptiness of the night. Once again, she prayed Laura would understand that Nathen did not belong in her world, that he was much better off in Burwood. He'll have a life there. Tanya stopped at the end of the pier, then turned to catch one last glimpse of Nathen, but both he and William were gone. Sadly, Tanya turned around and continued to make her way down the quiet streets that she called home, knowing deep in her heart that she had done right by Nathen. She only hoped that when Nathen discovered the truth, he would be able to understand her motives and find room in his heart for her.

ABOUT THE AUTHOR

Christine Frances was born July 29, 1958, in Halifax, Nova Scotia, Canada. She was born to a military family, her father being in the Royal Canadian Navy. Her passion for writing started at an early age with her seventh-grade teacher, Sister Lambert, playing an influential part in developing Christine's love for short stories. After a period in Christine's life when she put down her pen to run her own business, raise two boys and become a grandmother, the desire to write once again took over, and the series Lord of His People was born.

www.ingramcontent.com/pod-product-compliance
Lightning Source LLC
Chambersburg PA
CBHW061304170626
46817CB00001B/40